To Roger,
A wonderful state representative. Thank you for the dynamic leadership you give our district. I greatly enjoyed serving as your secretary. I hope you enjoy Curve.

Joy & Peace
Madge
4-7-06

THE FINAL CURVE

by

Madge D. Owens

authorHOUSE™

1663 LIBERTY DRIVE, SUITE 200
BLOOMINGTON, INDIANA 47403
(800) 839-8640
WWW.AUTHORHOUSE.COM

First published by AuthorHouse 01/18/06

ISBN: 1-4208-9215-0 (sc)

Library of Congress Control Number: 2005909133

Printed in the United States of America
Bloomington, Indiana

This book is printed on acid-free paper.

DEDICATION

To my friends on the Hill. Especially, to the wonderful, dynamic elected officials for whom I have worked through the years.

In memory of Anthony Grogan, Mrs. Ethel Winfrey and Mrs. Mary Schell.

Also, in memory of Mona Lisa Grant and Natalie Leslie, forever in the hearts of the BTW Class of 1976. We miss you.

ACKNOWLEDGMENTS & DEEPEST APPRECIATION

To God Be The Glory!

The author is also grateful to the following persons and organizations for your continuous prayers, assistance, encouragement and support.

Dorothy Grant Owens, Mother
Talmadge Owens, Brother
Adrienne Owens, Sister-in-law and the Ebony Ya Yas Book Club
Mack Dennis, Richard Marion, Faye Marion, Cousins
Leishea and Carl D. Johnson, NIB-C (Not I, But Christ) Digital Imaging
The Reverend Frederick Gray and the Central United Methodist Church Family
The Reverend Curtis Williams, CUMC Source Newsletter
Krystal Evans, CUMC Source Newsletter
The Honorable Tyrone Brooks, President, Georgia Association of Black
    Elected Officials
Booker T. Washington High School Class of 1976
Hal Lamar, The Atlanta Voice Newspaper
Art Searles, Albany Southwest Georgian Newspaper
Mary Charles Ford, Delta Sigma Theta Sorority, Inc.
Brandon Massey, Author and Editor
Stella Taylor, Carolyn West, Hazel Scott and TLC Atlanta Book Club
Lynne and Robert Kuhn, and the Buckhead Couples Book Club
Stephanie and Cedric Brooks and Onyx Book Club
Donald Redic, Onyx Book Club
Mignon McDonald, Daphne Axam and the Southwest Regional Library Book Club
Chartavia Harris and the Soulful Minds Book Club
Lisa Brown, KISS 104.1
Shasta Rodgers and the SoulFull Readers Book Club
Brother Babatunde K. Abdullah, The Alley Pat Show
The Mays on Lynhurst Neighborhood Association

Juanita M. Eber, Clark Atlanta University National Alumni Association
Carrie Hamilton, CAU Office of Alumni Relations.
Julia Gilmore, Friends of the Southwest Regional Library
Diane Drake, East Point Black History Weekend Literary Café
Marvel Micheale, Atlanta Book Festival Literary Soul Café
Nia Damali, Medu Bookstore, Greenbriar Mall
Lisa Jamison, Lynn Graves and the Literary Ladies of Excellence Book Club
Tee C. Royal, L. Raven James and The RAWSISTAZ™ Reviewers
Tjames Scott, KADTS Ballroom Dance Club
Marcus Williams, Nubian Bookstore, Southlake Mall
Brian Christian, Brian L. Christian Photography, Author Cover Photo

Also, many thanks to: The Honorable Maretta Mitchell Taylor, The Honorable
    Winfred J. Dukes, Thelma Brown, Moses Few, Ella Green, The Reverend
    Willie Webb, Johnny A. Neal, Anita Hanshaw Wyatt, Dr. Jayan Allen,
    Debra Scarlette.

Readers Love *To Silence Her Memory*

" . . . a chilling ride through the pages of Hot 'Lanta."
–TLC Atlanta Book Club

"We had a wonderful time reviewing the book. Overwhelmingly people enjoyed [it] . . ."
–ONYX Book Club, Atlanta

"Truly one of the best books I have read in a while . . . this one was a page turner. I anxiously await Ms. Owens' next novel. This one was a gem."
–Lynn Graves, Literary Ladies of Excellence Book Club, Atlanta

"It was an easy read . . . a real page turner. The descriptions made you visualize the characters."
–The Ebony Ya-Yas Book Club, Columbus, Ohio

"Every time I thought I had it figured out, you threw me a curve. I like a good mystery, and this one was first rate."
–Reginald Stanfield, Decatur, Georgia

"Oh my goodness! I just finished this book and it was wonderful! I just know . . . there's going to be a sequel."
–Pennisi L. Glover, Stone Mountain, Georgia

"To Silence Her Memory was a good read . . . It had more twists and turns than Lombard Street, the [most] crooked street in San Francisco. I enjoyed reading it, from beginning to end."
–Baji Daniels, Westport Way Homeowners Association

"It was FANTASTIC!!!!!! The ending took me by surprise which is a great way to end a story. I LOVED IT! I was on an emotional roller coaster ride and enjoyed every minute of it."
–Phyllis Ivey, College Park, Georgia

"I just finished the book, it was a great who-done-it, every time I thought I knew you tricked me."
–Valencia (Val) Perry, Clarkston, Georgia

"I really enjoyed reading To Silence Her Memory. The familiar places in Atlanta made me feel like I was right there with the characters. The suspense kept me on the edge of my seat."
–Gwendolyn J. Hudson, Plano, Texas

"I enjoyed it very much! The ending was quite a BIG SURPRISE. I truly fell in love with the characters (Doreen, Byron, Matt and Bootsie). The plot kept you on edge... Thanks so much for allowing me to be a part of the reading circle for your premier novel."
–Wanda F. Wynder, Atlanta

"On a scale of one to ten with ten being the highest. This one rates a nine."
–The Southwest Regional Library Book Club, Atlanta

January 1990

*H*enry Perkins was desperate to clear his name. As he drove down the highway, blinding sheets of rain sliced down so hard he could barely see one foot in front of him. His quick breaths formed a steamy fog across his windshield. The bourbon he'd consumed didn't help matters, and he struggled to hold on to what was left of his concentration and his sanity.

How had it come to this? And only a few years away from retirement. He had worked hard for the state of Georgia, taken all kinds of humiliation and abuse. And for what – to be framed by some upstart kid who wanted his job? His wife, Martha, was devastated. He thought she might have a stroke. She had battled hypertension for years, and this kind of stress wasn't good for her health. What would they do now? His job and his pension were gone. Not that he had much, but he treasured what little he *did* have. It was everything to him and his family. Besides disgracing Martha and his granddaughter, he had only one other real regret.

Hot tears of anger blurred his vision. He was almost blinded by the glare of oncoming headlights and struggled to keep the car from veering into another lane.

Everything started when Marcus was hired as his assistant. He had groomed Marcus like a son – taught him everything he knew. And in the end, it was Marcus who betrayed him for a low-level position as mail services director. If it hadn't been so sad, he would have laughed out loud.

Not one of his co-workers believed his side of the story! That's what hurt the most. After all his years of dedication, the people he had gone out of his way to serve chose to believe Marcus. The one person who did believe him was powerless to help because he had no real proof that Henry was framed.

And the one person who knew the truth was a coward who chose to remain silent. Some pal Jesse Higgins turned out to be.

Henry was not a man who would intentionally wish bad luck on anyone, not even Marcus. But still he knew that Marcus would eventually be forced to pay for his deceit. Henry would not be around to see it, but he knew in his heart it would happen. And although Marcus had maliciously twisted the knife in his back, the thought still made Henry sad. No one escaped justice, and Marcus' day would surely come.

Henry tried his best to remember a poem by one of his favorite writers, Langston Hughes. The poem was entitled "Final Curve." It was a short poem: something about turning a corner and running into yourself and not having any corners left to turn. Yes, one day Marcus would hit that final curve. He would turn that final corner and face himself and all that he had done.

That was Henry's last thought as he hydroplaned and lost control of the car, plunging over the guard rail and into the dark, unforgiving ditch below.

~Ten years later~

CHAPTER 1

$\mathcal{T}$he first day of the legislative session on the second Monday of January was always a frenzy of activity at the Georgia State Capitol. The building, a virtual cocoon of tranquil dormancy for the last nine months, was now bursting with renewed life and energy. Reporters and camera crews hustled to get situated in the designated media areas in the House and Senate Chambers. Lobbyists, who didn't opt to sit in the fourth floor galleries, were staking out their positions in front of the closed circuit television monitors on the third floor. Impressionable college interns, officious-looking legislative aides, and ambitious law clerks scurried to check in and report to their various office assignments. On the main floor, school children and adults of all ages were assembling in their respective groups to begin tours designed to enlighten them about the history and government of their state. Combined with the normal activity of year-round Capitol employees, the first day of the session could easily be described as controlled pandemonium.

That's the way it always looked to Lessye Yvonne McLemore, the Capitol tour director. Lessye had been a tourist information specialist at the State Capitol for the last ten years, and the excitement on the first day of the session was still exhilarating.

"Lessye, do you want me to take the next group?" asked Tracey Allen, referring to the school group entering the front door.

"I prefer the big groups, so I'll take them," Lessye said. She exited the tour booth, a convenient, well equipped and functional space situated behind the security check point on the main floor.

Lessye looked at her watch. "You cover the desk until Jon returns. His tour should be over in about five minutes. Your group will be a combination of ten college students and twenty senior citizens. They're beginning to gather now."

"Sure. You know I do much better with the smaller ones," said Tracey, a bubbly brown-skinned stunner, in her usual personable manner. Lessye was blessed to have a highly motivated, enthusiastic team to work with. Their smiling faces were the first impression many visitors got of the state of Georgia, and it was always a good one.

Lessye warmly greeted the group of one hundred eighth graders with a friendly, professional manner and immediately commanded their silence and attention. She introduced herself and welcomed them to the State Capitol, then led them into the rotunda to begin her lecture. Lessye spoke forcefully through the hand-held microphone.

"Georgia was founded on Yamacraw Bluff in Savannah on February 12, 1733 by James Edward Oglethorpe and 114 settlers. It was the 13th and last of the British colonies and the fourth state to ratify the United States Constitution on January 2, 1788. Our state has had five capital cities: Savannah, Augusta, Louisville, Milledgeville, and Atlanta, which became the capital in 1868.

"The rotunda is the center point of our building. The Senate Chamber is on the third floor on the east side of the building over the back entrance. And the House of Representatives is west over the main entrance. On the last day of the legislative session each year, the curtains are open on each side of the rotunda on the third floor," Lessye said, gesturing back and forth with her right hand. "The doors of both of the Chambers are open wide so when the Speaker of the House and the Lieutenant Governor, who serves as the President of the Senate, bang their gavels ending the session, they can see each other across the rotunda. There are two hundred thirty-six members in the Georgia General Assembly: one hundred eighty representatives and fifty-six senators. They always convene on the second Monday of January and meet for forty working days each year.

"From the main floor where we are standing, it is approximately two hundred thirty-seven feet and four inches to the inside of the dome," Lessye said, pointing upward. "The outside of the dome is covered with sixty ounces of twenty-three karat gold leaf from Dahlonega in the North Georgia mountains. That was the site of America's first gold rush in 1828. The dome is seventy-five feet in diameter, making it one of the largest gold-covered domes in the nation. The Greek-inspired statue on top of the building is called Miss Freedom. Standing fifteen feet tall, in her left hand, she holds a sword honoring Georgia's war dead. In her right hand, the torch, which is dedicated to those who have given their lives for freedom." Lessye's strong, clear, voice resounded through the building. As usual, the students, captivated by her charm and eloquence in delivering the information, found it almost impossible to believe that she knew it all from memory. The teachers and parents were impressed by her articulation, in-depth knowledge of the subject matter, and the fact that she could hold the attention of one hundred restless eighth-graders for more than five minutes.

"The Capitol interior includes one and one-half acres of Georgia marble. The outside is constructed of Indiana Limestone. It took five years to construct this building which opened on July 4,1889. At the time it was built, it cost less than one million dollars. There was approximately $118.43 left in the state treasury. The Capitol weighs approximately 70,300 tons and cost Georgians about fourteen dollars and twenty-two cents a ton, which was less than one cent per pound." Lessye glowed at the appreciative smiles.

She led the group to the north and south wings, telling them about the famous Georgians represented by marble busts included in the state Hall of Fame, the portrait and contributions of her hero, Dr. Martin Luther King, Jr., and the portraits of past Governors. At the grand stairs in the south wing, she instructed the students to get in a single-file line so they could proceed in a quiet orderly manner up to the fourth-floor House gallery.

On her way back down to the tour booth, she ran into her best friend, Tanya, a secretary in the Legislative Office Building across the street.

"Girl, what are you doing over here so early?" Lessye said. "I know it must be important for you to leave your desk before session starts."

"You know that's right. Brad has a couple of student Pages who had to come today. Instead of their parents bringing them straight to the Capitol — like I instructed them in the confirmation letter — they showed up at the suite a half hour late. These people won't follow directions."

"I know that from experience," Lessye said, remembering the many times she had given tour groups explicit directions which were ignored.

"You coming over for lunch today?" Tanya asked.

"Yeah. If you're not too busy."

"I am. But I'll still meet you in the break room at noon."

"See you then."

They parted on the second floor, and Tanya exited the Capitol through the south door closest to her building.

As Lessye walked briskly to the tour booth, she heard the familiar bell signaling all members to gather in the House Chamber. It was official. The General Assembly was about to begin. Lessye couldn't help but wonder what new challenges this one would bring.

CHAPTER 2

Not without a considerable amount of effort, two Georgia State troopers and a recovery team reached the car that had plummeted into a ravine on a deserted stretch of Mableton Parkway. The wreck happened the night before, but because of the position of the car, it was not spotted until after day break.

There was only one person in the vehicle, and he appeared to have been dead for some hours. The police suspected that he had been drinking heavily; an empty bottle of bourbon was found in the car.

The special tag on the car prompted the troopers to immediately notify Major Juan Hanlon of the Georgia State Patrol. The dead man was well known in state government. He was Senator Killian Drake.

When Juan arrived on the scene, investigated the accident, and saw the bourbon bottle, his mind traveled back to an accident ten years earlier. It was on a rainy Sunday evening the night before the beginning of the legislative session. A former Capitol employee, Henry Perkins, had been drunk on bourbon when he lost control of his car, plunging to his death.

CHAPTER 3

*R*enae Dolores Stewart hoped she would get through the morning without having a nervous breakdown. This was her first session as a legislative secretary, and she feared the heightened pressure would reveal her secret.

Renae suffered from narcolepsy, a disabling neurological disorder of unknown causes that affects one's ability to control sleep and wakefulness. She had suffered with the disease since shortly after her fifteenth birthday. The sudden and unexpected blackouts lasted sometimes for only minutes, other times for hours.

From the time the condition began until she was eighteen, Renae's grandparents had eked out enough money to take her to several doctors, all of whom had given the identical diagnosis and said the same thing: Although narcolepsy is an incurable, life-long condition, Renae could have a near-normal lifestyle with adequate medication. The problem with Renae was that she suffered terrible side effects from the amphetamine-based medications. The results were always the same: terrible chronic headaches, constant nausea and severe stomach pain. Because the medications only slightly reduced her symptoms, she gave up taking them at all.

Since beginning her job as a House secretary, she had suffered short spells, but they came at times when she was alone in the office suite – except that one time when Lena had been there. She always feared the day would come when she would pass out in front of everyone. Renae could not afford to lose her job. And the forty days of the General Assembly were no time to have a secretary who might drift off to sleep at any given moment.

It had happened again early last evening. Renae had blacked out and didn't regain consciousness until almost three hours later, waking up with a terrible headache and intense stomach pain. It was shortly after she left the Wild Hog Legislative Dinner, the annual barbeque dinner at the historic Georgia Freight Depot in the Underground Atlanta area.

She had felt dizzy and wanted to go home. She had gone outside to hail a cab when Senator Killian Drake approached her. He was leaving early and offered to give her a ride. Renae disliked and distrusted Killian – and for good reason. But she was feeling much too awful to argue with him when he insisted, and the last available cab had left with a fare. Besides, this was the least he could do to make up for his past sins. She reluctantly got into his car, and that was the last thing she remembered until she woke up in her apartment hours later groggy, disoriented, nauseous, and in pain. What had happened during that ride, and why couldn't she remember?

Now, Renae looked across the room straight into the eyes of her suite mate, Clarice Montgomery, who was staring at her curiously.

"Is everything all right, Renae?"

"Yes, I'm okay. I have a lot on my mind. This is my first session, and I want to make a good impression. Maybe I'm a little nervous."

"Don't be. You're going to do fine. You're a great worker, and you get along with your representatives in spite of how difficult some of them are. You come to work on time and rarely take a lunch hour. I mean, as far as I'm concerned, you're the perfect secretary."

"Thanks."

Renae logged on to the Internet and set her computer on the Real Player to pick up the audio and video of the House of Representatives. The morning devotional period was over, and they were beginning the day's business.

She decided her next task would be to tackle sorting the large volume of morning mail. As Renae bent down to pick up the mail basket on the floor beside her desk, she noticed a newsletter on top. It was the *Capitol Reporter*, the one put out by that nosey Sean Ryan. There was a familiar face staring off the front page at her. It was a picture of the man she hated most in this world, Marcus Norwood. Renae scowled at the image, her anger so intense that it was a wonder the paper didn't burst into flames.

After proofreading several letters, Tanya corrected her errors and printed them on the appropriate legislative letterhead.

Tanya Cecily Ivey, at age thirty-two, was about five-six and a firm and shapely size twelve. She had a glowing pecan complexion, playful nutmeg-brown eyes, and thick ebony hair which fell to her shoulders in soft cascading curls. A seasoned veteran of the Georgia General Assembly, she was a legislative secretary in a suite of eight members.

Tanya's temporary legislative assistant, Amber Brown, had worked with her the previous three sessions. They had an excellent rapport, and Tanya was happy that Amber was still available to temp another year. Tanya trusted Amber because she knew Amber always had her back and was a gem in helping her handle the abundance of extra work.

They were chatting about office issues when Lena Lawrence, legislative aide for Brad Austin, sashayed into the suite, leaving a scented trail of her expensive perfume. Built like an hour glass, Lena had a radiant olive complexion, exotic features, and mysterious hazel eyes that seemed to change colors with her wardrobe, as well as her moods.

"Good morning. How's everybody today?"

"Fine and you?" Tanya said.

Amber, a smooth chocolate pudding-brown beauty with huge almond eyes and a short curly afro, nodded with a quick grimace but did not speak. Amber didn't like Lena, and when Amber didn't like someone, it was obvious.

"Fine," Lena said to Tanya, ignoring Amber's lack of response. "Has Brad been in this morning?" she asked, lingering on his name.

"No. Not yet. He went straight to the Chamber. He has two Pages over there who came in late and missed the orientation. I took them over this morning. You need to go over and let him know they're here. They want a photo with him and the Speaker."

Lena gave her a sharp look but quickly changed back to her pleasant expression. "Well, I'm on my way. See you girls later." She was almost out the door when she stopped, flipped her hair, and said, "Oh, by the way, while I'm at the Capitol I'm going to stop in and see Marcus in the Governor's office. So if anyone is looking for me, that's where I'll be. Bye." With another flip of her mass of long brown hair, she swished out the door.

"Bye, Barbie with a tan." Amber said under her breath. "Isn't it a joy to have our own fifth-floor sex symbol?"

Tanya giggled and playfully admonished her. "Pull in the claws, Catwoman. You know that's not nice. What has Lena ever done to you?"

Amber raised an eyebrow. "Besides being a Marilyn Monroe wanna-be with a butterfly tattoo? She rubs me the wrong way. Did you notice the way she looked at you when you told her to go tell Brad about his Pages?"

"You know I don't miss much. Lena doesn't like it that Brad has her taking orders from me and not the other way around. She wants to boss us."

"If that happened you'd be looking for another assistant. And what about that last statement? You know it was aimed at you. You know Lena knows Lessye dates Marcus sometimes. She's rubbing it in that there's something going on between her and him. She's a troublemaker, and I don't trust her."

Amber, as usual, was right. That's another thing Tanya loved about Amber. She told it like it was. Lena was a troublemaker.

CHAPTER 4

*M*arcus Norwood had come a long way from the dilapidated dump in Vine City where he grew up in one of Atlanta's toughest and poorest neighborhoods. He leaned back in his comfortable leather chair in his office, only a few doors from Governor Robert Baker on the main floor of the State Capitol.

At thirty-three, Marcus was the first African-American, and probably the youngest, chief of staff in the state's history. He was happy to be among several unprecedented firsts in current Georgia government, which included the first black Chief Justice of the State Supreme Court, first black state Attorney General and first black Labor Commissioner, each of whom were elected statewide. Marcus was appointed by the Governor.

The taut muscles in his arm flexed as he squeezed his favorite red "power stress ball."

Marcus had worked hard to get to this rung on the political ladder and still sometimes found it hard to believe that he was on a first-name basis with the Governor of the state. He had aspired to a position in state government, not necessarily in order to serve people but to have power over them. Marcus learned early that as long as you knew the right people and stayed on their good side, you could get anything you wanted in state government.

Marcus was a diligent chief of staff who made everything in Robert's administration his concern. He knew, first-hand, everything that affected Robert. His main duties included overseeing the Governor's discretionary fund, scheduling important meetings and events, serving as the Governor's liaison to several state agencies and closely conferring with the Governor on all major policy and legislative decisions. All senior staff members reported directly to him.

On the Hill, Marcus was envied for his power, as well as his looks. Handsome by anyone's definition, Marcus was tall and tempting – six-two, with solidly built muscular legs, well-toned biceps, and rippling six-pack abs. He had a smooth bronze complexion, hypnotic light brown eyes, and full sensuous lips. His curly hair was cut in a conservative fade, edged to perfection. It complimented the long, sweeping eyelashes that made his deep, wide-set eyes even more alluring.

When Marcus finished college, he turned down several promising entry-level positions in the private sector to take a job as a mail clerk in the office of Secretary of State. He would have much preferred starting as a legislative aide or special assistant in the Secretary of State's office, but Marcus was realistic. Although he had served in the Legislative Intern Program, established himself as a diligent worker, and gotten acquainted with a few movers and shakers, he knew qualifications and experience didn't mean anything unless you had something to back them up with – a rich influential daddy, ability to contribute heavily to political campaigns, a residential address in their hometown, or willingness to sleep with the right people. Marcus' major marketable asset was his exemplary brown nosing skills, which he used liberally. That was enough to get his foot through the door. His skills in information gathering moved him up the ladder.

Marcus saw another tremendous plus in working for the Secretary of State. It gave him the opportunity to work side-by-side with Henry. He had a score to settle with Henry, and he settled it in a big way.

Now after ten years, that mess with Henry was coming back to haunt him. He thought about his last conversation with Killian and closed his eyes tightly. It seemed that everyone was having a touch of conscience. Marcus had come too far to let anything stop him now.

His thoughts were interrupted by a knock on his door.

"Come in."

"Hey. I stopped by to say hello," Lena said seductively.

"Hey," he said, rising from the seat behind his desk and walking slowly toward her. Reaching behind her, he closed and locked the office door, then pulled her close to him and kissed her hard. Lena was a flavor of the moment. She was also his best source of information about Renae Stewart.

CHAPTER 5

*A*t noon, Lessye grabbed her purse and leather jacket, and announced to everyone that she was breaking for lunch.

She walked briskly across Mitchell Street to the main entrance of the Legislative Office Building, dubbed LOB, which mainly housed office suites for members of the Georgia General Assembly.

Lessye took the elevator up to the sixth-floor cafeteria, purchased a chicken tenders basket with French fries and arrived in the fifth-floor break room to find Tanya already there waiting for her.

"Hey, girl. What took you so long? I was about to give up on you today," Tanya said, as she munched on a grilled chicken sandwich and chips she brought from home.

"The line in the cafeteria was backed up. They only had two cashiers on duty," Lessye said, grabbing a complimentary soda from the refrigerator, taking off her jacket, and plopping down in a chair across from her friend.

"You'd think they would hire some extra help for the session. I knew I made the right decision bringing my lunch today."

Lessye opened her lunch, said grace, and started chewing the first of four chicken strips that she dipped in the sweet and tangy honey mustard sauce.

"I saw Aunt Rose in the gallery when I was at the Capitol this morning; she's keeping the other doorkeepers straight as usual," Tanya said. Rose McLemore was Lessye's aunt on her father's side, and Tanya started addressing her in the endearing manner when she and Lessye were freshmen in college. After Rose was hired as a House doorkeeper, all of Lessye's friends at the Capitol began referring to her as Aunt Rose, as well.

"She was on break when I took my first group up this morning. I saw her on my third trip. I offered her a ride home, but she'll probably leave early after the House adjourns."

"They usually don't meet longer than two o'clock during the first few weeks. There's not much on the calendar, but they still manage to keep us busy," Tanya said, then bit into her sandwich. After she chewed, swallowed and took a long swig of her soda, she said, "I know it's only the first day of the session, and I shouldn't complain, but I will be glad when it's over and we can get back to our usual, quiet routine. I'm already sick of the lunatic phone calls and a couple of pushy lobbyists who are always hanging around."

"Okay. You can trade places with me. How would you like to tour one hundred twenty ninth graders at one-thirty?"

"Never mind. I'll take the mix ups with Pages, endless thank-you letters and sore feet from walking at least ten miles around the building before noon any day."

Lessye and Tanya traded small talk about their jobs, co-workers, weight-loss issues and current gossip.

"How's Kevin? Lessye asked. You two love birds getting adjusted to married life?"

"He's fine, and we love it! You know I told you we were looking at this house in the Junipers subdivision.   We've qualified for the loan, and we're closing this week."

"I'm so happy for you.   I've been praying that everything would come through. And the best part is we'll only be a few blocks from each other."

"Thanks, Lessye."

"Thank me by inviting me to your first cookout. I haven't had any of Kevin's grilled steaks and tilapia in a long time, and I'm way overdue."

"Consider yourself invited, and you can bring Marcus.   How *is* Marcus?"

"He's fine as far as I know."

"Well how are *you* and Marcus?"

"There is no *me* and Marcus."

"You two have been out several times. Don't tell me that you're not attracted to him. When we first started working for the state, you thought he was real cute, but you were married to Russell and couldn't move on him. Now, you're free. What's the problem?"

"There's no problem."

"Well then, isn't it about time you at least considered dating him or somebody seriously? After all, it's been five years since you and Russell broke up. You can't stay alone and lonely all your life."

"Stop right there. I'm low key when I want to be, and when I want to be active, I do that, too. It's my choice, and right now I'm enjoying my solitude."

"Yeah, I know. You've always done your own thing."

"I may be alone as far as a relationship is concerned, but I am never lonely. There's a difference. Besides, I like my freedom. In high school, I dated the same guy from the ninth grade through senior year. When I left home to come to CAU and we broke up, not a year passed before Russell and I became serious. After Russell and I split, it was the first time I was on my own and had the opportunity to experience dating other people. I'm enjoying a breather from steady relationships for once in my life."

"But don't you want to have children? You'd be a great mom."

"One day, but not this minute," Lessye said.

"You know what I mean."

"Yes I know, and maybe that contributed to my breakup with Russell. He was ready, and I wasn't. But although he wanted children, I think it was for the wrong reasons. A lot of his friends' wives were pregnant, and he wanted me to be in that number. But I didn't feel Russell was stable and dependable enough to bring a child into the world. And I was right."

"You made the right decision. What would possess Russell to quit a good management position and move to California to be a visual artist? And the boy can't even draw."

"Go figure," Lessye said, and laughed. "But getting back to Marcus, to be honest, I don't think he's looking for an exclusive romantic relationship. I don't think marriage is on his agenda. He's too much into his career, has been since I've known him."

"Who said anything about exclusivity or marriage? All I'm saying is heat it up. Have some fun. Go out more. Get to know him better. You're taking Salsa classes. Invite him out to one of those hot Latin clubs."

"I think Marcus has all the heat he can handle for the time being."

"You mean Lena."

14

"Yes. Lena."

"I wouldn't worry about her," Tanya said. "Marcus likes you a lot. He always has. So my advice is go for him. All you have to do is give him the slightest encouragement, and that man is yours."

"Tell me something," Lessye said. "You're usually the one who's so cautious and suspicious of everyone. Why the sudden switch when it comes to Marcus? Are you so desperate to get me hooked up with a steady man with a good income that you'd push me toward anybody?"

Tanya stretched her eyes in feigned shock. "What a thing to say! I wouldn't push you toward anyone – only Marcus. And that's because I know how long you two have had a thing for each other. Every time I run into Marcus, he says, 'Hey, Tanya. How's your friend? Tell her I asked about her.' And he always has that dreamy look in his eyes. I happen to think you two would be good for each other."

"In spite of his reputation?"

"That's debatable. Around here, you've got to know the difference between fact and fiction. You know how state employees love to gossip. They're nosy and don't mind dipping in other people's business. And what they can't find out legitimately, they don't mind making up. Think about it. Our friend, Lola, on security is the source of most of our Marcus rumors. And you know I love Lola, but that girl can exaggerate up a tidal wave."

"You got that right," Lessye said.

"Marcus could have a quiet disagreement with a staff member in the back corner of the Governor's private conference room and after Lola got through blowing it up, you'd think it was a fistfight in the middle of the rotunda. You can only believe so much of what she says."

"We get a lot of news from Rod, too," Lessye said.

"Oh yeah, Marcus' biggest fan. Rod may not be prone to exaggeration, but he's hardly objective either as far as Marcus is concerned. You know he can't stand Marcus."

"I know. And I don't understand why Rod will never give him a break. He thinks Marcus is the most ruthless man in state government. What do you think?"

"Marcus has never shown me that side. I think Rod is confusing ruthlessness with ambition. Marcus is ambitious. He's got a tough job. Sure he's going to have to irritate some people. And people who disagree with him are going to run him down, especially these jealous white boys who think they should have his job. Marcus is a walking target."

"You're right about that. I know it took a lot of hard work for him to rise from a mail room clerk to chief of staff for the Governor of the state. Marcus is a strong man, and I admire him for having the guts to reach his goals," Lessye said.

"If Marcus had backstabbed as many people as Rod seems to think, he'd be on death row. Rod needs to stop hating and try to support a brother."

Lessye sighed. "I tell him that all the time. But he doesn't listen. Rod never misses an opportunity to tell me about the number of women Marcus is supposedly dating."

"More Capitol fiction. Marcus has a hectic schedule trailing the Governor all over Georgia. When would he find the time?"

"But do you believe he's seeing Lena?"

"Now that one, I do believe is true. Knowing Lena she probably hounded him to the point he was almost stumbling over her every time he turned around. He probably broke down and gave her some to shut her mouth. She made a point of telling me she was going to see Marcus this morning, and she hasn't come back to the suite yet."

"I saw her when she came strolling through the main floor. She made sure she got my attention. She waved."

"And flipped the hair."

"You know."

"Nobody can accuse Lena of being a shy, retiring flower."

"Or not going after what she wants," Lessye said.

"And in this case, what she wants is Marcus."

"You can't blame her. Marcus is fine, smart and eligible. And she's an impressionable, idealistic young woman who is caught up in the whole government scene. Marcus is a powerful man at the center of it. Besides, I don't own him. We're not a couple. We go out to a few state-related functions on occasion."

"Don't make the mistake of thinking Lena is naive. Lena knows exactly what she's doing. That girl gets around. While you're sitting back playing it cool and talking about how idealistic she is, she's working overtime to snag Marcus. And he's not the only one. Amber and I believe she's after Brad, poor man. Brad is so nice. I hope he doesn't make the mistake of getting tied up with her."

"Girl, please. I've got to go now. See you later," Lessye stood, gathered her trash and threw it in the waste basket.

"Okay, girlfriend. But don't say I didn't try to warn you."

CHAPTER 6

*M*arcus watched Lena straighten her tight knit dress and prepare to leave, as if getting busy in his office was another normal part of her daily schedule. She fished in her purse for a small mirror, lipstick, and powder, and touched up her makeup.

"See you later, Marcus," she said, in a breathy voice.

"Yeah. See you."

"When?"

"Soon. I'll call you," he said to get rid of her.

Marcus, ready for her to leave his office, tried to tune her out. He was relieved to be interrupted by the intercom buzzer.

"Yes?"

"Marcus. The Governor needs to see you right away. It's important."

"Thank you, Shonna." Thank goodness for his secretary.

He turned back to Lena. "I have to go. Are you ready?" He wasn't about to leave her behind to snoop in his office while he was gone.

"Yeah, baby."

"Then let's go."

They walked out of the office and Lena swished through the rotunda toward the south wing. Marcus headed for the Governor's office.

"Come in, Marcus. Please close the door and have a seat," said Robert as soon as Marcus entered his executive office. Of all the power offices in the building, this was Marcus' favorite with its rich wood paneled walls, soft peachy-beige chairs, elegant silk- covered sofas and love seats, ornate book cabinets, and end tables. A plush Oriental rug covered the hardwood floor. Souvenir nicknacks sent to the Governor from well-wishers throughout the state as gifts of appreciation were scattered on end tables, the fireplace mantel and in the finely finished cabinetry. Antique lighting fixtures illuminated the room. Marcus loved this office, not because it was probably the most expensively decorated but because it radiated elegance and power in a tasteful and subtle way.

After Marcus sat, Robert said, "I have some bad news. I'm almost saddened beyond words." Robert's usually jovial bright blue eyes were cloudy and downcast, and his sturdy shoulders were stooped as if he was straining under a heavy load.

Marcus had never seen Robert look this beaten down. He took a deep breath and prepared himself. "What is it, Robert? What's wrong?"

"Killian is dead."

"Dead? What? How did it happen? When?" Marcus, although relieved the news had nothing directly to do with him, managed to look and sound appropriately shocked.

"It was a car accident. Juan called me a little before noon. It was a single-car accident on a deserted stretch of Mableton Parkway. He said it probably happened sometime last night. But the car wasn't spotted until early this morning."

Marcus got up and walked over to where Robert was seated behind his desk and gave him a consoling pat on the shoulder. "I'm so sorry. I know how close you were. This is a shock."

"This is more than a shock. It's a tragedy. You haven't heard it all. And this is between you and me. Juan tells me that they found an empty bottle of bourbon in the car."

Marcus' face fell into the same crunched expression it always did when he anticipated trouble. And a dead ally of the Governor found in a wrecked car with a drained liquor bottle was potential for disaster. His head began to throb.

"Do they suspect he was drunk?" Marcus asked as he made his way back to his chair.

"Juan didn't want to speculate. They should know definitely after lab tests."

"Did he seem intoxicated to you last night at the Wild Hog Dinner?"

Robert shook his head. "No. He was stone sober. Killian was never a big drinker, even when we were classmates and frat brothers at UGA. While we were kegging, he was studying. That's why this is so puzzling."

"I remember him leaving early. Do you think he could have gone somewhere else afterwards?" Marcus asked.

"I don't think so. Killian wasn't much of a night owl. He probably would have gone straight home to prepare for today."

"Did he leave with anybody?"

"Not that I know of. I told you, Juan said he was in the car alone."

"Has Sean or the other media gotten hold of this?"

"They don't know anything about the bourbon bottle yet. Juan was called to the scene and removed it before the press began nosing around. But that hasn't stopped them from speculating about intoxication. Juan heard some mumbling to that effect. And if Killian's blood shows a high content of alcohol, we're not going to be able to keep it quiet. Have you seen the latest issue of Ryan's rag?"

"No," Marcus said.

"Well, congratulations, your picture is on the front page," Robert said dryly and handed him a copy. "Sean's regular yada-yada about too much unchecked behind-the-scenes power in state government punctuated by his usual jabs that I'm running this office like an emperor, of all things."

Marcus took the copy and looked at it with disdain. "He enjoys baiting us. Like that's going to make me tell him more than I want him to know. He's probably still pissed off because I told him he would not get a copy of your budget address in advance of the other media. He can't seem to grasp the concept that he doesn't run this office. I take it the mainstream media hasn't broken any news about Killian's accident, yet. Have you heard from Hazel?"

"Yes. She called me a few minutes ago. She said that her contact at WSB said they were going to break the story at six. Although Killian doesn't have any close family, the State Patrol still cautioned them not to break anything until they had sufficient time to notify Killian's out-of-town relatives, some distant cousins. The AJC won't have it in print until tomorrow."

"What about the radio stations and wire services?"

"Nothing is going to be reported before this evening."

"They're going to call you for a statement. You, Michael and Hazel need to get together on something appropriate."

Robert grimaced. "I don't need a speech writer and press secretary to give me an appropriate statement for Killian. He was my friend. I'll speak from my heart."

"I'm sorry. You know I didn't mean anything by that. Of course you'll speak from your heart. I meant . . . how can I say this?"

"Go ahead and say it, like you do everything else," Robert said.

Marcus chose his words carefully. The last thing he wanted to do was upset Robert at a time like this. But some things had to be said. "You know . . . that if alcohol is found in Killian's blood, he's going to be considered a drunk driver. That's going to raise other questions about his character, and you know the press. They'll have a feeding frenzy and start digging into every aspect of his life. I'm only saying that if that worst scenario is found to be true . . . you're going to have to be tactful about what you say. It's all about perception. If you appear to be too close to him, you may be dragged down into the scandal, and it could damage your reputation."

Robert rose from his chair behind his desk, moved around in front of it and sat on the edge of the desk with his arms folded across his chest.

"But I *was* close to him. And to try to distance myself from him now, no matter what the circumstances, will be hypocritical — unconscionable. I'm not about to turn my back on a friend in order to save my behind. You would understand that if you had any friends."

Marcus let Robert's last remark pass and chalked it up to a combination of his grief at losing a friend and his nervousness over the upcoming budget address. The Governor sometimes lashed out and used him as a verbal punching bag on the rare occasions when he was extremely uptight. After all, that's what he was getting paid for. Taking a private tongue slapping every now and then was well worth the payoff, power and prestige that came with his position. Besides, Robert had not said one thing that was not true.

"You're right, Robert. But it's my job to protect you and to point out all the variables and suggest options, whether you agree with them or not. You're not paying me to agree with you or for my charm and wit. You're paying me to give you honest advice on delicate situations. And thus far, I've never led you wrong."

"Okay, you've made your point." Robert ran his hands through his thick, dark hair and paced across the floor several times. Finally, he said, "I wish

I could put this off. But let's face it, as sad as I am about Killian, he's not going to be any deader two days from now than he is today. Some decisions have to be made, and I don't want them hanging over my head until after the budget address."

"Believe me, I understand," Marcus said in a low, consoling voice. He couldn't relate, but what else could he say?

"Here's another delicate situation for you. I've got to decide which one of the assistant Senate floor leaders will be promoted to fill Killian's position and decide on a new assistant floor leader. Do you have any ideas?"

Marcus thought for a moment. "Why don't you promote Shannon Coble to floor leader? And to fill the assistant floor leader slot, it's probably wise to choose a moderate, but popular, Republican."

Anybody who knew Robert knew you didn't get away with making a suggestion without a sound reason to back it up. "Shannon has more seniority in the Senate than the other assistant," Marcus said. "Plus she's a woman, she's a moderate, she comes from a strong politically connected family, and she's extremely popular in south Georgia. Her appointment will also be a first for a woman. It will bring in a lot of female votes come re-election time. Also, you can break more ground by being the first Democrat to appoint a Republican assistant floor leader. Choose someone popular from north Georgia. How about Tyler Bowman? He's young, clean cut, a go-getter. A poster boy for the new Republican Party. The word *liberal* is beginning to stick to you like a fungus, you've got to do something to deflect your potential opponents. Show them that you're fair enough to cross party lines in your administration without alienating your political base."

Robert nodded in agreement. "You've made some sound points."

"When will you make the announcement?"

"Tuesday. I'm sure Killian's services will be held by then. It would be in poor taste to make a public announcement before then. And I definitely don't want to do it on the King Holiday."

"I agree. I'll prepare the executive order for all flags to fly at half staff until after the service and get it to Rod Jennings."

"Good." Robert smiled faintly. "Killian would have liked having the flags lowered in his honor."

"Also, the writ of election calling for a special election to fill Killian's Senate seat must be issued to the Secretary of State within ten days. And remember the date on the writ for the special election can't be less than thirty and not more than sixty days after its issuance."

"I won't forget," Robert said as if it were a foul taste in his mouth.

"How's everything coming with the budget address?"

"It's going fine since the last time we got together with the analyst to hammer out the final figures. Michael and I have been putting the finishing touches on this thing. I've added a few more notes I want him to work into the speech. He should be finished with the final draft this evening."

"I need to see the finished product. It may need some tweaking," Marcus said.

"You don't trust Michael's judgement?"

"Not when it comes to something as sensitive as the state budget address."

Robert's eyebrows arched. It was common knowledge there was no love lost between Marcus and the ambitious young speech writer who aspired to have his job. Marcus knew he could not make this into something personal, so he softened his approach.

"Don't get me wrong. It has nothing to do with his expertise. Michael Peyton is an excellent speech writer, probably one of the best in the business. I have every confidence in his ability to construct an intelligible and effective sentence, but sometimes his phrasing can be too hard-edged for your style, too confrontational. The budget is a delicate matter. It calls for tact and diplomacy. You can get the same points across but in a much gentler way. That's my department." Marcus was pleased that Robert nodded his approval at his line of reasoning, especially since he had thrown in his favorite alarm word, "confrontational." Marcus knew that if there was anything Robert hated, it was unnecessary confrontation.

"All right, Marcus, as always, I'm leaving it in your capable hands. Let's go with Coble and Bowman."

"Good. I'll handle the notification."

"I want to have everything in place by Friday so that Tuesday all I'll have to do is make the announcement, with them smiling on each side of me. Make sure our photographer knows I want some good photos."

"Fine, and I think we should arrange the press conference for ten so it will make the noon news. I'll get Hazel on it immediately. However, the official news releases won't go out until late Friday afternoon."

"Great. Thank you. Is that about it for now?"

"Don't forget that the Peterson family will be here for a VIP tour at four. They will want a photo with you here in the office. If at all possible, please make yourself available."

"I could never forget the Petersons. Jim Peterson is one of my strongest south Georgia supporters. That's why I selected him for an appointment to serve on the board of Industry, Trade and Tourism. Who's giving the tour?"

"Lessye McLemore."

"Yes. I know Lessye. She does an excellent job. I'm sure they will be impressed."

"I'm sure they will."

"Why don't you join them on the tour. I think that will make a special statement. Don't you think so?"

"Yes. I was planning to join them."

"Good. Then, I'll see you later."

As Marcus left Robert's office, he had a satisfied smirk on his face. He did not see Killian's fatal accident as a tragedy at all. He saw it as a positive twist of fate. Now there was one less potential thorn in his side.

CHAPTER 7

*R*epresentative Randy Joe Reynolds relaxed in his sixth-floor office in the LOB late that evening while he waited for his running buddy, Senator Tyrell Buford. Their close associate, Nathaniel Tucker, a lobbyist for a group called Citizens for a New American Agenda or CNAA, was also joining them. The purpose of the meeting was to put the finishing touches on their agenda for the legislative session. The primary goal of their agenda was the development of fool-proof, anti-affirmative action legislation and any other strategy that would successfully put the blacks back in their place for good.

Randy Joe, who held the House seat once held by his daddy and granddaddy, had a lot of experience keeping blacks in their place.

The first three things Randy Joe's daddy ever taught him were how to make a noose, shoot a gun, and hate niggers — not necessarily in that order.

Later, his daddy taught him how to swindle money and steal land, especially heir property from blacks. Through the years, Randy Joe's greedy and ruthless family had swindled and outright stolen so much land from poor, unsuspecting black farmers that they could have chartered their own town.

The Reynolds men were in the droves of angry white Republicans who deserted the Party and turned Democrat in protest of Abraham Lincoln, Reconstruction, and the idea that any "civilized society" would even consider allowing blacks to compete for political power. However, after a short stint as "Dixiecrats," they returned in the mid-1960s when the ultra conservative wing of the Republican Party offered them an alternative to the more liberal-leaning post-FDR Democratic Party, which passed the Civil Rights and Voting Rights Acts of 1964 and 1965, respectively.

Randy Joe was a gangling, rawboned man, with a wrinkled, ruddy complexion, thin lips and a sharp beak-like nose. His crew cut strawberry blond hair was as short as his temper. His engaging, deep-set emerald green eyes looked conspicuously out of place amid his other crooked features. He boasted of being a direct descendant of John Reynolds, the first of three Royal Governors who presided over Georgia government in the mid-1700s, but no one (including Randy Joe) could prove it. Still, Randy Joe was proud of his Southern heritage and never let anyone forget it.

Randy Joe was a millionaire, but no one would ever guess from looking at him in his inexpensive, ill-fitting business suit, western string tie, scuffed cowboy boots, and well-worn hat. As much as his wife tried to improve his fashion statement, he was comfortable looking more like a hapless cowboy than the owner of one of the most profitable peach farms in Georgia.

Randy Joe was confident this would be the year they would have the votes to pass their anti-affirmative action legislation and push Georgia blacks back a giant step.

Although African-American businesses still only received less than two percent of all state contracts, Randy Joe and his "good ole boy" cronies thought that even the crumbs were too much.

This was a legislative election year, and with the right strategy, they could push this into a major issue and pick up several Democratic seats in the process, especially in the rural areas of north and south Georgia. The way he saw it, the blacks had already inflamed many Southern whites by systematically dismantling sacred symbols of their heritage. Randy Joe would die before he would sit by and let a handful of loud-mouth agitators rewrite his history.

During the legislative session, Representative Alonso Steele and the other forty-nine members of the Black Caucus met each Monday at five in the evening in a Capitol conference room. As usual, they waited until the first week of the session to hammer out their legislative agenda and plan their annual Taste of the South Barbeque Cook-off and Talent Show, which was always one of the most popular events of the legislative season.

This particular meeting was characterized by strong disagreements and seemingly endless bickering. The only consistently cool heads belonged to Alonso and his diligent, no-nonsense supporter, Representative Della Harden, who had not yet arrived.

The personalities of the Caucus membership were as diverse as their numbers. To make matters more complicated, they now had a conservative Republican member. Bernard Benton, representing a majority-white northeast Georgia district, was the first black Republican elected to the House since Reconstruction. He insisted on being included in the Caucus and attended most of their meetings, which angered many of the other forty-nine members because they were sure he reported everything they did back to the Republican leadership. His strong conservative positions against affirmative action, majority-minority voting districts and hardline attitude against the poor further alienated him from the Caucus of majority liberal Democrats.

Accusations were flying and Alonso, fed up with the personal attacks, interrupted before some of the more opinionated members could reload.

"Look. This arguing is getting us nowhere," Alonso said. "We're here to develop an agenda. Something, I might add, we should have done back in November. I personally sent out notices for a meeting and only about five of you showed up. Since we procrastinated, we need to get down to business now and stop picking each other to pieces with these nonproductive personal attacks."

Everyone was quiet as they absorbed his words. Alonso was tall and regally thin with a booming voice that resounded long distances and cut to the bone. He had studious sepia eyes under wire-rimmed glasses, a strong prominent chin, and high cheekbones, evidence of his Indian ancestry. His facial complexion was rich red-brown, as was his thick curly hair. Orphaned at a young age, Alonso was a product of the foster care system which instilled in him a special sensitivity to mentoring youth and an abundance of compassion for the poor and downtrodden.

"We have our differences," Alonso said, "and we also have our common ground. There is place on our agenda for all ideas and issues which will benefit our constituencies and all the people of Georgia. Most of us have majority African-American districts, and all of us are African-Americans. When we took our oath of office, we did not take it just to serve black people, we took it to serve all the people of Georgia.

"There's a lot of ground to cover. And I've said this before, and I'll say it again: We *all* have to work together. That means putting our petty differences aside for the good of our constituencies. They don't send us here every two years to argue among ourselves. They send us here with a mandate to address their concerns and work to pass laws that will raise their quality of life. If we're not up to that challenge, then we should not be here. So, please let's get to work."

They took his advice and got down to business, discussing their position on education reform, predatory lending, business and economic development, reapportionment, teen driving, the criminal justice system, increasing the minimum wage and Temporary Assistance for Needy Families (TANF). They had decided on seven of the ten major points on their agenda when Della arrived late with a startling announcement. She told them she had heard on the news that Killian was dead. He was killed in a fatal car accident sometime after the Wild Hog Dinner the night before.

The room fell silent. This was one thing they all could agree on: They were sorry Killian was gone.

CHAPTER 8

*T*here were two sizzling topics on the minds and lips of everyone under the gold dome by Wednesday morning: the Governor's State of the Budget Address and Killian's untimely death. The buzz was everywhere, especially around the tour booth.

Lessye always tried to arrange tours so they would be lighter on the mornings of joint sessions. The four small adult groups currently on tour were divided between Tracey, Jon, and the college interns. This left Lessye alone at her desk answering questions, giving directions, scheduling tours, answering the phone lines, and checking e-mail.

The tour booth was a popular hangout for members of the security staff who were on break. At present, Captain Rod Jennings, the Capitol police chief, was leaning over the spacious marble-covered counter shooting the breeze with Lessye.

Roderick Danvers Jennings was a native Atlanta and proud grandson of a retired homicide detective. An officer with the Capitol Hill Police Department for twelve years, he had served as chief for the last five, supervising a staff of over seventy-five police and security officers. He was medium height with a solid, husky build and thoughtful, dancing ebony eyes. His creamy smooth complexion always reminded Lessye of melted chocolate.

"That was some shock about Killian," Rod said.

"I know. It's so sad. He was a good guy. I got to know him when he was director of personnel. We used to talk a lot. He gave me a lot of good advice and insight into state government. He always requested me to guide his special tour groups. I sure will miss him."

"He was cool. His ego wasn't puffed up like a lot of these guys around here. He was real people all the time, down to earth."

"The news report mentioned there's suspicion Killian's accident may have been alcohol related," Lessye said. "Is that true? Have you heard anything else?"

"No, nothing confirming it, but when has that ever stopped the media? I talked with Juan yesterday. He said we won't know anything conclusive until the GBI releases the toxicology report."

"I'm praying it's not true. He was too good a man to end his life in a cloud of suspicion." All of a sudden, Rod's facial expression shifted from serious to mildly disturbed. Lessye had known him long enough to know that something was wrong.

"What is it, Rod? Is there something you're not telling me? If so, spill it."

"How long have I known you, Lessye?"

"Ten years."

"And during that time, I've confided in you a lot over the years and have never known you to break a confidence."

"I know. What's your point?"

"I'm going to tell you something and with the exception of Tanya, please don't tell anyone else."

"I won't, and you know you'd have to drag Tanya by her well-manicured nails before she would give up a secret. So tell me."

He leaned closer to her. "Juan told me that his guys found an empty fifth of bourbon in the car with Killian. But although he got to it before the media, rumors are still flying. He didn't come out and say it, but I believe Juan thinks Killian had been drinking heavily."

"But as I remember, Killian was never a big drinker. A group of us from the office used to socialize often at a lot of the receptions when I first started working here. I never saw him take more than two cocktails at a time, if that much. Has Juan told anyone else about the bourbon?"

"I'm sure he told the Governor. And if the Governor knows, then Marcus knows." Rod was staring at her oddly.

"What are you thinking? I know there's more."

Rod looked over his shoulder to make sure no one had come up behind him.

"I don't think he mentioned this to the Governor, but Juan also told me that Killian's accident reminded him of Henry's accident ten years ago."

"Go on."

"The week before the legislative session was to begin, we were called in to investigate a theft involving Henry in the Secretary of State's office."

"I remember. He was accused of theft and mail tampering. I always liked Henry. I didn't know him that well, but he seemed to be a nice man. It was hard for me to believe he could ever do anything like that."

"But your friend, Marcus, confirmed it. And the powers that be believed Marcus."

"You never did," Lessye said. She knew this was a sensitive subject with Rod and hoped it would not lead to a disagreement between them about Marcus.

"I believed Henry was innocent, but I couldn't prove it. When we were called in to investigate, we found stolen money and open mail that had never been delivered. It was in a drawer at his desk among his personal belongings. He was the only person with a key. Alonso was assistant Secretary of State at that time. He handled it internally. They didn't press criminal charges, but they fired him immediately and stripped him of his pension only four years away from retirement."

"That was a blow to him and his family," Lessye said. "He died in a car accident less than a week later. And I heard that his wife, Martha, died of a massive stroke not long afterwards. I guess the grief was too much for her. It was a sad, sad story. I still regret not going to his funeral. But I was new, it was on a work day and my supervisor discouraged it because of the scandal."

"Don't feel too bad," Rod said. "I didn't go either. I was on special duty that day."

"Now that I think about it Killian and Henry both died on a Sunday night, before the beginning of a session."

"That's not all. When Henry was killed, an empty bottle of bourbon was found in his car. And both of them worked in the same office at one time."

At that moment, Lessye noticed that a small school group was at the main door.

"Well, duty calls. Time to get back to work."

"Yeah. Me too. I need to check out the fourth floor to monitor crowd control up in the House gallery area. You remember the day a couple of years ago when there were so many people crowded in the building for the budget address that the fire marshal had to clear the fourth floor.

"How can I forget?" Lessye said, and laughed. "That's the same day about one hundred fifty high school seniors showed up without an appointment, and I gave the whole tour lecture outside on the Washington Street steps. See you later."

"Later, Lessye."

═══════════════

Marcus was on a serious high. He had gotten Robert through the first major hurdle of the session, and from the positive responses he observed from the leadership in both parties, he was confident that Robert had set exactly the right tone in his speech. His agenda was on point. The next hurdle would be the State of the State address later in the session.

On his way back to the office for a luncheon meeting with Robert and department heads, Marcus walked by the tour booth and observed Lessye.

He always thought she was fine with her pretty oval face, deep dimples, and sensual heart-shaped lips. He loved her shoulder-length brown hair that fell loosely in thick, silky waves. At five-eight, Lessye was a curvaceous gingersnap beauty who seemed to get more attractive as she grew older. When they first met ten years earlier, Lessye was twenty-two, fresh out of college, and a newlywed. He was a struggling nobody in the mail room. She was always so nice to him, even then.

Now Lessye was divorced, and he, although not an elected official, was the second most powerful person in state government. A poor black boy from the slums of Vine City, was now advising the Governor of the state on policy affecting people throughout Georgia.

He caught Lessye's eye, and she smiled warmly and waved at him. He waved back. He felt the familiar consuming heat he felt every time he saw Lessye or even thought about her. She was everything a man could want. And the girl could cook. Her husband must have been a fool to leave her.

Well his loss was definitely Marcus' gain. Although Marcus had no intentions of settling down with any woman, he honestly enjoyed being around Lessye. Hearing her voice and touching her hand excited him. He found himself drawn to her and thinking about her more and more . . . What was happening to him? He was acting like a simple, silly, love-sick school boy. This kind of thing was dangerous. He had to snap out of it and come back to reality quick. He had a lot to accomplish and could not afford to allow any woman to make him soft now. Not even if that woman was Lessye.

CHAPTER 9

*G*us Stanton had listened to the Governor's speech via closed circuit television on the Capitol third floor before heading for the shoe-shine stand. Gus had heard many budget addresses during his time and thought Robert's was among the best – regardless of their difference in Party affiliation. At age eighty, Gus was undoubtedly the oldest and most experienced lobbyist under the gold dome. He currently represented the interests of pharmaceutical companies, carpet manufacturers, and a senior citizens organization.

One could safely say that Gus had witnessed every major event to take place in the Capitol during the second half of the twentieth century.

He would never forget the three Governors debacle of 1947. When Governor-elect Eugene Talmadge died before taking office his fourth term, M. E. Thompson, Ellis Arnall, and his son, Herman Talmadge, all claimed rights to the executive office. Secretary of State Ben Fortson "sat on the state seal," refusing to relinquish it until the issue was resolved, taking it home with him each night under the seat in his wheelchair. The matter was not resolved until March 19, 1947, when the Georgia Supreme Court ruled 5-2 that M. E. Thompson should serve as acting Governor until the next general election in 1948.

Gus witnessed the day that 38th District Senator Leroy Johnson took the oath of office in 1963, making him the first African-American to serve in the legislature since the Reconstruction Era.

Gus was there on the proud day in 1965, when eight African-Americans were sworn into the House of Representatives. They included the late

Special Judiciary Chairman Julius C. Daugherty, a good friend whom he still missed.

Old Gus also remembered the hoopla over the Governor's election of 1966, when neither candidate received fifty-one percent of the vote and the outcome of the election had to be decided by the House of Representatives.

Gus was a proud Lincoln Republican as a nod to his great grandfather, Christopher Augustus Stanton, for whom he was named. Gus considered himself conservative on some issues, liberal on others and moderate on most. But above all, he firmly believed in fairness, justice and equality for all.

With a healthy head full of silvery gray hair, a rosy peach complexion, a medium frame and spry gait, he could easily pass for a man at least twenty years younger. The vision in his kind hazel eyes only needed slight correction provided by the hip designer glasses his grands had picked out for him.

Gus was a walking and talking volume of Georgia history who knew every corner in the state house. He was sometimes known to stand with his back to one of those corners when discussing important private business so he could easily detect who was edging up on his turf. He would hold a folder covering his mouth when he talked because from years of experience, he could almost swear that some people at the Capitol possessed the ability to read lips.

From the shoe-shine stand where he was seated on the third floor, he looked down the hall in front of the House Chamber and saw Randy Joe with his trademark scuffed cowboy boots and cheap rumpled business suit; Tyrell, with his perpetual sour scowl; and their lobbyist friend, Nathaniel. Gus had never much cared for any of them and was disgusted by the divisive rhetoric and ideology of their ilk polluting his political party. Gus knew that Tyrell and especially Randy Joe were capable of almost anything, and with the help of Nathaniel, who knew what devilment they could stir up. Nathaniel was a slick, suave, corporate-groomed racist who wore expensive suits and did his dirty work from the boardroom. Gus had talked with him on several occasions, and each time, he found his ideology more and more disturbing.

Gus knew that although Randy Joe and Tyrell had degrees from UGA, they were still ignorant, crazy rednecks. But Nathaniel's intelligence and cool-headed, calculating mind corrupted by an insatiable lust for money beyond all reasoning made him downright sinister. Gus knew that whenever those boys cooked up something, somebody always got burned.

When Marcus returned to his office after his meeting with Robert, Lena was waiting for him. Up to this point, his day had been going too good. Robert's speech was fantastic, and Lessye was lingering on his mind.

He knew from the expression on Lena's face that she was ready for a repeat of Monday, but he wasn't in the mood for mischief; besides he had something more important to discuss with her.

"Come in, Lena. Sit down."

Lena entered the office and sat on the sofa adjacent to his desk. Marcus, refusing to take the hint, settled in the seat behind his desk.

"Why are you being so unsociable?" she asked, tossing her hair and crossing her legs. "I would think you would be in a good mood."

"I am. That's why I'm still sitting at my desk. Besides, there's a time and place for everything."

She leaned back and licked her lips seductively. "Funny, you didn't say that on Monday."

"That was Monday, and this is Wednesday. And it's time for business. What else can you tell me about Renae?"

"Why are you so interested in Renae? I thought it was Lessye who struck your fancy?"

Marcus did not respond. He stared at her with a cold and detached look in his eyes.

"Okay. I told you that Renae stays nervous all the time. I thought it was because of what happened to her grandparents. That has something to do with it, but there's more. Renae told me she has narcolepsy. It's a sleeping disorder that– "

"I know what it is. And?"

"She had an episode at work. We were alone in her suite, and I convinced her to confide in me about it. She said it wasn't the first time."

Marcus leaned forward. "When?"

"When, what?"

"When did she have the episode?"

Lena ducked her head and looked at him sheepishly. "Last Tuesday or Wednesday. I can't remember what day."

"And you waited until now to tell me? I saw you Monday. Why didn't you mention it then?"

"So much was going on Monday. We got sidetracked, and it slipped my mind," she said, alluding to their intimate time together. "Then you had to go to the Governor's office and —"

"Stay focused! This is important to me. I want to know exactly what you know, as soon as you know it. Got it?"

"Sure, baby."

"Is there more?"

"She's terrified it will happen again and people on the job will find out. She doesn't want anyone to know. And she's nervous about something else. Yesterday she told me she had one of the attacks Sunday evening after the Wild Hog Dinner. She was in the car with Killian at the time. Renae said all she could remember was leaving the dinner after feeling ill, and Killian offered her a ride home. That's all she remembered until waking up in her apartment several hours later."

"Why is she nervous about that?"

"She's afraid because she thinks she may have been the last person to see Killian alive."

"So what if she was?"

"Why don't you ask her yourself?"

"Is that all?" Marcus asked, ignoring her, his facial expression not changing.

"Yes, for now."

"Good. I want you to stay close to her. Be her best friend. I want to know her every move. Oh, and one more thing. Remember, this is strictly confidential, only between you and me."

"Why?"

"That's my business."

"Whatever you say. What are you doing this weekend?"

"I'm busy. I'm attending some King Week activities with Robert. I'll be tied up all weekend."

"You can't squeeze in a little time to see me? If you come to my apartment, I'll have something good for you. Or, I can always come to you."

"We'll see. Now run along. I've got work to do."

CHAPTER 10

*A*fter returning from Killian's memorial service Friday morning, Lessye took an early lunch so she would be back at the Capitol a half hour before the King program started at one. She called Tanya in advance, who arranged to join her.

When Lessye arrived in the break room, carrying two grilled chicken salads she had purchased in the cafeteria, she found Tanya already there and waiting with two ice cold bottles of water.

"How was the memorial service?" Tanya asked.

"It was a nice tribute – and brief. The church was packed. I barely got there in time to get a seat on the back row. The few cousins who blew in from out of town looked like it was a duty call. They didn't seem too broken up. I think the Governor and Mrs. Baker took it harder than they did."

"That's too bad," Tanya said, then quickly changed the subject. "You have any special plans with Marcus this weekend?"

"Down girl. Marcus is busy this weekend. He's accompanying the Governor to several King Week activities. And I'm taking it easy. I'm planning to get some sleep. After dance class this evening, I'm going to go home and crash. And if things work out like I've planned, I will be resting comfortably in bed and won't leave the house again until time for church Sunday morning. After church and dinner with Aunt Rose, I'm cooling out for the rest of the evening and all day Monday."

"*That's* exciting," Tanya said. "I was hoping you and Marcus might hook up."

"Maybe next week."

"Have you two made a definite date?"

"No. But maybe I'll call him next week and see if he's free for dinner next Saturday. He's invited me out several times, and it's about time I reciprocate by treating him to dinner."

"Good girl. Do it. I'd call him Tuesday if I were you."

"I know you would. You are so fast."

Tanya gave her a sly look. "Yes, Ma'am. You know the old saying. The early hen catches the fine rooster."

"Girl, you made that up."

"Regardless," Tanya said, not missing a beat, "you better get to work and catch Marcus. You need to spend more time with that man away from the Capitol. And I don't count going to the Governor's dinner."

"You said away from the Capitol, and the Governor's Mansion is away from the Capitol."

"I mean away from the whole state government culture. How else are you going to get to know Marcus unless you spend some time alone with him?"

"You're right."

As they munched on their salads, they chatted about the usual challenges that come with the first week of the session and the latest gossip passed on by Lola.

Lessye remembered her conversation with Rod, and after swearing Tanya to secrecy, told her everything he said.

"Bourbon bottle or not, I don't believe it's true about the drunk driving," Tanya said. "We've been to dinners and receptions with Killian and never saw him order more than one or two drinks. If he was an undercover drinker, he did a good job of hiding it."

"That's what I told Rod."

"And I haven't thought of Henry in years. I remember how upset you were over his death. It was real sad. Who else has Juan told beside Rod?"

"Only the Governor. And if the Governor knows, then so does Marcus," Lessye said.

"I know Rod had something smart to say about Marcus."

Lessye nodded. "He reminded me that everybody believed Marcus over Henry and he knows I did, too. Of course, he always stops short of outright accusing Marcus."

Tanya sighed and shook her head. "Tell Rod I said, *Please, stop the hating.*"

Suddenly the door to the break room flew open and Clarice ran in like she was being chased by a maniac with a machete. She was frantic and out of breath.

"Clarice. What's the matter?" Tanya asked, as startled as Lessye.

"It's. . . it's Renae!" she said breathlessly. "She passed out at her desk, and I had the hardest time waking her. She was unconscious for almost thirty minutes!"

"What?!" Tanya and Lessye said in unison.

"The girl passed out. I was so scared, I called the nurse at the medical aide station, and she came over with a doctor. They were able to revive her, and tried to convince Renae to go back with them to the medical aide station, but she wouldn't do it. The doctor is a cool guy from Della's district. He did everything he could, but Renae would not budge." Clarice took a quick breath. "Renae seemed so terrified by all the attention, she looked like she was ready to pass out again." Exhausted from the excitement, Clarice draped her small frame on a chair and pushed her braids out of her chestnut-brown face, shining from light perspiration.

"Do you know why she passed out?" Lessye asked. "Is she sick?"

"I don't think so. One minute she was working on an assignment. I turned away for a moment to answer the telephone. The next thing I knew she was slumped over on the floor unconscious."

"What did the doctor say?" Tanya asked.

"There wasn't much he could say. She didn't hardly want to answer his questions. He checked her blood pressure and heart rhythm and took her temperature, and she checked out okay. Renae tried to play it off as an attack of nerves. One of her representatives had been riding her earlier."

"Where is she now?" Lessye asked.

"Lena came in as the doctor and nurse were leaving. She took Renae out for a while to get some air and some food in her stomach."

"Lena to the rescue," Tanya said.

"Lena was a big help!" Clarice said with tears in her eyes. "I don't know what I would have done without her. Amber couldn't leave the suite, and I was almost hysterical. I thought Renae was dying!"

Tanya handed her a couple of napkins to dab her eyes and face.

"But everything is okay now?" Lessye said. "Renae wasn't dying. She's okay."

"Yes, but it still worries me," Clarice said. "Renae is hiding something from us."

Tanya's need-to-know antenna went up. "What makes you think that?"

"Because, Lena was so cool and calm. It was as if Lena knows what's going on with Renae. I could tell by the way they looked at each other when I told Lena what happened."

"You think Renae has a secret concerning her health?" Lessye asked.

Clarice shrugged. "I don't know. But she refused to go to the infirmary. Now if I had fallen out all of a sudden like that, I would be scared out of my mind."

"Yes, we know," Tanya said, cutting her eyes at Lessye. "After waking up you'd probably have called for an ambulance to take you, sprawled out on a gurney, to Grady's trauma center."

Clarice stood up. "It's not funny, Tanya. This is serious!"

"Okay. You're right. I'm sorry," Tanya said. "It does sound strange. Maybe she does have something to hide."

The three of them looked at one another, and there was no need for further conversation. If Renae was hiding a secret and Lena knew about it, then it was their duty in the grand tradition of nosey state employees to find out.

Marcus purposely kept Senator Windsor "Sammy" Nokes waiting in the reception area for over an hour before allowing him to be ushered into the Governor's office.

Sammy impatiently strode into the executive office expecting a meeting with the Governor. Who he got instead was Marcus.

"Wait a minute. What's going on?" Sammy asked as Marcus spun around in the Governor's chair to face him.

"Good afternoon, Sammy. Come in and have a seat."

Sammy looked as if he were ready to spit. "What are you trying to pull, Marcus? I've been trying to get an appointment with Robert since Wednesday and getting the run around. I've been sitting in the front office for over an hour. Now I want to see Robert."

"That won't be possible. Robert had to leave on an emergency. He's doing a helicopter fly by of flood damaged areas in Southeast Georgia with GEMA. He asked me to take the meeting. So you have two choices: You can tell me what you want or you can leave."

Sammy reluctantly took his seat.

"Okay. If that's the way you guys want to play it. I have a serious problem with Robert's budget and some of the local items he's left out. During the last campaign, I made my constituents two promises. One was that I would bring a state-of-the-art medical center to our area. The other was that I would get 10 million dollars in local assistance grant money to match local funds in building a new tri-county library. If I don't deliver on those promises, I may as well kiss my Senate seat goodbye come next election."

Marcus stared at him coldly. "Those are issues you should be discussing with the House and Senate Appropriations chairs."

"Don't try and screw with me, Marcus. You know the chairs were handpicked by the Governor and rubber-stamped by the Speaker and Lieutenant Governor. They are Robert's boys and they're planning to support his budget down the line. If I want something in the budget, I've got to get your boss' okay. Or . . . is it you I should be worried about?"

Marcus laughed. "I'm only the chief of staff. I'm here to listen to your appeal and then give Robert recommendations. Incidently, how are you getting along with your majority leader these days?"

Sammy flinched, and Marcus knew he had struck a raw nerve. Sammy resented the Senate Majority Leader, who was the first African-American in history ever to hold the position – a position that Sammy felt was rightfully his. The two rarely agreed on anything, and their relationship was contentious at best.

"What do you think?"

"I think you're not a team player. You ignore the authority of important members of our team, but yet you have the nerve to come in here demanding our help."

"What do I have to do to get your boss' attention? Switch parties?"

"That's about the only way you're going to raise enough money to mount a gubernatorial campaign. The Democrats would not stand for you challenging an incumbent. So realistically, you'd have to run to the Republicans, that is if right-wing radicals like Randy Joe and Tyrell would have you."

Sammy began to squirm in his seat. "What are you talking about?"

"I hear you're a man of great ambitions — big aspirations. A little bird told me you might be thinking about challenging Robert in 2002. You can't honestly think I'd sit back and let you pose a threat to him getting re-elected to another term."

Sammy sat back in surprise. "I don't know where you got your information from, but I assure you—"

"Come on. I don't have to be a Rhodes scholar to figure out your plan. And I don't necessarily have to depend on your loose-lipped cronies to tell me what I need to know. Let's look at recent history. During the last election cycle, you avoided Robert like a bad case of the flu. Every time we came to your district, you had another pressing engagement which took you out of town. You were unopposed, but according to your campaign disclosure statements, you raised more money than any other legislator in your area. Yet, you didn't donate one cent to help Robert get elected. You're aligning yourself with conservative Democrats and moderate Republicans in an area of south Georgia that gave Robert less support than anywhere else in the state. You're disloyal. And if you are not loyal to us, how do you expect us to be loyal to you?"

"I'm a good Democrat, and you know it! I support you guys on every vote even though your boy keeps his foot in my face at every turn. I don't ask for much. Never have. But I need these two items in the budget. I might not have been with Robert during his campaign stops, but I seem to remember reading in the paper that he promised my district a medical center and a library. He said he would support the projects. He gave his word. What's it going to look like if he goes back on his word? The people want a Governor with integrity."

"And that's exactly what they have. I never said Robert has gone back on his word. In fact he is in strong support of these projects. So strong that he's planning a trip to your area in a couple of weeks. He's been invited by Representative Todd Bankston. I'm sure you know him — energetic young go-getter in his third term in the House. A real rising star in the Party. Can you see the photo-op of that clean cut young man standing shoulder to shoulder with Robert when he announces to your constituents that they will have a new medical center and library solely due to the efforts of Bankston? Can't you see the publicity? With that kind of positive publicity alone, Todd could probably get elected to any office in the district he wanted. I hear Todd also has ambitions. He might even decide to run for the Senate seat in his district next time. Oh . . . my bad. I forgot. That's your seat, isn't it?"

What little color he had drained from Sammy's face. "You can't give someone else credit for projects I've been fighting for. And you can't threaten me with my Senate seat out of spite."

"We can do whatever we want to. Robert's poll numbers reflect an eighty percent approval rating. The full weight of this office supports those who support us. If you don't wise up and join our team your constituents will replace you faster than a snotty handkerchief. You'll be standing on a street corner shaking a cup with the rest of the bums when we get through with you."

From the look on Sammy's face, Marcus knew he had the distinguished senator by the most tender part of his male anatomy and took great pleasure in squeezing – hard.

The life of a state legislator was a precarious one if they intended to get re-elected. They walked a tight rope of tough decisions to make. And it was impossible to please everyone. If a legislator's district had a strong position on a controversial issue, they put pressure on their duly elected official to vote in their favor. But if the leadership opposed that position, the legislator risked not ever securing another dime in local assistance grants or discretionary funds if they bucked the powers that be. When it came down to it, nothing outweighed money pouring into a district from the annual state budget. No matter how courageous a legislator might be, come election time, what they could tangibly deliver to the community trumped a few forgotten votes.

There were the exceptional rare mavericks like Alonso who commanded everyone's respect and were known as advocates for the poor and downtrodden. They personally fought the battles of their constituency, always introducing legislation with implications of protecting their rights. Their constituents couldn't have cared less how much money came to the district as long as they were available to draft the occasional letter on their behalf and join a picket line protesting unfair treatment at a moments notice. Unfortunately, Sammy was not in that league.

Sammy gave a sigh of defeat. "All right. You win. What do I have to do?"

"Start by recommitting your loyalty to the Party," Marcus said in an upbeat manner, not too unlike a college pep squad leader. "Robert could as easily come to your district at your invitation. During a big public rally, you could put your arm around his shoulder and in front of all the television cameras, declare your unwavering support for him. Talk about your commitment to making sure Robert's legislative package is successful and pledge to work amicably with your majority leader. Dispel all rumors that you're planning to switch parties and run for Governor. Deny it emphatically. Knowing Robert, he will be so overwhelmed with your outpouring of loyalty and support, I wouldn't be surprised if he made the announcement then and there that your medical center and library were not only in the budget but you are the man to thank for it."

Sammy's raven eyes seemed drained of their usual fierce energy. "Does this also include a hefty contribution to his next campaign?"

"Let your conscience be your guide."

Sammy rose to leave. Marcus walked him to the door. "I understand," Sammy said, struggling hard to muster an agreeable team-like posture.

"We'll look forward to hearing from you," Marcus said, sending him off with a friendly pat on the back. "Isn't it wonderful to understand each other?"

Sammy grunted and was gone. Another problem solved, Marcus thought to himself.

Marcus would return to his own office for his last meeting of the day. It would be with Representative Todd Bankston. The boy was in a serious moral dilemma: whether to vote in favor of the citizens who elected him or support the will of the Governor who could make sure he had something to take back to his district. It was time for another lesson in loyalty.

CHAPTER 11

*A*lonso was beginning to think he would never get on the road to Savannah on Sunday afternoon. After an unexpected visitor, combined with other last-minute complications, he wound up leaving an hour late for his at least four-hour drive from Atlanta. Alonso was an ordained minister, whose duties as an elected official precluded him from accepting the responsibilities of a full-time ministerial position. He did, however, frequently travel around the state making speeches and delivering inspiring sermons always evoking a chorus of amens from spirited congregations.

That evening he was scheduled to deliver a sermon during a special King Week service at a local Baptist church followed by a rally at Savannah State University. On Monday, he would participate as grand marshal in the annual parade down Martin Luther King Jr. Boulevard.

This trip was just what he needed to relax his mind and connect with people who supported his mission to uplift the quality of life for African-Americans. He would deliver a strong message of unity, participation and service to the community.

As Alonso drove along at a moderate speed, he thought about his unexpected visitor and the meetings he reluctantly attended on his way through Macon. He knew he'd better get plenty of rest during these few days away, because he would need all the stamina he could muster upon returning to Atlanta.

Alonso could tell this was shaping up to be a difficult year. It had kicked off with the workshop he attended with Brad and Killian in New York. He could hardly believe that Killian, a priceless ally in the Senate, was gone forever. But in the midst of his grief, there was still work to be done.

There was a situation with Marcus that had to be handled immediately. He would definitely have his hands full keeping the Caucus agenda focused and on course. He would have to fend off attacks by racist right wing conservatives like Randy Joe who were determined to dismantle all the gains that minorities had made since 1970. He knew now, without a doubt, that Randy Joe and his crew would make another attempt this year to abolish affirmative action. This time, they would not only have the full support of their party members – which now included the conservative black member – but Alonso knew for a fact that several moderate Democrats were also leaning in that direction. If they succeeded, minorities and women in the state of Georgia would surely lose ground. The Black Caucus would have to stick together this year, or they would be sunk.

Alonso was barely twenty miles from Macon when he began feeling nauseous and a sharp pain gripped his stomach. He unbuckled his seat belt to try and ease the pain. The next exit was miles away, and he pondered whether it would be a good idea to pull to the shoulder of the road for a few minutes. He looked at his watch. It was almost four. He could easily make it to Savannah in time for the program that evening. A few seconds later he suddenly lost consciousness and his sedan spun out of control, flipped over the guard rail, and landed upside down in a deep ravine.

Lessye spent Sunday with her Aunt Rose, returning home after six in the evening. She checked for telephone messages. There was only one, a frantic message from Clarice asking her to call as soon as possible.

Lessye immediately dialed her number, and the phone was snatched up on the first ring.

"Hello!"

"Clarice? This is Lessye. I got your message. What's up?"

"Lessye, thank goodness you called! I tried to call Tanya and Lena but neither of them were home either."

"What is it? What's the matter? Your message sounded almost hysterical."

"It's Renae. She called me sounding crazy and disoriented. She's stranded at the bus station in Macon!"

"I'm on my way."

Lessye jumped in her Ford Contour, picked up Clarice and off they went to Macon as fast as the speed limit would allow. Traffic was light, and it would have been an enjoyable ride if they hadn't been so worried about Renae.

When they arrived at the Greyhound bus station in Macon, Renae looked like she had been in a fight. Her navy suit was wrinkled and smudged with dirt, and her hair was sticking up all over her head like she had barely escaped a dog pack.

"Renae, what happened to you? How did you get here?" Clarice tried to pat her hair down and brush some of the dirt off of her clothes.

"Lena was driving down to Macon to visit her aunt. She asked me to ride with her. We had an argument, and she dropped me off at the bus station. She left before I realized I didn't have enough money to get back home."

"Lena just left you here? Did you two have a fist fight?" Clarice asked.

"No, we argued, that's all."

"About what?" Lessye asked.

"It's personal, and I'd rather not say."

"You and Lena are good friends," Clarice said. "Now you're telling us that she would leave you stranded in Macon? I can't see her leaving you here no matter how mad you got. Are you telling us the truth?"

"Yes. What reason would I have to lie? Lena and I spent the day together. She was depressed this weekend so I invited her to go to church this morning and then afterwards we picked up some food and took it back to my place because the restaurant was crowded. After dinner, she asked me to ride with her to Macon. While we were here, we argued."

"Renae, are you sure you're telling us everything?" Lessye asked. "And what's the story on your fainting spells?"

Renae glared at Clarice. "You told her?"

"Yes, I told Lessye and Tanya. I was worried about you."

"We all were," Lessye said. "Now talk to us, Renae."

"All right. I fainted, that's all," Renae said with tears in her eyes. She rubbed her stomach. "I appreciate you coming to get me. Please, can we go home. My head is pounding, and my stomach hurts."

And go home they did. Because Renae wasn't feeling well, she didn't want to be alone in her apartment, so Lessye invited Renae to stay with her since Clarice's apartment was small, and she already had two roommates.

After dropping Clarice off at her place, Lessye and Renae swung by Renae's apartment so she could pack an overnight bag. When they arrived at Lessye's, she took Renae to her upstairs guest room, and that is where Renae parked and stayed for the remainder of Sunday night. On Monday, she stayed in bed all day, barely getting up to creep downstairs and nibble on some salad and drink some juice and then return upstairs.

Lessye spent her morning watching the live telecast of the King Ecumenical Service, and the afternoon reading and thinking about Renae and her trip to Macon. Lessye realized that Renae remained holed up in her guest room to keep her from asking any more questions about it. She barely responded when Lessye knocked on the door to try and tell her about Alonso.

Tuesday morning, when Lessye awakened, to her surprise, Renae was already gone. She left a note thanking her again for picking her up and for her gracious hospitality.

Lessye picked up the telephone to call Renae, then decided against it. Lessye had to face the fact that Renae didn't trust her enough to confide her trouble. And if Lessye didn't get a move on she was going to be late for work.

CHAPTER 12

*A*lonso's death had subdued the mood at the tour booth. Everyone knew Alonso had been a favorite of Lessye's, and they were especially sensitive to her feelings.

"Lessye, are you all right? Is there anything I can do?" Jon asked, before leaving the desk to begin his first tour.

"No, I'm fine. Thank you for asking. You go ahead and start your tour."

But everything wasn't fine. The morning had not started well for Lessye, who was deeply upset over Alonso's death. She hardly slept last night after hearing the news. When she finally fell into a fitful sleep, she woke up late because she didn't hear her clock alarm. Lessye had taken her shower and dressed so fast that she wondered whether she remembered to put on deodorant. She was having a horrendous hair day. And to top it off, she pulled a run as wide as a MARTA train track in her last pair of panty hose. *What a morning!*

Renae's desperate situation Sunday evening and hasty departure that morning were still on her mind, too.

"Lessye, wake up." It was Rod. He had come up quietly behind her.

"Hey, Rod, Why don't you get some taps on your shoes so a sister can hear you coming?"

"I wasn't tipping."

"Maybe my mind is somewhere else. Have you heard anything else about Alonso's accident?"

"That's what I stopped by to tell you," he said. Rod stared into Lessye's tearful eyes, and she guessed what he was going to say.

"There was a bottle of bourbon found in his car, wasn't it?"

"Yes," he said. "According to Juan, the bottle was empty."

———

Brad Austin sat doodling on his legal pad in the Appropriations Committee room in the Capitol. But his mind was not on the first of a steady succession of state department commissioners and agency heads who were scheduled throughout the week to plead cases and defend budget requests. His thoughts were about the sudden death of his friend and colleague, Alonso. The death of his friend, Killian, had only started to sink in, and now Alonso was gone.

Along with mourning his friends, Brad had someone else on his mind: Marcus. Brad had known Marcus since the two worked together in the office of Secretary of State, and he had never forgotten the Perkins incident. Brad never cared much for Marcus, but he truly believed Marcus' story about Henry being guilty of theft. They all had. Marcus was so convincing. But Henry was the one telling the truth after all. Marcus used him, Killian, and Alonso in a malicious plan to get rid of Henry, and now there was proof. The new revelation came ten years too late to save poor Henry, but Brad's conscience would not allow him to keep quiet, no matter how much Marcus wanted him to. Henry was cheated out of his pension and his granddaughter deserved compensation. Henry deserved to have his name cleared. Brad felt obligated to do what he could to right this wrong. Brad also thought it his duty to tell Robert, who had a right to know the truth about what happened ten years earlier. He had a right to know that his chief of staff was power hungry, ruthless, and dangerous.

Brad's thoughts turned to his aide, Lena, another potential problem of a different kind. Brad found out about Lena's attraction to Marcus, but in warning her away from him, he seemed to have given her the mistaken impression that he wanted her for himself. Lena had been coming on strong since his trip to New York the first week in January and with the exception of a misunderstanding concerning her college alumni participation, she had been all but dripping honey.

Lena was smart, beautiful and provocative, with a reputation with men that preceded her. Brad was old enough to be her father and not the type of man to mix business with pleasure. Starting a romantic relationship with an employee was only asking for trouble down the line. Brad was determined to keep their relationship on a professional level.

He remembered the surprise he had for her, something he came across on his recent trip. It was intended to be only a friendly gesture, but now he wondered whether he should still give it to her for fear of sending the wrong signals. The last thing he wanted to do was give her the wrong impression.

"Why didn't you return any of my messages over the weekend, Marcus? I must have called you about twenty times."

Marcus glared at Lena, who'd burst into his office. His light brown eyes suddenly took on a fierce quality. In a cold voice he said, "Lena, you know better than to enter my office without knocking, and because you are an intelligent girl, you also know it's not wise to talk to me in that tone of voice."

"Save your intimidation tactics for the weak-spined legislators you bully. You didn't answer my question."

"I told you I was busy. I didn't have time for you or anyone else. So get off my back!"

"You can't treat me any way you want to and get away with it."

"How am I treating you?"

"Like a tramp."

"Well, if the thong fits, tug it on, princess. I haven't done anything to you that you didn't want. You're a spoiled brat who thinks that men should be at your beck and call because you look good. Well look around you, baby. There are plenty of women on the Hill who look good, many of them better than you. So get over yourself."

"I suggest you get over yourself. You're far from the most popular brother on the Hill. So it wouldn't be wise for you to alienate the few friends you have. Brad has disliked you since you worked together in the office of Secretary of State. He knows about some underhanded mess you pulled back then. He saw us together one day and warned me not to trust you. And I might tell my good friend, Renae, that you are spying on her for some reason. Maybe she can figure out why since you won't tell me —"

Before she could finish the last sentence, Marcus lunged across the room, grabbing Lena and pinning her arms painfully behind her back.

"Stop it! You're hurting me!"

"What happened to all that bravado? I believe it's melting into fear." He pressed his face to hers, and she could feel the heat of his breath. "Lena, baby, you have no idea what hurt is. If you even think of crossing me, you'll be sorry the thought ever entered your mind."

"Marcus, please let me go. I'm sorry. I didn't mean it."

"That's better." He released his tight grip on her and smiled as he gently caressed her face. "Now, I know what you want, and I have about an hour to kill before my next appointment. I'm going to give it to you. Get on the couch."

Lena did as she was told as Marcus locked his office door. He was about to join her when his secretary buzzed him. The Governor wanted to see him immediately.

CHAPTER 13

$\mathcal{D}$r. Gordon Sizemore, director of the GBI Division of Forensic Sciences Toxicology Section, was extremely agitated because he had not uncovered the real reason for Killian's death. Yes, it had been established that he expired from injuries sustained in the car crash. But what precipitated the accident in the first place? What happened prior to the crash that made Killian lose control of his car? Why wasn't he wearing his seat belt?

Prior to the case reaching Gordon's department, the car Killian had been driving was thoroughly inspected and found to be in tip-top condition. An autopsy failed to reveal any physical explanations, such as a stroke, heart attack, or seizure. So there were only two other possible reasons: alcohol or drugs. Although an empty bottle of bourbon was found in his car, careful analysis of his blood proved conclusively that all the missing alcohol was not in his body. The percent of his blood alcohol content was less than 0.08 gm. The next step was to check for drugs. Killian was not on any prescribed medications. And on first examination, no evidence of any illegal substance was found. Gordon was not satisfied. He would not be satisfied with the explanation that Killian fell asleep behind the wheel. His behavior had definitely been influenced by something.

Another priority case was now on his desk. Representative Alonso Steele died of injuries sustained in a single-car accident, and a bottle of bourbon was also found. But none of it was in his system. Another legislator, who knew the dangers of driving without a seat belt, had failed to buckle up. Two legislators dead of similar circumstances in seven days? Something was going on, and it was Gordon's mission to find out what it was.

CHAPTER 14

S ean's eyes darted across the desk of the Appropriations secretary, Rita Kirk, as his ears tuned in to several conversations going on in the room. He needed an interview with the committee chairman and hoped to pick up any other juicy tidbits for the *Capitol Reporter*. His newsletter was appropriately named due to the fact that Sean was an excellent reporter, and he reported everything he knew. He carried a small tape recorder (in case a disgruntled subject developed a sudden case of direct-quote amnesia) along with his laptop and camera, which were never out of his sight.

The color of caramel candy with brooding brown eyes, he sported a short tight Afro. His plain, uneven features were balanced by an unnerving charm and mischievous smile that could sometimes be deceiving. He was a hopeless flirt whose reputation with the women was almost as legendary as his adept news-gathering skills. Although he was not tied down in a steady relationship, he was rumored to have made some pretty top-shelf conquests on the Hill during his time.

"I'm sorry for the interruption, Sean. I couldn't get out of taking that call. It was urgent."

"That's all right, Rita. You know I don't mind waiting for you, beautiful. Seeing you always makes my day."

"Here comes the sugar. What do you want this time, Sean?"

"Only a private interview with the chairman. I know he's busy this week, so it won't take more than five minutes of his time. I need to ask him a couple of questions. But I would rather it was in his office than out in the hall or in the Appropriations room. Fewer distractions."

"In that case, I'll schedule you for a quick meeting here in the office at twelve-thirty. The chairman is having lunch catered in today. So he should have a few extra minutes before the hearings begin again at one."

"Thanks, Rita."

"Isn't it sad about Alonso? Right on the heels of Killian."

"Yeah, it is."

"What's going on around here?"

"I don't know . . ."

"But I'm sure you're going to find out."

Sean smiled. "Well, I certainly will do my best."

Sean left the office and circled the third floor, listening for conversations for him to eavesdrop. He was especially keeping his ears open for any information he could find out about the deaths of Killian, and now, Alonso. He interviewed the Lieutenant Governor, several legislators, as well as the Governor and his trusty sidekick, Marcus, about Killian last week. The stiff interviews with Marcus and The Emperor piqued his curiosity. It wasn't what they said. It was what they didn't say with the same element of mystery. The Governor and Killian were friends, yet he was picking his words carefully and counting the minutes until the interview was over. Those two were definitely hiding something, especially Marcus, who worked overtime to make it difficult for him to get information from the Governor's office. So much for looking out for a brother.

Now, just a week later, another prominent legislator was dead. Both killed in car accidents, both died on a Sunday, both previously worked in the office of Secretary of State, both were currently powerful men of liberal politics in the state legislature, both men were single.

Sean decided to leave the third floor and go check out what was happening on the second floor. Maybe he would hang around the Governor's office for a while. The Capitol was Sean's stomping ground, and with the exception of old Gus and that cute tour guide, Lessye, he probably knew more about the Capitol than anyone else currently working there. He had numerous contacts in the building, as well as other state agencies.

Sean made it a point to scoop all the other media people who covered the Capitol beat, and it was easy for him because everybody knew him. Most importantly, he was their pal, a cool confidant, who never revealed his sources. Sean possessed a unique talent. But most importantly, he was relentless and resourceful, which, in the long run, would get him farther than mere talent and an Irish name ever would.

CHAPTER 15

*J*esse Higgins was a sick man, physically and spiritually. On the physical side, years of smoking resulted in lungs first crippled by emphysema, now consumed by rapidly spreading cancer. Equally as many years of hard drinking had fried his liver.

Jesse knew — long before the doctors told him — that he was a man not long for this world, and he desperately wanted to make it into the next with a mansion and a crown. This forced him to look hard at his spiritual side and get himself right with God. Jesse still had one more account to settle before checking himself back into Grady Hospital for what he knew would be his last time. Only when he did what he should have done ten years ago would his conscience be clear. Only then would he be able to close his eyes for the last time and rest in peace with the angels.

He had broken his ten-year silence and told his beloved Mattie Mae. She encouraged him to do the right thing. Jesse sifted through a battered tin box that held his keepsakes – the cards, letters, photographs, old coins, medals, and mementoes which, combined, pieced together the tender threads of his life. His most valuable treasure was an old gold wedding band, the remnants of his first and only attempt at marriage. He would give this to Mattie Mae during their next breakfast.

Jesse was a coal black runt of a man with tired bloodshot eyes and thinning gray hair. His chronic illnesses left him frail and wiry, with a lingering chill that ached deep in his bones and an aggravating hacking cough that chopped at the pit of his throat.

He sat tentatively at the battered makeshift wooden desk in his sparsely decorated two-room apartment in the Open Arms assisted living center on Simpson Road and began scrawling the last of four important letters. Three others had already been sent. They were addressed to Senator Killian Drake, Representative Alonso Steele, and Representative Brad Austin. Jesse had been shocked to learn of the sudden deaths of Drake and Steele and prayed they had gotten the letters in time.

He addressed the last letter to his friend, the only person from the Capitol who cared enough to call and come to visit him. He loved Rod like a son. Rod would visit him this coming Sunday, and he would put the letter in his hands. It was past time to reveal the truth. Marcus would pay for his crimes.

Unlike the secretarial staff, which had a mini-breather during the week of recess, Lessye's week had gotten off to a fast and busy start. There were so many tour groups, news conferences to coordinate, and choral and band groups to assist, Lessye didn't catch her first wind until Friday. It was so hectic, she hadn't been able to join Tanya for lunch once that week and calling Marcus about dinner had slipped her mind. She didn't think about it until she ran into him in front of the floor leader's office on the first floor Friday morning.

"Hey, Lessye, you've been a busy lady this week. Every time I call the desk, you're either on tour or I get the voice mail."

"Why didn't you leave a message?"

"I kept intending to catch you at home. But Robert's schedule has been tight. I've been attending functions almost every evening and usually get home too late to call." Marcus moved closer to her and whispered in her ear. His face was so close to hers that she felt his lips gently brush her ear which made her tingle with excitement.

"How do you do it?" he asked.

"What?"

"Always manage to look and smell as sweet as a fresh garden rose?"

"Thank you. You say the sweetest things." She blushed.

"That's because you give me wonderful inspiration."

"I've been meaning to talk with you this week, too."

Marcus' eyes lit up. "Really."

"Yes. I know it's late notice. But do you have plans for tomorrow evening?"

"No. And if I did, I'd break them. What's up?"

"How about dinner at my place?"

"Are you cooking?"

"Yes."

"Then that sounds great. Early in the day, I'm attending Alonso's funeral with Robert. Dinner with you will be just the thing to raise my spirits. What time?"

"I'm going to the funeral, too, and will probably do some shopping after that. How about eight? That will give me enough time to have everything prepared."

"Sounds good. I can't wait."

"See you then."

CHAPTER 16

*G*eorgia peach production was a booming industry that made the nickname "Peach State" well deserved and Randy Joe's family millionaires for generations.

Peaches were first grown in Georgia in the 1700s during the colonial period. By 1800, some farmers were said to have approximately 5,000 peach trees, and by 1889, some Georgia peach orchards stretched for 3,000 acres. Presently, there were more than 2.4 million peach trees in the state with each tree having the potential to produce a commercial crop for up to 15 to 20 years.

A variety known as "Elberta," first grown in middle Georgia, was the first peach to be successfully shipped to distant markets. Red Haven was now the most widely planted and marketed variety in the United States.

Randy Joe had an intimate love-hate relationship with the temperamental fuzzy fruit that, if not pampered, could easily send one plummeting from riches to ruin.

Peaches were an extremely difficult fruit to grow. Conditions must be nearly perfect to ensure a full crop. Too much or too little rain, not enough chilling hours, a late frost, disease, insects and wind, and not enough sunshine for the ripening process could wreak havoc on the size and quality of a crop. There were also considerable risks in packing and shipping peaches, which bruise easily, and could be damaged if not handled properly. Not to mention the short shelf life.

From the veranda of his four-story, antebellum-style mansion, Randy Joe surveyed the dormant buds of his orchard. Reynolds Farms was among the seven major growers within 20 miles of Fort Valley. With more than 617,000 trees producing more than 40 commercial varieties of peaches, Peach County had the highest concentration of peach trees in Georgia. Until the late 1980s, the peach-picking workforce on Reynolds Farms had been predominantly black. But as more and better opportunities opened, they aspired to better jobs that did not subject them to the scorching 100-degree temperatures of peach orchards. Now the work was done by migrants, some of whom boasted picking up to 120 bags a day in the sweltering conditions. Randy Joe only tolerated them slightly more than he did blacks.

The blustery January breeze drove Randy Joe off the veranda and back into the house where he went downstairs to see how his wife was progressing with plans for the dinner meeting with the Citizens for a New American Agenda. He wanted everything to be perfect, and no one could make that happen better than his wife, Miss Pearl.

Looking at Pearl now as she directed the servants in preparing the mammoth dining room table for the elaborate buffet-style meal, Randy Joe appreciated the fact that after twenty years of marriage, she was still as gorgeous as the first day they met with her raven-black hair and peaches and cream complexion.

Randy Joe was pleased with how quiet the house was for once. The only movement was the hustle and bustle of the servants. The kids were gone. Their youngest, Tim, was on a weekend scouting sleep over. Their daughter, Kelley, was in Macon with friends probably running up Randy Joe's credit cards shopping. And his oldest, Ronnie had pulled his weekly disappearing act, leaving before the rest of the family woke up Saturday morning.

Randy Joe's thoughts were interrupted by the strong door chime that played the first line of "Dixie." It was Tyrell, closely followed by Nathaniel. They would meet briefly before the others arrived. Tyrell was slightly shorter than Randy Joe, also thin, with straight, rusty brown hair and menacing, snake-like pale blue eyes. The sour look puckering his thin lips gave the appearance that he was always sucking on lemons. He had weak-looking sloping shoulders and a rough complexion, pockmarked from a mixture of acne and a childhood bout with chicken pox. He was non-athletic, with a body that would have been flabby if it wasn't so lean.

Nathaniel was a big man, an imposing figure with a body like a stone building. His huge head and thick neck looked like a square block perched on top of a tree stump. Despite his solid bulk, Nathaniel could easily be described as attractive in an odd sort of way. His dreamy brown eyes and wavy black hair enhanced by appealing features, would have been considered handsome on another man of less bulk. Unlike Randy Joe and Tyrell, who wore their prejudice like a badge, he had a deceptively affable countenance that concealed the danger lurking underneath.

"Come on in, boys. Let me pour you a drink. Name your poison."

"Bourbon, straight," said Tyrell.

"Scotch and soda for me," Nathaniel said.

The men gave their coats to one of the servants and made pleasant conversation with Miss Pearl before she went upstairs. Randy Joe went to the bar and poured their drinks, and they settled in the massive den for their meeting. The den was paneled in cedar wood and included built-in bookshelves containing volumes of books on cars, hunting, fishing, and boats that Randy Joe never so much as cracked open. The walls held a hideous assortment of stuffed heads of wild game that formed an eerie menagerie combined with other garish trophies he had collected through the years. There was a huge display case that held an heirloom gun collection passed down from his great granddaddy. There were expensively framed oil paintings of cowboys on the range and Civil War battle scenes. The fully stocked bar, which traveled the length of one side of the room, was equipped with a mirror and swivel chairs; the maple wood counter glossed to a high sheen. There were two huge leather sofas, coffee tables, comfortable leather club chairs, a billiards table and a wide screen television. Animal skin rugs hugged the hard wood floor. Randy Joe's favorite, yet battered, reclining chair, occupying a prominent corner of the room, served as a tarnished throne for him to reign as king of his castle.

"How's life on the plantation?" Tyrell said as soon as Miss Pearl was out of ear shot.

"I can't complain." Randy Joe eyed the servants, warning them it was time to make themselves scarce, quickly.

Nathaniel settled his big body in one of the leather club chairs. "That was some news about the Right Reverend Steele, wasn't it?"

"Good news if you ask me," said Tyrell. "One less aggravating nigger to impede our progress."

Randy Joe raised his glass. "I'll drink to that."

"Let's not get too excited yet," Nathaniel said. "The jury is still out, whether Alonso's death will work for – or against – us."

"What are you talking about?" Tyrell's pale snake eyes were beginning to darken. "We all know what a shambles that Black Caucus is in. Alonso was their leader, their only strength. Now he's gone. There's nobody in that group who can take the reins and lead that pony across the finish line."

"I wouldn't be so sure of that," Nathaniel said. "They have several potential candidates."

"Who? Bernard Benton?" asked Randy Joe. They all had a good laugh. "But seriously, boys, I haven't noticed anyone with balls like Alonso."

"That's because the person I'm thinking of doesn't have balls," Nathaniel said. "The word is that Della Harden may be the heir apparent."

"Oh, yeah," Randy Joe said. "I forgot about Della. I've seen her in action. That pretty little wench has some juice. She might be a problem. I hear she learned everything she knows from Alonso."

"Wyatt Harvey's name is also being tossed around," said Nathaniel.

"How'd you happen by this information?" Tyrell asked.

"It's my job to know. That's what you boys in the CNAA are paying me for. As a lobbyist, I have to talk to everybody. I don't have the luxury of staying in selective cliques of my conservative brethren. I've observed those two on more than one occasion; they're no pushovers." Nathaniel took a long sip of his drink. "Like Alonso, they've got more clout than the Caucus chairman, who as far as I'm concerned is a figure head. It's the Whip who wields the real power in that outfit. And Della and Wyatt have got it."

"I don't care how strong they are," Tyrell said. "They can't hold that bunch together. And they'll probably raise such a ruckus fighting over the position that they divide the Caucus in half." Tyrell, who had plopped into a swivel chair at the bar, was on his second glass of straight bourbon, and the liquor was beginning to have an affect.

"I wouldn't bet on it this time," Nathaniel said. "And they probably won't have to hold the Caucus together either. Maybe Alonso will hold them together better than he ever did before."

Randy Joe looked at Nathaniel as if he had lost his mind. "How's a dead man going to hold anybody together?"

"The King factor."

"What?" Randy Joe asked. Nathaniel might as well have been speaking in a foreign language.

"By the force of his memory," Nathaniel explained calmly. "Alonso is not any dead man. In the eyes of the civil rights community, he's another dead martyr, like King."

"I hadn't thought of it in that light," Tyrell said and scratched his head. "I'd say it's about time we lit a fire under our new Republican 'soul brother.'"

"Has anyone talked to Bernard?" Nathaniel asked.

"I'm still trying to feel him out, find out what side of the fence he's playing on," Randy Joe said. "We've got a lot of support for this bill this year. Much more than last time. The anti-affirmative action movement is growing, especially in the more conservative rural areas in north and south Georgia. We've got a lot of solid support from Republican strongholds in Cobb and Gwinnett counties right outside Atlanta. A lot of moderate Democrats see our argument, and those who don't are feeling the pressure from their constituents. They're running scared of a backlash at the polls."

Tyrell vigorously nodded his head in agreement. "And with the backing of the CNAA and other strong conservative organizations, we've got a good shot."

Randy Joe took a healthy swig of liquor. "Once we get it on the open floor for debate, we're home free. But we've got to get it out of committee. That's where Bernard comes in. The House Judiciary vote will be close. Bernard better come through."

"I think he knows better than to sell us out. But you better keep the heat on, and don't trust him," Nathaniel warned. "Republican or not – that's a nigger you better watch out for."

CHAPTER 17

*M*arcus arrived at Lessye's house with a bottle of champagne in one hand and two dozen yellow roses in the other. Lessye thought he looked sharp in a royal blue shirt, black wool slacks and black alligator loafers. His thick leather jacket was soft as butter.

Lessye greeted him with her most radiant smile. "Hey, Marcus. Come in."

"These are for you." Marcus said, handing her the bouquet of flowers and the bottle of champagne, then kissing her on the cheek.

"Thank you. How thoughtful. These are lovely. I'll put them in a vase and chill the champagne. If you don't mind, hang your jacket in that closet." She gestured toward the hall closet on her way into the kitchen.

Marcus hung up his jacket, then followed Lessye into the kitchen where she was filling a vase with water. Without the jacket, Lessye could see how well-built Marcus was. His powerful muscles bulged through the blue shirt, and he filled out the wool slacks nicely.

"Everything smells so good, and you look gorgeous," he said admiring Lessye, who was wearing a striking lavender dress that showed off her shapely legs and dangling gold hoop earrings that she loved. The vibrant color complimented her ginger complexion. Her hair fell soft and loose to her shoulders.

"Thank you," she said, placing the flowers on the coffee table in her den. "Make yourself comfortable. I'm serving wine with dinner, but would you care for something stronger?"

"What do you have?"

"Bourbon, scotch, cognac?"

"Bourbon is fine with water and ice."

Lessye went to her bar and prepared his drink. "I hope you have a big appetite."

"Yes, ma'am. My mouth has been watering for this all day." Marcus gave her a suggestive smile. For a moment Lessye didn't know whether he was referring to her cooking or something else.

"Well then, I won't keep you waiting any longer." Lessye took his hand and led him into the dining room, where she seated him at the elegant mahogany table topped with exquisite place settings. The room was spacious with a bay window. West African drums, benches, masks, and colorful fabric enhanced the decor.

"You have several new art pieces since the last time I was here."

"I love my African art. I'm in Densua's at Greenbriar almost every week."

Off the kitchen to the left was a cozy nook of a den that some people now referred to as a keeping room. Healthy green plants in colorful ceramic and clay pots added warmth to the space. There were paintings, basketry, sculpture, and dolls that were a mixture of Afro-centric and Western Indian art she had collected through the years. To the right of the kitchen was the dining room that flowed into the living room.

Lessye served the spinach salad with a warm bacon and ginger dressing, then poured them glasses of a cool, fruity blush wine. Next was the main course: roasted Cornish hens with a sauteed mushroom herb sauce, wild rice, French cut green beans, corn pudding, and rolls made from scratch. For dessert, Lessye went back to her roots and one of her grandmother's favorite recipes, homemade cherry cheese cake.

"Girl, you can throw down," Marcus said after his last bite. "It's been a while since I've tasted your cooking. If possible, I think your skills have improved."

"You can thank Aunt Rose. She and my grandma taught me the art of Southern cooking. I enjoyed watching and helping them in the kitchen."

"I'll remember to thank her the next time I see her in the gallery. She was off this week, wasn't she?"

"Yes. Recess week. The House only had a skeleton crew of doorkeepers working the Appropriations meetings. She'll be back Monday."

Lessye observed Marcus: how strong his hands were and his gentle manners, the masculine heat oozing from him. He seemed to be a perfect gentleman in every way. She wondered why some lucky woman hadn't snagged him by now. She had heard he was romantically involved with Lena. But she never saw them out anywhere together. It was Lessye he occasionally invited to accompany him to the Governor's dinner and other state functions. He seemed to genuinely like her and to enjoy the times they spent together. As far as Lessye knew, she was the only woman with whom he openly flirted. But there was always something that kept him from getting too close, as if he was afraid of revealing too much of himself. Marcus was definitely an enigma.

"We've known each other a long time," Lessye said. "But there is still so much I don't know about you."

"I'm all yours. What would you like to know?" His words always seemed to have a deeper meaning. He had a way of looking at her like she was the only woman on earth, the only one who mattered. In some strange way, he made it seem like he was giving himself to her – the part he wanted her to have.

"Where did you grow up? Where'd you go to school? What about your parents? What are your likes and dislikes?"

"Hey, slow down. One at a time." Marcus laughed.

"I'm sorry. There are so many things I want to know about you. The few times we've gone out, you always steer the conversation toward me or talk about what's going on in politics. I don't even know whether you like to dance. Do you?"

"Definitely yes to the last question. And I can't wait to get you on the dance floor to see what you've learned from those Salsa lessons."

"I'll look forward to it."

"Now to answer your other questions. I'm a Grady baby. I grew up in an area called Vine City, not too far from Clark Atlanta University. I graduated from Booker T. Washington High School with an honors diploma. I had some great teachers who guided me and helped me get into Georgia State University. I wanted to go to Morehouse but a state school was more in line with my budget."

"What was your major?"

"Political Science. I was a loner who studied all the time because I didn't have many friends to hang out with, and I always had a job. The studying paid off because I graduated magna cum laude."

"I'm impressed. And with your looks, brains, and personality I would think you would have been a popular man on campus, especially with the ladies."

"Thanks. But you'd be surprised."

Marcus became pensive. "My mother died when I was seven. Her family didn't want to keep me, so they sent me to my father's people. We were poor and struggling. They were rough. My dad had a revolving door romance with prison. Not the kind of people you would have come in contact with growing up unless they were mugging you."

"I'm so sorry about your mother." She took his hand in hers. "Maybe there was some other reason her family couldn't keep you. No one would want to give up a wonderful guy like you."

"Thanks. And about my mother . . . well . . . it's been a long time. I don't think about it much anymore. Now you see why I don't talk about myself."

Lessye broke the momentary tense silence between them. "Why don't you open the champagne while I put on a CD."

"Good idea. It should be chilled by now," he said, rising to retrieve it from the refrigerator.

Lessye went into the den, thumbed through her music collection and put on one of her favorite CDs, *The Best of Sade*. The mellow sound of the music drifted behind her into the dining room. Marcus opened and poured the champagne, and she invited him to sit beside her on the comfortable living room sofa. They sat close together, their legs touching ever so gently as they sipped champagne, grooving to the sound of Sade's smooth, hypnotic voice.

"Dance with me," Marcus said. Bathed in the soft lights of her living room, Marcus took her in his arms, and they glided across the floor.

The brother was smooth. The champagne on top of the bottle of wine had taken an effect on Lessye, and she could tell they were both lightheaded.

"You still haven't answered one of my questions," she said.

"What's that?"

"What are your likes and dislikes?"

"Well," he said, "I like holding you in my arms. I like your perfect lips being so close to mine. I don't like the fact that mine are not touching them." At that moment, before Lessye could utter another word, his full lips had covered hers for a long kiss.

Many thoughts twirled through Lessye's mind as she folded closer into Marcus' body: the steadiness of his chest, the softness of his touch, the commanding tenderness of his mouth on hers. Lessye enjoyed the kiss, but there was still the issue of Lena dangling on the edge of her mind. As much as she liked Marcus, she was not about to allow herself to become intimately involved with a man who was sleeping with someone else.

Marcus, sensing her hesitation, pulled away and they retreated to the sofa. "Now it's your turn," he said, pushing back a tendril of her hair. "I know you grew up in Philly. Is that where you were born?"

"Yes, but when I came South to Atlanta to go to CAU, I never left."

"Is that where you met Tanya?"

"During our freshman year. Tanya was fresh off the bus from Hawkinsville, Georgia. We were in the same orientation week huddle group. Then we sang together in the Philharmonic Society. Our bond of friendship and sisterhood grew even stronger when we pledged and became members of Delta Sigma Theta Sorority sophomore year."

"So you fell in love with my hometown?"

"Tanya wasn't about to give up the bright lights and excitement of the city, and as for me, I loved it long before I came to Clark. I spent at least three weeks here every summer when I was in elementary and high school. First, we'd go on a family vacation in June. I'd do the boarding camp thing in July. And in August, I would visit my aunt and grandma."

"Ahhh, rich kid from Chestnut Hill."

"I never thought of it like that. We were blessed with a lot of things, but I didn't get everything I wanted."

"But you sure came close. Your daddy's a judge, and your mom's a teacher. What they gave you was much more than things. I would have given almost anything for a life like that . . . for parents who loved me. Did you mention one time that you have an older brother?"

"Yes, Brian, whose fifteen years older. He and his family live in Philly. He's an attorney. Brian is more like an uncle than a brother. He's always looked out for me. I also have four nephews — two in high school and two in college. They're always getting into something. How about you?"

"I have a half sister, but we don't have contact with each other."

"Does she live in Atlanta? What's her name?"

Marcus took a sip from his glass. "It's not important," he mumbled, shifting his eyes.

Sensing she was stepping into off-limits territory, Lessye didn't press it when he changed the subject.

"I'll bet you're one of those good girls who calls home every Sunday."

"I'm a good girl, but I don't have a special day to call home. I call whenever I feel like talking to my folks. And that's almost all the time. I miss them."

"Do you go home often?"

"Aunt Rose and I go up for Christmas and Mother's Day. Aunt Rose never married or had any children, so she's a second mom to my brother and me. I also spend a couple of weeks at home every summer."

Marcus poured the remainder of the champagne, dividing it equally between both their glasses. Then he took a long sip from his glass.

"Lessye, how long were you married?"

"Five years."

"If you don't mind me asking; what went wrong?"

Lessye sighed. "I failed. I failed Russell, and I failed myself."

"I think you're being too hard on yourself."

"I don't. Not when I measure my marriage by the example of my parents' and my brother's. My parents have been married for forty-nine years – my brother has been married twenty-four. I couldn't even keep mine together for ten."

"Maybe the trouble is that you're measuring your life and relationship by someone else's. You're unique, and you had problems unique and specific to your marriage. Besides, it takes two to breakup a relationship. You can't take all the blame yourself."

"But I just can't help feeling that way sometimes."

"If you weren't getting along, it was better that you part than stay together and be miserable."

"That's true."

"Do you still love him?"

"As a friend. We had known each other since we were children. He grew up a couple of houses from my aunt near Washington Park, and we were playmates when I would visit in the summers. We didn't have a bad breakup and still talk on occasion. But I'm not in love with him and haven't been for a long time. That's the main thing that contributed to our breakup. We fell out of love among other things."

"Like?"

"Russell and I wanted different things at different times. When we married he wanted to immediately have a child. I didn't want a child. Then after about three years he wanted us to move to LA. He quit his job to be a full-time visual artist. I was grounded in my life here. At the time we didn't have the money for a move like that. So we grew further apart."

"You don't want children?"

Lessye's mind flashed back to one of the hardest and worst decisions of her life, a secret that would remain between her and God forever. "Sure I do, someday. But Russell and I weren't ready for the responsibility at that time. Neither of us was mature enough."

Marcus sipped his champagne. "Do you feel you're mature enough now?"

"What do you think?"

"I think you'll make a wonderful mom."

"Thank you. And what about your fatherly instincts?"

Marcus got a far away look in his eyes. "If I knew that I would be a better father than the one I had. My parenting role models sucked. Having a child is the most important thing a person can ever do. I don't even know whether I have it inside me to be someone's dad. But I do know I don't want to mess it up. I don't want to be responsible for ruining a little person's life."

Lessye looked at him tenderly and rubbed his hand. "I think you'll be a fantastic father because you have the desire to be. You won't make the same mistakes your father did, because you're a different person, a good person. You may not see it, but I do. You don't give yourself enough credit. There's a lot of tenderness stored up in there," she said placing her hand gently on his chest over his heart. "You just need to let it out."

He took her hand and brought it to his lips and kissed her palm. "Thanks. But let's get back to you. I suppose now the only thing missing in your equation is the right man."

"Do you have any suggestions?"

"Sure, but first there's something I need to know. Are you seriously dating anyone right now?"

"I'm keeping my options open."

"Well, are you accepting applications?"

"That depends on you. Are you interested in the position?" she said.

Marcus took her face in his hands and gave her another long kiss. "You've got me, baby," he said when they separated for air.

Lessye took another sip of her champagne. Now it was time for some serious dipping. "There's something I need to ask you, and please give me an honest answer. Are you dating Lena?"

"No. We're not dating. I don't take her out."

"Are you sleeping with her?"

"Would it make a difference between us?"

"Not if our goal is to be platonic friends. But if we take this relationship to a more intimate level, then it definitely would. You didn't answer my question."

"I'm not one to kiss and tell, but since it's so important to you . . . yes, I am. But it's not serious. I'm not interested in pursuing an emotional relationship with her. It's only physical."

"I think it's a great deal more than that on her part."

But I'm interested in you. I have been for a while. If you're interested in being with me, dating me on a regular basis and ending it with Lena is what it takes to make that happen, then consider it over."

"Won't that cause you problems? I believe she cares for you. And although I'm interested in you, I don't want to get in the middle of anything."

Marcus gently cupped her face in his hands. "Don't worry. There won't be any problems. I told you, it's just physical, no attachments."

They finished their champagne, and Marcus gave Lessye a long, lingering kiss good night before heading home.

As Marcus drove his Lexus onto Interstate 20 East, en route to his midtown loft, he wondered whether he had done the right thing. Lena was a handful in more ways than one, and it wasn't going to be easy getting rid of her. But he wanted Lessye. He couldn't risk procrastinating and letting her become involved with someone else.

He smiled when he thought of Lessye's persistence in getting to the bottom of his relationship with Lena. The determined expression on her face when she questioned him reflected a quiet strength. She didn't intend to let him off the hook without an answer. Normally Marcus would not tolerate anyone prying into his personal business. But he couldn't seem to refuse Lessye. She was one of the rare individuals who had the art of drawing the truth out of a person whether they wanted to tell it or not. Between the food, wine, music, the feel of Lessye in his arms, and the smell of her hair, he had practically lost his mind. He was sure Lessye had somehow bewitched him. Whatever she did, he hoped it wouldn't stop.

CHAPTER 18

*I*t had been a tumultuous two weeks for Brad: the sudden deaths of his friends Killian and Alonso, the letter from Jesse, and now another problem that demanded his immediate attention.

He sat on the porch of his Unicoi, Georgia cabin sipping a cup of strong, black coffee and enjoying the clean beauty of God's mountain nature. Lacking the will power to kick the habit for good, he still smoked occasionally and inhaled the smoke of his fourth cigarette, exhaling rings that floated like tiny halos to the roof of his porch overhang. Regardless of the temperature, Brad always found time to enjoy his porch. He craved the rush of the cold air to keep his senses acute and give him the courage to do what had to be done. Truth that should have been told ten years earlier was finally going to be revealed. He would show Robert the letter from Jesse. Brad had already confronted Marcus and guessed that the argument they had would pale in comparison to what was waiting for him when Robert found out. He would not be able to weasel his way out of this one. Brad had warned Robert about flaws in Marcus' character, but Robert liked Marcus. He trusted him. Brad never had solid proof to back up accusations against Marcus. Now he did.

Brad thought about old Jesse and remembered a few brief talks they had years ago. Jesse had worked pushing a broom and mop for the state for over half his life. Brad suspected that old Jesse was a heavy drinker because whenever they talked, he could smell it on his breath. Sometimes the odor seemed to seep through his pores. Henry had gone out on a limb and covered for him on more than one occasion. But when the time came for Jesse to return the favor, he had been a coward.

Now according to his letter, Jesse was dying and he wanted to set the record straight. He could not bring Henry back, but he could make sure that Marcus got what he deserved. Brad tried several times to reach Jesse by phone to thank him, but there was no answer. He would try again later.

Alonso's funeral affected Brad deeply: the moving Spirituals; his own words of respect and the other heartfelt tributes; the dynamic eulogy; seeing the body of his friend now enclosed in that shiny mahogany box on a mule-drawn wagon passing the Capitol he loved for the last time. Like Robert and himself, Alonso had wanted so much for Georgia to live up to her potential. He knew what the people of Georgia were capable of and knew in his heart what could be achieved if people let go of racism, hatred and oppression. He never stopped fighting for justice and equality. Now Alonso's fight was over. He did not live to see his dream come to fruition. Life was so unfair and its sister, Death, a cruel enemy.

Brad thought about the other pressing matter he was now forced to handle, one that could be potentially more explosive than the situation with Marcus. But no matter what, he was determined to settle it today.

The biting north wind swelling from the mountains tore through his jacket, and it was time for him to go inside and wait for his visitor to arrive.

After attending church, Rod stopped by a soul food restaurant and picked up a couple of dinners he would share with Jesse. Since Jesse had been ill, he had been too frail to leave his apartment for long periods of time and rarely attended church. So on the Sundays Rod didn't have to work, he would usually bring Jesse dinner and share what happened during his church services. He spoke with Jesse on Friday morning and at that time, he told Rod he had something for him. Rod tried to get him to tell what it was, but Jesse was feeling weaker than usual and began coughing so badly that all he could manage to say was that he wanted to put it in Rod's hands.

It was about two when Rod arrived at Jesse's door at Open Arms. He knocked several times, but there was no answer. While he was there, Jesse's neighbor, Mattie Mae Clark, an elderly, heavy set woman with bluish-gray hair, was coming in from church. He could tell by her friendly expression that she also remembered him from visiting often with Jesse.

"How are you, son? You looking for Jesse?"

"Yes, Miss Mattie Mae, I'm fine. I hope you are."

She nodded.

"Do you know where he is?"

Her eyes watered into tears. "Yes. He took a turn for the worse Friday evening. The ambulance came, and they took him to Grady. I visited him yesterday and sat with him most of the day. His visitors are restricted to family, and I'm the closest thing to family he's got. But I'm sure he would love to see you. You'll have to talk to the nurse on duty because there's a *no visitors* sign on his door." She gave him Jesse's room number.

"I'm sorry about Jesse. Thank you, ma'am. I'm on my way." Before leaving he said, "Miss Mattie Mae, I picked up these dinners for Jesse and me. Would you like to have them?"

Her dim eyes brightened through the glistening tears, and she looked as if he had offered her a million dollars.

"Thank you, baby. God bless you. The good Lord sure provides for his children. I appreciate it."

The only resemblance between Ronnie James Reynolds and his father were his mesmerizing emerald green eyes. Where they looked out of place on his father, Randy Joe's, ruddy, rawboned face, they found an excellent home among the delicate features and smooth complexion Ronnie inherited from his mother. Ronnie was taller than his father with the solid build of an athlete. His jet black, wavy hair fell lazily to his broad shoulders. Years of weight lifting had given him huge biceps and ironing board-tight abs. A horseback riding accident at the end of last summer prevented the handsome eighteen-year-old from enrolling at the University of Georgia in the fall, but he planned to enter as a freshman the following year. For now, he was content to help his father on their sprawling peach farm.

Ronnie left home early Saturday morning to spend the day with his girlfriend. He was also eager to be away from the house this particular Saturday to avoid any confrontations with Tyrell, Nathaniel and that other group of ignorant racists who called themselves Citizens for a New American Agenda.

Unlike his father, Ronnie was not a racist, and he staunchly refused to let his father mold him into one. He remembered when he was in the third grade – one of his last memories of attending public school. His favorite teacher had been an attractive young black woman. To show her his admiration,

Ronnie decided he would give her a gift of a basket of peaches from his family orchard. When his father found out, he warned Ronnie never to take any peaches from his home to that teacher again.

"Why?" Ronnie had asked.

His father bent down and looked him square in the face before hissing, "Because peaches ain't for niggers. That's why."

That same year, another incident happened when Ronnie invited a black boy and girl to his birthday party. Afterwards, his father pitched a fit. He sat his son down and lectured him on the evils of associating with "those people" and warned him never to invite another black person to his house again. His father's twisted philosophy didn't make sense to Ronnie even when he was a child. Ronnie had said, "But we have black people in our house all the time. They help us, and we love them. If they can come in our house, what's the difference?"

"There's a big difference!" his father had said. "You'll learn as you grow older."

Well, now Ronnie *was* older and after several beatings, transfers to private (all white) academies, and endless lectures from his father's cronies, Ronnie still hadn't learned. To Ronnie, people were people. Some you liked and some you didn't like, but it had nothing to do with their color and everything to do with what was on the inside.

Ronnie returned home on Sunday morning in time to shower, dress, and join his family downstairs for the weekly breakfast before church. Randy Joe had certain rules that must be adhered to if one lived under his roof. So unless you were in the hospital or dead, you ate breakfast and went to church with the family every Sunday morning, regardless of the weather.

As Ronnie stood beside his father this Sunday morning singing one of his favorite hymns, "What A Friend We Have in Jesus," Ronnie knew his father would blow a blood vessel if he knew about his girlfriend. She was black. Her name was Tamika Rae Layton, and Ronnie was in love with her.

He first met Tamika in September when he went with friends to a Fort Valley State University football game. Tamika was a cheerleader. She stood out with her short cropped hair cut and gorgeous figure. Ronnie had never laid eyes on a girl who radiated such confidence and beauty, and he met her after the game.

Their first date had been a dream come true. When Ronnie took her home afterwards, they sat in his car and talked until almost daybreak.

Ronnie confessed to her about his father's racist attitude. He didn't want to begin a relationship with a lie between them. His honesty touched Tamika. She told him she had heard of Representative Reynolds but was surprised to know they were related. She also told him that although her family was liberal on most issues, interracial dating was not one of them. Her father had been a Black Panther back in the day.

"But I like you," Tamika had said. "And if you like me, too, isn't that all that matters?" It was certainly enough for Ronnie. Their date ended with the sweetest kiss Ronnie had ever tasted.

A smile tickled his lips as he thought about the first time he and Tamika made love. It was during the Christmas holidays and they had seen each other almost every day since Thanksgiving. Tamika prepared a soul food dinner, and they exchanged gifts. She gave him a nice gold-plated watch inscribed on the back: *To Ronnie, Love T.*

"Now when you look at your watch, you'll think of our wonderful times together," she said while twirling his thick hair through her fingers.

He gave her an expensive solid gold charm bracelet with only one charm, a large golden heart that had the word *yours* and his initials engraved on the back. Because, indeed, his heart did belong to her.

When he took her in his arms, it seemed time stopped. There was no one else in the world who mattered but the two of them. Ronnie had never seen anyone so beautiful. She was dark like Hershey chocolate and twice as smooth. Her small frame was accentuated by soft curves and her delicateness felt magnificent against the hardness of his body. Ronnie could almost taste Tamika's lips right now.

His thoughts were interrupted when his father nudged him and whispered, "Boy, you want to stop that daydreaming and pay attention to this service. And whoever this girl is who's keeping you out of my house and that smile glued to your face, don't you think it's about time you brought her home and introduced her to your family?"

Rod arrived at Grady Hospital and located Jesse's room, but the *No Visitors* sign posted on the door that Mattie Mae warned him about stopped him from entering. He went to the desk to speak with a nurse.

"Excuse me. I'm here to see Mr. Jesse Higgins, but there's a no visitors sign on the door." Before Rod could give her his name, she said something that made him reconsider.

"You must be Marcus," she said with a pleasant smile. "Mr. Higgins has been calling for you since he was brought in Friday. He's been moved out of intensive care, but his visitors are still restricted to family. That's the reason for the sign. Are you related to Mr. Higgins?"

"His nephew." Rod hated to lie, but he had to get in to see Jesse. This might be his last chance, and this was the only way. Besides, Rod knew that Jesse would want to see him. Rod could not count the times that Jesse had told him he was like a son to him.

"Go on in. He'll be happy to see you."

Rod went into Jesse's room. He was on oxygen and hooked up to a heart monitor. Tubes were running intravenous liquid into his veins. Rod pulled up a chair as close to the bed as possible and sat down. Jesse seemed even smaller and more frail than usual. He looked like a raisin stuck in a bowl of whipped cream, his small, dark body swallowed up in the stark white linen and blankets covering the bed.

Rod looked back over his shoulder to make sure the nurse did not follow him in the room, then said in a low voice, "Jesse. Jesse. It's me, Rod. How are you feeling? Please open your eyes. Talk to me."

Jesse used his last ounce of strength to open his eyes. His lashes fluttered for a moment before his red eyes managed to focus on Rod.

"Marcus," he said in a small voice that seemed to be coming from some deserted place far away. "Marcus."

"I'm not Marcus, Jesse. I'm Rod. You told me you have something for me. Remember?"

"Marcus," he said again weakly.

"No, Jesse. I'm Rod, Rod Jennings from the State Capitol police. Please remember, Jesse. I come to visit you almost every Sunday. We were going to have dinner today. And you were going to give me what you mentioned on the phone. Is it about Marcus? Do you have something to tell me about Marcus?"

"Marcus," he kept wheezing out the name over and over. "Marcus."

Suddenly the hacking cough began more violently than Rod had ever heard. It was followed by convulsions. Before Rod could push the call button, two nurses and a doctor burst into the room and converged on Jesse's bed, almost knocking Rod over in the process.

The desk nurse, who had been so warm and friendly to him a few minutes earlier now said in a polite but stern voice, "Sir, Mr. Higgins is in a crisis. You'll have to wait outside."

Rod paced the hall for only ten minutes before he saw the nurse one last time. She was accompanied by the doctor, who came to inform him of the news he dreaded. "I'm so sorry, sir," the doctor said. "Mr. Higgins has passed away."

CHAPTER 19

*H*ey, Randy Joe. This is the day we've been waiting for," said a colleague and co-signer of the anti-affirmative action bill. He patted Randy Joe on the back as he took his seat beside him.

"Yeah, buddy. You bet," said Randy Joe.

The Speaker of the House called the day's session to order.

"The hour of convening has arrived. All members please take seats and cease audible conversation," the Speaker said, banging his heavy gavel. "Clerk will ring the bell. All members please take seats and cease audible conversation. Clerk will please continue to ring the bell. Call the roll! All members present please vote their own and only their own machines aye. Someone can vote Mr. Harvey's machine. He's up here with the chaplain. Clerk will unlock the machines." He paused for a moment, then said. "All members now voted?" He repeated, "All members now voted? If so, the Clerk will lock the machines. Doorkeepers close the doors and keep them closed. Our chaplain of the day will be introduced by Representative Wyatt Harvey. Scripture reading and prayer by the chaplain, after which we will have the pledge of allegiance to the flag."

The first Monday back after recess week was always a busy one. The day's calendar was full and after the morning invocation they got down to "the people's business," as they frequently referred to it.

The general order of business was dictated by House Rules, and the Speaker made sure the rules were strictly adhered to.

It was still early in the day, and the Clerk was in the process of announcing first and second readers. Among the first readers would be a bill sponsored by Randy Joe and co-sponsored by several other of his cronies seeking to prevent the state of Georgia, its agents, or any of its political subdivisions from using race, color, creed, gender or national origin to grant preferential treatment to any individual or group.

Randy Joe was proud of himself as he leaned back in his comfortable high back chair at his antique cherrywood desk on the floor of the Georgia House. He waited for the sparks to fly.

Before the Clerk announced his bill, however, the Speaker interrupted them with an important announcement. Representative Brad Austin's SUV had run off the road Sunday evening as he was returning to Atlanta from his Unicoi, Georgia, cabin. He was dead.

Rays from the brilliant sun streamed into the Capitol rotunda each time the door opened on the east side of the building. Standing majestically on the periphery of Atlanta's bustling downtown business district, the Georgia State Capitol was a beautiful Greek Revival-style building. Reflecting its original grandeur, it sparkled like a priceless antique jewel.

If Lessye had been any higher, she would have floated. With the exception of her grief at the loss of Alonso and his funeral Saturday, her weekend had been great: the date with Marcus on Saturday and dinner with Tanya and Kevin Sunday. Tanya's new house was beautiful, and Kevin outdid himself with the steaks.

Lessye confided in Tanya about her conversation with Marcus and his promise to end his tryst with Lena. Tanya was so excited that Lessye thought she might start suggesting china patterns but settled for inviting them to dinner the next Sunday.

As Lessye sat at her desk computer checking e-mail and thinking about the way Marcus kissed her, Tracey came rushing back to the tour booth with tears in her eyes.

"Tracey, what's the matter?" Lessye moved quickly toward her.

"Oh, Lessye, I was in the House gallery and heard some bad news. Representative Austin is dead."

Renae had another of what she had begun to describe as her lost Sunday evenings. This was the third one in a row. This time she had awakened, head and stomach aching, in a vacant motel room in Helen, Georgia. Again, she had no idea how she got there or how long she had been there. This time she had a strange dream, as well. Luckily, she was able to reach Lena on her cell phone, and she drove up to pick her up. Lena was so sympathetic. And unlike Lessye and Clarice, Lena did not interrogate her.

Renae wondered whether, on top of everything else, she was now losing her mind. There was no other way to explain her loss of long spans of time. Yes, the narcolepsy caused her to have sleeping spells, but that didn't explain why she was finding herself in places she had never been. And her narcoleptic episodes never left her in pain. And why, all of a sudden, was she finding things in her purse she didn't remember putting there?

She briefly considered seeing her doctor but was afraid to. She was not prepared for his nosy questions or any more medical tests. What if he thought she was crazy and sent her to a psychiatrist? No. Renae would handle this on her own.

She remembered the previous Sunday evening when Lessye and Clarice picked her up in Macon. She had lied to them. The truth was that Renae couldn't remember how she got there. The last thing she remembered was sitting down alone to watch some television in her apartment after church and dinner with Lena. It was after Lena went home. But she couldn't admit that to the girls. They would think she was crazy. It would lead to questions she did not want to answer. A person doesn't get from her apartment in Atlanta to the Greyhound bus station in Macon without knowing how she got there. She remembered that Lena once mentioned having an aunt in Macon and built her lie around it, mixing in a little truth. She thought her story sounded convincing, but those girls were smart, and Renae knew they believed she was hiding something.

Renae thought about her grandparents and how much she missed them. She needed them right now like never before.

"Renae, have you been listening to your Real Player!" Clarice said as she came bursting into the suite looking crazed and frantic, braids flying in the air. She had been across the hall visiting with Tanya and Amber.

Renae snapped out of the cloudy fog of her thoughts and focused on Clarice. "No, what's wrong?"

"Transfer the lines to Tanya's suite. They need us over there. Brad was killed last night in an accident close to Helen, Georgia. Lena is practically hysterical!"

The color drained from Renae's face as she slumped into unconsciousness.

———————————

Upset about Jesse's death, Rod was anxious to get his hands on whatever it was Jesse had for him. All Sunday night, he tossed and turned with horrible dreams about Jesse, with that coal black skin and fire-red eyes, dragging his portable oxygen canister with one hand and a gnarly, accusing finger of the other pointed, jumping up out of the hospital bed chasing after him, screaming Marcus' name at the top of his lungs.

As he sat at his desk in the spacious security office on the Capitol first floor, he thought about the events of the previous day. After the doctor informed him that Jesse was dead, he immediately went back to Open Arms to tell Jesse's neighbor, Mattie Mae, but there was no answer when he knocked on her door.

He stopped by to inform the manager of Jesse's death, but was told the hospital had already called. Mattie Mae and some other residents had gone to the hospital. Jesse didn't have any close relatives and the manager – a tall, slender, stoop-shouldered woman named Mrs. Lane – informed him that they were holding his small insurance policy and had been instructed to make all the necessary arrangements at the time of his death.

Rod told her that he visited Jesse often and that he would appreciate being informed about the time and location of his services. He gave Mrs. Lane one of his cards, included all his contact numbers, and let her know that the last time he and Jesse had spoken by phone, Jesse told him he had something for him. She promised to relay his message to Mattie Mae and call him if they found anything.

As Rod thought harder, he knew whatever it was involved Marcus. But what could it be? There was a knock at his office door.

"Come in."

The door cracked open, and Gus peeped inside.

"Hey, Rod. If you're not busy, can I talk with you for a moment?"

"Sure, Gus. Come in and have a seat. How are you doing?"

"Fine for an old man."

"I should be doing as well as you are. Want some coffee?"

"No thank you. I don't want to take up much of your time."

"What's going on?"

"I heard something this morning that I think you should know. Have you ever heard of a drug called GHB?" Gus asked, removing his glasses and cleaning the lenses with a handkerchief he plucked from his pocket.

"Yeah. A date rape drug, something like Rohypnol."

"Right," Gus said, putting his glasses back on and the handkerchief back in his pocket. "It's also popular with people with narcolepsy. Some of the pharmaceutical companies I represent are experimenting with it."

"Yeah. I've heard that, too. If you don't mind me asking, why the interest in GHB?"

"Because of a conversation I overheard this morning between two interns in the House gallery," Gus said. "Now, I'm not trying to start anything or spread any rumors, but I thought it was only my duty to pull your coat tail."

Experience told Rod some juicy news was forthcoming. In all the years he'd known Gus, he always prefaced juicy news with those words. He had always been a nice guy. And through the years, Gus never failed to keep him informed about happenings around the Capitol he thought Rod should know.

"One of the girls told the other that she had seen someone on the Hill with GHB. She named Randy Joe."

"Do you believe it?"

"Between you and me, yes. From some of the things I've heard about Randy Joe, I can definitely believe it."

It had been a rough morning for Tanya, Amber, and Clarice. In the midst of their mini celebration about Tanya's new house, they heard the news about Brad. From that moment, everything spiraled downward. Lena became almost hysterical and when Clarice ran across the hall to tell Renae, Renae passed out. Tanya and Amber had taken turns crying all morning. They loved Brad. He was one of their favorite representatives. Now he was gone, and they would miss him.

At lunch time, no one was in the mood to eat, but Lessye came over anyway and spent her hour trying to console her friends. Lessye had worked closely with Brad in the office of Secretary of State, so she took his death as hard as the others.

On her way back to the Capitol, she ran into Marcus, who looked handsome in a well tailored black business suit, charcoal shirt and black and gray silk tie. He was waiting at the Mitchell Street guard shack to accompany the Governor on a speaking engagement.

"Hey, Lessye. I guess you heard about Brad."

"Yes. It's awful. What's going on around here?"

"Baby, I wish I knew." He took her hands in his. "I know you're upset. Is there anything I can do?"

"No. I'll be okay. But thank you."

"I enjoyed dinner Saturday evening. I'm looking forward to us getting together again soon."

"I am too."

"How about this weekend? I'd love to take you dancing."

"There's Salsa at the Duplex on Fridays. Are you busy?"

"No, Friday is perfect. I'll call you, and we can work out the time." The Governor and his bodyguard were coming, and Marcus had to leave. "See you later."

"Bye."

Before she walked up the steps to the Capitol, something drew her attention, and she glanced back at the double doors of the LOB. Lena was standing there, staring at her with a vicious look on her face.

CHAPTER 20

The 40-day session of the Georgia Legislature was a combination of hard work and equally exhausting play. It was as easy to find a reception or party as it was to put your hands on a House Bill.

Randy Joe's main reason for coming to Atlanta, beside devising schemes to thwart minorities, was attending receptions and chasing young aides and interns. He and his running buddy, Tyrell, were proficient at skirt chasing. After the receptions and dinners were finished for the evening, they hosted private parties. They would pay certain Capitol employees under the table to deliver complimentary soft drinks, whiskey, and other "party favors" to their hotel rooms. They also had plenty of cash to make playing with them well worth any money-hungry young woman's while.

Randy Joe was a man of two faces. One Randy Joe was a devout church-going family man who loved his wife and children more than life itself. Ms. Pearl came to Atlanta on the first and fortieth days of the session. And while she was there, he was the perfect husband and treated her like a queen.

Days two through thirty-nine belonged to the other Randy Joe and whichever fresh, young intern or aide he chose to spend it with.

Tonight, he was cutting Tyrell loose.

Randy Joe drove several blocks to a stylish apartment in midtown.

"Hey, baby. I had almost given up on you this evening," said the provocative young aide who opened the door.

"I'm here now. What you got for me?"

She pressed up close to him and kissed him on the lips. "Come in, sit down and relax."

"Pour me a drink," he said taking off his coat and slinging it across a chair. He took a wad of bills from his pocket and put it on her coffee table.

She went to the bar and poured him a half a glass of bourbon over ice.

"Now come sit here."

She walked slowly over to the sofa where he was seated handed him his drink, and sat on his lap.

He caught her by the chin and turned her face to his. He wanted to see her eyes. "I called you the other night and you weren't home. Where were you?"

"I had to go to Macon on urgent business."

"You telling me the truth?" His grip on her face was like a vise.

"I wouldn't lie to you. I know what you do to people who get on your bad side."

"Remember that. You better not be seeing another man. Because if I ever come here and catch you with someone else . . . there's gonna be hell to pay. You understand me?"

"I understand."

"I brought you something," he said referring to the money on the table.

Her eyes lit up. "Thank you, baby. You want it now?"

"Later," he said and gulped his drink. "Now take off that gown so I can get a good look at you."

Lena slowly stood up and did as she was told.

===

Originally the Black Caucus decided to cancel their meeting the first Monday after the homegoing service of their beloved Alonso and on top of it, the shock of the news about Brad. But there was a serious problem looming: the anti-affirmative action legislation. An issue they thought had been put to rest when an attempt to amend the state Constitution a couple of years earlier failed had now resurfaced like an insatiable shark and was threatening to devour them. All members were present at this important meeting except Bernard, which the other members thought was just as well because he would be no help in their fight to save affirmative action.

The first order of business was to elect a new Caucus whip. Without much discussion the group unanimously elected Representative Della Harden, who was feisty and petite, with golden honey-toned skin, dark alert eyes, and shoulder-length, copper-brown hair. Being the closest ally of Alonso, the members felt that's what he would have wanted. Della was also the only one who possessed his unique ability to calm the turbulent political waters, his high level of integrity, and butter-sizzling charisma.

After the general meeting Della had a private discussion with the chairman, Charles Colson.

"We're going to have to keep it from coming out of the House Judiciary Committee," said Charles. "The makeup of that committee has changed drastically. Two of our biggest supporters are now dead. And Bernard will definitely vote with the conservatives."

"Maybe Mr. Speaker will cut us some slack and appoint new Judiciary members who share the vision of Alonso and Brad," Della said.

"Wishful thinking. We all know our Speaker is not the most liberal-minded person. Just because we lost two of our strongest liberals doesn't mean the Speaker is going to appoint others to Judy. He's got the last word on his House Committees, and right now, I think he's more interested in making points with the conservative arm of his district. His district is fast shifting from majority Democratic to majority Republican. I think his appointments are going to be conservative Democrats or moderates."

"The bottom line is, if we don't stop this bill in committee, it could pass if it gets to the House Floor," Della said. "The longer it stays in play, the more momentum it's building up because of media attention. I'm already being flooded with e-mails from folks on both sides of the issue. I can only imagine the pressure on all the members if it makes it to the House floor for open debate."

"The right wingers are salivating. Randy Joe and Tyrell and that lobbyist, Nathaniel, are pushing hard to get the votes. They are working every legislative event with all the zeal of horny college jocks during freshman orientation week. We've got to hold the line, because we definitely don't have the strength in numbers to stop it in the Senate."

"But Robert would surely veto it, if it passed the General Assembly."

"Knowing Robert, he would want to. But if it gets that far, the pressure on him might be too great. He's got to look forward to re-election in two years, and deep south Georgia will make or break him. That's heavy anti-affirmative action territory. He could leave it on his desk and do nothing if it passes. And as we know, forty days after the legislature adjourns for the year, it will automatically become law without his signature. So it's got to be stopped, now."

"I'm going to talk with Marcus. Robert still has considerable influence over the Speaker and the Judiciary chairman. Maybe with some pressure from the Governor's office they will table it."

"Good idea. But whatever we do, we better do it fast. Because if it comes up for a full committee vote, we can't afford to let the deciding vote fall into the hands of Bernard."

═══════════════════════

Juan Hanlon's official title with the Georgia State Patrol was Special Operations Adjutant, giving him direct supervision of the day-to-day operations of several units including the Specialized Collision Reconstruction and Special Weapons and Tactics teams.

At forty, he possessed a swarthy complexion, thick raven hair, and the smoldering, inky black eyes of his Latino mother – a coloring that the devoted husband and father of three passed on to his children. His lean build, edgy personality, and keen features were inherited from his Irish father, whose grandfather had dropped the O and apostrophe from their family name. Seventeen years of on-the-job police experience, nine of which were with the State Patrol, told Juan that there was something sinister going on in the deaths of the three legislators. And Juan was determined to find some answers.

Unlike the first two accidents where the wreckage was left for the most part intact, Brad's vehicle plunged off the side of a curvy mountain road and burst into flames upon impact. But lucky for them, everything was not consumed in the flames. Beside Brad's mangled body, an overnight bag had been thrown clear of the wreckage. In the bag, tucked between the cushion of Brad's clothing, Juan found an empty bottle of bourbon, the only solid connection to the other deaths. As with the others, latent print analysis failed to turn up any suspicious fingerprints.

Other than a strong coincidence, there was no other tangible evidence that would point to these deaths being anything more than freak accidents. But Juan was suspicious. Maybe it was the close resemblance to Henry's death and the connection these men had with Perkins that triggered his senses.

Although Juan found no evidence that would lead him to call for a criminal investigation, he found something else: an empty envelope addressed to Brad with a return address for Jesse Higgins.

CHAPTER 21

$\mathcal{I}$t was early Wednesday morning before Rod received a call from Mrs. Lane, the manager of Open Arms, concerning the services for Jesse. The funeral would be Saturday at 1 p.m. at Mattie Mae's home church on Simpson Road, not too far from the center. Rod planned to attend. However, to his disappointment, Mrs. Lane failed to find anything in Jesse's apartment addressed to Rod.

"Give me a sign, Jesse," he said to himself after hanging up the phone. "I know you had something to tell me. Please, give me a sign."

"Marcus, what have you found out from Juan?" Robert was in a foul mood, still deeply grieved over the loss of three good friends and political allies. Sean and other members of the media were nagging him for answers to these "bizarre" coincidences, as if he had any.

"I spoke to Juan yesterday. There's still no evidence of foul play, and he doesn't have any more to report than he did the day before—"

"Well, call him again today and keep calling until he comes up with some answers! Our forensic sciences division boasts about being one of the best in the nation. Now's the time to prove it. Who's the guy over toxicology?"

"Gordon Sizemore. I hear he's the best—"

"I'm not interested in what you hear or what people say about him! I'm interested in what he can produce! Call Juan and Director Shaw. Tell them to build a fire under Sizemore and fan the flames until he comes up with something. And call a meeting here in my office for ten o'clock Friday morning with Hanlon, Shaw, Sizemore, and Jennings."

"You want Jennings involved?" Marcus had never liked Rod and knew the feeling was mutual. Marcus knew that Rod always suspected him of being more involved in the Perkins situation than he was telling. Rod irritated Marcus with his snide remarks and suspicious glances, and he didn't want him around.

Robert cut his eyes in Marcus' direction. "Yes, I want Jennings. Is there a problem?"

"No. . . no problem. But why include him at this point?"

Robert's icy stare bore through him. "Because he's our police chief. He should be in on all the meetings. Does that answer your question?"

"I'll set it up." Great, Marcus thought. This is all I need.

"Remember, Marcus, I want answers by Friday. No more excuses!"

═══════════════

His nose for news, plus a reliable tip, led Sean to the State Crime Lab on Panthersville Road. The source informed him on Thursday morning that Gordon was working around the clock and would have an answer to the mystery surrounding the deaths of the legislators in time to present his findings at a ten o'clock meeting with the Governor on Friday.

Sean was almost drooling. "The Emperor suspects foul play, doesn't he?"

"I don't know. No one has said definitively. But the heat is on like August in south Georgia over here. And if I had to guess, my feeling would be, he does," said the source.

Ten minutes after receiving the call, Sean was on I-20 East heading toward Decatur. It was a cold, crisp sunny day with clouds floating across the sky like puffy white pillows. Well before the noon lunch hour, traffic was lighter than usual, and the drive from Atlanta was easy.

Sean knew without a doubt that his source was reliable, and when Gordon finished his report, he would have a copy before the Governor. All Sean had to do was be in the right place at the right time.

═══════════════

Gordon was sure he found what he was looking for.

Gamma hydroxybutyric acid was more popularly known as GHB – a date rape drug. It was also used to treat narcolepsy. The three legislators who died were not naive teenage party girls, nor were they afflicted with the sleeping disorder. However, they all died due to reactions caused by an overdose of the drug. GHB metabolized quickly, making it difficult to detect.

Since making his discovery, Gordon had done his homework on the drug.

GHB was odorless and tasteless. It depressed all brain functions and came in a variety of forms: liquid, powder, tablet, and capsule. It could be taken orally, smoked or snorted. Its more common street names included: Liquid Ecstacy, Everclear, Scoop, G, Goop, G-Riffick, Georgia Home Boy, Liquid X and Cherry Menth. If taken in large doses, GHB could induce a coma.

Gordon's findings were that the three legislators died as the result of loss of reflexes and loss of consciousness caused by an overdose of GHB. Because Gordon thought it highly improbable that three prominent legislators who knew they would be traveling some distance on three consecutive Sundays would intentionally take an overdose of GHB, he decided that at the meeting with the Governor, he would suggest an immediate criminal investigation – an investigation into possible murder.

Gordon finished scribbling his notes and rushed out of the lab and handed several pages to his secretary.

"Please stop whatever you're doing and type this report ASAP. I need it for a meeting tomorrow morning."

"Yes, sir. I'll start on it immediately."

Less than an hour later, a copy of Gordon's final report was in Sean's hands.

CHAPTER 22

*Y*ou've been avoiding me all week, and I want to know why!" Lena took the liberty once again of bursting into Marcus' office unannounced and uninvited, which she knew annoyed him. Lena wore a tight black dress that hugged her curves and exposed far too much cleavage for the workplace. It was accessorized with dangling gold earrings, a matching bracelet, and the sexy black butterfly tattoo in the middle of the back of her neck. Her hair was pulled back from her face in a sleek ponytail. She stood glaring at him with her hands on her hips. Her usually vibrant hazel eyes appeared to be charcoal gray.

Marcus had gotten chewed out by Robert for the fourth time that week and was in no mood to play games with Lena.

"I haven't been avoiding you, Lena. I've been busy. Some people work around here."

"No kidding."

"You might have missed this in that you're only concerned with how you look in the mirror, but three legislators are dead under mysterious circumstances, and believe it or not, I have more to do than hold your hand."

"What's so mysterious about a car accident? Or do you know something that I don't?"

"And what would that be?"

"I didn't come here to match wits with you about three dead legislators."

"Your compassion is touching."

"Let's get back to the subject of hand holding. You weren't too busy to hold Lessye's hands Monday by the guard shack. I saw you!"

"Excuse me, I must be confused," Marcus said, making a point of looking at himself up and down. "I don't seem to be wearing a sign that says property of Lena Lawrence. Who I hold hands with is none of your business. And for a person who was supposedly on the verge of hysteria over Brad a few days ago, you sure have recovered fast."

"I guess your girlfriend told you that, too!"

"No. She didn't have to. Gossip travels on the Hill."

"Like your date Saturday night?"

Marcus bristled.

"Yes, Marcus. Gossip gets around to me, too."

"Do I have to repeat myself? That's none of your business." Marcus felt his temper rising, and Lena was giving him a headache. "By the way. Weren't you Brad's aide?"

"You know I was."

"Well then . . . Since he's dead, why are you still hanging around?"

"You dog." She moved toward him, raising her hand as if to slap him.

He caught it in mid swing. "Careful. Temper. Temper. I'd hate to have to call security and have you thrown out of here."

"I'd like to see you try. Why don't you call your *friend*, Rod? I'm sure he'd love to hear all the mess I know on you . . ."

"What do you know on me that you think you can get away with telling?" Marcus' voice was low and threatening. His light brown eyes narrowed into menacing slits.

"Marcus, let's calm down. We've both said some things we don't mean," she said softly.

"You know me. I never say anything I don't mean."

"Baby, listen . . ."

"No, you listen. This thing between us . . . it's not working out. It's obviously draining both of us. . . What I'm saying is . . . it's over. Don't come to my office again. Understand?"

"This is about her, isn't it? Sweet, precious Lessye doesn't want to share you with me."

"You have to first have something in order to share it. You've never had me. And you never will. Now please leave, and don't come back."

"I care for you. Didn't I befriend Renae because you asked me to? You know, baby, I've done a lot for you. I would do anything for you. What will I do if you send me away?"

Marcus looked at her coldly. "Well . . . you can always go back to that redneck, Randy Joe."

"What . . . ?"

"Yes. The secret's out. I know all about your romance with that cracker. How you could associate with a man like that is beyond me."

"You've got me all wrong. I don't care about Randy Joe. I love you. I want you!"

"Well that's something you can't have. You are a beautiful woman. But you're also a trashy slut who's no good for any man. Get out."

"Why do you take pleasure in humiliating me? Why do you use me and spit the love I have for you back in my face?"

"For the second time – Get out! Don't let there have to be a third."

Lena glared at Marcus one last time, then turned abruptly and left his office. She slammed the door behind her so hard that she startled his secretary whose desk was located in the reception area in the outer office. Lena managed to make it out to the second floor hall before the tears burning beneath her eyelids began pouring down her face.

Marcus had planned to end it differently, gentler. But with Lena's temperament, the only way it could have ended was badly. Lena never failed to bring out the worst in him. He thought about Lena as opposed to Lessye, who brought out his best side. How different those two women were, so much so it amazed him.

Marcus refused to dwell on Lena's ruffled feathers, especially not now. He had to psyche himself up for an important meeting with Robert, and there was Brad's memorial service to get through.

His mind wandered to thoughts of Lessye and the wonderful weekend ahead. They would go dancing on Friday and Tanya had invited them to dinner on Sunday. Marcus found himself anticipating spending time with Lessye more and more.

Sometimes he couldn't understand what was happening to him. Often he would stop in the middle of what he was doing and think of Lessye. On a couple of occasions, he even found himself losing track of what Robert was saying to him, but fortunately Robert was so caught up in whatever subject he was expounding on at the time, he didn't notice. Unlike with Lena, Marcus had more than a physical attraction to Lessye – much more. He was attracted to her mind, her humor, her compassion, and her gentleness. He loved the way she smiled and laughed with him. He thought about their date on the previous Saturday evening— how comfortable and natural it was. Lessye was different from any woman he had ever known. With Lessye, he was content with being in her presence.

The intercom buzzer followed by the soft voice of his secretary interrupted his thoughts. "Marcus."

"Yes, Shonna."

"Gordon Sizemore is on line one."

"Thank you."

After speaking with him briefly, Marcus was confident he would definitely be ready for the meeting with Robert.

———

Tyrell slammed down the telephone in his LOB third floor office for the fourth time. His temper was getting on Randy Joe's nerves, and it never took much to do that.

"Does everyone in The Emperor's office screen their calls?" Tyrell said.

"Yeah, son," said Randy Joe as he propped his feet up on the opposite side of Tyrell's desk. "Important people can't be caught answering the phone for every Tom, Dick and Tyrell who happens to call." Randy Joe thought some humor might extricate Tyrell from the funk he had slid into, but he was wrong.

"I'm important, too, and when I call somebody I want to hear more than a voice mail recording. This is another liberal plot to drive us crazy."

"I'm sick and tired of that arrogant Robert and his uppity black boy, Marcus, running roughshod over the Governor's office. Those boys are sending this state to hell minus the handbasket."

"I know," said Tyrell. "I can't hardly wait for the next election to roll around. There are going to be some big changes. You wait and see. I'm going to do all I can to make sure they're both booted out on their butts." There was nothing like venting about Robert and Marcus to raise the roof on some righteous Republican rancor.

Tyrell glanced at the large Confederate Battle flag mounted on his wall above the symbolic bale of cotton which rested on the floor. "Those sure were the days."

"I'll second that," said Randy Joe, who had slid into the same funk as Tyrell. "Where's Nathaniel? He should be here by now."

"I'm right here," Nathaniel said, his large frame filling the doorway.

"Come in and sit down. We've got a lot to talk about. For one thing, *Bernard* Benton." Randy Joe always twanged out special emphasis on the first syllable of "Bernard."

"He was real evasive at our meeting the other day. I'm worried about that boy," Tyrell said, his snake eyes beginning to twitch.

"I don't think we have anything to worry about at this point," Nathaniel said. "I believe he knows what will happen if he tries to cross us."

"I'll put a bullet in him!" Randy Joe said. "That's what will happen."

"Settle that temper of yours down, Randy Joe. You know if there is anything to be handled, that's my department," Nathaniel said.

The three men talked for another thirty minutes then completed their meeting.

After Nathaniel and Randy Joe left Tyrell's office, Nathaniel pulled Randy Joe aside. "How's Ronnie doing?" Nathaniel asked.

"He's fine. Wearing his hair like a hippie. Staying out all night and driving that Mustang too fast. Lord knows I love that boy, but sometimes he gives me a big pain where the sun don't shine."

"Who's he dating now?"

"I don't know." Randy Joe shrugged. "It seems to be some big secret."

"If it is . . . I know why."

Randy Joe's eyes darkened. "What are you talking about, Nathaniel? And why is my boy's love life so important to *you* all of a sudden?"

"Now calm down. You're not going to like what I'm about to tell you. But please try to stay cool."

"If you know something about my boy I should know, you best spit it out, now!" Randy Joe's lips twisted into a snarl, leaving Nathaniel with the frightening thought that in the next few seconds, he might take off one of his scuffed cowboy boots and beat an answer out of him.

"I got a call from one of the members of the CNAA this morning."

"So? What does that have to do with my Ronnie?"

"Well . . . this member told me that last Saturday evening his boy was at the movies in Macon and he saw Ronnie there, and he wasn't alone."

"Well, tell me! Who was he with?"

"He was with a black girl, and they were kissing."

CHAPTER 23

*W*hat was planned as a private meeting turned into an impromptu press conference, thanks to Sean's revelations in a special edition of the *Capitol Reporter.* Shortly after the meeting began in the Governor's office, his press secretary rushed in with a copy. Gordon could save his breath. Most of his report was in the *Capitol Reporter.*

Media representatives from news organizations throughout the metro area and as far away as Savannah and Valdosta had deserted their coveted positions in the House and Senate Chambers to cram into the reception area of the Governor's main office on the second floor of the Capitol. They were demanding answers. The situation in which Sean placed them left the Governor little choice. The word was out. So what should have been a private strategy session turned into almost thirty minutes' worth of questions and answers about the impending investigation.

The one question that rang in everyone's ears came from Sean's lips: "Isn't it an odd coincidence that three prominent legislators would die in car accidents on consecutive Sundays and GHB is involved?" Everyone knew the answer to that question. Coincidences rarely came in threes.

=====================

"Rod, you got a minute?" Juan said as they were leaving the Governor's office.

"Sure, what's up?"

"There's something I need to talk with you about. I didn't want to bring it up during that sideshow in the Governor's office."

"Man, I feel you. Let's have lunch. I'm on my way to the Towers."

Rod and Juan had known each other many years, had an excellent working relationship, and were friendly. When Rod first joined the Capitol Hill Police Department, Juan had trained him. Juan later moved on to the State Patrol. They both worked under the large law enforcement umbrella of the Department of Public Safety and their immediate supervisor was the Lt. Colonel, who served as commanding officer of Special Operations and Support Services. So through the years they remained in close contact and frequently discussed and worked major cases together.

The state cafeteria, located in the James "Sloppy" Floyd Memorial Towers, took up most of the twin buildings' bottom floor. Its potpourri of selections included meat and vegetable dishes, short order items, soups and sandwiches, salads, fresh fruit, pizza and desserts.

Both men opted for short order, Rod having a cheeseburger and Juan a steak and cheese sandwich. Both had fries and a cola.

"You remember an ex-Capitol employee named Jesse Higgins?" Juan asked, no sooner than they were seated in the spacious cafeteria that included numerous tables and decorative planters.

"Yeah, Jesse was an old friend of mine. He passed away last Sunday. His funeral is tomorrow. Why do you ask?"

"Man, I'm sorry about your friend. The reason I'm asking is because I found this envelope addressed to Brad among his belongings at the scene of the accident." Juan handed Rod a plastic bag containing the envelope. He examined it and handed it back to Juan, who laid it on the table. "The return address is from Jesse."

"What was in the envelope?"

"I don't know. It was empty. I don't know whether this has some significance in these cases or not, but it's one of the only pieces of evidence that distinguishes them. I'm curious to know why Jesse contacted Brad after all these years."

Rod told Juan about his last conversation with Jesse and about his visit with Jesse at the hospital. "He kept repeating the name Marcus."

"Was he referring to Marcus Norwood?"

"I think so. That's the only Marcus he knew. At first I thought he mistook me for Marcus, but Jesse and Marcus were never friendly. As I thought about it more, it seemed more like he was trying to tell me something *about* Marcus."

"Like what?"

"That's what I'm still trying to figure out. I have a strong feeling it has something to do with that incident with Henry ten years ago," Rod said between bites of his burger.

"Or you're hoping it does. You always had doubts about Henry's guilt and suspicions about Marcus' involvement."

"I still do. Between you and me, I always thought Henry was framed. And Marcus was deep in the mix. Jesse and Henry had been real tight. Jesse always cleaned the Secretary of State's office so everyone got to know him pretty well, but he and Henry were especially close. Henry suggested I question him, but Jesse said he didn't know anything. I got the feeling he was afraid to talk. Through the years, he never said anything to me and became uneasy whenever I would bring up Henry's name during my visits. I wonder how much he knew about the Perkins incident."

Juan took a king-size bite of his sandwich. After washing it down with some cola, he said, "Now I'm more intrigued than ever about what was in this envelope. Do you think it might be connected to whatever it was he said he had for you?"

"I don't know. I'm going to Jesse's funeral tomorrow and hopefully after that, I'll have some answers."

═══════════

What was that boy thinking about? Randy Joe fumed to himself as he drove toward Fort Valley, Georgia at almost 90 miles an hour Friday afternoon. He didn't know whether he was angrier about the fact that Ronnie was dating a black girl or about the fact that he had been seen in public kissing her. And knowing that Nathaniel knew something about his son first added fuel to the fire.

He couldn't wait to get a hold of Ronnie, but he couldn't blame him either. The taste for forbidden fruit ran like blood in the family vein. Reynolds men had craved brown sugar for generations. Hadn't his own daddy and granddaddy done it? And Randy Joe himself was right now sleeping with that sexy aide, Lena. Sometimes life was a paradox, Randy Joe thought. Talking white by day and sleeping black by night. But he refused to see himself as a hypocrite.

Randy Joe was experienced with his hidden life. He could sleep black without it affecting him personally. But he knew Ronnie was different. That boy couldn't handle it. He was one of those hand-holding, Kumbaya-singing, all-men-are-created-equal, bleeding-heart liberals. Ronnie was a loving, sensitive kid, and Randy Joe knew that it was impossible for him to sleep black without it getting under his skin. He knew that if Ronnie was seeing her in public and kissing her out in the open, he was in love with her.

Randy Joe had always protected his children, and he was not about to sit back and let some little black strumpet derail his emerald-eyed prince. He had too many plans for Ronnie's future, and those plans did not include any nappy-headed grand children. Randy Joe would save Ronnie from himself. In doing so, he would also save his reputation.

Everyday after the session ended, four House doorkeepers were on rotation to monitor the Chamber until 4 p.m., and it was Rose McLemore's turn to keep watch. She didn't mind so much because she rode home with her niece, Lessye, on her late days.

Lessye had been a godsend and Rose thanked God everyday that Lessye decided to make her home in Atlanta. She was a great help to her aunt. Rose always thought of Lessye as a younger version of herself. Her gentle, attractive features, inherited from her father and other generations of McLemores gave her more the look of Rose's daughter than her own mother's. This was one more thing that bound Rose closer to her niece.

Through the years, Rose made lots of friends at the Capitol. One of her dearest gossip buddies was a member of the housekeeping staff – Neveleen Scott, a short, chubby, dark brown-skinned woman with whom she frequently shared lunch.

"Did you hear about Jesse?" Neveleen asked, as they ate their sandwiches on the long wooden bench outside the House Chamber.

"Lessye mentioned it, and I saw the obituary notice in the newspaper today. We're planning on going to the funeral tomorrow after the memorial service for Brad. How about you?"

"No, chile. I don't do funerals no more," Neveleen said as if it were the source of an allergy. "I haven't been to a funeral since Henry died ten years ago. I get too upset, no matter who it is, close or not. And with my pressure going up and down, that's not good." For the next few minutes, Neveleen rattled on about funerals, Jesse, how sad it was about the dead legislators and how their situations reminded her of Henry. She hardly took a breath.

Rose enjoyed talking with, or rather listening to, Neveleen because she had only to ask her a few key questions to get her in conversational gear, and Rose never failed to glean a wealth of previously unknown information.

"You remember Henry?" Neveleen asked.

"He died before I began working here. My niece got to know him a little. She was real sad about his death–"

"Henry's funeral was the saddest thing I've ever seen. I felt sorry for his wife, Martha. I thought she would have a stroke and fall on the floor and die any minute. It took two of the funeral home attendants to hold her back from jumping over into the casket. Girl, it was a mess. Those Negroes showed out, hollering and screaming and running up and down the aisles. His granddaughter took it real hard, too. She passed out, poor thing. Slumped right down on the pew. They had a heck of a time waking her up to go to the cemetery. She had a tendency to pass out all the time like Harriet Tubman."

"What do you mean?"

"You know, Harriet Tubman used to fall out like that when she was on the Underground Railroad. It's some kind of disease. Oh, don't tell me." She frowned up her weathered brown face in thought. Suddenly a light of remembrance flashed in her eyes. "Noc . . . clepsy! It's where you pass out unconscious and don't know it."

"Oh, do you mean narcolepsy?"

"Yeah. His granddaughter has it." Neveleen didn't try and struggle with the pronunciation again. "Henry was real secretive about it. He didn't want people to know, almost like it was something to be ashamed of. I found out by mistake, and when I mentioned it to him, he made me swear I wouldn't mention it to anyone else. I think the only other person at the Capitol who knew was Jesse. And although he was known as a talking drunk, he never let that slip. Jesse was at the funeral crying like a bald-headed baby. And the music was so good that a couple of Henry's sanctified church members got the Spirit and shouted. Not too many people from the Capitol came other than the housekeeping staff because of the situation with the stealing and all. Did your niece tell you he was fired for stealing and messing with the mail?"

"Yes. I believe she did mention it. But she couldn't believe —"

"Neither could we, chile, neither could we. Now old Jesse was another matter. You know he was a drunk and a thief. God rest his soul. But not Henry. Henry was a good man. His wife, Martha, dropped dead of a stroke not too long after he died. Now it's only the granddaughter, and a grandson he lost touch with years ago. The girl seems to be doing all right though. She works for the state. I see her pretty often when I'm over in the LOB.

Rose looked surprised. "What's her name? Lessye might know her."

"Her name is Renae, Renae Stewart."

CHAPTER 24

Saturday was a beautiful crisp winter day with warming rays of sun that kept the sting of the brisk wind at bay. The small, subdued funeral for Jesse in the tiny A.M.E. church was a stark contrast to Alonso's public, spirited homegoing a week earlier and the private memorial for Brad which had just ended across town.

Lessye picked up Aunt Rose earlier that morning, and they were among the few Capitol support staff invited to attend Brad's service at eleven, sharing a pew with Tanya, Kevin and Amber. Lena came alone but made it a point not to sit anywhere near them. From a distance, they could see Marcus, who accompanied the Governor, down front in the section reserved for Brad's General Assembly colleagues and other VIPs. Lessye and Aunt Rose left Brad's service as soon as it was over to make it to Jesse's funeral on time. Rod was the only other person from the Capitol who came to show respect for Jesse, and after viewing Jesse's body, the three sat together on a back pew. Lessye was glad she was there to support Rod, who was feeling the loss of his friend deeply.

The people at Open Arms did a good job putting Jesse away. Although at a glance, one would immediately realize that his was not the most expensive casket, it was extremely nice and tasteful. It was covered with a blanket of red and white carnations, and a sparse number of flower arrangements and plants were sprinkled on both sides. Rod sent a beautiful wreath of red and white roses with a banner that read: *With love from your friends at the State Capitol.*

The funeral was brief, with the reading of Jesse's favorite scripture, a couple of solos, a soul-stirring sermon in place of a eulogy, and a medley of his favorite hymns. After the funeral, Lessye and her aunt kissed and hugged Rod goodbye and went to have a late lunch. Rod declined to join them and went to the cemetery.

During their meal, Lessye told her aunt about the wonderful time she had out dancing with Marcus the previous evening, and they also talked about Renae.

"I had no idea that Renae was Henry's granddaughter," Lessye said, still stunned by the news her aunt shared with her the day before. "She has never even mentioned the name of her grandparents. She only said they died some years ago."

"Maybe she's ashamed. Because of the circumstances under which Henry lost his job. Maybe she felt that she would get along better on her job if the people at the Capitol didn't know about the connection."

"You could be right about that. But why couldn't she confide in us about her narcolepsy, especially since she's passed out at work several times? She nearly scared everyone half to death, especially Clarice who was so rattled she almost passed out herself."

"You've got me on that one. Maybe Renae is a secretive girl."

"You can say that again." Lessye told her aunt about the Sunday evening she and Clarice drove to Macon to pick Renae up at the bus station and how antisocial she was when she stayed at Lessye's house. "She gave us some lame story about going to Macon with Lena and getting stranded after they had an argument. She purposely avoided me so she wouldn't be forced to answer any more questions. She left a thoughtful thank you note, but it would have been nice if she had said something to me face to face."

"You don't believe her story?"

"I wouldn't say I don't believe any of it, because I know how moody Lena can be. But I still think there is something that Renae is holding back."

"Maybe she has something to hide."

"Well, judging from what she has concealed from us already, I would said you're right on target. I wonder what it could be."

Lena picked up Renae after Brad's service and the two of them headed to Lenox Square for some shopping, a late lunch, and a movie. Lena knew

Renae had no use for Brad and hadn't bothered to invite her to the memorial. Lena had expensive tastes but also knew where to find some good sales. It was after dark when they returned to Renae's apartment. Lena insisted on coming in to help Renae with her purchases.

Although the apartment was too small for Lena's taste, she appreciated Renae's wise use of space that made the rooms appear larger. There were a few well-preserved old pieces of furniture in the living and dining rooms that to Lena's eye looked like valuable antiques: a Queen Anne sofa, an exquisite maple-wood china cabinet and buffet, a hand-painted armoire and a bookcase that included photographs on a couple of the shelves. The walls were painted a light egg-shell beige that matched the carpet. The plants, basketry, and a few colorful wall paintings brightened the space.

Renae had gone to her bedroom to drop the load of packages when Lena picked up a beautifully framed photograph she had noticed and studied several times before. In the photo was a pretty young woman cradling a little girl in her arms, and a small boy was standing beside her.

"What a gorgeous lady. Who is she?" Lena asked Renae when she returned to the living room.

"Thank you. That's a picture of my mother. She died when I was young. That's me she was holding. I guess I was about two."

"I thought so. I can see a lot of her in you. You have her exotic cheek bones, dark wavy hair, and light brown eyes that almost match your complexion."

Renae smiled. "Thanks for the compliment. My grandmama always said I was the image of her girl."

"What was her name?"

"Roslynn Dolores Perkins. I have her middle name. My grandmama told me she never married my father, but I have his last name."

Lena was still staring at the picture. "Who's the handsome little boy beside her?"

Renae shrugged. "I don't know, probably some kid from the neighborhood."

"Didn't you ever ask your grandparents?"

"No. I didn't find this picture until after my grandmama died. That's why its so special to me. It's the only picture I've ever seen with my mama holding me."

Renae took the photograph from Lena and gently placed it back in its position of prominence on the bookshelf.

As Lena drove home to her spacious apartment in Midtown, she thought more about the handsome little boy in the photo. His big, beckoning brown eyes were familiar and she had seen them before – in a photo album not too long ago. That was not some kid from the neighborhood as Renae thought. It was Marcus at age seven.

Rod had read the letter at least seven times since Mattie Mae gave it to him when they left the cemetery after Jesse's funeral.

"Jesse gave me this letter addressed to you along with his special box of keepsakes during our last breakfast together," she had said, pressing the letter into his hand. "He had wanted to put it in your hands himself, but started feeling poorly. He gave it to me in case . . . Jesse told me if anything happened to him to give it to you on the day we put him away." Her eyes watered like shiny pools and the cool, gusting wind whipped her blue-gray hair over her head. "I believe this is what you are looking for."

After reading the letter for the eighth time, several thoughts swirled in Rod's head. He folded the letter and placed it back in the envelope. He felt like kissing Mattie Mae. Yes, this was exactly what he was looking for! Now he knew the contents of the envelope Juan found in Brad's belongings. He received a letter from Jesse. According to Jesse's letter, so did Alonso and Killian. Now all three were dead under questionable circumstances. His suspicions about Marcus had been right after all. Henry's firing began his rise in state government. If the information in this letter were revealed, it could precipitate his downfall. The question was: Would Marcus kill to keep the truth from ever being revealed?

CHAPTER 25

*T*he worst possible thing that could happen to Ronnie did so when he was on his way home from Tamika's on Sunday morning: a flat tire. It was a cold and soggy day, and he had snuggled under the covers with Tamika until he had to go. Now with the extra time it took for him to change the tire and extricate his car from the mud puddle from hell, he was sure to be late. He could see his father's face, all red and swollen, simmering like a coffee pot ready to percolate. Breakfast was always served at eight sharp. The family left for church at nine on the dot so they could first attend Sunday school, then the morning service. No excuses and no exceptions. Ronnie had already left the house before his father returned from Atlanta on Friday and instead of coming home, he decided to spend the night and all day Saturday with Tamika. Her sisters had gone to Atlanta for the weekend. It was on rare occasions that they had the apartment all to themselves and when they did, they took advantage of it.

Ronnie arrived home at ten-thirty-five . . . and his father was waiting for him.

"Boy, where have you been! Dragging in here this late on a Sunday morning looking like you've been wallowing in a pigpen!"

Ronnie thought he could probably be heard all the way in Macon.

"I'm sorry, Daddy. I know I look a mess. But my car got a flat, and it's raining out. I got muddy trying to change it."

"I've been calling you all weekend. Why didn't you return my calls?"

Ronnie, who always turned off his cell when he was with Tamika, said, "I turned off my phone and forgot to check messages."

"Get upstairs, now! Wash and dress for church. We're going to be late, thanks to you, but we're going. I'll deal with you later!"

Church service was a nightmare. Ronnie could barely concentrate on the sermon for listening to his father's heavy sighs of anger and exasperation. Ronnie understood the importance of coming to church, but he didn't see the sense in bringing all that anger into the house of the Lord. Ronnie, however, had sense enough not to say that to his father for fear of Randy Joe knocking him under one of the pews.

When they arrived home from church, Randy Joe said, "Meet me in the den, now!" and stomped off. Ronnie knew that this was his cue to follow. He heard his stomach growl and remembered he had missed breakfast. He guessed dinner would be late today, too.

When Randy Joe slammed the doors shut behind them, he turned on his son.

"Ronnie, are you trying to embarrass me or something?"

"No, Daddy. I'm sorry about church. But I don't think being late on one rainy Sunday is going to ruin your reputation in the community."

"You better watch your smart mouth, Junior."

"Daddy, I— "

"Shut up! Just shut up!"

Ronnie hadn't seen his father this angry in a long time and was beginning to sense it had more to do with than being late for church.

"You don't think," Randy Joe said. "Because if you did, you would pay more attention to the company you keep."

"What are you talking about?"

"Who are you sleeping with these days, Ronnie?"

"What?"

"It's a simple question. I know you heard me. You may have gone stupid, but I don't think you've gone deaf in the last five minutes."

"I don't see where that's any of your business."

"Oh, it's my business all right when somebody tells me they've seen my boy out in public kissing some black gal!"

"I date who I please! And who has the nerve to spy on me and report back to you?"

"That's the least of your problems, boy. Don't worry yourself about who told me. It could be any number of people since you are so indiscreet that you parade your business around in public."

"I don't call kissing parading around in public. And if I feel like kissing my girlfriend and she approves, then that's between us, not you or your spying friends."

"Your girlfriend?! Boy, we better rush you to the emergency room and get your head checked out. Have you lost all your mind? You're not even trying to deny it. You can't have a black gal for your girlfriend. Sleeping with her in the dark is one thing. She's dark so you keep her in the dark. But parading her in public like she's some kind of queen? Boy, you've gone too far this time. This is a reflection on our whole family, and it's got to stop. Now!"

"No! You don't know what you're talking about! I love her, and she loves me. Our relationship is our business, it's not hurting anyone. This is the first time I've ever been in love, and you're not taking that away from me!"

"We'll see," Randy Joe said, looking as if he were going to explode any second. "You better end it now or I will!"

"What are you talking about? Don't you say anything to her! Don't you go near her!"

"I'll do whatever it takes to keep me from having a litter of nappy-headed, half breeds. So you better call your project slut, Tamika, at Fort Valley State University." Randy Joe paused at the surprised look on Ronnie's face. "Oh yeah. You didn't think I knew her name, did you? Well I do. Your daddy makes it his business to know everything that concerns you, boy. Remember that."

"Don't you dare talk about Tamika like that. She's not a slut, and she's not from the projects. And if she was from the projects, there wouldn't be one thing wrong with that. She's a nice girl from a good family. She's the sweetest person I ever met. Are you so hateful, bitter and close-minded you can't even give her a chance?"

"Give her a chance to do what? Slither her way into our family? Wake up, boy. You're rich and good-looking — the prince of the county. That gold digger is after one thing: your money."

"That's a lie! Tamika doesn't need my money. She's never asked me for a dime. Anything I give her is because I want to."

"That's her plan, boy. Do you expect her to walk around with a gold digger sign stuck to her back? I'll bet you that slut is daydreaming right now about seeing her name on your bank account. All she has to do is get pregnant and call a press conference and say it's yours. I hope you've had sense enough to use some protection."

"She's not a slut, and I'm not listening to any more of this," Ronnie said, turning to leave.

Randy Joe moved between Ronnie and the double doors, blocking his path. "Oh yes, you will listen. I haven't finished with you yet. Did you know her daddy is a Black Panther radical?"

"He's not a Black Panther anymore. That was a long time ago. And Tamika told me about that on our first date."

"Once a radical, always a radical!" Randy Joe moved closer to Ronnie and narrowed his eyes. "How long you think he's going to put up with you sniffing around his daughter? Those niggers are crazy and violent. They might do anything."

"You're the one whose acting crazy. Listen to yourself. You're acting like a raving lunatic—"

"A lunatic who is determined to protect you. Whether you like it or not . . ." Randy Joe lowered his voice almost to a whisper. "Do you hate me, Ronnie? Do you want to kill your daddy? Do you want me to have a heart attack and die?"

"No, Daddy, I love you. You know that."

"Well, you're not acting like it. You know what I believe? I believe you're seeing this girl to get at me for some reason. Deep down, you resent me, and you know that dating a black girl is the worst thing you can do to hurt me. So if you want to kill me, keep seeing her. It's either her or me, boy — her or me."

Ronnie looked at his father with new eyes. His father was toying with him. When he couldn't get what he wanted by yelling and screaming, he resorted to manipulation and guilt.

Ronnie walked across the room away from his father as he struggled to keep his voice calm. "My seeing Tamika has nothing to do with you. It has everything to do with me. Get one thing straight: I love Tamika. I have loved her since the first day I saw her, and I will love her forever. All the manipulation in the world is not going to change it. And if you can't deal with that, then I don't know what to tell you."

"You better start by telling me it's over! This is your last chance to get that leech out of our lives!"

Ronnie was so mad his whole body was throbbing. "Now let's get this straight. According to you, I'm the prince of Peach County; Tamika is not good enough for me because she's black; she's a manipulative gold digger who wants to trap me with a baby; her daddy is a crazy, violent radical; and if I keep seeing her, I'm killing you. I think you know what you can do with that sickening racist bull —"

"Boy, I should have shipped you off to military school years ago. I will slap your sassy tongue all the way down your throat!"

Randy Joe took off his suit jacket and slung it across one of the huge couches and began advancing toward Ronnie, who was standing his ground. The way Ronnie saw it, Tamika was his lady, and he would defend her honor, even if it meant coming to blows with his own father.

"What's going on in here?" Miss Pearl burst into the room. "We can hear you hollering and screaming all over the house. Randy Joe, you calm down this instant. The children are afraid you're going to kill Ronnie. And I'm worried, too."

Miss Pearl's words grabbed Randy Joe and stopped him in his tracks.

"We're having a civil conversation, Miss Pearl," Randy Joe said.

Miss Pearl cut her eyes at Randy Joe. "I know exactly what you're having, and it's hardly civil," she said. "I think you two have talked enough for one day. You both need some time to cool off, especially you, Randy Joe. We don't need this dissension in our house on a Sunday, and I don't want you driving up that dangerous highway to Atlanta angry. Now come on, baby, let me draw you a nice bath so you can relax before dinner is served."

Randy Joe went to the couch and snatched up his jacket, but before leaving, he whispered to his son, "You can thank your mother for saving your behind. But, remember, this is not over by a longshot." He then walked toward Miss Pearl and put his arm around her shoulders. As they left the room, Miss Pearl turned and told Ronnie, "You sit in here a while and cool down. We'll talk later."

Ronnie did as his mother instructed and plopped down hard on the same sofa where his father's suit jacket had just been. As he sat fuming and trying to get his adrenalin under control, a small bottle of clear liquid caught his eye. He had seen bottles of this kind, often at clubs and raves. It had obviously fallen from his father's jacket pocket because it hadn't been there before.

Ronnie picked it up, wondering: What would my daddy be doing with a date-rape drug?

Marcus spent Sunday morning with Robert, who was delivering the Men's Day speech at a small Baptist church in the Pittsburgh area of southwest Atlanta. There would be a reception afterwards. Marcus didn't know exactly how long it would be before he could leave, so he called Lessye to let her know he would meet her at Tanya's house at three. She gave him the address and directions, and told him to call her on her cell phone in case he got lost.

Lessye arrived at two to give Tanya a hand and was there to greet Marcus when he arrived with fifteen minutes to spare, carrying a bottle of expensive champagne as a gift for his hosts.

The conversation was lively and animated. Marcus and Kevin took to each other immediately and Marcus, with beer in hand, accompanied him in the back yard, where Kevin was again demonstrating his grilling expertise. The menu included grilled Tilapia, Teriyaki chicken and mixed vegetables. The ladies busied themselves preparing pasta salad, deviled eggs and rolls.

During the meal, they talked about a variety of subjects from music and sports to politics. Kevin shared some of the daily trials of being a high school assistant principal, and told them about some upcoming gigs for his jazz band, the Hep Cats, composed of several friends from his college days at Morehouse. And Marcus talked about his hectic morning with Robert and the ups and downs of his position as the governor's chief of staff. Tanya mentioned the elaborate reception following Brad's memorial service. Lessye filled them in on Jesse's funeral. When Lessye brought up the subject of Renae, Marcus' eyes slightly twitched, and he became silent.

"So that solves a lot of mystery surrounding Renae," Tanya said. "I can't wait to tell the girls. Now when she passes out at midday, we'll know why."

After dinner, they relaxed in the Ivey's cavernous family room, drinking wine, playing spades, and listening to Wynton Marsalis CDs. Too soon, it was time for the evening to come to an end because they all had work the next day.

Tanya thought about Marcus as he pulled off, trailing Lessye home to make sure she got there safely. She had been closely observing him during dinner and hadn't failed to notice the fleeting expression that swept across Marcus' face at the mention of Renae being Henry Perkins' granddaughter. As quickly as the look appeared on Marcus' face, it disappeared when Kevin changed the subject to talk about Samuel L. Jackson's latest movie. Tanya thought to herself that Marcus' look was like a dark cloud passing over the sun.

He was definitely a fine hunk of man. He seemed to adore Lessye, and she returned his admiration. He was witty, down-to-earth, and he knew how to do and say exactly the right things to ingratiate himself. But still . . . there was something missing that Tanya couldn't put her finger on. Or was it something there in plain view that she couldn't grasp? Whichever the case, there was definitely more beneath the surface of Marcus than met the eye. Tanya thought about how many times she had so eagerly pushed her best friend in his direction and for a brief moment hoped she hadn't pushed her onto a land mine.

CHAPTER 26

*M*onday began with a sigh of relief that no one had been killed on Sunday night. The Governor called for an investigation into the deaths of the three legislators, and Director Shaw would announce the name of the GBI agent assigned to handle the case during a press conference later that morning. Everyone was still buzzing over Sean's article, and the Governor made it clear to Director Shaw that departmental leaks must be found and plugged.

Marcus was summoned to the Governor's office first thing, partly for their morning meeting on the week's agenda and partly, as Marcus predicted, for him to be used as a sounding board.

After they reviewed the agenda, highlighting appointments and activities in order of importance, Robert said, "Ever since Sean's article broke, I've been catching it from both ends. The civil rights community has turned on me, and Brad's family is extremely upset. His father called me at the mansion yesterday evening, screaming in my ear. Thank goodness we don't have to deal with Killian's greedy cousins. They're so busy fighting over his property, they don't have time for anything else. We've got to bring this thing to closure before it ends my career."

"This situation is hard for all of us, but especially for you. You've lost three close friends and colleagues. You shouldn't have to be subjected to this abuse. I'll tell your secretary to direct all calls concerning this matter to me. I'll screen them."

"That's going to look like I'm avoiding them."

"No. It's going to look like you're doing exactly what you were elected to do – handle the business of Georgia. And because this matter is of the utmost importance to you, you have instructed your right hand man to take charge and insure that everything possible is being done. I'll call them everyday with updates to demonstrate that our first and foremost priority is solving this case and that we're committed to keeping them informed about its progress. I'll call them so much, they won't have time to harass you."

Robert's face collapsed in relief. "Nobody but you and my wife know how difficult this has been for me. I'm in deep grief, but can't give in to it. I'm the Governor, and I still have to appear strong and look like I'm in control. I can't show an ounce of weakness or my enemies will smell blood. Now on top of everything, thanks to Randy Joe, we've got a repeat of this anti-affirmative action crap to deal with, and I haven't even gotten started on my State of the State address."

"I have everything under control. We'll get through this. And after we do, you'll be more popular than ever before."

"Thank you, Marcus. What would I ever do without you?"

"Let's hope you never have to find out."

===

Marcus was practically gliding as he left the Governor's office. He was gaining more power over Robert by the minute, and the feeling was exhilarating. His weekend dates with Lessye had been phenomenal. He didn't know that another human being could feel so good in his arms. Marcus was almost whistling when he entered his office, tripping over an envelope that had been slid under his door.

Inside was a short typed note: *I know you framed Henry Perkins, and I know why. The three dead legislators knew it, too. Could that explain their accidents? It won't be long before everyone else knows.* Included with the note, was a copy of Jesse's letter, minus a salutation. Marcus froze. Those tumultuous dark clouds had once again covered his brilliant sun.

===

Due to a GBI press conference earlier in the day and a couple of routine crisis situations Juan was expected to handle personally, he didn't get a chance to come to Rod's office until late Monday afternoon.

"Man, I should be a firefighter considering the number of blazes I have to put out," Juan said, and plopped down in a chair opposite Rod's desk. "These folks are running me ragged. You wouldn't believe the day I've had. This is the first time I've been off my feet since I drove in this morning."

"Well your day is about to get better."

Juan's dark eyes lit up with curiosity. "What's up?"

Rod handed him the envelope containing the letter from Jesse. "This was hand delivered to me by a Ms. Mattie Mae Clark, one of Jesse's neighbors. I saw her at his funeral. He asked her to give it to me if something happened to him."

Juan read the letter, then looked back at Rod, his eyes looking like light bulbs that had suddenly been switched on. "So now we know what Jesse had to tell Brad after all these years. He was hiding in the office and eyeballed Marcus the night he sneaked back In and planted the incriminating evidence in Henry's desk drawer. And that part about Marcus being DeMarco Norris, Henry's own grandson. Man, that's deep. If it's true, that means Marcus put the fix on his own grandfather. That's cold. Do you think this is true, or could it be a case of sour grapes?"

"I believe it, all right. Jesse was not a man to play with God. He wrote this to clear his conscience before he died. He never cared much for Marcus, but I don't believe he'd lie about something this important. And there's something else. Jesse mentions Henry had a granddaughter. I found out her name is Renae Stewart. She's a secretary over in the LOB. According to a friend of mine, it seems her relationship with Perkins has been some big secret."

"Jesse's letter says Henry only had one daughter who had two children by different men," Juan said. So if it's true about Marcus, Renae is his half sister."

"Poor girl. As if she doesn't already have enough problems. I hope she never turns her back to him. She might find a knife in it."

Juan laughed. "It seems that your theory about Marcus framing Henry is true. We have an eye witness. A now dead witness, but a witness just the same." Juan got up and walked to the small refrigerator in Rod's office, got a cold bottle of water and returned to his seat. "I think we better give this letter to Claude as soon as possible," Juan said after taking a long sip.

"I saw the press conference on TV when Director Shaw announced he was the agent in charge of handling the case. I've met him several times.

He seems to be a good man. Haven't you worked with him on a couple of Ops?"

"Four to date. Claude's been with the department a stretch. No prima donna. He's fair and thorough. The type who makes sure he has all his ducks in a row before he starts quacking accusations. You'll like working with him."

"I'm looking forward to it. Will you arrange a meeting?"

"Yeah. Claude will love to get his hands on this. It's the first break in this case. And it fell right in your lap. Jesse says in this letter that he sent one to Killian, Alonso and Brad. So this is the first piece of evidence that goes to a possible motive for murder."

"My only concern is that the Governor wants play-by-play updates on this investigation, and Marcus is the point man. If he gets wind of this, or it's leaked to the press before we can corroborate it, we'll be cleaning the mess off our clothes until next year this time."

"I'm sure Claude will handle this discreetly until we can make some sense of this thing." Juan took another long sip of water and looked at the letter again. "All three of those legislators got a letter from Jesse and now they're dead. I know Marcus is ambitious and sneaky, but could he be a killer?"

"I don't know. It's never been a secret that I don't like Marcus, but the last thing I want to do is accuse someone unjustly. According to Jesse's letter, though, and if his assumption is correct, this could be a guy who is so cold and corrupt that he framed his own grandfather. I believe if he could do that, he's capable of almost anything."

Juan sighed. "Man, I've got a real bad feeling about this."

"And I'm afraid it's going to get a lot worse before it gets better."

―――――――――――――――

Tanya, Amber, and Clarice formed their own mini-version of a Capitol Hill walking club, more aptly described by Tanya as the "walk until you sweat like horses but still never lose a pound club." After starting out with ten secretaries from the Capitol and LOB, their numbers had dwindled to the three faithfuls who walked every day, rain or shine, summer or winter. Lessye declined joining them from the beginning, citing that walking up and down stairs with tour groups all day and her dance classes were enough exercise for her.

Monday was a relatively warm winter day that gave an enticing glimpse of Spring. During their ten laps around the Capitol building, Tanya shared her news about Renae, and they all agreed that they would not discuss it with Renae unless she specifically mentioned it first. The short winter days brought an early darkness that made Tanya pine for the long, lingering days of summer. After their walk, Amber and Clarice headed straight for the parking lot, but Tanya returned to her suite to change her shoes and get her purse. The suite reception area was dark, and it was obvious the cleaners had already come and gone, because the waste baskets were empty, the carpet vacuumed, and the furniture dusted.

She noticed a solitary stream of light coming from Brad's old office and wondered why. That office had been cleared of his belongings and was currently vacant. Tanya, still wearing her athletic shoes, walked quietly to the door. When she got to the office door and saw it was cracked open, she peeped in. Lena and Randy Joe were on top of what used to be Brad's desk. As she backed away, Tanya instantly realized they had more on their minds than listening for her footsteps.

CHAPTER 27

*G*us was almost breathless when he caught up with Rod on Tuesday morning.

"I saw the intern who was talking about the GHB. She's in the gallery now."

Rod followed Gus to the House gallery where Gus pointed out an attractive brunette with purplish blue eyes.

"Thanks, Gus, I'll take it from here." Rod approached the girl who was quietly chatting with two male interns and tapped her gently on the back of the shoulder. "Miss, could you please step outside for a moment? There are some questions I need to ask you."

The girl looked at him, then at the guys, who appeared equally as puzzled, and then back at Rod. "Sure."

Once outside the gallery, Rod, who always dressed in smartly tailored business suits, introduced himself and produced his ID.

"My name is Anita Colburn. How may I help you, Chief Jennings?"

"It has come to my attention that you had a recent conversation with someone concerning a drug called GHB. Is that true?"

"Yes. What do you need to know about it?" A nervous look was creeping into the corners of her eyes.

"Well frankly, Miss, everything you do. And let me preface this by saying you are not in any trouble. I need this information."

"Will you have to tell where it came from?" Her face was now a mixture of nervousness and fear.

"I promise I will handle this discreetly. Your name will not be mentioned unless it is necessary. Now please tell me what you know."

"There are these parties at the Coach House Hotel almost every evening, usually given by legislators. Almost all the interns know about them."

"What legislators?"

"Senator Tyrell Buford and Representative Randy Joe Reynolds."

"Have you ever seen them or anyone else in possession of GHB?"

She began to bite her lip.

"It's all right," Rod said. "Please don't be nervous."

"I saw Representative Reynolds with a bottle of it."

"When?"

"During the first week of the session. He invited me to a party in Senator Buford's hotel suite. I didn't want to go alone, so I took a friend. I saw him with a bottle then."

"How did you know what it was?"

"My sorority sponsored a drug prevention seminar that included a lecture about date rape drugs last semester. The bottle looked the same as some of the pictures and exhibits we were shown."

"Generally, people don't advertise the fact they're getting ready to spike someone's drink with GHB."

"Neither did Representative Reynolds. I saw it by accident. On my way to the bathroom I mistakenly opened the wrong door and saw him and Senator Buford talking. Representative Reynolds was shaking the bottle and laughing. I wasn't close enough to hear what they were saying."

"Does he know you saw him?"

"No. I don't think so, at least he didn't say anything when he came back to where I was sitting."

"Do you know whether Representative Reynolds used that drug on anyone?"

"Now that I think back, I believe he originally planned to use it on me. But when he found out who my friend was, he decided to use it on her instead."

"What gave you that impression?"

"By the way he was acting. Strange vibes. He asked me who she was and who she worked for. When I told him, he got real interested. Then he disappeared. The next thing I knew, she told me she had two drinks and was starting to feel woozy. She went outside to get some air. Later, I saw Representative Reynolds leave, too. I didn't think much about it then. The music was blaring, and we had all gotten high off the wine and liquor. I didn't see her anymore that night, so I assumed she decided to ditch me and go home."

"Did you see Reynolds anymore that night?"

"No. Not that I remember."

"When is the next time you saw your friend?"

"A couple of days later. I asked her why she left me, and that's when she told me what happened. Her drink was spiked and she was . . . raped." Anita's eyes melted into watery blue pools.

"I understand, Miss Colburn. I only have one more question: Who is your friend?"

"Her name is Courtney Maxwell, she's an intern for Representative Bernard Benton. She is his goddaughter."

===

Marcus was seated at the polished mahogany desk in his office, watching videotapes of the Governor's speeches with the sound on mute so he could focus on Robert's facial expressions and mannerisms. He immediately put his executive buffer plan into action. Between tapes he made some telephone calls.

His first call was follow-up contact with Claude. Marcus was serving as the official liaison in the Governor's office, and he reiterated that any and all information concerning the progress of the investigation should come directly to him. He would expect daily updates.

The second call was to Brad's father, assuring him that the case would have a swift resolution. He also promised to give him daily updates and encouraged the elder Austin to call as often as he wished.

The third call was to Della to find out her progress in arranging a meeting with the Black Caucus and representatives of the civil rights community at the Capitol, which he hoped could take place as soon as possible. She in turn had gotten a firm commitment from Marcus that the Governor would support the Caucus in their fight to save affirmative action.

Troubleshooting, combined with his other duties, hadn't left much time for him to dwell on who sent him the note and letter. But it was still simmering in the back of his mind. Someone is trying to mess with me, Marcus thought angrily. Whoever it was had been clever enough not to leave a trail and had gotten the envelope into his office past his secretary. It would have been easier for Marcus to narrow down if he knew which legislator received this particular copy. But he did know one thing: All three had received one because each of them had confronted him.

And as for whoever was trying to mess with his mind, if they had plans to send the letter to Robert, he was almost sure they would have by now. Marcus guessed that they wanted something else. Maybe they thought they could make a quick buck by blackmailing him. Or maybe they didn't want money at all.

He ejected one tape, slid in another one, and pressed the play button.

His initial impulse was to blame Lena. Sure. She was Brad's aide, and he had probably shown her his letter. Lena was angry with him for dumping her and would do anything for some get back. He couldn't wait to get his hands on her. His thoughts turned from Lena and focused on Tanya and how she looked at him when Renae's name came up during dinner on Sunday. At one point, Tanya caught his eyes, but he shifted them in another direction. For that brief moment, it was as if her eyes had cut right through him and were raking over his bare soul. Tanya was Lessye's best friend, and she had been Brad's secretary. Did she also have a hidden agenda?

What about Della? Marcus thought she sounded a bit stiff and stilted on the occasions he spoke with her about setting up the meeting. Alonso told her everything. But did he tell her about the letter?

And there was that old used up secretary of Killian's who had been almost rude to him when he called to arrange that last meeting with Killian. Does she have an axe to grind? Then there was another possibility: Rod. Marcus knew that if that old drunk, Jesse, wrote the legislators, he shot his mouth off to the golden boy as well. And last, but most certainly not least, Renae. Now, if anyone had a reason to get back at him, she did. He was the one who encouraged Lena to keep tabs on her. Had Lena told Renae in order to get back at him? Marcus opened his desk drawer, took out his power stress ball and began squeezing it hard.

Renae – that pampered little princess – raised in a loving, nurturing family with two doting grandparents. She had the life he should have had in a warm, clean home in a nice neighborhood. It was a glaring contrast to the roach-infested, rat trap where he had lived – with relatives who didn't much care whether he lived or died – in constant dread of getting shot in a drive by. But as things change, in the end Renae suffered the worst loss of all. Marcus was now on top of the world, and he intended to stay there.

Marcus played it over and over in his head like a popular tune one soon tired of hearing. He vowed to find out who was doing this to him, and when he did . . .

CHAPTER 28

Special Agent Claude Henderson, assigned to the Americus office, was one of approximately 400 employees who composed the largest division of the Georgia Bureau of Investigation. The Investigative Division employees worked in regional offices, regional drug enforcement offices, and other work units that provided specialized services in criminal investigations, including crimes such as homicide, rape, child abuse, armed robbery, fraud, drug offenses and other felonies.

Claude was a tall, solidly appealing man with coal black hair and a rich, peanut-colored complexion. He had large gentle hands and deep brown eyes that his wife, Carmen, always told him reminded her of what sweet dreams were made of. His quick wit kept his two college-age boys on their toes. He was tough, determined and professional with a flowing well of compassion that rivaled Niagra Falls. For a career agent who had handled his share of grisly homicide and rape cases, the fact that his strong faith in God prevented him from becoming jaded was rare in itself.

Following the press conference Monday morning, he opened a temporary office in the state-of-the-art GBI Atlanta Headquarters to be more accessible to the Governor and his chief of staff, as well as to conduct interviews with anyone at the Capitol who could shed light on this baffling case.

Unlike most temporary offices that were a hastily thrown together assortment of scuffed up and mismatched furniture, the comfortable, smartly polished furnishings for his office had been carefully selected and coordinated: his equipment, top of the line. Director Shaw assigned his special assistant, Karin Roberts, to help Claude organize his work space and to act as his assistant during the investigation.

The Director wanted daily updates as did Marcus, so Claude was expected to hit the ground running. No one told him directly, but he sensed that the Governor wanted this case settled before the end of the legislative session. He did not want the legislature going home for the year with this mystery still unsolved. Also, legislators were edgy. There was possibly a killer in their midst, and no one knew who might be targeted next. Security was being beefed up.

Although Claude felt a certain amount of pressure, he would not let it dictate how he would handle this case. He would work in his usual painstaking, methodical fashion that never failed him. He was as anxious as anyone to find the guilty party, but he would not settle for a scapegoat.

The telephone rang, and he picked it up on the second ring.

"Claude Henderson," he answered firmly.

"Agent Henderson. My name is Leah Clemons. I was the secretary for Senator Killian Drake. I have some information I think you should have. Should I fax it?"

"No, Ms. Clemons. I'm on my way to the Capitol. I'll come to you. What's your room number?"

"I'm in room 109, the Administration Floor Leader's office."

Looking at his watch, he said, "I'll try to be there in twenty minutes."

Claude grabbed his jacket and headed out the door.

Renae rarely went inside the Capitol building — for any reason. She dreaded it. That building caused memories of her grandparents to come flooding back through her with currents of raw sorrow so forceful, they threatened to wash her away. Today, there was no getting around going inside. One of her representatives asked her to hand-deliver letters to several key offices and news releases to the press boxes in the House and Senate as opposed to sending them through interoffice mail or via e-mail. She also had to reschedule some Pages who had changed their date of service at the last minute.

She first delivered some of the news releases to the press corps offices in the LOB, and then went across the street to the Capitol where she made all her deliveries, saving the office of Secretary of State for last. Because of what happened to her beloved granddaddy, Renae swore she would never set foot in that office, even if it meant losing her job.

"Hey, Renae," Lessye said. "It's been a while since I've seen you in the Capitol. Can I help you with anything?"

"Hi, Lessye. I had to come over here to deliver some letters and news releases. If you're not busy, you can do me a big favor."

"Sure."

"Could you deliver this letter to your boss?"

"I'll be glad to," Lessye said, taking the letter before going into the office.

"Thanks."

While Renae waited for Lessye to return, Marcus exited the Governor's front office holding some papers he was reading. The look in Renae's eyes hardened into a burning intense hatred. Renae was concentrating so hard on Marcus, she didn't hear Lessye return.

"Renae? Do you know him? You're looking like you hate him. Has he done something to you?"

Renae was startled, then momentarily upset that Lessye had seen her.

"No . . . No, I don't. See you later," she said and was gone.

As Renae walked away she thought to herself that Lessye was so nice, and she hated lying to her. Yes, Renae new exactly who Marcus was: the man who killed her grandparents, the only man in the world she had ever hated. He was also a man who would eventually get what he deserved.

Rod located the intern, Courtney Maxwell, who confirmed Anita Colburn's account of the incident the night of the party at the Coach House. She informed him that she had no idea who spiked her drink, molested her, or moved her to a vacant hotel suite. She did remember walking outside and someone joining her later, but she could not be sure it was Randy Joe. She told Rod she poured her own glasses of wine, but admitted she must have become distracted after placing her glass unattended on the bar a couple of times. Rod knew that turning your back on a drink for a second was all the time needed for someone to spike it. Whenever he spoke to youth groups, he always stressed to them the potential danger of leaving any liquid unattended at social gatherings.

Rod immediately relayed this latest information about the interns and GHB to Juan who called to arrange an appointment with Claude. Juan was informed by Claude's assistant that he was currently out of the office and the earliest he could see them would be the next morning.

Karin was waiting for Claude when he returned to the office that evening.

"Agent Henderson, you have some messages." She handed him several small, pale pink squares of paper torn from a duplicate message pad. "One is an important message from Major Juan Hanlon of the State Patrol. He and Capitol Police Chief Rod Jennings want to meet with you as soon as possible concerning the case. I scheduled them for eight tomorrow morning. They will be your first appointment. Is that all right?"

"That's fine. Thank you. And please call me Claude. We're going to be working closely together. No need for formalities."

"Thank you, Claude. Is there anything else you need before I leave?"

"No. I'm fine. You go ahead and have a nice evening."

Karin organized her desk and placed a few items in her leather attache case.

She walked swiftly to her black BMW, checking the time on her watch. She was late for an appointment. Even if she drove like a maniac, in metro Atlanta traffic, she would not make it from Panthersville Road in Decatur to south Fulton County on time. Before pulling off, she made a quick call on her cell phone.

"Hello," the familiar voice filled her ear.

"Sean. I'm leaving work now. I'll get there as soon as I can."

"I'll be waiting."

Claude stayed at the office long enough to recap the events of his day and put some things into perspective.

After his meeting with Killian's secretary, he made an impromptu courtesy call on Marcus, whom he had first met shortly after Robert was elected Governor. Later at the GBI crime lab, he did his own inspection of the vehicles of Killian and Alonso, and what was left of the wreckage of Brad's SUV. However, he failed to find anything inconsistent with the extremely thorough report issued by the Division of Forensic Sciences. The latents on all the bourbon bottles were smeared beyond identification and only trace amounts of the alcohol were found in the systems of Killian and Brad. What happened to the rest? And although an empty bottle of bourbon was found in Alonso's car, none was found in his system.

He would spend the evening poring through the toxicology report submitted by Gordon, the same report that wound up almost verbatim in the *Capitol Reporter* even before the Governor received his copy. Marcus had shown him the newsletter and informed him that finding the leak at GBI Headquarters would be among Claude's major priorities.

Claude knew it would definitely be his number one priority. He would not allow a case of this magnitude to be compromised in any way, especially by some meddlesome journalist.

He thought for a moment about Marcus. In the last few hours, he learned a lot more about the Governor's chief of staff. He was a smooth operator who had defied the odds and clawed his way up the good-ole-boy state hierarchy in his unprecedented rise from a mail clerk to one of the most powerful men in the state. He was intelligent and, no doubt, equally as ruthless, if the information Claude had obtained was true. He speculated on Marcus' true motives for becoming the buffer between the Governor and this investigation. It was worth a little digging. Claude sat down at his laptop and popped in a diskette. His first day on the job had been most productive.

CHAPTER 29

*H*ey, Red. You couldn't be in a better position if I had put you there myself," Sean said to Karin as she slid into the booth facing him. It was obvious he had been waiting for a while. He was finished with his second beer and about to start on a third.

"Hello, Sean. That's what you're paying me for." Karin scanned the bar to see if she saw anyone she recognized from the bureau. Rio Tavern was a small, but always crowded, "Cheers" - like, bar located on a lonely and secluded stretch of highway near the Atlanta suburb of Hapeville.

"See anyone you know?" Sean asked, watching her closely.

"No, but it never hurts to be sure," she said, flipping back long strands of her thick copper-colored hair. "The last thing we need is to run into someone from my office and they realize where you're getting your information."

"They're too busy fighting crime to stop for a beer. Besides have we ever seen anyone here we know?"

"Well, I can remember one night during our college fling that we almost got busted by our intern coordinator from GPTV."

Sean laughed. "I almost forgot about that. How long did our romance last?"

"Long enough for us to realize we were better at business than pleasure. How's it going with your book deal?"

"Why, you want to sabotage it?"

"Believe it or not, I'm probably one of your biggest supporters. I can't wait to read about your experiences in government over the past ten years. And . . . the more money in your pocket means . . ."

"There it is. The bottom line – always something in it for Karin."

"A girl's got to look out for herself."

"Which you do oh so well. You want a drink and some hot wings?" Sean asked.

"I can stay for a beer but no wings for me. I've got a late dinner date."

"Shaking down another gullible old man?"

She flashed him a coy smile. "What a sense of humor. It's none of your business. But since you're incurably nosey, this one is strictly pleasure."

The waiter appeared and Sean said, "A Corona with lime for the lady and an order of hot wings for me: Three Mile Island."

"One day your tongue is going to go up in flames," Karen said.

"I like my wings and my women hot," Sean said and winked. As soon as the waiter was out of earshot he turned serious. "You have anything for me?"

"Not today, but definitely tomorrow. Claude met with Killian's secretary today and early tomorrow morning he has an urgent meeting with Juan Hanlon and Rod Jennings."

"Hummmmm. Leah Clemons is one of the Capitol old timers. She more than likely had a mouthful to tell him. And Rod Jennings. This is getting better."

"Yeah, this has the potential for being the juiciest story you've ever covered in your little rag. It should be worth double the usual."

"My girl – ever the calculating opportunist. Let's not let our greed get ahead of us. I'll have to see what you've got first."

"After all these years. You don't trust me?"

"Sure I do . . . to find any angle you can to rip me off."

The waiter reappeared with a beer for Karin and again disappeared through the crowd.

"What time can we meet tomorrow?"

"I'll call you. Claude has got to submit daily reports to the Director and the Governor. I'll have to wait until he's out of the office and sniff around for what I can find." Karin squeezed in her lime and took a long sip of her beer.

"I want the whole report."

"I'm not sure I can get it all at one time. You might have to settle for a part of it."

"Not good enough. I can get eked out bits on the six o'clock news. It's the whole report or nothing."

"All right. I'll do my best. But remember the Governor and the Director are on a mission to find the leak. I think that's going to be one of Claude's main priorities. So I'm going to have to watch my back. Depending on the heat, I might have to cool it for a while after this one."

"Well, you make sure you don't have to cool it too long. This story is smoking, and I want to know how it unfolds before I read about it in the AJC."

CHAPTER 30

*J*anuary passed as swiftly as a bullet. A month that usually crept by like a lazy snail had suddenly taken wings. It was now the second day of February. Atlanta's fickle weather, unpredictable even in deep winter, could be icy one day and balmy the next. The sun shone like a golden spotlight, illuminating the capital city with a teasing warmth that beckoned for shirt sleeves. The only reminder of winter was the starkness of the trees. When Rod and Juan arrived at Claude's office at GBI Headquarters a few minutes before eight, he was already hard at work pecking on his laptop. Claude immediately rose from behind his desk and greeted them. They shook hands with the warmth of longtime colleagues and strong men who shared mutual professional respect.

"I knew we were going to get together at some point this week. But what was so urgent it brings you guys by this early in the morning?" Claude said, sitting down behind his desk and leaning back in the chair.

"We have some information pertinent to the case," Rod said. "But we don't want it to seem like we're stepping on your turf or trying to run your Op. We want you to know we're available to assist in any way we can."

"Not a problem. I'm not one of those arrogant, know-it-alls who feel like I'm superior to everyone else in law enforcement because I can wear a jacket with GBI on the back. I'm an easy man to get along with, and I don't get into that turf crap. Our foremost goal is to solve this case, and it is imperative that we work together in order to do that. The Governor and the Director wanted me on this case because of my longevity on the Bureau and because I'm on a first-name basis with most of the movers and shakers on the Hill."

"Not to mention your stellar success rate," Juan said.

"Thanks, Juan. It's men like you who through the years have contributed to that success.   I want you two in the loop and to play important roles on the task force. Rod your position at the Capitol is key, and your experience is valuable, especially in light of some information that has come to my attention. What's your take on Marcus Norwood?"

Rod and Juan filled Claude in on everything they knew about Marcus and the Perkins incident. Rod gave him a copy of Jesse's letter and informed Claude of his passing. Claude, in turn, gave Rod and Juan copies of Killian's memo to Marcus he got from Leah and told them what she said about the last meeting Killian had with Marcus being a heated confrontation. Rod filled them in on the revelations from the two interns concerning GHB use on the Hill and the allegations against Randy Joe and Tyrell. They also discussed Renae's relationship to Henry and speculated on the reasons why she kept their relationship a secret.

As they concluded the meeting, Claude said, "Rod, why don't you find out all you can about Renae and keep following up on the GHB lead. Juan, I need you to find out if Jesse's supposition is true – whether Marcus is in fact DeMarco Norris, the grandson of Henry Perkins and half brother of Renae. I'm going to talk with the secretaries and staff persons of Brad and Alonso and find out if they also had meetings with Marcus about that letter. I'm also going to put a plan in action to get rid of the leak in our department."

They planned to meet again Monday morning and traded cell and pager numbers in case anything urgent came up before then.

═══════════════

Representative Bernard Benton missed his three o'clock Insurance Committee meeting on Wednesday to keep a more pressing appointment. It was less than a ten minute drive from the Capitol to the unpretentious office building of Harlin Burr he was looking for on Peters Street.

Bernard arrived at Burr's office promptly at three and was unprepared for the ragged runt of a man with thick features, close-set eyes, ashy dark brown skin, unkempt hair, scraggly beard, and a shiny gold tooth in the front of his mouth. He looked like a rumpled skid row bum who had just crawled out of a pasteboard box. He was a pitiful contrast to the impeccably dressed Bernard: tall and distinguished, with deep, rich ebony skin; appealing features; neatly trimmed salt and pepper hair with matching mustache and beard and bright, gold-flecked sepia eyes.

"Come in and have a seat," Burr said. When he smile, his gold tooth shined like a miniature nugget, reflecting the solitary light illuminating the rather large warehouse-type room he used for an office. Burr's handshake was hard and commanding, and despite his bedraggled appearance, Bernard immediately recognized him as a man confident in his intelligence, skills, and expertise. Although Burr's office, even for its size, was somewhat cluttered, Bernard noticed it contained expensive-looking furniture and cutting-edge equipment – from the sleek cedar desk smothered with papers and folders to the high-tech computers, printers, fax machines, scanners, color copy machines, paper shredders, radios, tape recorders, camcorders, television monitors and security and still cameras dominating one side of the room.

Bernard took a seat in one of the lush, leather armchairs opposite Burr's desk.

"Thank you for seeing me on short notice," Bernard said. "You were highly recommended, and I know your time is limited, so I won't take much of it."

"You're welcome. You can also thank our mutual friend for his referral. Now as both of us are busy men, Representative Benton, let's get down to business."

Bernard explained his problem and his preferred solution. He handed Burr a piece of note paper containing all the information Burr needed to complete the task and what Bernard would need.

"When can you do it?" Bernard asked.

"For you, Representative Benton, immediately," Burr said, memorizing the contents of the note paper before feeding it to a small paper shredder close to his desk.

Bernard sighed with relief. "I know you're one of the best in this business and your services don't come cheap. What about the fee?"

"Thank you. But the fee will be taken care of by our mutual friend in California. In that way, my services will be in no way connected to you."

"Also, this is a highly sensitive and confidential matter," Bernard said.

"I understand," Burr nodded. "Representative Benton, I run an exclusive business. This is an extremely delicate service and complete discretion is of the utmost importance."

"All right. When can I expect some results?"

Burr swept away some papers covering his desk calendar. After studying it for a moment, he said, "Call me next Friday, the eleventh. I should definitely have something for you by then." Burr handed Bernard one of his gold embossed business cards.

"Thank you for your time, Mr. Burr. I'll contact you then," Bernard said, rising to leave.

"You won't be disappointed."

CHAPTER 31

*G*et me my information, Karin. I'm paying you good money, and I expect results."

Sean could be so irritating sometimes, Karin thought. He thought every piece of news was his by right.

"Cool your jets, will you? You'll get it as soon as I do. Claude is working on the first report now. I'll get my hands on it as soon as he leaves the office."

"You better. Remember, I have a deadline to meet."

"Don't try to strong-arm me, Sean. Everyone knows that the *Capitol Reporter* is a one-man show. You can run a special edition anytime you get ready. So chill out and wait for my call."

There was a sharp click and the connection was broken.

═══════════════════════

Renae took a short break to go buy some stamps at the U. S. Post Office on the first floor of the LOB and to buy a bottle of apple juice from the snack bar. Before she returned to her suite upstairs, she stopped at the pay phone around the corner from the snack bar to make a call. She fished in her purse for the scrap of paper with the number, dropped in her coins and then dialed.

"Hello," said a smooth, relaxed voice on the other end of the line.

"Hey. This is Renae. What's taking so long? I think it's time."

There was a long pause followed by an impatient sigh.

"Calm down. I have everything under control. It will all be over soon."

"That GBI agent has been snooping around and asking questions, so has Rod. I'm almost sure it's about me."

"So what? They don't know anything and won't know anything as long as you keep your cool."

"I'm getting anxious. Please do it now."

"Consider it done."

CHAPTER 32

*W*ednesday afternoon, Tanya's supervisor called to inform her that Brad's old office would remain vacant until after the General Election in November. Tanya and Amber had already packed up all of Brad's personal belongings which had been delivered to his family. After all the office furniture was moved into storage, Tanya and Amber began the task of setting up their own inner-suite break room.

By Friday morning, Brad's once professional legislative office had been transformed into a comfortable lounge, equipped with sofa, end table, lamp, microwave, toaster, coffee maker, small refrigerator, and color television. All the items except the sofa, which Tanya and Amber hauled from the suite reception area, were supplied by Tanya, Amber and Lessye. Amber brought in a couple of old sofa pillows and a colorful quilt she wasn't using at her apartment, and they were set.

When Lessye arrived to see the finished product and join them for lunch on Friday afternoon, she remarked that all they needed now was a fireplace. Tanya and Amber were delighted because now they had a pleasant alternative to that drab, smoke-filled break room.

The telephone was still hooked up, so they could catch the lines. Also, they kept the door cracked open so they could easily hear if anyone entered the suite.

"If Lena could see this place now, she and that nasty Randy Joe could get seriously busy in here," Amber said, as the three of them ate sandwiches and watched the first half of "The Young and the Restless."

Tanya winced. "Please don't talk like that while I'm trying to eat my lunch. Besides, you shouldn't hate on our former fifth floor Marilyn Monroe."

"More like Scarilyn Monhoe," Amber said.

"Seriously, Tanya, what if Lena does come back for a second act?" Lessye asked.

"Unless she has suddenly turned into David Copperfield, she'll have to break the door down. The only reason she was in here the day I caught them was because she had hung around piddling in Brad's office after hours. When we left to go walking, she probably thought I was gone for the day. That girl never had a key to this suite. That's one firm rule all my representatives agree to: Aides in this suite do not have keys."

"Thank the Lord," Amber said, her voice mimicking a televangelist.

"No one knows about this place but the three of us," Tanya said. "We keep the door locked when we're not using it so nobody will stumble in here by accident and start asking questions. We never know when we might need somewhere to escape from the representatives. So let this be our secret."

"What about Clarice and Renae?" Lessye asked.

"No," Tanya said. "Don't get me wrong. I love both of them. But Renae is close to Lena and has been acting stranger than usual lately, lurking around like a deranged racoon. And Clarice, bless her heart, is too hyper besides being a loyal Lena fan. They might let something slip and the next thing we know, there will be a call from the Speaker's office. You know Lena is desperate to score points over there these days."

"And I thought she wanted to get a job in the Speaker's office to score floor privileges inside the Chamber," Amber said.

"What?" Lessye asked.

"Yeah," Tanya said. "Lena sucked up on a pity position as girl gopher in the Speaker's office for the remainder of the session. Everybody felt bad about Brad, and they decided to help her out since she was so desperate to stay on the Hill. I'm just glad she's out of here."

They heard loud voices at the front of the suite, and Amber immediately left the office to see who it was.

"Well, lunch is over ladies," she said when she reappeared after a few seconds. "A couple of lobbyists are making courtesy calls. I better go up front and keep them company before they start snooping."

"Thanks, Amber." Tanya said, "I'll be out in a minute."

Amber grabbed the remainder of her sandwich and grape soda and returned to her desk, closing the door behind her.

"What's up with you?" Tanya asked Lessye when they were alone. "Where did that gloomy look come from when Amber brought up Lena's name?"

"Is it that obvious?"

"Yes. I notice everything. It's in my job description. Now what's up?"

"I had a long talk with Rod yesterday. He thinks Marcus is still seeing Lena, and I could not convince him it's over. He thinks Marcus is only after one thing, and I should take it slow with him. He said everything he could to warn me off him. I know most of that's coming from the fact that Rod has never liked Marcus. But what do you think?"

"Rod has never been long on tact when it comes to Marcus. His opinion is anything but objective. But that doesn't change the fact that he sincerely wants the best for you. I think you need to pray about it, then follow your heart. Rod and I can give you all the advice in the world, but this relationship is between you and Marcus, and it's your call."

"What would you do?"

"I'd keep my eyes open. I would continue to date him, but there would be no pillow tag until I was sure there's no double dipping."

"I hear you. What do you think of Marcus now that you've gotten to know him better?"

"I like him okay. You know I always thought Marcus was cool. I still think you make a good couple."

"I sense a *but.*"

"Well, when he was at the house it struck me that there is a lot we don't know about him. I had the feeling he was showing us the Marcus he wanted us to see. That kind of worries me. Second to Kevin, you're my best friend in the world. I'm the one who's been pushing you forward with this relationship. It would kill me if you got hurt and it was my fault."

"I'm not going to get hurt. And whatever happens, it won't be your fault. I'm seeing Marcus because I want to. Are you saying you think I should back away from him?"

"No. But I am saying that you should let your common sense work for you — head first rather than heart first. Be careful."

"Rod said almost the same thing."

"Well, you know what they say about great minds. What did Rod say about his role in the GHB connection?"

"He was vague, which isn't like him. He was more interested in getting information from me."

"Did he say anything about Marcus in relationship to the case?"

"No. Why?"

"Agent Henderson asked me for a list of everyone who met with Brad the week before his death. He was especially interested in Marcus' last meeting with Brad. All I could do was confirm they met because I was on my way out when Marcus came in. I'm pretty sure he also talked to Lena, because he asked me how to contact her. I thought he may have said something to Rod."

"If he did, Rod didn't tell me. He asked me some questions about Renae and gave some lame explanation about everybody being questioned at this point. Rod is keeping something from me, and I'm almost certain that he already has at least one suspect in mind."

Marcus was thoroughly pleased with his damage control. The dreaded meeting with Black Caucus members and civil rights activists to lament Alonso's death and discuss the subsequent criminal investigation, which could have disintegrated into disaster, was a great success thanks to the wise intervention of Della. Marcus managed to pacify them by addressing their gripes and concerns. Robert, still floating on the success of his Budget Address and most recently the State of the State Address, impressed the crowd by making an impromptu appearance. He pressed every palm in the room, assured them that the case was top priority and reminded them they were in capable hands with his chief aide. Then, he was off to handle yet another crisis that needed his immediate and personal attention.

Della came through for him, so for the time being, Marcus dismissed the idea that she sent him the copy of Jesse's letter.

After the meeting, Marcus paid a courtesy call to the Austin family at their Buckhead mansion. He met Brad's parents, his two brothers, who were sturdy replicas of their serious stone-faced father, and his sister, Kaye, in the cavernous oak-paneled library of their elegant home. Kaye, with her kind, down-to-earth manner, and Brad, with his genuine concern for the working class, had been the mavericks in this bunch.

Marcus' polite air of authority and intelligence commanded their respect. He promised them he and Robert would not rest until Brad's killer was brought to justice. Marcus also assured them that they were on the verge of finding the leak at the GBI. When they did, the Austins would be the second to know.

Marcus' day was most productive, and there was one other item on his agenda. He parked his car in his reserved parking space just outside the Capitol on MLK Drive, and as always, before entering the building, he admired the sign at the curb beside his parking space that warned in big bold lettering: DON'T EVEN <u>THINK</u> ABOUT PARKING HERE.

He entered the building with a confident swagger, passing his office suite and strutting in the direction of the tour booth. Lessye was away on tour. He could hear her lovely voice floating through the main floor. He looked in the rotunda. She was there dressed in an attractive teal pant suit and relating Georgia's history to about seventy members of Alpha Kappa Alpha Sorority. It was their day at the Capitol sponsored by their dynamic and illustrious soror, Della.

Marcus stood planted there, admiring her beauty and intelligence, watching her every move. When Lessye was ready to take the ladies to another area, she noticed Marcus staring at her and smiled that effervescent smile. Marcus smiled and winked at her before continuing on his mission.

He arrived at his destination in good time. As he approached the Speaker's office on the third floor, Lena was on her way out to run an errand.

"Lena, I need to talk to you."

"Hello, Marcus. How are you?"

"Now!"

"Please watch your tone. There's no need for you to be loud and rude. And I can't imagine why you need to talk to me since the last time I saw you, you made it clear it was over between us and you had nothing further to say. You hurt me. But now you want to talk to me?"

Marcus lowered his voice. "Yes, we need to talk." He knew she was waiting for an apology. But she wouldn't get one, because he meant every word he said. Marcus was not about to waste his hypocrisy on the likes of Lena. Disingenuous cow-towing was reserved for those who could further his financial or political ambitions.

Lena fished in her purse for a mirror to check her makeup.

"This is serious," Marcus said. "There's something I need to know."

"And what might that be?" she asked, admiring her reflection in the small mirror.

"Did you happen to send me a love note dripping with venom, recently?"

"I don't know what you're talking about. You have to be more specific. But before we get into that, aren't you afraid your girlfriend might see us?" Lena said, alluding to Lessye, who was leading her tour group into the south wing below where they were standing.

"This has nothing to do with her. It's between you and me . . . and Jesse Higgins. Does that name ring a bell?"

"Should it?"

"Lena, I'm not playing," Marcus said in a chilling voice that could make ice cubes shiver from the cold.

She again reached in her purse to fish out a tissue to dab at her lips when a key fell out and hit the floor. She waited for him to pick it up. When he hesitated, she said, "Do you mind helping a sister out?"

Marcus grunted in exasperation and bent down to pick up the key. "If you kept your keys all together on a key-ring like everybody else, you'd keep up with them better."

Lena rolled her eyes at him. "Don't worry about how I handle my keys, thank you. Drop it in my purse," she said, opening the small bag. Marcus did as she requested, and she put in her tissue and the mirror and closed the purse.

"Now back to Jesse," he said.

"Who?"

"Jesse Higgins!"

She flipped her hair. "All right. Maybe I do know something. But I can't talk about it here."

"Where then?"

"Your place this Sunday."

"No, I don't think —"

"It's either your place or no place. Make up your mind. I don't have all day. I have to run an errand for the Speaker."

"Okay. Why don't you come Sunday at —"

"I'll decide the time when I call you on Sunday. You be at home and available all day. I'm calling you one time at home. If you are not there, forget it."

"You'd better not be pulling my chain to get into my loft. Bad things happen to people who jerk me around."

"You might be jerked around," she said purposely glancing in Lessye's direction. "But it's not going to be by me. See you Sunday." She flipped her hair in his face before briskly walking away from him.

Gus was around the corner buying stamps at the Legislative Post Office when he saw Marcus approach Lena, looking none too friendly. Inquisitive man that Gus was, he figured that this would be a conversation worth listening to, and he was right. But what could Marcus need to know involving Jesse Higgins?

"Have you spoken to Ronnie anymore about that situation?" Nathaniel asked as he and Randy Joe relaxed in Reynolds' office sipping straight bourbon.

"Not since the blowout last weekend. I swear, that boy is trying my patience and is determined to send his old daddy to an early grave. He's dug in his heels, and the boy ain't flinching."

Nathaniel sipped his drink. "Well, at least I've heard she is a cute little thing."

Randy Joe scowled at him after gulping a big swig of bourbon. "Is that supposed to be some kind of consolation? I don't care if she's Miss America. My boy ain't hooking up with no black gal!"

"Calm down. Can't you take a joke?"

"Not about this, and not when it comes to my boy," he said gulping down one glass of bourbon and starting another.

"Hey, boy, you'd better slow down. Remember, you've got to drive down the road a piece to get home. Miss Pearl wouldn't appreciate having you splattered all over the highway."

"Don't worry. I'm not about to end up like my late colleagues. I know my limit."

Nathaniel observed him for a moment. "Speaking of your late colleagues, I can't help but wonder whether you've been doing some freelance problem solving without my knowledge."

Randy Joe took another long swig of liquor and narrowed his eyes. "One thing's for sure . . . I'd never kill and tell."

Nathaniel thought that given Randy Joe's current mood, it would be best to let it drop. "Where's Tyrell?" he asked.

"He's already gone for the weekend. He's meeting with his county sheriff. Some niggers at the jail have accused him of brutality. It's a mess. They've called in the SCLC, ACLU, NAACP and any other militant agitators they can think of. And while I'm on the subject, did you know that of all the black girls to get mixed up with, Ronnie had to go and pick the daughter of one of the most notorious militants in Peach County? Her daddy is a Black Panther civil rights worker of all things – agitating all over the county and the rest of Georgia."

Nathaniel sighed. "Yes, I know. I'm the one who told you, remember?"

"Oh yeah, yeah. That's right. I forgot. This situation with Ronnie is about to make me lose my mind."

Not to mention the liquor you're drowning it in, Nathaniel thought, then looked at him. "Do you want me to take care of it?"

Randy Joe eyed him cautiously. "How . . . exactly would you . . . take care of it?"

"You know I can't go into details. But be confident that if you give me the go ahead to handle it, this situation will be handled for good," Nathaniel said, his usual jovial countenance turning hard and sinister.

"I'll let you know. I'm not ready to commit to anything." Randy Joe said and shivered.

The temperature in the room suddenly dropped twenty degrees. It was chilling. Almost like death had walked through the door and taken a seat between them.

CHAPTER 33

*B*arry Cornelius Layton was by profession a political consultant and executive director of a powerful middle Georgia equal rights organization. By passion, he was a writer and fervent public speaker on the subject of civil and human rights in the tradition of his hero, Dr. Martin Luther King, Jr.

When Dr. King was assassinated in 1968, Barry rebelled, moving to Oakland, California, where he became a member of the "Black Panther Party For Self Defense." After a few years of government harassment and one too many close calls with the police, Barry returned home and earned a master's degree in social work at Atlanta University. He married his Morris Brown College sweetheart and moved to Fort Valley, Georgia where his girls Tarrah, Tammi, and Tamika were raised.

Barry dearly loved all three of his girls, but Tamika was special. She was his baby, and her current romantic relationship was especially disturbing. Of all the young men in Fort Valley, Tamika had gone and given her precious heart to a white boy. And if that wasn't already bad enough, this wasn't any white boy: Ronnie was the son of one of the most hardcore racists in Peach County.

By reputation throughout the county, Randy Joe was a vile, hateful man who could be vicious when things didn't go his way.

Barry heard many horror stories about the antics of Randy Joe and his sidekicks, Tyrell and Nathaniel, from his friends Alonso and Della. Barry's organization was currently involved in a civil rights battle against a racist middle Georgia county sheriff, whom Tyrell strongly supported. Barry knew people who had been victims of the Reynolds' ruthless land grabbing. There were also rumors that Randy Joe could be physically violent.

Barry thought sadly about his dear friend, Alonso, and his tragic, untimely death. He wished that his friend was still here. He would be the perfect person with whom to discuss this delicate situation. Alonso had great wisdom. He was already deeply missed. Barry also subscribed to the *Capitol Reporter* newsletter that he received via Internet, and after reading that GHB was involved in Alonso's death, he knew there had to be some foul play. And now there was a criminal investigation underway. He was confident that Della would keep abreast of the investigation and get some answers. Someone murdered his friend. Could Randy Joe and his hateful crowd have had anything to do with Alonso's death?

No, this white-boy situation was not good at all. Barry brought up every point he could think of when trying to talk Tamika into getting out of this relationship. He prevailed upon her common sense by insisting the boy was using her, detailed his family's rogue history, explained to her the potential danger if his father found out, and implored her to think about her racial pride and her ancestors. He even used the parents' best weapon: guilt. But Tamika's mind was made up. She wasn't giving up Ronnie. She loved him, and she was sure that when her family got to know him, they would, too.

So Tamika was bringing her "redneck Romeo" home for dinner Sunday and had pleaded with her father to be on his best behavior. He reluctantly promised her he would, after all, he would not be rude to any guest in his home. But the Lord knew that Barry loathed the idea of his daughter dating a white boy. He practically got physically ill whenever he thought about Ronnie touching her. Barry knew the slave master mentality of white men and their "forbidden fruit." And no matter how nice Ronnie might be, Barry could not believe that an apple, or in Ronnie's case a peach, could fall that far from the family tree, especially if the tree was one as rotten as Randy Joe.

═══════════

Although Marcus dreaded his meeting with Lena, sticking close to home gave him a chance to think about Lessye and his feelings for her. He had prepared dinner for her at his loft on Friday evening after her dance class. When he looked into her eyes through the candlelight, he knew that what he felt for her was unlike any feeling he had ever had for anyone in his entire life. He felt like he would do anything for Lessye, anything to have her love and respect him. Anything to keep her in his life. These unfamiliar emotions made him feel vulnerable and frightened him. But at the same time, he felt happier than he had ever been. He felt free, for the first time, to let down his guard, remove his mask and share the real Marcus and still be sincerely cared for. It was a fantastic feeling.

Marcus was thankful that for the first weekend since the session began, Robert did not have some important appearance that required Marcus' presence. So he spent all day Saturday with Lessye and a leisurely Sunday thinking about her, and watching basketball games, listening to his collection of Stevie Wonder CDs, and waiting for Lena to call.

By 8 p.m., when he finally heard from Lena, he was seriously considering whether he should strangle her as she walked through his door or after she gave him the information he needed. Because of Lena's refusal to give him an exact time for their meeting, he turned down an invitation to attend church with Lessye and asked for a rain check. He wasted a whole day waiting for Lena, who rang his doorbell exactly one hour after her call.

"What took you so long?" Marcus said when he opened the door.

"You have a real problem with formal greetings, don't you?" She brushed past him and walked inside his loft. As usual, Lena was provocatively dressed, leaving almost nothing to the imagination. She was wearing sleek, black riding pants that were so tight they looked like they were laminated on; a low-cut, skin-hugging black ribbed sweater, a black leather jacket with matching boots and driving gloves. Her long brown hair was pulled back in a ponytail. She was carrying a large black leather bag.

"I'm sorry I'm late. I intended to get with you earlier today, but I had an emergency. Peace offering." She held out an ornate cologne bottle that she had taken from her bag.

"What is this?"

"As I said, just a peace offering to make up for being so late. It's your favorite cologne, Mystique. Sorry I didn't have time to get it gift wrapped."

"This isn't a Mystique bottle," he said, taking it from her and examining it.

"I know it's not, and that's part of the present. I went to this delightful boutique called Perfect Scents in Greenbriar Mall. They precisely copy all major brands for a fraction of the price. The best thing about the place are these exquisite keepsake cologne bottles."

"I didn't know you shopped at Greenbriar. I thought Lenox was more your style."

"Renae lives close to there; I go with her on occasion."

"Well, thank you. That was thoughtful. But you shouldn't have." Marcus wanted to say he wished she hadn't, but he had to admit it was a thoughtful gesture.

"You're welcome. Besides I know you have other plans for Valentine's Day this year," she said with a sly smile. "So I thought I'd give you your present early."

"Let's get down to the business of this visit."

"Okay. But first I need to use the bathroom, and I could use a chilled glass of wine, if you have some. "

Marcus exhaled deeply. "You know where it is. And do me a favor: take this with you and leave it on the counter," he said, handing her the cologne bottle. All I have is some burgundy."

"That's fine," she said, sauntering in the direction of the bathroom.

Marcus went to the kitchen and took an almost empty bottle of wine from the refrigerator. After pouring the burgundy liquid in a glass for Lena, he went to his bar and poured himself a stiff bourbon and water and gulped half of it down. This was shaping up to be a long evening.

They both arrived back in his living room at about the same time.

"All right," Marcus said as he handed her the glass of wine. "You've given me my token, gone to the bathroom, and here's your wine. Now it's time to talk. Who sent the note?"

She took a long sip of wine. "This is good," she said, stalling for time.

"Come on, Lena. I want the name, now!"

She grinned at him wickedly. "Probably the one woman who hates you even more than you hated Henry . . . Renae."

———

Not only did Ronnie leave home before his father returned Friday evening, he was gone all day Saturday and also defied his father by not even returning home for church Sunday morning. Ronnie was asserting his independence. But what the boy failed to take under consideration was as long as he resided under Randy Joe's roof, he would obey his rules – or else. Randy Joe would teach his son a good lesson for disobeying his authority. He would understand that his loyalty was to his father first and family and to the white race, not some black slut he was shacking up with.

On his way back to Atlanta on Sunday evening with still no sign of Ronnie in sight, Randy Joe used his cell phone to make an urgent call.

"Hello."

"Nathaniel, it's Randy Joe. You remember what we discussed on Friday?"

"Yeah."

"I think it's time for you to take care of it."

"Okay."

CHAPTER 34

*M*arcus checked his e-mail first thing Monday morning , then thumbed through his most recent stack of U.S. mail before his meeting with Robert. He came across the complimentary tickets for Robert and his staff to the Black Caucus barbeque and made a mental note to call Lessye and let her know he had tickets for her, Tanya and Kevin. Next he came to an inter-office envelope marked confidential from Claude and hastily opened it. He hoped that Claude was sending him an update on the case, something he could report to Robert. After he tore into the envelope, his eyes opened wide with a perplexed expression. Inside was only a blank sheet of letterhead.

Claude managed to get his hands on one of the first copies of the *Capitol Reporter* to reach the Hill. After reading the first page, his suspicions were confirmed. He immediately called Director Shaw.

"Yes, sir. Yes, sir. I understand. We're on our way." Claude hung up the phone and stepped outside to the desk of his assistant. "Karin?"

"Yes, Claude."

"The Director needs to see us in his office immediately. There are some issues we need to discuss before my meeting with Rod and Juan."

Sean was on the Hill bright and early Monday morning to see first-hand the response to his most recent victory in investigative journalism. The article concerning what he had dubbed the GHB Connection started with Sean's conspiracy theory that the deaths were all somehow connected to the Perkins case. He wrote about the empty bottle of bourbon found in each instance, a tidbit he held back from his first article covering Gordon's report. Sean brought up the bourbon, not because of any connection with the cause of death but because of the striking similarities with Perkins, and the fact that the three legislators played prominent roles in Perkins' firing when they all worked together in the office of Secretary of State. The fact they were all single and had prominent, influential and liberal positions in the state legislature also fueled the theory of similarities.

However, the focal point of his piece was the contents of the memo that Karin leaked to him. Sean explained that a memo updating the case had been sent by Agent Claude Henderson to the GBI Director informing him that after another thorough search of the wreckage, a small bottle of liquid thought to be a controlled substance had been found under the passenger seat in Killian's car. An unnamed source had reported the bottle contained GHB, but this had not yet been confirmed. The liquid was currently being tested for contents and the bottle checked for latent prints.

Sean could ascertain that the whole Capitol was buzzing and speculating about these new revelations. The deferential nods and awe-filled smiles were evidence that he again scooped the elite of Atlanta's premier news agencies. He almost felt like whistling as he walked down the main floor toward the Governor's office. Sean figured the Emperor was probably meeting with Marcus. He would politely ask the Governor's press secretary to check and see if he had a response to the article. Sean knew he would, he always did. It would be good to see the dumb-struck expressions on the faces of the Governor and his temperamental top aide when he stuck his tape recorder in their faces and asked for a comment.

As his hand was about to grasp the door knob of the Governor's front office, his cell phone rang.

"Yeah," he said.

"Sean . . . this is Karin."

"Hey, Karin. My girl! Have you seen the newsletter?"

"Yes."

"Well? What do you think?"

"I . . . I don't have to think . . . I know."

"What? What does that mean?"

"It means . . . we've been had."

"What are you talking about, and why are you sounding so strange?"

"Let me put it this way. As of this morning, you won't find any more drippy faucets at the GBI."

"We caught everything on tape," Claude told Rod and Juan during their meeting. "The hidden surveillance camera we installed to monitor the office caught her in full color snooping around my desk and laptop. I left the diskette containing the bogus memo where I was sure she would find it after a little searching. The sealed interoffice envelopes that I gave her with instructions to send to you guys and at least nine others contained only blank sheets of letterhead. This prevented her from casting doubt on her guilt by shifting the blame to someone in another office. Fortunately for us, Karin believed the envelopes contained the fake memo and felt she was home free giving that hogwash to Sean, because she was secure the source could not be traced. The Director called her in and fired her on the spot. He will decide whether to take further action against her after this case is cleared up. I, for one, am satisfied with her dismissal. So, gentlemen, we can safely say that our leak is officially plugged."

"Good work," Juan said. "I can't believe Karin traded away a good job, to leak information to Sean."

"That's what greed will do for you," Rod said. "Sean had to be paying her. She was dipping from both ends and as a result, she's lost it all. I wish I could have seen the look on his face when he found out that tip was bogus."

"Now that would have been worth some money," Juan said and laughed.

"Well, at least now we can concentrate our full efforts on the case," Claude said. "What do you guys have for me?"

Rod related the information he had gotten from Lessye, Tanya, Clarice and Neveleen about Renae, her sleeping disorder and the Macon trip.

"Have you heard any more about the GHB?" Claude asked.

"No," Rod said. "But I did pick up some information from Gus. He told me he overheard some interns talking about a big party happening tonight at the Coach House in celebration of CNAA Day at the Capitol. Randy Joe is hosting this one in his suite. If possible, we need to get an undercover agent in there. It should be someone young enough to pass for an intern and attractive enough to get attention from the right people."

"I'll arrange it," Claude said scribbling a note to himself.

Next, Juan informed them that a thorough background check confirmed that Marcus Norwood and DeMarco Norris were indeed the same person, the grandson of Henry and Martha Perkins. "His name was legally changed before he went to college at age eighteen. His father, Quentin Norris, is a career felon currently doing a quarter at Coxsackie Maximum Security Prison in Greene County, New York, for armed robbery and drug possession. And get this, when Norris was caught, among the drugs found in his possession were cocaine, heroin and Rohypnol."

"I wonder if the Governor knows about his boy's old man's prison history?" Claude said.

"I doubt it," Rod said. "Marcus came up through the ranks in state government, starting in the college intern program. Everyone got used to seeing him around, knew he was a good worker, and took him on face value."

"That's right," Juan said. "It wasn't like he was going to work for the GBI or another police agency. No fingerprints or background check were required."

"So Marcus and Renae are definitely half siblings," Rod said. "And they're both Henry's grandchildren. This sheds a new spotlight on Marcus."

"And it keeps getting brighter," Claude said. "I spoke with the secretaries of the dead legislators. Each of them confirmed that Marcus met with the legislators the week before their deaths. I talked with Brad's aide, Lena Lawrence." Claude glanced at his notepad. "She was reluctant to talk at first, but she told me that Brad and Marcus had a heated argument the Friday before he died. The name Jesse Higgins was shouted around. She told me that she and Marcus were friends. When Brad found out about their friendship he warned her about him, and she stopped seeing him. She says Brad showed her the letter from Higgins."

"From what I hear, she and Marcus were a lot closer than friends," Rod said. "The word on the Capitol grapevine is that she and Marcus were romantically involved. And I have personally seen her going in and out of Marcus' office on numerous occasions. It was Marcus who put the brakes on that relationship. I know for a fact he's now dating a good friend of mine."

"For a woman whose been dumped, she sure is good-natured about it," said Claude. "It's interesting she omitted the romance part and the fact that he broke up with her."

Claude was thoughtful for a moment. "Marcus is currently at the top of my list of suspects because of the Perkins incident. He has a lot to lose if the word gets out. He knew about Jesse's letter and argued with the legislators about it. Next in line is the half sister, Renae, a secretive girl who could be out for revenge. The three legislators were responsible for the firing of her grandfather, as was Marcus."

"Then wouldn't she also want revenge against Marcus?" Juan said. "You think she might make a move on him?"

"Only if she knew for a fact that Marcus arranged the frame-up."

"She knows," Rod said. "Henry told me what he suspected about Marcus, but neither of us could prove it. I know he told his family what happened. Also, Lessye McLemore at the tour booth told me about an incident recently when Renae was delivering some letters at the Capitol. She saw Renae give Marcus a look that could boil water. Renae definitely knows."

Claude scribbled a note on his pad. "I'm going to arrange for an agent to tail her. Keep an eye on what she does and who she does it with." After a sigh, he said, "All right, our last candidate is Randy Joe. Getting rid of three powerful and influential political enemies could play into his hands and besides motive, he's also been seen in possession of GHB."

"Then our next step," Juan said, "is finding out whether Marcus and Renae had the opportunity and whether either of them has ever been in possession of GHB."

"Another thing," Rod said, "Gordon's report said that GHB metabolizes quickly when it enters the system. That means whoever gave it to the legislators had to have been close to them not too long before their deaths. I think it would be a good idea for me to start talking with anyone who saw Killian at the Wild Hog Dinner. We need to know who was paying especially close attention to him. Also, we need to know if he left with anyone."

"Good point," Claude said. "I'll start talking with Alonso's neighbors and associates and take a drive up to Unicoi and do some sniffing around about Brad." Claude reviewed his notes, then said, "That's all for now. Let's plan to get together again Friday."

Ronnie dreaded another volatile confrontation with his father, so he decided not to return home until late Monday morning. After being greeted by his mother, who couldn't conceal her concern, they had a long talk during which Miss Pearl pleaded with him not to push his father too far.

"Please be more understanding, honey. Your daddy thinks he's doing what's best for your welfare."

"Mama, Daddy thinks he's doing what's best for his image and reputation. Trying to control my love life has nothing to do with protecting me and everything to do with protecting his position in the CNAA."

She sighed. "No, honey, you're wrong. It's not all about his reputation, regardless of what you might think. Your daddy loves you. And he's basically a good man. He loves his family. But he is extremely proud, and when he feels he's being pushed in a corner he comes out like a tiger. Your daddy's not one to easily compromise. I don't think he's going to bend on this situation."

"So you're saying I should give up Tamika to please Daddy because she doesn't happen to be the right color for him? I love her."

"No, baby. All I'm saying is don't rub your daddy's face in it. Like, for example, this weekend. Staying out all weekend and not even coming home to attend church with the family. You know how he is about Sundays."

"Then why doesn't his Christianity ever pour over into Mondays?"

"Don't be fresh."

"I'm sorry but he says he's a Christian. Why doesn't he act like one? Why can't he love all people like you do?"

"I don't know. Those are questions I guess only God can answer. We have to continue to pray for him." Miss Pearl paused for a moment choosing her words. "Maybe it will be a good idea for you and Tamika to cool off for a while."

"No. That's a promise I can't make—"

"Now, hear me out before you get excited. You and Tamika are still so young. You have plenty of time to be together. In the fall, you'll be going away to UGA. When you're away at school, your daddy won't expect you to come all the way from Athens to go to church with the family on Sundays. Living on campus, you'll have your freedom. You'll be free to see whoever you want without your daddy interfering. Think about it. Wait a few months." Miss Pearl kissed him on the cheek before leaving him alone with his thoughts.

His mother had given him some wonderful advice. But there was only one problem: Ronnie did not want to wait. He was in love with Tamika, and he wanted her now.

Sunday dinner at the Laytons had gone much better than he ever imagined. Although Tamika's father had been cordially aloof, he welcomed Ronnie into his home and seemed to have appreciated his honesty in answering numerous questions. Barry was a tall distinguished man, with regal posture, graying temples, and the intelligent bearing of a college professor. In spite of a slight paunch in his mid section, his maroon-brown eyes and cinnamon complexion were a perfect compliment to Tamika's mother, Gloria Layton, a petite, curvaceous woman with milk chocolate skin and large adorable brown eyes. She was an older version of Tamika. Mrs. Layton was a charming and thoughtful hostess, and was genuinely warm to him. In many ways, she reminded him a lot of his mother. Tamika's sisters, Tarrah and Tammi, were cool with their relationship. Ronnie had met them on several occasions, and they got along great.

That dinner had made it easier for Ronnie to make his decision. He took out the velvet covered jewel box he had been carrying around with him for a couple of weeks. It held an exquisite two carat diamond ring. On Valentine's Day, he would ask Tamika to be his wife.

Marcus hoped that his foul disposition during the morning meeting had not offended Robert, but he couldn't help it. His meeting with Lena the previous evening had been a bombshell. He should have known it was Renae. First Henry had thrown him away like some cheap, discarded old rag doll. Now his crazy granddaughter was trying to get him fired. Lena had explained how Renae had gotten hold of Jesse's letter to Brad.

"She saw it on Tanya's desk, slipped it out and made several copies and then replaced it before Tanya knew it was missing," Lena had said.

"How did she see it on Tanya's desk? Renae and Tanya don't work in the same office."

"Renae can be sneaky when she wants to be."

"Why didn't you tell me when you first found out?"

"After our last conversation, I honestly didn't think you wanted to hear anything from me. I wasn't going to volunteer anything. But since you asked, I figured I'd help you out."

Marcus thought about how strangely Tanya stared at him during dinner at her house. He wondered if she told Lessye. Maybe not. Marcus knew enough about Lessye to know that if she had seen the letter, she would have told him. Lena kept stressing the point that Renae still had several copies. Marcus wondered what he should do. Approaching her would probably lead to a volatile confrontation. That was the last thing he needed, especially in the middle of this investigation. He couldn't risk her throwing a screaming fit and passing out on the floor in front of him. When she came to, she would probably lie and say he assaulted her.

No, the only thing he could do now was wait. He hated to admit it, but Lena was his only hope. Maybe she could talk some sense into Renae as he asked her to. Or if not, maybe she would at least warn him before Renae did something stupid.

"Hello."

"This is Renae. Did you do it?" Renae was again using the pay phone around the corner from the LOB snack bar on the first floor.

"I said I would. I told you before, there's no need for you to worry."

"When are you going to make the call?"

"Maybe next Tuesday."

"Why not sooner?"

"Settle down. I'm sure you of all people enjoy seeing him squirm."

"Have you sent the note we talked about?" Renae asked.

"Yes. It should be delivered today. Let's give it a chance to sink in, and then we'll move on to the next step."

"Rod and that Agent Henderson have been asking questions."

"Good. Let them ask."

The line went dead.

CHAPTER 35

O n Wednesday afternoon, Rod caught up with Gus, who told him that Marcus and Randy Joe were paying especially close attention to Killian during the Wild Hog Dinner.

"They stayed so close on his heels, it looked like Killian was dragging them around," Gus said. "I was telling that young lobbyist, Kwame Jordan, that he probably left early to get away from those hounds. Kwame had been trying to catch up with Killian all evening to have a private chat about tort reform. But before he could ever corner him, Killian was distracted by either Marcus or Randy Joe. While Kwame and I were talking, he saw Killian head for the door and took off after him. He still didn't have any luck. Kwame said he was getting into his car by the time he made it outside the Depot."

"Did Kwame mention whether he was alone?"

"No. But if you want to ask him, he's on the third floor in front of the House Chamber. If you hurry, you can catch him."

Rod found Kwame right where Gus said he would be.

"Hey, Kwame, you got a minute?"

"Sure. What's up?"

"Gus told me that during the Wild Hog Dinner, you tried several times to talk with Killian."

"That's true. I wanted to get his take on the new tort reform legislation slated to be introduced in the Senate. But I couldn't get to him for Randy Joe and Marcus. Gus and I laughed about it then. But after Killian was killed, I felt real bad. You know, man, if I had tried harder to catch him, maybe he wouldn't have had that accident."

"You can't beat yourself up."

"Yeah. I know."

"Gus said you saw Killian leaving. Do you remember if anyone was with him?"

"Yeah, I saw one of the LOB secretaries getting in the car with him. Her name is Renae Stewart."

As soon as she received the urgent call from Claude Monday morning, Agent Valerie Carr dropped everything and headed to the main office in Decatur. It took her little time to make the drive from the Regional Drug Enforcement Office in Macon where she had been assigned for four years. After arriving and having a quick lunch, she was briefed on her assignment for Monday evening. Valerie, an attractive blonde, was to pose as a Governor's intern and attend a party in Randy Joe's hotel suite at the Coach House and find any evidence of GHB or other illegal drug use. She was only to gather information and evidence. No arrests were to be made at that time because the surveillance was in conjunction with a larger investigation.

As she sat in Claude's office the following Wednesday morning watching him peruse the detailed typed report she had prepared, Valerie was as pleased with her work as Claude seemed to be.

"Excellent work, Valerie. Excellent."

"Thank you, Claude."

"It can't get any sweeter than this. A Georgia state senator spiking the drink of a GBI agent."

"Senator Tyrell Buford at his lowest," she said, her lips spreading into a broad smile. "Representative Randy Joe Reynolds was also in possession of the drug. Buford was hugging me closer than a cat suit. I had to do some slick maneuvering to shake him long enough to get out of there with a liquid sample."

"I knew you were the one for the job. Thanks again for your good work. We'll take it from here."

As Valerie prepared to leave his office, she said as an afterthought, "I'm surprised you guys didn't already have a lot of the shenanigans in that suite already on tape."

"Why do you say that?"

"You do have it under electronic surveillance."

"No, I haven't requested or authorized electronic surveillance."

"Well if you haven't, then somebody has."

"Maybe you better tell me how you got that idea."

"I'll be glad to."

After a brief press conference in the Governor's office to refute the information in the *Capitol Reporter,* announce that the GBI located and contained the source of the information leak, and that the investigation was making progress, Claude spent most of the day Tuesday interviewing Alonso's neighbors. He found out that a young man fitting Marcus' description driving a red Lexus visited Alonso the Sunday he died.

Following his Wednesday meeting with Valerie, Claude went to the Capitol and paged Della and then tracked down several other of Alonso's close colleagues. As he sat at his desk at GBI headquarters, he mapped out his plan for Thursday when he would go to Unicoi near Helen in North Georgia then down to Macon. He planned to start early and would be out of the office all day.

Before leaving the office Wednesday evening, he packed the necessary items needed for his excursion in his briefcase and checked his evening mail. There was one envelope containing a note that read: *"You don't have to look any further than the Governor's office to find your man. The killer is Marcus Norwood. He's responsible for Henry Perkins, and he killed those three legislators to keep them quiet. Jesse Higgins knew it. You should, too."*

Accompanying the note was a copy of the letter from Jesse, minus the salutation. There was no return address on the envelope, and the note was not signed. Claude carefully placed the note and letter in a plastic bag. He would drop it off by the Latent Print Section for fingerprint analysis on his way out.

Gus, accompanied by his young protégée, Kwame, were among the first to arrive for the Natural Resources and Environment Committee meeting Thursday morning. There were always numerous conversations to be overheard prior to the beginning of the meetings. Lobbyists, interns, aides, law clerks, and legislators were chatty people. There were lots of useful, informative tidbits to gather, and Gus had an excellent memory for storing them. Gus was in the process of teaching Kwame what he referred to as the delicate art of effective political maneuvering.

Gus saw in Kwame a lot of himself at that age. He was savvy and most of all sincere, a genuinely rare quality in a sea of political sharks. Gus immediately took a liking to Kwame, and there was rarely a day that passed that he didn't share with him at least one valuable gem of wisdom.

As they stood talking before the meeting was scheduled to begin at nine, Kwame's lesson would be how to carry on one conversation while effectively eavesdropping on another.

Gus' antenna was in excellent form. He had honed in on a conversation between Randy Joe and Tyrell. A Senate Bill sponsored by Tyrell concerning the location of landfills in southwest Georgia, all "coincidentally" set for placement in African-American communities, was on the day's agenda for a House committee vote. If it received a "do pass" recommendation from the committee, it would go to the full House for consideration. Several members of the Black Caucus who served on the committee were poised and ready to oppose the bill. A couple of local civil rights leaders were also on hand to speak against it. This should be a good one, Gus thought.

"You should know," Tyrell said to Randy Joe with his usual sour sneer, "it's all over the CNAA about Ronnie and that girl. What do you plan to do?"

Gus recognized the name, Ronnie, as belonging to Randy Joe's oldest son. He could tell by the stilted manner of his speech that Tyrell perceived *that girl* he was referring to as a problem. Gus had heard rumors that Randy Joe's son was seeing a black girl but dismissed them as being far-fetched, especially considering Randy Joe's racist ideology and mean spirit. Sometimes the Capitol rumor mill spun out of control. And this had to be one of those times. Or was it? Could it be true? Was Ronnie Reynolds, the prince of Peach County, involved with a black girl? Gus wondered who the girl was.

"I have it under control," Randy Joe said, failing in his attempt to keep his voice at a whisper.

From Randy Joe's countenance and short answer, Gus observed that this was a subject he'd rather not discuss with Tyrell. Trouble in paradise? Gus thought.

Tyrell plowed on in his crude manner, seemingly oblivious to Randy Joe's attitude. "Boy, you better do something quick. I talked to several members of the CNAA when they were here Monday. They don't like it. They say this thing is getting way out of hand."

Randy Joe's face twisted into a nasty snarl. It had the appearance of wrinkled stone. "Do you think I like it? I told you before. I'm handling it."

"But some of the members are questioning your leadership. They say that if you can't handle your kids, then maybe you can't handle . . ."

Randy Joe's eyes looked like green ice as he froze Tyrell with a disarming stare causing his words to trail off. Randy Joe said, "Is that the members talking, Tyrell, or you? You're being pretty cocky this morning for someone who needs my vote for his bill to pass out of committee."

Tyrell was ignorant, but he was no fool, Gus thought. He had to know that he had overstepped his bounds with Randy Joe. And that was something that no sane person did. That boy had better start back peddling and pumping, hard.

"I'm sorry, Randy Joe. I didn't mean anything by it. Of course that's not me talking. Boy, I wouldn't even think something like that. But as a friend and colleague, I thought it was my duty to let you know what people are saying, that's all." Tiny beads of perspiration were breaking out on his forehead, though the room was cool.

"No harm done. I've been so pissed off over this situation I can't hardly think straight."

"If it was me, I don't know what I would do."

"Well, I know what I'm going to do. And it's going to be done next week. Nathaniel's handling the details."

"Then I know for a fact it will be handled."

"I don't care who her daddy is. If that tramp thinks she's going to derail my boy's future, she's got another thought coming."

Gus' face went pale and his body tingled as if he had suffered a mild electric shock. For as long as he could remember, that was the way his body had warned him of danger. That feeling kept him alive in the Navy during WWII and had never failed him since. Randy Joe was planning something bad.

"Gus? Are you all right?" Kwame asked. "Do you need something to drink?"

"No. I'm okay. Nothing for you to worry about."

The chairman called the meeting to order as Gus replayed Randy Joe's words in his mind: *Well I know what I'm going to do. And it's going to be done next week. Nathaniel's handling the details.* If only they had said the girl's name. As the chairman called up the first bill on the calendar for discussion and vote, Gus hoped like everything that this one time, his premonition of doom was wrong.

CHAPTER 36

*U*nfortunately, the latent print analysis of the anonymous note and letter turned up no fingerprints," Claude said during the Friday morning meeting with Juan and Rod. Claude gave them a copy of the report from Valerie and an update on his trip.

"A gas station attendant at a small service station near Helen, Georgia, serviced a red Lexus the night Brad was killed. The driver was described as a 'young black dude' who paid with cash, seemed kind of nervous and rushed him to 'hurry it up.' The attendant said the car has a vanity tag — *Marc 1*. It belongs to Marcus. He positively identified Norwood from a copy of his driver's license photo.

"In Macon, a waitress and the cashier at Dot's Restaurant close to the interstate remembered seeing Alonso when he passed through on his way to Savannah. He met with an arrogant white man with blondish hair and green eyes who drove a Ford truck, a good looking young black man in a sharp business suit, who drove a red Lexus, and a young white woman with a stylish short hairstyle. She was thin, dressed plainly in a dark suit and wore dark shades. They didn't get a look at the vehicle she was driving. They said Steele had heated conversations with the two men but not with the woman. I showed them a copy of Renae's state ID photo. They couldn't be sure if she had been there or not because according to the cashier, 'almost everyone who came in stopped and had a word for Alonso.' They did, however, definitely identify Randy Joe and Marcus from the copies of driver's license photos.

"A visit to the Greyhound Bus Station revealed that a young woman described as black with a medium bob and a dark suit showed up there the Sunday Alonso died. No one could tell when she came in, but one of the ticket agents noticed her because she was nodding on a bench. When the agent approached her to find out if she was all right and she realized where she was, she looked nervous and disoriented like she didn't know how she got there. The agent was sure she had seen the woman leave with two other young ladies. The agent also confirmed that the young black woman was the same one on the ID photo."

Before adjourning, they agreed that Marcus, Randy Joe, and Renae were definitely worth following up. It was time to ask some questions and they were sure one of these three had the answers.

Ronnie packed a bag with enough clothes to last through Tuesday. Although his mother pleaded with him not to push his dad any further, he didn't feel like being around when he was home. It would only lead to another ugly argument. His father would have to understand that this was his life, and he intended to live it the way he pleased. No matter how much he loved his daddy, if Randy Joe could not accept the woman he loved, then Ronnie would have to go.

Ronnie, always practical and conscientious, had thought out everything. Although he was currently working for his daddy, which certainly would not last after his marriage, Ronnie was by no means hurting financially. He was thrifty with his money, and on his eighteenth birthday, a large trust fund inherited from his grandfather became available to him. Ronnie would have plenty of money to support himself and Tamika comfortably until they both finished school.

Ronnie looked at the beautiful watch Tamika gave him and realized time was passing swiftly. He finished packing and headed down the stairs. He intended to be out of there long before his daddy showed up. Ronnie was planning another wonderful weekend with Tamika and her family, and Valentine's Day was Monday. He didn't want anything to spoil it.

"I want you to call Sean today!" Renae said.

"Why don't you chill out before you have an episode? First things first. Wait until after they search his place."

"Why? Why should we wait?"

"So they can pull him in for questioning before we put the final nail in his coffin. If I call Sean today, he'll call Marcus for a response. Marcus will panic. He may run. You don't want him to get away before the cops get him, do you?"

"No."

"Then please be patient, or you could ruin everything. Are you going to Tanya's party?"

"You know about that?"

"I know a few people who got invitations."

"I'm not going. I told her I was busy. Besides, Marcus will probably be there with Lessye. And I can't risk giving anything away."

"Good girl. Now spend this weekend relaxing. Next week is going to be explosive."

———

Barry had been distracted all week, lost in his own thoughts. He hoped it was possible for him to have a good weekend, but the chances of that were unlikely. This situation with his baby girl was pressing on his mind.

The dinner the previous Sunday had not been the disaster he expected. Barry had been prepared to dislike Ronnie, to serve him so much frigid iceberg politeness that he would leave their home and Tamika, never to return. But to his surprise, Ronnie was genuinely nice. He dearly loved Tamika as much as she loved him, which radiated in his twinkling green eyes. Barry had asked Ronnie numerous rapid-fire questions that he answered frankly, without hesitation.

When Barry pulled him aside and practically accused him of being in league with his father to use Tamika to get at him, Ronnie looked him squarely in the eyes and told him he would never use Tamika and would sooner die than let anyone hurt her. He confided to Barry how he and his father had almost come to blows over their relationship.

The iciness of Barry's resolve chipped away bit by bit, and by the end of the evening he began to warm up to him. Between his wife, Gloria, and Tamika, they had persuaded Barry to invite Ronnie to dinner again the following Sunday. So the eldest son of the biggest bigot east of the Mississippi River, would again be a guest at his dinner table this weekend.

Barry thought more about Ronnie. He definitely was not using Tamika. That Barry could have handled and exposed. But Ronnie's sincerity brought him face-to-face with a potentially bigger problem: If he was this much in love with Tamika, would he be foolish enough to consider marriage? Barry's baby girl was only eighteen years old and he had miles of plans for her future, none of which included her marrying a white boy, no matter how nice he seemed to be. *No. No. Hell no!* Ronnie was far more dangerous now than he was when Barry thought he was only after her body.

Tamika and Ronnie were like two reckless trains headed straight for each other. It was up to Barry to cool off their hot little engines before it was too late.

CHAPTER 37

The ringing telephone yanked Lessye from the seductive arms of a deep sleep. She was dreaming of Marcus. They had spent a beautiful day together on the beach, and were just about to . . . Then she was abruptly awakened.

"Hello," she grumbled, annoyed at being awakened from her best dream in months.

"Rise and shine, sleepyhead," Tanya said. "You know today is the big day."

"What are you talking about? And what time is it?"

"It's eight o'clock. I've been up for over an hour."

"Good for you. Haven't you learned by now that Saturdays are meant for sleeping late and shopping?" Lessye asked, refusing to move an inch from the comfortable spot in her queen-size bed.

"I was too excited to sleep late."

"Excited? Excited about what?"

"The party, of course."

"Party?"

Tanya sighed. "Please don't tell me you forgot about my party this evening? You're supposed to come over early to help me out."

"Uh, uh."

"You did forget!"

"I'm sorry. It's been a hectic week, and I've had a lot on my mind."

"Don't worry about it. All is forgiven as long as you're coming. Are you bringing Marcus?"

"You know I'll be there. But I'm not sure about Marcus since I forgot to ask him. What time?"

"Get here at seven. That's the same time I told Clarice and Amber. The party doesn't start until nine, but I need you to come early and help me out."

"What about Renae?"

"Renae's anti-social. I don't think she likes parties that much. Besides she said she can't make it because she has other plans. Guess who Amber is bringing?"

"Who?"

"That darling Kwame."

"That cute chocolate-brown lobbyist with the cut body and pretty eyes who gave her tickets to the Caucus barbeque?"

"Yeah. It's about time those two hooked up. They look so cute together. Kwame is the only lobbyist Amber encourages to linger in our suite. Now what's this about you not being sure about Marcus? Aren't you two still attending church together tomorrow?"

"Yes. As far as I know."

"And aren't you still his date for the Governor's dinner next week?"

"Yeah, I guess . . ."

"Then there shouldn't be any problem inviting him to my party. Call him, now."

"But it's so early."

"Good. The earlier the better. Girl, catch him before he gets out for the day. See you later."

"Bye."

Lessye sat up in bed, pondering whether to take her friend's advice and call Marcus. She hadn't spoken with him since Tuesday when they attended the Black Caucus Barbeque. She tried to fight it, but she was beginning to feel insecure. Monday was Valentine's Day and Marcus hadn't mentioned any plans. Although she didn't put much confidence in Valentine's Day as a barometer of one's true feelings, she wanted to see how Marcus would handle it. As much as she hated to admit it, this would be the test of whether Marcus had truly made a clean break from Lena. Well, she thought to herself, if Marcus is planning to be MIA this weekend and on Valentine's Day, I might as well find out now.

She tentatively dialed his home number and Marcus answered on the second ring. Well at least that was a good sign. He wasn't screening his calls.

"Hello, Lessye. How are you?"

"I'm good. How about you?"

"I'm fine now," he said in a husky voice. "Where have you been hiding? I've missed your pretty face and sweet smile."

Marcus certainly knew how to turn on the charm even this early in the morning.

"I miss you, too. The Black History Celebration and Georgia Founders Day Program kept me away from the desk . . . I hope I didn't wake you."

"No, you didn't wake me. Robert is speaking to a group of black elected officials at Paschal's today at noon. I'm meeting him there. They're gearing up for their statewide convention at the end of the month. It's going to be a luncheon meeting. Would you like to come?"

"I wish I could, but I have some running around to do. Are you busy this evening?"

"Not if there's something you want me to do."

"That's so sweet of you to say. I know you have a busy schedule. And I apologize for asking you at the last minute . . ."

"I mean it. I'd drop anything for you. And you never have to apologize for asking me something at the last minute. What is it?"

"Tanya is having a . . . a party this evening, and she wants us to come." Lessye almost said Valentine's party, but caught herself. She wanted any mention of Valentine's Day to originate with Marcus.

"That sounds nice," Marcus said. "She specifically said she wants me to come?"

"Yes, sure. She likes you. Why wouldn't she want you to come?" Lessye was puzzled by his question.

"No reason . . ."

"Marcus? Is everything all right?"

"Sure, baby. Everything is fine. What time should I pick you up?"

"Tanya wants me to be there at seven to help out. The party doesn't start until nine. So, if you want, you can meet me there."

"What I want is to pick you up. I've missed you and can't wait to see you. I'll be at your place at six-thirty."

"I'll be ready."

"Good, and while I have you on the line, will you do me the honor of joining me for a special dinner on Monday evening? Because in case you didn't already know it, you are my Valentine."

"Yes, I'd love to," Lessye said, blushing from ear to ear. For a moment, she was happy that Marcus couldn't see through the telephone.

"I can't wait to be alone with you again."

"I'm looking forward to it, too. See you later."

"Absolutely."

Marcus was relieved to know that Lessye didn't have any hurt feelings about not hearing from him since their last date. She was the same sweet, understanding Lessye who was beginning to turn his closely guarded world upside down. Marcus was also relieved to know that Lessye hadn't suddenly started avoiding him because of something Tanya might have told her about Jesse's letter.

If Tanya had seen Jesse's letter like Lena said, wouldn't she be trying to warn Lessye off him instead of inviting him to a party? Lessye was her best friend. Tanya would certainly have told her about it. He reasoned that maybe Tanya would wait until tonight to tear into him.

He knew above all else Lessye appreciated honesty, and for their relationship to have any hope of a chance, he would have to come clean with her about his past and about the letter from Jesse. He would have to tell her about his true relationship to Renae. Marcus knew that he risked losing her, especially when he confessed about framing Henry. As much as she had liked Henry, Lessye had believed Marcus. She believed that he was telling the truth. Now to find out that he lied and had been lying all these years would be a tremendous blow of deception. But Marcus knew that now he had to tell the truth, and it was important that he tell her before Tanya or anyone else did.

Now the only question was: When would he do it? Not today before Tanya's party. Maybe tomorrow after they attended church together? No. She might refuse to see him on Valentine's Day. He had a treat for her. And if she did end their friendship after the revelation about his sins, at least they would have that wonderful night to remember.

Marcus decided he would tell her on Tuesday. After work, he would go to her house, and they would talk.

He knew this much. It better be soon. Renae was a loose cannon firing in his direction, Marcus thought with despair. God only knew who she would send that letter to next.

CHAPTER 38

*M*onday, February 14th, started as normally as any other day at the Capitol during the legislative session. Groups were entering in a steady procession for guided tours. The usual news conferences calling attention to the latest crisis in state government were in full swing. Issue-oriented delegations and special interest groups who weren't demanding a meeting with the Governor were, along with the hoards of school children and senior citizens groups, lining up for photos with their legislators. Members of the broadcast media were scampering around pursuing interviews. Gus was looking for yet another conversation on which to eavesdrop. Sean was snooping around for possible stories . . . And Lessye was in love.

She was staring at two dozen perfect red roses that were delivered to her at the tour booth. The attached card read: *From my heart to yours, Marcus.*

Lessye received compliments on the beautiful roses all morning, especially from the members of Delta Sigma Theta Sorority, who had converged on the Capitol for their annual Delta Day. The building was a beautiful sea of red and white. The ladies were gathering in the lobby for a photo with the Governor and then a guided tour, given by their soror, Lessye. Later they would be recognized in the House and Senate Chambers and host an elegant luncheon at the Garden Room. Lessye had hoped that Tanya would be able to come over and join them for their tour, but she was much too busy working on an urgent project.

"Good morning, Lessye," Rod said as he approached the tour booth. "Beautiful roses. I guess I don't have to ask who they're from."

"You know they're from Marcus."

"Well, my Valentine's token certainly can't compete with a rose garden, but Happy Valentine's Day." Rod kissed her on the cheek before handing her a humorous card and a small box of chocolate candy.

"Thank you. You're so thoughtful."

"Yeah, well that's what they tell me," he said with a slow smile.

"How's the investigation coming?" Lessye asked, hoping he'd reveal his thoughts on any possible suspects.

"Moving right along. I wouldn't be surprised if something breaks this week."

Bernard had spoken with Harlin Burr the previous Friday, and they arranged to meet at Burr's office on Monday at 9 a.m. When Bernard arrived, he found a different man than the one he'd first met. Burr's hair was neatly trimmed. Gone was the unattractive layer of lotion-starved ash. It had been replaced by rich, dark brown skin with a healthy glow. Instead of rumpled clothing he wore an expensive black business suit, silk tie, and starched snow-white shirt. Even the shining gold tooth was missing from his million dollar smile. Burr couldn't help but be amused by Bernard's shock at his dramatic transformation.

"What can I say?" he said. "I adapt my appearance according to the specific job." He handed Bernard an envelope. "I think you'll be pleased with the results."

After looking at Burr's work, he could not have been more pleased. Burr had followed Bernard's instructions to the letter. There were, in all, ten packages waiting for him. Two he would keep. Eight would be anonymously delivered to their appointed destinations. Burr had recommended a discreet agency to handle deliveries, one that was untraceable. Bernard would make all arrangements with them personally. This meant he would probably miss the morning roll call. So be it.

Claude arranged a meeting with Randy Joe, who agreed to see him during the noon recess. During the stiffly cordial, bum's rush meeting that lasted all of five minutes, Claude sized up the thin, angular man peddling his phony Southern gentility. He was the kind who could string a noose around your neck between dinner and dessert. Claude decided that Randy Joe was a man of little patience who enjoyed wielding his power.

Claude also surmised that Randy Joe's arrogance would cause him to make a huge tactical error: underestimating his competence as an investigator. Claude had run up against many of the ilk of Randy Joe during his years with the GBI. In the early days, it would have been difficult for him to decide whether Randy Joe's effusive greeting was meant to be excessively courteous . . . or subtly condescending. At this point, Claude had no doubt, and although he could not judge his guilt or innocence, he knew he didn't like the man.

After the meeting, Claude made a few notes in his pad. All he managed to get out of Randy Joe was a confirmation that he met with Alonso at Dot's Restaurant in Macon at 3 p.m. the Sunday he died. According to the smug Randy Joe, the meeting was about his anti-affirmative action legislation. He seriously thought he could make Claude believe that there was a chance that Alonso would change his position on working to defeat the bill. Randy Joe had met with Brad on January 21st and had almost come to blows with Killian during the Wild Hog Dinner over the same anti-affirmative action legislation. According to Randy Joe, he had no knowledge of GHB use on the Hill and even managed to look appropriately shocked.

Claude smiled to himself. He had gotten exactly the response he had expected. Randy Joe failed this preliminary inquiry. He was insincere, evasive, and a liar. Strike one. Now on to Renae.

This was the first week of the session that Nathaniel's huge brick-like frame had not been looming on the Hill. He was out of town handling urgent business on behalf of Randy Joe. The two men had known each other since their days as classmates at UGA. After graduation, Randy Joe returned home to reign as scion of his family peach empire, while Nathaniel relocated to the metro Atlanta area to try his hand as a businessman. Seduced by the excitement of state politics, he became a consultant, offering practical advice and public relations services to aspiring conservative political candidates throughout the state. He had singlehandedly been the force behind Randy Joe's election to the State House.

Eventually, he opened Tucker and Associates, a high-profile, highly sought-after lobbying firm that currently handled the lobbying efforts for a wealthy consortium of home builders, carpet manufacturers, and mortgage bankers. He had been governmental affairs director for the CNAA for the past ten years and had personally sponsored Randy Joe and Tyrell for membership in the organization. Unlike them, his brand of racism was rooted more in economics than in social ideology. There was big money to be made from people deluded by their own arrogance, those who sincerely believed in their superiority and sought to force others (no matter how historically unsuccessful) to believe it, too. The only thing Nathaniel believed in was the dollar bill, and he worshiped it accordingly.

Although he would never consider Randy Joe a good friend, they had always been close acquaintances through the years, and because of his firm belief in the power of American currency, Nathaniel had always made himself available to discreetly assist Randy Joe in handling sensitive issues for a fee. His business in Fort Valley this week was by far the most sensitive to date.

Nathaniel's call came through on Randy Joe's cell phone no sooner than Claude left his office.

"Randy Joe. It's Nathaniel. Ronnie is still here. What do you want me to do?"

"Wait until he leaves. I don't want him anywhere around."

"Okay."

"Are you working alone?"

"I hired some people. They're going to do the work per my instructions."

"Can they be trusted?"

"Of course," Nathaniel said dryly. "They can be trusted, and they are discreet. That's the only reason I use them in delicate situations. They are well qualified so don't worry."

"The only thing I'm worried about is my boy. He's not to be involved in this in any way. You better make sure he's long gone before you make your move."

=======

Claude closely observed Renae as her curious light brown eyes alternated between frightened and extremely suspicious. He could easily see the resemblance between her and Marcus. The deep, wide-set eyes, satiny bronze skin, and exotically high cheek bones were so similar. Her delicate femininity softened the look that on Marcus took on a hard, masculine edge.

Renae was inexpensively, but neatly dressed in a plain hunter green pant suit and flat black leather shoes. Her hair was stylishly trimmed and she wore little makeup. The small diamond stud earrings that glittered in her lobes had probably been a special gift, perhaps from her grandparents. His first impression of her was that of an insecure young woman who, though sweet by nature, could turn sneakily vicious if provoked.

Unlike his strategy with Randy Joe, Claude had not called her in advance to schedule an interview. He decided to make an impromptu visit to her suite after his meeting with Randy Joe and hoped she was available to talk with him a few minutes. He was glad he did.

Claude learned considerable information from Renae, who was probably the last person to see Killian alive and could not hide her seething bitterness for Marcus whom she held responsible for her grandparents' deaths. She had no idea of the blood relationship between them. She had argued with Brad's aide, Lena, over Lena's friendship with Marcus during a trip to Macon. It was the day that Alonso was killed, but she denied seeing him while she was there. She confirmed that Lena left her stranded that evening and when she realized she didn't have enough money for the return trip, she immediately called Clarice. According to Renae, she felt betrayed that Lena would consider a relationship with a man who wronged her grandparents, but their friendship was still intact. Claude noted that Renae's account of her "calm" demeanor during the Macon excursion was somewhat different than that of the Greyhound Bus Station attendant, who described her as nervous and disoriented. She denied nodding off on a bench or anywhere else. Renae told him she had never been prescribed the drug GHB nor did she know of anyone on the Hill who used it. She had concealed information about her disease from everyone except Lena to protect her job.

Claude had carefully observed Renae. She handled herself well for a person who was obviously concealing something, leaving Claude only one question as he stood in the hallway writing in his note pad after their meeting: What was it that Renae had to hide?

Renae hated to leave Clarice alone with the phones, but she had to take a break after her conversation with Claude. She had to call and warn Lena. She had to tell her everything that she said to that agent so Lena would be prepared to back her up. She called Lena from her favorite pay phone downstairs.

"Lena, I need to see you, now!"

"Renae. Calm down. What's wrong?"

"I'd rather not say over the phone. Where can we meet?"

"Are you in the suite?"

"No. I'm around the corner from the snack bar on the first floor of the LOB."

"Don't move. I'll be right over."

As Renae hung up, she prayed Lena didn't run into Claude on the way.

Before returning to GBI Headquarters, Claude stopped by the Speaker's office to speak with Lena, but he just missed her. She had stepped out only seconds before he got there to run an errand. Instead of waiting, he decided he would catch up with her the next day after his much anticipated visit with Marcus.

When he returned to the office on Monday evening, Rod and Juan were anxiously waiting for him. Rod was holding a videotape.

"Claude, this is something you've got to see."

CHAPTER 39

*A*s Marcus drove over to pick up Lessye, he anticipated their evening and thought about what a wonderful time he had over the weekend. The party at Tanya's had been both fun and enlightening. He learned through conversation with Tanya that she had not seen a letter to Brad from Jesse and that Brad or Lena opened all Brad's mail. Then how was it that, according to Lena, Renae had taken the letter from Tanya's desk to make copies? Had Lena been stupid enough to lie to him? Anyway, he was somewhat relieved that Tanya didn't know the contents; he could still be the first to tell Lessye.

On Sunday morning he enjoyed accompanying Lessye and Aunt Rose to church. It had been a long time since he had been in church – when it didn't have something to do with campaigning, accompanying Robert on a speaking engagement, or otherwise as an opportunity to further his career – and it felt good. The spirited music, fervent prayers and praise, heartfelt testimonials, and dynamic sermon fed his hungry soul in ways he didn't realize needed to be nourished. He realized that Lessye's devout faith had a lot to do with her inner joy and peace. He wished that one day he would be able to feel it, too.

When Lessye opened the door to greet him, her beauty almost sucked his breath away. She was dressed in a shimmering red cocktail length dress that hugged her magnificent curves in all the right places. It dipped low enough at her cleavage to be provocative and alluring but not cheap and easy. She was wearing sexy red heels and diamond stud earrings that sparkled like tiny stars.

"Oh, baby," is all he managed to utter as he handed her a box of candy and another bouquet of roses. He leaned forward and tasted the sweetness of her lips.

"Oh, baby yourself," she said after their brief, but urgent kiss. "And thank you for all the beautiful roses. You look so handsome." Marcus was wearing an expensive black Armani suit, elegant white shirt, and red silk tie that complimented the red rose bud in his lapel.

"I have something for you, too, " Lessye said, handing Marcus a small, but lavishly, wrapped gift box. "I hope you like it."

"I know I will," Marcus said as he tore open the package to find a beautiful set of gold cuff links.

"Thank you. This is so thoughtful. I want to wear them tonight." He removed the ones he was wearing and put them on. "Perfect," he said, and they shared a long kiss.

Velvety blackness draped the city as Marcus and Lessye arrived at his fabulous loft apartment in Midtown. It was decorated in bold blacks, browns, and burgundies, with overstuffed leather chairs and sofa, dramatic wood furnishings and hand-carved, African-inspired statues. Definitely a manly man's domain.

Marcus could hardly take his eyes off Lessye.

They enjoyed an exquisitely catered dinner for two, compliments of Robert as a gesture of appreciation to Marcus for all his hard work. By candlelight, they began with a double appetizer of jumbo shrimp with cocktail sauce and a cream of broccoli soup, followed by a spinach salad. The main course consisted of grilled salmon steaks with fennel sauce, rice pilaf, and mixed vegetables, accompanied by a bottle of champagne. For dessert, they enjoyed generous slices of red velvet cake.

After dinner and the caterer left, they floated across the floor to the soulful crooning of Teddy Pendergrass, sipped warm brandy in front of the crackling hearth, and allowed themselves to flirt with a fiery passion that, if unleashed, could consume them. But as much as Marcus wanted her, he could not start a relationship with Lessye this way – under a cloud of lies and deceit. It was not fair to her. They could share a blissful night together engulfed in the warm glow of budding love. But then, tomorrow would come, and Marcus would have to make the hardest confession of his life, and she would despise him for leading her on only for a cruel letdown. Lessye would be heartbroken. She would feel used. She would never trust him again. And the accusatory look that would be in her eyes. Marcus would not be able to stand it. No, he *had* to wait for his sake as much as Lessye's. Even if it meant losing her forever after his confession, that was the chance he had to take. At least Lessye could leave with her dignity and self respect. And suddenly that was the most important thing in the world to Marcus.

He gently disentangled himself from her embrace and pulled away.

"Marcus? What's wrong?"

"Nothing, baby, everything is fine," he said, sweeping a few tendrils of hair from her face with his fingers.

"Then why did you stop? You feel so good," she said, cuddling closer to him. The smoky look in Lessye's eyes made it difficult for him to fight the desire to lose himself in her sweetness.

He moved away from her. "I think it would be better for both of us if we cool it tonight, and I take you home." He hadn't meant to, but the turmoil and frustration he was feeling made the words come out abruptly. Lessye recoiled with a weak, embarrassed smile and sank back on his comfortable couch. The sudden look of hurt and rejection in her eyes stung him deeply. Marcus wanted Lessye – bad. He had for a long time. And he would not have her leaving there thinking he didn't. He took her face in his hands.

"You've got to know I'm crazy about you. I care for you deeply. I desire you. I want to make love to you more than anything. But I have my reasons. There are some things . . ." Marcus struggled to gather his words. "There are some things that you don't know about me: Some things that if you knew – or should I say when you do – will make you change your mind forever."

"I can't imagine anything being that bad. You know how I feel about you, and you know you can tell me what's bothering you."

"I want to tell you everything. I was planning to tell you tomorrow. That's the reason I pulled away tonight. We can't get deeper in this relationship with these secrets hanging between us. I respect you too much. I always have." Marcus had the most forlorn and yearning look in his eyes. He was vulnerable to her, and this was something new to him.

"Talk to me. If you were planning to tell me tomorrow, you can tell me now."

"I wanted tonight to be special. I don't want to spoil your Valentine's Day. Even if you decide tomorrow to leave me, I wanted us to have tonight."

She caressed his face. "We'll always have tonight and many nights after this one. Tonight is special to me because I'm with you. Our times together are always special. This is a wonderful time for us to get everything in the open. But I can't imagine that you could tell me anything that would make me stop caring for you."

She looked at him so sweetly, it made him want to cry. Lessye was so pure and trusting. She had faith in him, and the pain of it was, that was all about to come crashing to an end.

"You will when you hear this." His voice was low and choked like his throat was constricted, and could not contain all of the emotion.

"Does it have something to do with your relationship with Lena?"

"No, baby. This has nothing to do with Lena or anybody else. You are the only woman in my life. No, this is about me and some bad choices I've made. It's about some awful things I've done in the past, that are now catching up with me. . . some things I'm ashamed of." Marcus sucked in a deep breath while struggling to hold on to his courage. Encouraged by the warmth in Lessye's eyes, he began.

"Do you remember me telling you that my mother died when I was about seven and that I was sent to live with my father's people?"

"Yes. I remember."

"Well, what I didn't tell you was . . . who my grandparents were . . . my mother's parents . . . the ones who gave me away. They were . . . Martha and Henry Perkins."

"What?" Lessye's expression changed to one of shock and bewilderment. "Henry from the mail room . . . was your grandfather?"

"Yes. I kept it a secret from everyone . . . including Henry. They were my biological grandparents."

Lessye squeezed his hand and said, "Go on, I can tell there's more."

"Marcus Norwood is not my birth name. I adopted the name Norwood from the former law firm Stanhope, Norwood, and Hargrove. Marcus is another slant on my real first name. I was born DeMarco Norris. My mother's name was Roslynn Dolores Perkins. She never married my father, Quentin Norris. My mother had two children. One was a girl. I'm sure you know her – Renae Stewart."

"Renae is your sister?"

"She's my half sister. We had different fathers. My mother never married Renae's father either. But both of us were given our father's names. When our mother died, her parents kept Renae but they sent me away to be raised in a dump.   My father was a lazy thug and dope dealer who lived off his sisters when the dope money dried up, or when he showed up between prison terms.   He stayed in and out of prison all my life.   He's in prison somewhere now.   And his sisters were some of the nastiest, most immoral women you could ever imagine.   I grew up hating them and hating Henry even worse – him, his wife, and Renae.   I felt that they had thrown me away, and she had somehow stolen the love and care that should have been mine. I remembered them through the years, knowing one day I would have the opportunity for payback."   Marcus' eyes glistened with tears.   Lessye held on to his hand.

"When I was eighteen, I began reinventing myself.   I legally changed my name to Marcus Norwood.   And I began snooping around to find out all the information I could about Martha and Henry.   I got a couple of jobs under my new name when I was in high school, and by the time I entered college, I had become that person.   I won a full academic scholarship to Georgia State.   I got the Georgia Incentive Grant to cover my books and part time jobs to cover my living expenses.   I moved away from Vine City, and I've never been back. During my senior year, I served as a legislative intern and started planning my revenge against Henry and his family.   After I graduated, I used a few contacts to get into state government in an entry-level position in the Secretary of State's mail room.   I was offered better positions in the private sector.   But the mail room was exactly where I wanted to be, with the man I hated all my life.   Henry taught me everything I knew about the job, he introduced me to people and showed me how to survive in the quirky state government culture.   To his credit, he treated me well.   If I hadn't been so consumed with hatred that clouded my reasoning, I could have liked Henry," Marcus said sadly.   By now Lessye had both his hands in hers.   She squeezed them gently.   It was as if she knew what he was going to say next, but needed to hear him say it.

"I bided my time waiting for what I thought would be the perfect opportunity to get even with Henry.   I decided I would get him fired.   I lifted money and other personal items from office staff, specifically Killian, Alonso, and Brad. They were in positions of power in the Secretary of State's office with the authority to fire him.   I also confiscated some incoming mail and planted it in a way that it would appear he was also guilty of mail tampering.   As mail services director, he had a key and open access to every office.   If items were missing, he would be the logical suspect. My perfect scenario was that he would be fired and brought up on criminal charges. I figured that the time he would serve in prison would be equal to the time he had sentenced me to my hellish childhood. But it all went wrong. Henry was killed in a car accident. He was despondent and had been drinking. He skidded away on that cold, rainy night. To make matters worse, I heard his wife died of a stroke soon after. She couldn't bear the loss and the grief. I had been directly responsible for the deaths of both of my grandparents. My self-centered hatred had killed them. But instead of allowing myself to feel the guilt and remorse, I kept trying to justify what I had done. When that didn't work, I tried to forget it, push it out of my mind. I channeled all my energies into plotting and scheming and clawing my way up the political ladder. I didn't much care who I had to connive, step on or over, back stab or push out of my way to get what I wanted. That's why I'm probably the most hated man in state government. You're probably one of the only people who ever saw some good in me and liked me. And God knows, I still can't figure out why. You believed in me. You believed me over an innocent man, and I deceived you. I lied to you, and I'm so sorry."

Before she could speak, he gently touched her lips with his fingers. "Let me finish before you say anything. There's more. What I didn't know was that on the night I planted those items in Henry's desk drawer, Jesse, a member of the cleaning crew, saw everything. He stayed quiet for ten years. Then to clear his conscience, he wrote letters to Killian, Alonso, and Brad, explaining what I did to Henry and his theory about me being Henry's grandson. I have to admit, I had discounted Jesse as a miserable old drunk, but he had some smarts. He figured out something that had never so much as crossed Henry's mind.

"Each of the legislators confronted me about the letter. I tried to deny it, pitting my word against that of Jesse, a known drunk. But they knew I was lying. Each of them had threatened to expose me to Robert . . . and each of them died in car crashes like Henry before they had a chance to tell," Marcus looked straight into her eyes. "Do you understand where I'm going with this?"

"Yes . . . I do . . ." Lessye said.

"Claude hasn't said anything yet. But I'm sure he has gotten his hands on a copy of that letter. I could be their prime suspect in this case. The motive is clear. And I couldn't blame them after what I did to my own grandfather."

Marcus fell silent and shifted his eyes away from her. Suddenly he couldn't bring himself to face her. He didn't want to look at her because he was afraid of the disgust he thought he would see in her eyes. He waited for her to speak, hoping with all that was inside him that she would find it in her heart to forgive him and understand him. He knew he was asking of her a tremendous task because that was something he had, as yet, not been able to do.

Marcus felt as lost and confused as he did when he was a little boy. He had opened his soul to her with this secret that had been laying on his heart all this time. Now he was carefully placing that tender, injured heart in her hands. For a moment Marcus was no longer in the comfortable, pampered adult world he had built for himself, he was again lost in the terrifying, uncertain world of a lonely little boy who had lost his mother and been torn away from a world of love and banished to a world of torment.

Lessye lifted his chin so that his eyes would again face hers.

"Marcus, first I want to thank you for confiding in me. I know it took a lot for you to confess this secret. My feelings for you haven't changed. I love you and real love just doesn't disappear overnight. I do understand that your actions were a result of the pain bottled up inside you since you were a little boy. But at the same time, I'm angry and disappointed in you. I'm disappointed that you would do something so cruel to Henry, and that you would lie about it for all these years. You don't know how many times I've defended you, and you were guilty all the time."

"Go ahead, let me have it. After what I've done, I deserve it."

"There's no use in me beating you up over what happened ten years ago because it won't change anything now. I see the hurt and guilt in your eyes. But . . ."

"Don't hold back. Say what's on your mind."

"I've always seen the best in you, believed in the best in you, regardless of how other people called you ruthless, calculating and manipulative, and talked about how you get rid of people who get in your way. Which leads me to wonder . . ."

"What?"

"Whether down the line I'm on your list of people to get rid of or manipulate. Or are you manipulating me now?"

"No. I've always cared for you. Always. You're the one person in my life that I can call my friend, and you are so much more. You're holding my heart. That's why I had to make this confession, even if it costs me your love and respect."

"Right now, I'm confused. I hear what you're saying, and I want to believe you. But you admit you've lied to me before. I don't know what to think."

"I know I'm going to have to prove myself to you – rebuild your trust. I'm prepared to do what it takes. But please believe I've never lied about my feelings for you. I can understand how right now you may have trouble believing my words. But actions don't lie. Think about the years we've known each other. Think about how I've always treated you."

"You could have slept with me tonight with this lie between us. We could have taken our relationship to a new level without me knowing. The fact that you didn't means a lot to me."

"Does it mean . . . you're still my lady?"

"Yes, I'm still your lady." They sat together quietly for several minutes.

"Did your father or his sisters ever tell you why Henry and Martha gave you up?"

"They said my grandparents didn't love me. They said they loved Renae better. They said Henry and Martha didn't want me," Marcus mumbled almost inaudibly.

"I don't believe that's true. And even if it was, they should never have said anything like that to a little boy. What your father and aunts did to you was as cruel as physical abuse. They probably hated your grandparents and wanted you to hate them, too. They didn't nurture you and give you the love you deserved. What should have been cultivated as love was twisted into hatred and revenge. Why didn't you ever talk to Henry and tell him who you were? Why didn't you ask him his side of the story?"

"I don't know. Looking back, that's exactly what I should have done. But I was young and impulsive. Honestly, at that time, hatred had a grip on me and I didn't want to hear his side. I didn't want to hear anything that would make me lose that lust for revenge. I didn't want to risk being rejected. And I wound up killing them."

"You got Henry fired, but you did not kill him or Martha. He made the decision to get drunk and get behind the wheel. There were many ways he could have handled his dismissal, but he chose to drink and drive on a rainy night. You did not kill him, just as I know in my heart you did not kill those legislators." Lessye's words had been a soothing, healing balm.

Tears were beginning to roll down his cheeks. "How can you be so understanding?"

"Because of my faith, and because all of us make mistakes. Marcus you're not the only person who's ever done something wrong and is guilty and ashamed. We all have. Contrary to what you might think, I did some pretty wild and reckless things in my younger years. One day in the future, I'll share with you some of the bad decisions I've made. But bad decisions don't make you a bad person. I've always seen the good in you. But you have to see the good in yourself."

"Do you forgive me, Lessye? Can you ever forgive me?"

"Yes. I forgive you. But you've got to forgive yourself. You're going to have to get rid of the resentment against Henry and his family and let go of the guilt about his death before it destroys you. You've got to confess your sin to God and ask Him for forgiveness and to give you the strength to move forward," she said, before hugging him tightly. Lessye went to Marcus' kitchen and made them both steaming cups of herbal tea with honey.

Marcus and Lessye talked for hours as he poured out his heart. He told her about the horrible things he had done in his life in the name of greed and ambition. He told her about how he was using Lena to keep tabs on Renae, and how Lena had told him Renae made several copies of Brad's letter and had sent him one.

"That's why I had to take a rain check on going to church with you last week," he said, after taking a long sip of the spicy orange-flavored tea. "I cornered Lena to find out if it was her, and she told me she would tell me only if she could come to my loft that Sunday. She refused to give me a time. She told me to be available all day but didn't show up until nine. I need to show you something. I'll be right back." Marcus went to his bedroom and returned with the copy of the letter from Jesse and the note he had been sent. Lessye read them both.

"Whoever sent this doesn't like you at all, and that would include Renae, especially if she knows your history with Henry. And my guess is she does. She was in the Capitol one day and when she saw you, she looked like she wanted to knock your head off. You were standing in front of the Governor's office reading some papers and didn't see her. When I asked her if she knew you, she took off, fast. How did Lena say Renae got the letter?"

"Lena said she got it from Tanya's desk."

Lessye shook her head. "That's not true. If Tanya had seen this, she would have told me. Besides, Tanya never opened Brad's mail anyway. Either he or Lena did. I remember Tanya telling me that was one less chore she had to worry about."

"I know. Tanya told me the same thing at her party Saturday night. The only reason I can think of that Lena would throw the blame on Renae would be to keep the heat off herself. Lena is angry at me for ending it with her. Maybe this is her way of getting back at me."

"You're probably right. How much do you know about Lena? Did you know she was sleeping with Randy Joe? Tanya told me she caught them in Brad's office."

"That sounds like Lena. I know about her and Randy Joe. A couple of times I went by her place and saw his truck parked there. But I don't know too much about her background other than she was originally from Boston and went to school in New York, some small university. I can't remember the name. I first met her when she worked as a volunteer on Robert's gubernatorial campaign. She had a crush on me. When she got a full-time job as Brad's aide, she went to work to take that crush to another level. And as I told you, I took advantage of her feelings and used her to achieve my own ends, finding out information on Renae."

"What were you going to do with the information you found out about her?"

"At first, I toyed with the idea of making her life on the Hill miserable until she either quit or was fired. But Henry haunted me. So then I thought it would be good to settle for having the satisfaction of knowing about her without her knowing about me. It was about having the power over her to use if I wanted to."

"Renae doesn't know she's your half sister?"

"No. Henry and Martha never told her. I know from my conversations with him about his family. He admitted he never told his granddaughter about her brother because he wouldn't know how to answer her questions. And since they weren't ever going to have any contact . . . what difference did it make?"

"That must have hurt?"

"Yes. So much so that I never brought it up again. Maybe if I had asked him his real feelings about his grandson, things would have turned out differently. Instead, I put the comment in the pile with all the other hurts and rejections."

"So, Henry never had any idea you were his grandson?"

"Not that I picked up on. Sometimes he said I reminded him of someone, but he never said who. And I never pressed him." Marcus told Lessye his fears about his impending meeting with Claude.

"You could be right. Some things are all coming together now. Tanya told me that when Claude asked her for a list of people who met with Brad a week before he died, he asked several questions about you and your meeting with Brad. He asked her how to contact Lena, so I'm guessing they talked. And now I know why Rod has been evasive about the case, and why he's been trying to warn me off you. I'm almost sure Rod has seen a copy of Jesse's letter. Rod and Jesse were close. He wouldn't have written letters to those three representatives, and not given Rod a copy."

"I'm sure Lena had a mouthful, and Rod, another member of my fan club. He always believed I framed Henry. Now he has the ammunition to prove it. When Robert finds out, my job is history. I'm sure Rod will hang that over my head as clear motive. He's working so close to Claude that he couldn't sneeze without some of his spit flying in Rod's face. And Robert is determined to keep Rod in the loop. I'm sunk."

"You know that Rod is also a dear friend of mine. He may not like you, but he's always fair. He would never use you as a scapegoat for something you didn't do."

"I know you and Rod are close. But I don't trust him to do the right thing by me. Sometimes things don't always turn out like we think they should. First, this is a high-profile case. You can't imagine the number of influential people who're pushing for it to be solved. That includes Robert, who I know wants the investigation wrapped up and the case solved by the end of session. The longer it remains unsolved, the more vulnerable he is to attack by his political enemies. They'll definitely use it as a weapon against him. I can almost envision Sammy Nokes rallying the troops now.

"I've been giving a lot of thought to how they can build a case against me. Killian, Alonso, and Brad knew a secret I'd been hiding that would probably cost my job. I had heated meetings with each of them within days of their deaths. Their secretaries can vouch for that. My red Lexus is anything but inconspicuous. And I have a vanity tag. I went to see Alonso at his home the Sunday he died. I also met with him in a restaurant in Macon later that same day. I got an urgent call from Brad to meet him at his Unicoi cabin the Sunday he died. When I got to the cabin, he was already gone, but I'll bet a number of people will remember the car being there because I stopped for gas. I argued with Killian in the middle of the Freight Room during the Wild Hog Dinner, and you know how many witnesses were there. All three men died in car accidents with empty bourbon bottles just like Henry. Everyone knows I'm a bourbon drinker. So we're looking at motive and opportunity – both of which I'm up to my waist in."

"But those legislators died as a result of some drug called GHB, not alcohol intoxication. You're not a drug dealer, and you're not a user."

"That's true. I've never been mixed up in drugs. I wouldn't even know how to get GHB or how it looks."

"Then you have nothing to worry about. The most important thing is that you tell the truth, no matter how bad it is. Everything is going to come out anyway. You have to be honest and answer every question truthfully. Remember, Marcus, the truth is always the truth. It never changes, and it always comes out the same way. I'm here for you and will be as long as you tell the truth."

Marcus looked at Lessye with love in his eyes. "After everything I've told you, you're not judging me. You're still my friend. I can't imagine what I've ever done to deserve you. I've never had a friend like you. I've never had any real friends."

"Well, you're stuck with me now," she said and kissed him lightly on the tip of his nose.

Before leaving, she took his hands, and they prayed together. When Marcus took Lessye home the next morning at daybreak, although they had not physically consummated their love, they both knew that on that Valentine's evening they shared much more than sex could ever give them. They lit a fire of friendship and trust that could never be extinguished. They shared a connection of spirits that could never be broken.

CHAPTER 40

On Tuesday, Claude planned to have another talk with Lena, this time about Renae's account of the Macon trip. He also anticipated his meeting with Marcus. Because of the explosive videotape, Tyrell and Randy Joe would be on program as soon as he could pin them down.

The videotape, anonymously delivered to Rod, included explicit and incriminating audio and video footage, as well as Tyrell spiking the drink of undercover agent Valerie Carr. It was all they needed to pull Randy Joe and Tyrell in to answer questions in conjunction with illegal drug possession and rape.

"Now we know why Randy Joe's and Tyrell's hotel suites were under surveillance," Claude said after viewing the tape. "I only wish we knew who set it up."

"God only knows how many unsuspecting young women besides Courtney Maxwell have been drugged and raped by those two, and this tape proves it," Rod said. "I guess whoever had it made was out to make sure they didn't get away with it again."

"Whoever it was paid a lot for this quality of work," Claude said.

"And to keep it discreet, it was sent anonymously," Rod said. "Not even a delivery company name on the package. I found it on my desk. None of my staff know how or when it got there. Someone sneaked it in."

"Very professional," Juan said.

"I'm going to have another chat with Valerie to see if she's had any luck coming up with a name for our mystery camera man," Claude said, making a quick notation on his pad. "This is some good information, but having an anonymous surveillance tape admitted as evidence is going to be shaky at best. Their attorneys will try to make it appear that we obtained it illegally and have a field day getting it thrown out."

"But we are going to try?" Juan said.

"Yes," Claude said. "We still have Valerie's statement and positive results on the lab tests of the drink sample she turned in. At best, the tape will be admitted as corroborating evidence. At worst, it won't be, but they will still suffer from the embarrassment when it's made public. And believe me, whoever took the trouble to have this made had to have more than one copy. I expect to see it turn up again."

"Do you think it could have been Bernard?" Rod asked. "Courtney Maxwell is his goddaughter, and he was furious about what happened to her. She told me she's not pressing charges because she can't positively identify who molested her. Maybe Bernard decided to take care of it in his own way."

"And if he did do it, he did it in a way that Randy Joe and Tyrell would never know it was him," Juan said. "How's that for sweet revenge?"

"And they deserve every bit of it," Claude said. "What I still can't believe is how Randy Joe and Tyrell laughed and talked about those innocent young girls like they were pieces of meat. Whoever edited this piece was a genius. They managed to record every incriminating conversation. These are the men who make our laws. And their arrogance makes them think they are above the law. Well, not for long."

It may not have been his birthday, but Sean sure did feel like he had received a present after viewing the steamy videotape that had been sent to him anonymously on Monday afternoon. This was what he needed to redeem himself after that fiasco with Karin. Representative Randy Joe Reynolds and Senator Tyrell Buford drugging and doing the wild thing with Capitol interns and aides . . . news at eleven. Thirty minutes of some of the most incriminating footage he'd ever had his hands on. This was too good to be true. He considered himself a good writer with a vivid imagination, but even he could not have dreamed up a scandal this good. He only wished the women's faces had not been edited out. Someone trying to protect the innocent, he thought.

He snooped around among the other reporters enough to realize he was the only one sitting on top of this bubbling volcano. The copies he was going to make and peddle to the television stations should net him a shiny dime. They'd have a field day clipping excerpts for their evening news. But before that, it was only his duty to be the first to break the news of its existence.

―――――――――

As Ronnie sped toward home early Tuesday evening, his thoughts were consumed with Tamika and how blessed he was she said yes to his proposal. Ronnie and Tamika knew they were facing some pretty stiff obstacles to their engagement – namely their fathers.

Tonight, however, was all about the celebration. His plan was to rush home, shower and change clothes, pick up Tamika and join their friends Tommy and Veda for a post Valentine's Day dinner. Their friends would be the first to learn of their engagement. Lifelong friends, Ronnie had introduced Tommy, a cool Cuban guy, to Tamika's best friend and classmate, Veda. The couples often double dated, and Ronnie loved climbing behind the wheel of Tommy's bullet-fast Camaro as much as Tommy envied his fire engine-red Mustang.

When Ronnie arrived home he found a package addressed to his mother propped against the front door.

"Hey, Mama, I'm home! There's a package for you!" Ronnie said as he entered the house.

"Hey, Ronnie," she said from the kitchen. "I'm on the phone right now. Why don't you go ahead and open it for me."

Ronnie eagerly did as she requested but was surprised to see that the package contained only an unlabeled videotape. His curiosity piqued, he immediately went to his father's den and popped it in the VCR. He stood rooted, stunned into silence, watching until he couldn't stomach any more. The mystery of why the date rape drug had fallen out of his father's jacket pocket was solved. Ronnie popped the video out of the VCR and with tape in hand, bolted out the front door.

―――――――――

"Are you sure he's gone?" Randy Joe asked Nathaniel one last time.
"Yes, he's gone. We watched him leave. He should be home by now."

"Good. Then do it tonight!" No sooner than he ended his call to Nathaniel, Tyrell burst into his office heaving like a horse, in a sweaty panic unlike anything Randy Joe had witnessed before.

"Settle down, boy. What's wrong with you?" Randy Joe said, slightly afraid of the answer.

"Have you seen . . . the videotape?"

"Videotape? What videotape? Boy, what are you talking about? You're scaring me. Calm down before you have a heart attack."

"Randy Joe, somebody bugged our hotel suites! They have everything on tape – picture, sound everything. They know about the GHB and the girls! My wife got a copy today, and that means Miss Pearl probably got one, too!" Tyrell howled as if he had been shot. "My wife called our lawyer before she even talked to me. He called me before I got a call from one of the executive board members of the CNAA. Hilton Lott, of all people, has a copy. He's going to have both our heads on a platter. We're as good as out of the CNAA, and we can forget about re-election. But those are the least of our problems because we're probably going to wind up in prison!"

Tyrell kept rambling on and on, bordering on hysteria, but Randy Joe had stopped listening. He turned pale, and his eyes clouded. All he could think of was that he had been exactly right to be afraid of the answer.

CHAPTER 41

Claude hadn't succeeded in doing nearly as much as he planned. He had seen Lena and Marcus, but he could never catch up with Tyrell. And Randy Joe had suddenly disappeared from the Hill. Claude suspected it was on purpose because of the videotape. Nevertheless, he would get them. He wanted to talk to Tyrell before revisiting Randy Joe because, from observation, Claude reasoned that Tyrell was the weak link and would be easiest to crack. The telephone rang, and Claude answered it gruffly.

"Agent Henderson. This is a friend. You'll find all the evidence you need against Marcus Norwood in his loft." The caller's voice was muffled. Claude could not ascertain whether it was male or female. He quickly glanced at the Caller ID which displayed *Unknown Name* and jotted down the number.

"Who is this?" Claude asked.

"I told you – a friend. A friend who's interested in justice. Marcus is dealing GHB on the Hill. He used it to kill those three legislators. Go to his loft. You'll find what you need."

There was a click, and the line went dead.

"How did the meeting with Claude go?" Lessye asked Marcus as they shared a glass of wine at her house on Tuesday evening. Marcus followed her home from work, and Lessye whipped up a light snack of sausage, cheese and crackers, and a mellow merlot.

"As smoothly as could be expected," Marcus said. "I answered all his questions truthfully. I told him everything I told you about my past, including why I changed my name, the Perkins incident and my meetings with Killian, Alonso, and Brad."

"Did he believe you?"

"It's hard to say. Cops are always skeptical, and GBI agents are the worse, next to the FBI. To his credit, though, he did seem impressed that I answered all his questions without hesitation. He seemed especially interested in the fact that Brad called and asked me to meet him at his cabin but was gone when I got there. Claude wanted to know why Brad would want to meet with me and why he would request an urgent meeting but leave before I got there. That's the only thing I couldn't answer because that was the night Brad was killed. I never spoke with him again."

Lessye sipped her wine. "Have you thought about what Brad could have wanted?"

"I had hoped it was to tell me he changed his mind about going to Robert with Jesse's letter. But I wondered why he wanted me to come up to Unicoi. There was no love lost between Brad and me. I'd be the last person on his guest list. I would think he wouldn't even want me to know he had a cabin. But then he told me he was leaving town for a few days on urgent business – catching an early flight Monday morning. So it was important that he see me Sunday night."

"Maybe he wanted to talk about something else."

"But what could have been so important that he couldn't tell me by phone or wait until he got back to Atlanta from his business trip?" Marcus sighed. "Now, we'll probably never know."

"Has Claude or Rod told the Governor about Jesse's letter?"

"I don't think so. Not yet. If they had, I certainly would have heard from Robert."

"Then I think you better tell him."

Marcus was hesitant. "This could mean my job. Everything I've worked so hard for all these years. How am I going to tell Robert I'm a prime suspect in these murders?" Marcus shook his head. Lessye slipped her hands inside his.

"You know it's going to come out. Renae or Lena or both of them are going to make sure the Governor knows. And Claude and Rod are not going to sit on this for long. As bad as it is, the Governor will appreciate it coming from you. You can't wait around and let him get his hands on a copy of that letter and confront you. What I know about Governor Baker is that he's compassionate and understanding. Break it down to him, like you explained it to me."

"You make some excellent points, and I know you're right. But I need to think about it."

"Okay, baby. But don't take too long," she said and then kissed him on the lips.

───────────────────

The fire at the Campus Row apartment complex in Fort Valley lit up the night sky and could easily be seen from the university campus only a few blocks away. Billows of thick, choking black smoke spiraled higher and higher. Campus Row was a small, intimate apartment complex catering primarily to university students and a few faculty members. The eight red brick buildings were well maintained and surrounded by beautifully manicured lawns, shrubs, and walkways. Each building contained four two-story, three-bedroom units with a cozy living room, convenient kitchen, and two full baths.

It was past midnight when the fire burst from one of the units and spread fast. Before firefighters could arrive, one of the buildings was almost gutted and the fire was threatening to leap to the building beside it.

Tarrah Layton, who had been cramming for an exam with her study group on campus, and her sister, Tammi, who had been to Macon with a couple of friends to see a play, both arrived at their apartment almost simultaneously to see it engulfed in flames. They had not seen their sister, Tamika, since dinner on Sunday, and they frantically searched for her among the swelling crowd of residents and other onlookers who had poured out into the street. Two hours after the fire was extinguished, the fire chief emerged from what was left of their building with a grim expression on his face. He stopped briefly to talk with two police officers and the apartment manager whose panicked eyes darted across the crowd and then settled on Tarrah and Tammi, whom he pointed out. As the fire chief and the officers slowly moved in their direction, the girls instinctively held hands and held their breaths.

CHAPTER 42

*A*fter leaving Lessye's place on Tuesday night, Marcus went home, showered and dressed for bed, prepared himself a stiff bourbon and water on the rocks, and lay awake for hours thinking about his life and how he would break the news to Robert. This was the week he and Lessye were supposed to shine at the annual Governor's dinner. Instead, he would be making one of the hardest confessions of his life and hoping he still had a job afterward.

He thought back to the first time he met Robert. They had been introduced by Killian, who at that time was working as personnel director in the office of Secretary of State. Robert was a member of the Georgia House, and he and Marcus connected so easily that Marcus volunteered to work on his next campaign.

Robert possessed a fire that Marcus appreciated. He was a rare breed in politics – a man of earnest integrity and honesty, a man who sincerely cared about the people he served and would not compromise his beliefs. Robert was a friend of the underdog – people like Marcus had been and in many ways still was. These were all qualities that Marcus lacked but greatly appreciated in his boss. Marcus saw in Robert his ticket to a prosperous future in state government.

In his role as campaign volunteer, Marcus was nothing less than impressive. He did door-to-door canvassing, posted yard signs and handed out campaign flyers, buttons and bumper stickers. He worked the polls on grueling hot and humid summer primary election days from seven until seven and manned manual phone banks. Clawing his way up to PR coordinator, he drafted constituent letters and other correspondence, news releases, and speeches, and arranged interviews also alternating as debate coach. He produced sharp television ads, appealing Web sites, and slick, eye-catching brochures.

On the dark side of political maneuvering, Marcus was not above leaking damaging information to the media about anyone who dared to oppose Robert. His bag of dirty tricks included having large volumes of unsolicited food or beverages delivered to the campaign headquarters of unsuspecting opponents. He planted volunteers in enemy camps to keep him apprised of their strategy and effectively turned it against them. His most diabolical strategy was his simplest: orchestrating the removal of their own campaign signs and blaming the enemy camp, then later replacing the same signs in other locations.

Marcus sensed that an idealistic visionary like Robert needed protection and buffering by a ruthless person who could watch his back and do the dirty work. Marcus was a savvy political organizer, astute in all the subtle nuances of Georgia government, so he appointed himself that person for Robert.

After a couple of years, Marcus moved from campaign volunteer to a paid, year-round staff position as chief legislative aide, which meant giving up the job he had stolen from Henry. He followed Robert from the House to the Senate and as campaign manager was one of the key engineers who steered Robert's gubernatorial train to victory.

Marcus was rewarded by being appointed the first African-American chief of staff in the state's history. Marcus was one of the handful of blacks in state government who had more than the illusion of power. He wielded real power. Anybody who wanted the ear of the Governor better snuggle as close as they could to his good side.

Now . . . it was all coming to an end. Even if he was exonerated of the crimes of murder, the Perkins incident combined with his shady family history would leave a cloud hanging forever over his head. And he knew that in politics, a dark cloud of suspicion was as terminal as outright guilt.

Marcus drifted off into the restless arms of sleep with one thought on his mind: There was no way out.

CHAPTER 43

*I*t was early Wednesday morning before Nathaniel returned home and called Hilton Bailey Lott, Jr., the newly elected national president of the CNAA, who was breathing fire and threatening to dismiss him as lobbyist if he didn't report to his office by nine. Nathaniel speculated about the true source of Hilton's foul mood as he quickly showered and dressed in a dark business suit and crisp white shirt.

Hilton's luxurious office was located on the top floor of Lott Tower, the crown jewel of Lott Enterprises, an accounting firm over which he presided. His secretary, who had been instructed to send Nathaniel in the moment he arrived, reached for his coat.

"He's been waiting for you," she said with an edge to her voice, nervously blinking her huge, doe-like brown eyes. Although often a ball of nerves resulting from Hilton's temperamental mood swings, she was ever the efficient assistant who knew the exact number, measurement and location of every bone in Hilton's closet. She alerted Hilton to his presence.

When Nathaniel entered the office, the tension in the room cut him like a razor. Hilton was seated at his desk. His back was turned to the door, and he was facing a huge window overlooking Piedmont Park.

"How thoughtful of you to finally return my calls and drop by for a visit," he said.

"Good morning, Hilton. I'm sorry it took so long to get back to you, but there was pressing business I had to take care of."

"More pressing than the business you're getting paid for?" Before Nathaniel could answer, Hilton spun around to face him. "Go over and turn on the television and push the play button on the VCR." Hilton gestured to an ornate satinwood wall cabinet that held the television, DVD Player, VCR, a stereo system and several CDs, DVDs, audio and videotapes. Nathaniel did as he was instructed, and then Hilton said, "Now sit down and watch carefully."

Nathaniel could not believe his eyes or his ears. He squirmed in his seat, hoping that it would end soon. But the thirty-minute tape seemed to drag on for hours. Finally, the sleazy videotape came grinding to an end. His only consolation was he was not the brunt of Hilton's anger. Randy Joe and Tyrell must have lost their minds. He had warned them about their recklessness with women, but he never imagined they could be this stupid. Nathaniel may have sponsored and made brief appearances at some of the parties, but he was in no way involved in this mess.

"From your expression, I can see that you're as speechless as I was when I first saw this filth," Hilton said. "Those crazy rednecks have gone too far this time. They might trash their own lives, but they won't take down the CNAA. Their criminal behavior could open all of us up to a government investigation, not to mention the hail storm of negative publicity. And we all know that when the government gets involved they'll either find the evidence they want or create some. But that won't happen on my watch."

All Nathaniel could do was nod as beads of perspiration began popping out on his forehead. Although Nathaniel had come to Hilton's office fresh from the shower, he now felt as sweaty as a field orchard worker on Randy Joe's peach farm. When he regained his ability to utter an intelligible word, he said, "I'm sorry about this. Believe me, I had no idea—"

"Of that I'm sure. If I had even the least suspicion you were a party to this travesty, we wouldn't be having this conversation now." Hilton rose from his desk and walked over to the VCR to rewind the videotape. Nathaniel was still glued to his chair, afraid to move. Hilton returned to his desk but did not sit down. Instead, he lifted his wrinkled hands making a sweeping motion indicating his spacious office.

"Do you know how many years it took my father to scratch his way out of the dirt, stench and degradation of poverty? How many years it took for him to build his small accounting firm and for me to grow that tiny business into the multimillion dollar empire Lott Enterprises is today?" Nathaniel did not speak because it was obviously a question Hilton intended to ask and answer himself. "More than sixty years combined, that's how long," Hilton said. "But for more years than that my family has revered the CNAA. I have achieved a status of which my father and grandfather only dreamed – to be national president of the CNAA. I take this honor seriously." He focused his steely, hawk-like eyes on Nathaniel, and his tight pasty face seemed to grow even harder. The strands of his thinning cotton-white hair stood on ends as if he were being electrocuted. "So you can understand that I will not allow anyone or anything to ruin my family dream," he said barely above a whisper.

"Yes, sir." Nathaniel said although they were on a first-name basis.

"You know people often ask me why we intentionally keep our membership numbers low – why we take great pains to screen our potential members. We could easily have ten times our one hundred thousand if we accepted anybody. But we are selective. The CNAA does not tolerate violence or scandal among its membership. That's what sets us apart from organizations who recruit common, tobacco juice-spitting, beer-belly rabble. Everyone does not merit membership in the CNAA. But sometimes as careful as we are, even we make a mistake and undesirables slip by. But we have means of dealing with these situations expeditiously." There was an odd faraway look in Hilton's eyes, bordering on the psychotic. His tone was hollow. For fear of opening his mouth and saying the wrong thing, Nathaniel nodded vigorously.

"Nathaniel, I don't have to remind you that the bylaws of the CNAA are specific in giving the executive board the power to take swift punitive action. We can immediately expel any member – or in this case members – who threaten the reputation and status of this organization. I have arranged a special meeting today at eleven to deal with the Reynolds and Buford matter. Your attendance is mandatory. Afterwards, you will personally have the honor of delivering the boards' decision to our former members."

Claude had just received a telephone call when he looked up and saw Rod and Juan at his door.

"What's the story on the tail on Renae?" he asked his caller, Agent Jason Grogan, as he gestured for them to come in and have a seat. Jason was an energetic, clean cut young agent still trying to make his bones within the bureau.

"Nothing so far," said Jason, who Claude had handpicked for his Op and assigned to tail Renae and keep her under surveillance. "She goes to work and goes home. Nothing out of the ordinary."

"Any visitors?" Claude asked.

"No, she's a loner. Doesn't seem to have a boyfriend or other visitors for that matter. I've only seen her with one person – some fly white-looking chick, with long brown hair, stacked up from the ground. You know her?"

"Yeah," Claude said, "That's a good description of her pal, Lena. Has she tried in any way to get close to Marcus either at the Capitol or at his loft?"

"No. She's a real quiet one. I might as well be bird dogging a nun."

"Stay on it," Claude said. "Report back to me if she does anything or goes anywhere out of the ordinary."

"Will do."

After hanging up the phone, Claude said, "That was Jason Grogan. His tail on Renae has produced nil so far. But I'm keeping him on it. You guys want to help yourselves to some coffee?"

Juan poured himself a cup of strong black coffee, while Rod opted for a steaming cup diluted with sugar and artificial creamer.

"Did Lena back up Renae's story about the Macon trip?" Rod asked.

"Every last word," Claude said. "Lena said she goes to Macon almost every Sunday to check on her aunt who's in an exclusive nursing home there. I called and checked it out. The chief administrator, Mrs. Sally Millen, verified that Lena visits her old aunt almost every Sunday and has been since she parked her there. It seems the old lady raised Lena, sent her to school and all. She had a stroke a few years ago which left her in bad shape. She's paralyzed on her right side and can't talk or communicate in writing."

"Lena's footing the bill for her aunt to stay in the home?" Rod asked.

"No, that money is coming from a trust fund. From what I understand, the old lady is loaded," said Claude. "Her husband had been wealthy and left her well fixed. Lena grew up in the lap of luxury and is still reaping benefits. Although she can't touch the trust fund, she has power of attorney over everything else which is a bundle."

"That all checks out with what I was able to dig up," Juan said. "Lena grew up in Boston where she lived with the aunt and uncle in the exclusive Beacon Hill section. She was an honor student at Branton University in Hartsdale, New York. After her aunt had the stroke, Lena closed up the Beacon Hill estate, and they moved south to Macon. Lena volunteered on

Governor Baker's gubernatorial campaign. That's how she met Brad and got a job as his aide. There are no fingerprints on file for Lena other than the one on her driver's license, and not so much as a traffic citation under her name turned up."

"Claude, did you hear anything else from Valerie about who she suspects did the surveillance tape?" Rod asked.

"Yeah, she kept digging and came up with the name Harlin Burr. I checked him out. He's a slick private detective and electronics genius with an office close to here on Peters Street. It looks like a dump on the outside, but the equipment is all high tech. The word is some of his A-list clients have contacts in high places. That's how he got hooked up doing hush-hush consulting jobs for the GBI and some federal government gigs. According to Burr, he was out of state on business on the evening Valerie says she eyeballed him."

"You believe him?" Juan asked.

"No. But his story checks out. He says he was in L. A. meeting with business associates. He gave me names and numbers, and they corroborated everything. And it all jibes right down to his airline ticket and hotel reservation, so I can't press him."

"So we're back to square one on the tape," Rod said.

"Not necessarily," Claude said. "I know he made it, but proving it and finding out who for is another matter. And right now, we have more pressing issues. I instructed a couple of guys to bring Tyrell in for questioning. He should arrive in a few minutes. They nabbed him in the parking lot when he arrived this morning." Claude took a long sip from his cup of coffee which had gone from piping hot to lukewarm. "Also, I received an anonymous phone tip late yesterday evening that Marcus is in possession of the drug GHB at his loft. According to the raspy-voiced caller, he's supposedly trafficking the drug on the Hill. I checked out the number. The call came from a public phone in Little Five Points."

"What?" Rod asked, almost gagging on a sip of coffee. "I know Marcus is capable of many things — but drug dealing? I'm not believing that."

"After considerable thought, I don't think so either. That tip could be on the level, or it could be some churl messing with Marcus because of his position. But with the other evidence against him, we're obligated to check it out. I spoke with Marcus before getting a warrant. He agreed to let us do the search without one. But I'm doing this strictly by the book. We couldn't get hold of a judge to issue one until this morning. Marcus arranged for his landlord to let our guys in when they arrived." Claude looked at his watch. "They should be there now. Depending on what they find, I may need to have another talk with Marcus after the meeting with Tyrell."

Their meeting was interrupted by Claude's intercom buzzer. "Yes?"

It was the secretary of the GBI Director. "Claude, Senator Buford has arrived. He's waiting for you in the Director's conference room."

Not a day went by that Gus did not read almost every newspaper he could get his hands on. After reading the bombshell exposed in the *Capitol Reporter*, he decided to thumb through one of the local daily newspapers as he waited for Kwame to join him on the third floor in front of the closed circuit monitor near the House Chamber. While scanning the metro section, Gus' attention was caught by a short article about a deadly fire in Fort Valley, Georgia, that claimed the lives of two people – one was the youngest daughter of the well known political activist and civil rights leader, Barry Cornelius Layton. The other was the oldest son of Representative Randy Joe Reynolds.

CHAPTER 44

*M*arcus had tussled with his thoughts and dreams all night. When his clock alarmed at five o'clock Wednesday morning, he felt like he had come up on the losing end of a wrestling smack down. He mechanically performed his morning exercise routine, followed by his grooming ritual – rinsed his mouth with hydrogen peroxide, brushed his almost perfect white teeth, shaved his prickly morning stubble, showered and dressed. As he brushed his hair into place and smacked on his favorite cologne, he noticed that his usually bright, clear brown eyes were bleary and bloodshot. He felt the faint pounding of an oncoming headache, the same nagging pain he got any time he was under a lot of pressure.

Marcus automatically turned on his television set to *Good Day Atlanta*, the morning program he watched everyday as he dressed for work, but his thoughts were distracted. Not even the hilarious antics of the Road Warrior managed to perk him up.

After dressing in a conservative charcoal business suit and imported black alligator shoes, he went to the kitchen to get some money from the cash stash he kept hidden in the refrigerator. That's one thing he learned from his aunts, who were forever scheming inventive ways to hide money from his dead-beat dad. His dad never looked in the refrigerator because he had always been too lazy to get himself a glass of water, Marcus remembered bitterly. If you wanted to keep something away from Quentin Norris, put it in either a book or the refrigerator. He would never find it. No one loved being waited on more than Quentin Norris. Marcus wondered what unlucky sucker he had pimped into waiting on him in lock up, wherever he was.

Marcus put seven hundred dollars in his wallet. He figured that after he told Robert his story, he needed enough money to go to the nearest hotel bar and get wasted after he was fired. He might even need to crash over night, and he felt more comfortable using cash than plastic.

When Marcus faced the early morning chill, he was happy he decided to wear his black, all-purpose coat with the heavy lining. The weather was cold, dismal gray and threatening rain. One of those dreary days that held no evidence of the colorful vibrance of spring in its near future. He threw his leather briefcase in the trunk of his spotlessly neat car and almost decided to remove his old leather jacket and a duffel bag packed with toiletries and clothes he kept in the car for impromptu changes. But the first drops of a stinging rain and the biting teeth of the wind changed his mind. Also, the few minutes it would take to walk back to his loft would make him miss his morning traffic window. In morning Atlanta traffic, timing was everything. A mere minute could be the determining factor in a smooth easy ride or hours stuck in traffic. Besides, if he got drunk and crashed in a hotel, the toiletries and change of clothing would come in handy.

Marcus had only a little nerve left, so he decided that he would tell the Governor first thing before their morning meeting.

━━━━━━━━━━━━━━━━

The silence between them after Marcus made his confession to Robert seemed to stretch for miles. Marcus left nothing out and gave him the same double-barrel, straight-up confession he first gave Lessye and then Claude. Marcus had done a lot of underhanded mess in his life, but would never, ever think of intentionally killing anyone.

While Robert regarded him in shocked silence, Marcus thought about his eager cooperation with the GBI search of his loft without having his attorney present. He wondered if he had made a mistake and hoped they weren't so zealous for a culprit that they would stoop to planting something at his place to frame him. Marcus had never trusted the police. The seeds of distrust had been planted by the knowledge of historical atrocities against blacks at the hands of police and reinforced by the many present-day police shootings of unarmed black men in their homes, on the street, driving while black, or for holding a wallet. He knew what law enforcement officers were capable of – especially when it came to dealing with black men whom they viewed as potential criminals. Yes, his father was a habitual offender who truly deserved to be in prison, but there were so many others there who didn't. Marcus did not want to be one of them.

Marcus also thought about Lessye: her pretty smile, warm, loving eyes and smooth brown skin. How would he be able to keep Lessye's love after he was fired, disgraced and black balled from state government? Lessye could not support him, and he wouldn't allow it even if she offered. In many ways he seemed to be a lousy heel, but he would never live off a woman like his father had. His father was a sorry, lazy man who lived off his sisters and any other woman who would give him the time of day. Marcus vowed early that his life would never go in that direction. He was still a man and did have some pride left.

It was Robert who broke the uneasy silence after pacing back and forth almost ten times. "Marcus, why didn't you tell me this before?"

"I was ashamed. I thought it would never come up again. The bottom line, I was afraid of losing my job."

"You must have known that Claude would get his hands on a copy of the Higgins letter and you would become a number-one suspect in this case. Do you understand the implications of your actions when word gets out that you're a suspect?"

"I'm sorry. I know I should have said something. I never should have put you in this potentially damaging position. I'll do whatever it takes to make it right. No one will blame you."

"You don't get it do you? It's not me that I'm worried about right now, it's you. The press, with Sean leading the pack, will try to crucify you with their subliminal messages and subtle innuendoes designed to turn public opinion against you. They'll devote segments of their prime time news programs to experts in the fields of psychology and law enforcement who will dissect your life, create some sort of new syndrome, and spew plausible reasons why you're the killer regardless of any concrete proof. That's all your enemies will need to pounce. They'll try to run you out of state government. Our opponents will demand that we hang you out to dry. After the press has put their spin on it, the loved ones of the victims will see your arrest as justice being served. This is a high-profile case, and people are demanding closure. They want someone they can blame. And if the media, the police, and your enemies can shape you into that someone, then they won't lose one minute of sleep doing it. The saddest thing is, all of this will happen regardless of whether you're guilty or innocent.

"I know you're not a murderer, Marcus. But, I wish you had told me the whole story sooner. It was wrong what you did to Henry. And you were wrong to keep it from me all this time. But I'm glad you told me before I heard it from someone else."

Marcus sighed. "Thank you for listening and believing in me. But I know I've let you down. Now, if you'll excuse me, I'll go clean out my desk and submit my letter of resignation, unless you want the satisfaction of firing me."

"Hold on. Have I asked you to resign or intimated in any way that you're fired?"

"No, but . . ."

"But nothing. Don't do anything right now. You've stuck your neck out for me almost on a daily basis. The least I can do is stand up for you when you need me. I'm no fool, and you may not realize this, but I know everything that goes on concerning my political life. Through the years on campaigns and to protect my back, you've done some questionable things, and I've turned my head. I felt that as long as it didn't get out of hand and the end results would benefit the greater good of the people, there was no need to interfere. I kept my hands clean while you climbed into the mud and became my hatchet man. I could chalk it up to being the nature of the political beast, but I'm not going to scapegoat. Some of it was plain wrong, and that makes me a hypocrite and as guilty as you."

"Robert . . ."

"Please. Let me finish. I'm always talking about integrity, but when it comes down to the nitty gritty of saving our political butts, how much true integrity do any of us have?" Robert put his hand on Marcus' shoulder in a reassuring, fatherly manner. "Marcus, I can't promise you that somewhere down the line in all this, I won't eventually be forced to accept your resignation. But what I can promise you is that I believe in your innocence and on that issue, I will never waver."

Marcus grasped Robert's hand. "Thank you. Thank you for everything."

CHAPTER 45

Tyrell did his best to dance around the truth but was fresh out of partners as far as Claude was concerned.

"Tyrell, I'm sure you know how much trouble you're in," Claude said. "Cooperating at this time will go a long way in your behalf. As it is, you're looking at a long stretch as guest of honor of the Georgia Department of Corrections, and I'm the man who will make that happen. You're looking at charges for possession of an illegal substance, the drug GHB, rape, and as far as I'm concerned you've moved up as a good suspect in the murders of three state legislators—"

"Now wait a minute!" Tyrell said in his heavy Southern twang, snake eyes squinting, his drawn up mouth looking as sour as ever. "I didn't have anything to do with any murder! You can't hang that on me."

"You had motive and possible opportunity, and this videotape proves that you were in possession of GHB, the drug used to induce their deaths. I think that this tape, combined with the other evidence we've collected, will give the Attorney General all the ammunition needed to charge you with drug possession, rape, and murder. What do you think?"

"I think . . . I think I need a lawyer present before I tell you what I know," Tyrell mumbled.

"I think that's one of the best decisions you've made in a long time."

=====

Rod returned to his office to find Gus waiting with a newspaper in hand.

"Hey, Gus. What's up?"

"Rod, I'm not trying to start anything or spread any rumors, but I thought it was only my duty to pull your coat tail. There's something important you need to know."

Rod had never seen the usually good natured, happy-go-lucky Gus look so serious, and it disturbed him. No, to be more accurate, it frightened him.

"What is it? Is it something about the case?" Rod slowly eased into the chair behind his desk.

"I don't think so, but it's awful just the same." Gus remained standing. "I read an article this morning, and I immediately spoke to Della, and she confirmed it." Gus reached across the desk and handed Rod the newspaper. He pointed to the brief article in the Metro section.

Rod gasped, after reading it. "My God. The daughter of Barry Layton was killed in a fire? It says that Randy Joe's son was killed, too. But there's something I *must* be missing here. What was Randy Joe's son doing in an apartment with Tamika Layton?"

"They were dating."

Rod's mouth dropped open. "Dating? Wait a minute. Are you standing here telling me that Randy Joe's son was dating a black girl?"

"Yes, he was. I had heard rumors. And now I know it for a fact because Della confirmed that, too."

"Well it must have been a secret to Randy Joe. That man would have pitched a fit."

"He knew, and he did," Gus said with the same somber expression dulling his usually bright eyes.

"My God," Rod said again shaking his head. "I still can't believe it. Two young people killed so tragically. Does anyone know what happened? What caused the fire?"

"Randy Joe."

"What . . .?"

"I don't believe that fire was an accident."

"What are you talking about? Why would you even think a thing like that?"

"Because I know Randy Joe. I overheard him having a conversation about putting an end to a relationship his son was in. He was talking with Tyrell last Thursday morning before a committee meeting. He was talking so low I had a hard time overhearing the conversation. Randy Joe didn't call any names but he said and I quote, 'Well, I know what I'm going to do. And it's going to be done next week. Nathaniel's handling the details. I don't care who her daddy is. If that tramp thinks she's going to derail my boy's future, she's got another thought coming,' end quote," Gus said. "I believe Randy Joe arranged to have that girl killed in that fire and that CNAA lobbyist, Nathaniel, was in on it."

"That's a strong accusation. I know Randy Joe is a ruthless individual, but even he wouldn't arrange to kill his own son."

"He probably didn't even know the boy would be there."

"Man, if what you believe is true, Randy Joe not only ended the relationship but killed his son."

"It's so sad," Gus said with tears in his eyes. "But like my dear grandmother always used to say, 'be careful when you dig a ditch for someone else to fall into, because you might end up being the first to slide in it yourself.'"

Excruciating was the only word Nathaniel could think of to describe the meeting with the executive board members of the CNAA, who took less than ninety minutes to enjoy refreshments, view the videotape, express their outrage, angrily discuss their options, and vote unanimously to throw Tyrell and Randy Joe out on their butts.

When he went to the Capitol, he was sucked into a storm equal to or worse than the one he left at Hilton's office. He got hold of a copy of the *Capitol Reporter* and heard the buzz about Tyrell being picked up by the GBI. The search was still on for Randy Joe, who was said to have left in a hurry due to an emergency at home. Great, Nathaniel thought to himself. His day had been sliding downhill with increasing momentum since the morning meeting. His cell phone rang.

What now? he thought as he said, "Hello."

"Nathaniel, this is Sonny Cole." His voice sounded weak as water, like he was battling the delirium of a devastating fever in order to stay coherent.

"I know who it is. Why are you calling me? You've got your money. Our business is concluded for now."

"Not quite . . . Ike and I . . . We need more money. We've got to get out of town . . . fast. "

"What are you talking about? Are you boys trying to shake me down?"

215

"No," Sonny said, sounding like he was about to pass out. "We'd never do that . . . this is serious–"

"Then what is it? And what's wrong with you? Are you sick?"

"Yeah. I've been throwing up."

"Sonny, I'm sorry you're sick but why—?"

"Have you read the paper or seen the news?" Sonny's voice was trembling, and it made Nathaniel's annoyance suddenly slip into a feeling of uneasiness.

"No . . . why . . .?"

"That Layton girl wasn't the only person killed in that fire last night."

Nathaniel's heart began a rapid descent to the pit of his stomach as beads of sweat began bursting forth from his forehead. "What are you talking about?"

"Ronnie was there, too. Nathaniel, he came back, and we didn't see him go in. He was in the apartment with that girl when she died. Do you hear what I'm saying? Ronnie was in that apartment. He was killed in that fire! If Randy Joe finds out about us we're dead! You've got to help us. Ike and I have got to get out of town before . . . "

Sonny was still talking when Nathaniel clicked off his cell phone. All he could think of was whether he could make it to the bathroom before vomiting all over himself.

———

"I want something planted in his office, today," Renae said to the person she had spoken to several times before from the downstairs pay phone.

"That's impossible. Enough is already in his loft. The GBI is conducting a search now. Please be patient. Marcus will be in jail before tomorrow at this time."

CHAPTER 46

*B*arry was colder than he ever felt. Cold and numb. So numb that he could hardly move. He had been glued practically to the same spot since Tarrah and Tammi arrived home early that morning accompanied by a police officer and the assistant fire chief, who was a friend of their family. They had all come to his home at two in the morning to inform him that his baby, Tamika, was dead. Tarrah and Tammi were too hysterical to speak coherently, their eyes swollen almost shut from crying. His wife, Gloria, screamed until the doctor arrived and gave her a sedative. Barry thought it was best she sleep as much as possible. Barry had done his share of crying while alternating between fits of rage and despair. Barry knew people who had lost children. A couple of their church members had gone through that pain. He always used empathy. He tried to put himself in their place and think of what it would be like if he lost one of his own children. Now he knew. It was a feeling past devastation, past hurt and pain. It was a feeling where your stomach churns with a sick hopelessness and nothing on earth could ease it — nothing on earth could make it right. This was so cruel and unfair. It was the most horrific unnatural order of life. He was not supposed to bury his baby – she was supposed to bury him.

No one should have to die that way, especially not his precious Tamika. His only consolation, if there could be any in a situation so profoundly devastating, was that Tamika had not faced death alone. She was with the man that she loved. He thought for a moment about the Reynolds family and the pain they must also be facing. He never liked Randy Joe, but the death of a child was something he would never wish on anyone. Ronnie had been a nice boy. He had truly loved Tamika as she loved him. Barry was also sorry he was gone.

Bad news traveled faster than a heat-seeking missile in a small town. Neighbors and friends started trickling in shortly after day break. Some brought food, others manned the phones and answered the door. Some worked in the kitchen to make space for what would eventually be an overflow of food and soft drinks. And others who were at a loss for words came and quietly sat with him. Co-workers came as they heard the news. Della called to express the sympathy from the Black Caucus, followed by calls from other friends on the Hill.

In the midst of everything, Barry did the one thing — the only thing that had gotten him through every tragedy in his life. He fell down on his knees and prayed.

CHAPTER 47

Special Agent Henderson, at this point, my client is not admitting anything. This tape you have as evidence will probably not be admissible in court when the judge finds out how it was obtained." The mouthpiece for Tyrell had arrived, and it didn't take long for the renowned Attorney Archer Wellington Paisley III to start throwing his considerable weight around. Archer, with his crooked receding hairline and thick flat nose, was a portly Perry Mason wannabe stuffed into expensive designer clothes. He had defended some of the most heinous criminals in the state's history and managed to get many of them off due to minor technicalities. Maybe he thought he could work the same magic in Tyrell's case, if he didn't split his pants first, Claude mused.

"There was no probable cause and no court order granting you permission to place video surveillance in my client's hotel suite or the suite of Randy Joe Reynolds in conjunction with any investigation," Archer said. "And, by your own admission, you don't even know who had their suites bugged or where the tape came from. *If,* that explanation is in fact true. We all know the many high-tech tricks people can play with photography. And as for the audio, other voices can easily be dubbed over the real ones to make it seem that a person is saying something they're not. This so-called evidence of yours will never hold up in court, if it gets there at all." Archer sniffed through his humongous nose. There was nothing like a pompous, pontificating defense attorney who was proud of himself. As for Tyrell, he sat there staring.

Claude had about enough of this two-bit shyster and could wait no longer to let him know it. "Mr. Paisley, If you think that our only piece of evidence against your client is that videotape, then you better go back to law school. Our investigation into GHB use at the Capitol began almost simultaneously with the investigation into the deaths of the three state legislators. We have a GBI agent who will testify that your client spiked her drink with GHB during a party in the hotel suite of Randy Joe Reynolds on the evening of Monday, February 7th. She saved a good sample. The lab analysis will also be presented as evidence. While we were awaiting your arrival, counselor, I got a call from the Fulton County DA's office. Three young ladies have already come forward to request formal charges be brought against your client. I'm sure they, too, will be willing to testify in court. We did have probable cause to get a warrant to search your client's hotel suite. A bottle with a liquid content our lab tested positive as GHB was found. Your client is looking at doing time for drug possession, rape, and possibly murder, and we both know that judges don't like it when public officials betray the trust of the people by abusing their power. So I wouldn't count on any leniency. If I were you, counselor, I'd give my client his money's worth. Advise him it will be in his best interest to tell me everything he knows."

Archer's nostrils flared, and he snorted his disapproval before whispering to Tyrell for a moment. Tyrell's dumb, sour look had been replaced by a pinched distress.

"If I talk, can I get a deal?" Tyrell asked.

"I'm not in a position to make you any deals," Claude said. "But your cooperation will be duly noted in my report, and depending on the information you provide, I might be willing to make a recommendation to the DA."

Tyrell and Archer huddled and whispered again.

"All right, I'll tell you what you want to know," Tyrell said.

"Where did you get the GHB?"

"I got it from Randy Joe."

"Do you know where he got it?"

"No, he never told me a name. He did say his contact is someone who works in the Capitol."

Did you have anything to do with the murders of Killian, Alonso, and Brad?"

"No! I told you before. I never killed anyone."

Tyrell glanced at Archer, who nodded slightly.

"But I know who did."

"Go on," Claude said.

"It was Randy Joe."

"Now, why do I get the impression that you're scapegoating Randy Joe to save your own skin?"

"It's true. Randy Joe is a murderer."

"And how did you come by this knowledge?"

"He told me."

"Randy Joe admitted to you that he killed the legislators?"

"Well, not in so many words. But he didn't deny it."

"That's not even your word against his. It's only supposition on your part. And an implied confession is hardly evidence."

"I also know for a fact that a fire in Fort Valley was no accident."

Claude leaned forward and considered him seriously. "What are you talking about?"

"Don't you read the newspaper? I'm talking about that fire near the university in Fort Valley at the apartment complex. Randy Joe arranged it. Nathaniel did the dirty work. Randy Joe meant only to kill that black girl, Tamika Layton, who was dating his son, but as it turned out, he ended up killing Ronnie, too."

Before Claude could respond any further, his cell phone rang. It was his men calling from Marcus' loft. They had found what they were looking for – a stash of GHB.

Marcus told Lessye about his meeting with the governor as she sat with him in his office while he prepared for another important staff meeting scheduled to begin at one.

"Robert was upset that I kept it from him, but he did say he was glad I told him before anyone else did. You were right. I do feel much better now that it's off my chest. So far, I still have a job."

"You made the right decision. I don't think you're going to lose your job. But we'll handle it if it comes. I've been praying for you. Everything will work out fine. We'll work it out together. You'll see." She kissed him lightly on the lips.

Marcus admired the glow of hope in Lessye's eyes, and he appreciated her use of the word *we*. Lessye was clearly committed to being in this with him, beside him. And that alone gave him a relief beyond words. He only wished that for one moment he could share her optimism, but he couldn't get rid of the nagging feeling that this was the calm before the storm.

———

"This better be good," Sean said after deciding to return Karin's calls.

"It's good to hear from you, too. Are you still in the market for news or are you on hiatus?"

"I don't have time for games. Do you have something that will interest me or not?"

"I don't remember us playing games for some time. And to answer your question: I've got info about the prime suspect in the GHB Connection. So you tell me."

"Okay, but it depends on what you have . . . and this better be on the up and up."

"Trust me when I tell you, I have two informative tidbits you'll be happy to get your hands on."

"It better be more reliable than that last GBI garbage. I can't afford to be embarrassed like that again."

"Give me a break. That only happened once, and only because you were impatient. The information I have for you is reliable, and it should be worth at least twenty-five hundred."

"All right, I'll be home in twenty minutes. Meet me there. And this better be good."

"The only thing you have to worry about is having my money when I get there – in cash."

CHAPTER 48

*O*n Wednesday morning, Kaye decided to drive up to Brad's Unicoi cabin and spend a few days.

Kaye missed her older brother desperately, and being at his favorite rustic retreat cradled deep in the woods always made her feel close to him. The cool, fresh smell of the thin mountain air was invigorating. The quiet serenity of nature was not disturbed by the incessant sound of piercing sirens, loud thumping music, and impatiently honking car horns.

On this particular excursion, she would force herself to begin the dreaded task of sorting and packing up Brad's belongings. Her mother couldn't bear to do it. Her father and brothers were much too busy making more money to involve themselves in mundane family issues. That only left Kaye, who had been closest to Brad.

As Kaye, with misty eyes, went through Brad's desk deciding what to keep, she came across an open envelope addressed to Brad from Vivian Staley of the Branton University alumni office. It contained an eight-by-ten glossy color photo of three young women dressed in cap and gown. One was Vivian. One of the others she recognized as Brad's aide, Lena.

Kaye remembered Brad mentioning that Lena graduated from Branton, which was also her alma mater. But during their few brief conversations, Lena never seemed remotely interested in staying current with alumni happenings or being included on the mailing list. Not being one to push or intrude, Kaye let it drop.

There was a short note attached along with Vivian's business card. The envelope was post marked in January, a few days after Brad's visit to Branton, where he Alonso and Killian had participated in a workshop on state government and politics. Kaye arranged the visit. Although an art project kept her from joining them, Kaye had called Vivian in advance and asked her to give them the VIP treatment.

Brad had attached a sticky note to the front of the photo that read, "frame for Lena." He died before he had a chance to frame it, Kaye thought, as fresh tears formed in her eyes. He wanted Lena to have this photo. The least she could do was make sure she got it. Kaye took out her cell phone and dialed a familiar number. This was the last thing she could do for her beloved brother.

———

Tanya was returning to her desk from lunch when the telephone rang.

"House of Representatives, Tanya speaking."

"Tanya, this is Kaye . . . Kaye Austin. How are you?"

"Fine, Kaye. How are you doing?"

"Getting a little better everyday."

Tanya wished that she could comfort Kaye by saying that she knew exactly how she felt, but she didn't. Tanya, an only child, had no idea how painful it was to lose a sibling. "We all loved Brad. You and your family are in our prayers."

"Thank you for everything. You were a wonderful assistant to my brother, and it means a lot to me that you thought so highly of him."

"You're kind to say that. If there's anything I can do for you, please let me know."

"Well, there is one thing. I've been going through some of Brad's personal items, and I found a photograph he planned to frame and give to Lena. Do you know where she's working now?"

"She's in the Speaker's office. Do you want the number and address?"

"No, but could you do me a huge favor?"

"Sure."

"I was coming down that way early next week on my way to the airport. I've been commissioned to do a painting in New York. If I drop it off at your suite, will you make sure she gets it?"

"I'll be glad to."

224

"Thank you. You know, finding this photograph made me curious about something. Do you know if my brother had been seeing Lena socially?"

Visions of Lena on Brad's desk with Randy Joe flashed through her mind, and Tanya winced. "What do you mean?"

"Was he dating her?"

Tanya thought about her conversations with Amber when they had wondered whether there was something going on between Brad and Lena. But they were not sure, and Tanya would not feed Brad's sister any gossip that might or might not be true.

"Not to my knowledge. They were friendly, but I don't know whether it was anything more than that. Outside of the office I've only seen them together at legislative functions and on the occasions Brad took us out to eat. I know that Lena seriously admired him, so much so that she didn't like it when he teased her."

"How so?"

"Well, for example, like the last time we all had dinner together. Brad treated Lena, Amber, and me to a celebration and welcome-back dinner for Amber, who had worked with us before. During the dinner, Brad was teasing Lena, and she seemed to get upset."

"Why was he teasing her?"

"We had gotten on the subject of universities because Amber is working on her master's. Brad was telling Lena that he had visited her alma mater, and he teased her about not being an active alum. He said he should have her picture posted on the Internet under dead-beat alumni. He was joking around and we all laughed, but Lena didn't think it was too funny. But then, she never did have much of a sense of humor."

CHAPTER 49

*M*arcus had just ended a staff meeting in the Governor's conference room on the Capitol first floor when Claude, Rod, and Juan entered the room.

"Marcus, we need to talk with you about some recent developments in the case," Claude said with a stern, foreboding expression that immediately set off warning signals in Marcus' head.

"Sure, come in, and sit down," Marcus said, as they walked in and took seats at the long walnut table in the neatly appointed conference room. "My meeting is over, and we can talk in here where we won't be disturbed."

Marcus cut his eyes in the direction of a couple of staff members who were lingering in the room, and they recognized it as their signal to leave, which they did quickly.

"Would you care for some coffee, tea or a soft drink?" Marcus asked.

"No, thank you." Claude said. "But we would care for some answers." He took out his tape recorder. "With your permission, I need to tape this conversation."

Marcus looked at the men. "Go ahead. That's up to you. This sounds serious."

"It is."

"What's this about, gentlemen?"

Claude clicked on the recorder. "First of all, you have the right to have an attorney present."

"No. Thank you. I don't have anything to hide. Please, get to the point and tell me what this is about."

"It's about the search of your loft," Claude said.

"Yes. The search that I authorized. What about it?"

"Do you suffer with a condition known as narcolepsy?"

"No."

"Then why are you in possession of GHB?"

"What are you talking about?"

"During the search this morning, our men found what they now have confirmed to be the drug GHB. The same drug that was used in connection with the deaths of the three legislators."

Marcus had trouble processing what he was hearing. "What? That's impossible. I've never been in possession of GHB or any other illegal drug. Your men have either made a mistake . . . or they planted it there."

"Marcus, there was no mistake and nobody at the GBI is trying to frame you," Claude said. "We are trying to solve this case. Now tell us about the GHB."

"I already told you. I don't know anything about any GHB."

"Then how can you explain two ounces of the drug in liquid form being found in the cabinet in your master bathroom and another two ounces in separate smaller bottles found stored in a box under your kitchen sink?"

"I . . . I can't explain it. All I know is, I didn't put it there."

"What I believe, Marcus," Juan said, "is that you hooked up with some of your daddy's old dope contacts and scored the drug, and then you used it to kill those legislators so they wouldn't blab to the Governor about what you did to your poor old grandpa Henry."

"What? I never killed anyone! And Robert knows everything. I told him this morning. And what's this trumped up notion about my daddy's drug contacts? Quentin Norris? You've got to be kidding now. I haven't even seen Quentin Norris enough times to know how to describe him if my life depended on it, not to mention any of his so-called contacts. For all I know, they're locked up with him, wherever he is."

"He's doing a quarter at Coxsackie maximum security prison in New York," Juan said. "When he was pinched, he was in possession of rohypnol, also a date rape drug in the GHB family."

"Well, that's news to me," said Marcus.

"Our guys found almost twenty thousand dollars hidden in your refrigerator. Explain that," Claude said.

"Why should I have to explain *my* money? I always keep a lot of cash on hand in case of emergencies, and I hide it in the refrigerator in case of a break in."

Claude, Juan, and Rod looked at one another.

"What do you keep all the bourbon for?" Claude asked.

"The bourbon—"

"That was found in your loft."

"I drink bourbon. I usually keep enough in my loft to have in case I'm entertaining guests."

"Isn't that a coincidence," Juan said. "You just happen to like the same kind of liquor that was found at the scene of all three legislator's deaths."

"And if I'm not mistaken," Claude said, "Our guys say that it's the same brand."

"Maybe I inherited a taste for good bourbon from Henry. A lot of people drink Jack. It's top of the line. Does that make them murderers?"

"We're not talking about a lot of people," Rod said. "Right now we're concentrating on you."

"We have witnesses who say that you had heated arguments with each of the legislators within days of their deaths," Claude said. "Killian could hardly turn around at the Wild Hog Dinner without bumping into you. The Sunday Alonso died, your car was spotted at his house in the morning, and there are witnesses who confirm that you had a brief meeting with Alonso in a Macon restaurant that afternoon, and it didn't seem friendly. Our witnesses also recognized your car, which is hardly inconspicuous. We have witnesses who can place you in Unicoi the Sunday that Brad died. Wouldn't you say that's too much of a coincidence?"

"What are you trying to say?"

"He's not trying, he's saying it," Rod said. "You had plenty of opportunity to slip all three of those men a lethal dosage of GHB which caused their deaths."

"You're wrong, I didn't kill those legislators. I don't know anything about any GHB."

"Why were you hounding Killian at the Wild Hog Dinner?" Juan asked.

"He received a copy of Jesse's letter and told me he was going to show it to Robert. I was trying one last time to convince him to reconsider, that's all."

"And Alonso?" Rod asked.

"I've answered all these questions before—"

"So answer them again," Rod said.

Marcus sighed. "It was the same with Alonso. I went to his house Sunday morning and met with him again later in Macon. He was understanding of my situation and apologized for the loud verbal disagreement we had after he received the letter. But he told me that I still had a responsibility to come forward and clear Henry's name. He reminded me that the truth would eventually come out, and that if I didn't stand up and do the right thing he would have to."

"You followed him to Macon?" Juan asked.

"No. I knew what time he would be stopping through. Robert had a speaking engagement in Macon that Sunday for King Week. He invited Alonso to attend, but Alonso had to decline due to a previous engagement in Savannah. He was only stopping through Macon long enough to have a brief meeting with Randy Joe and someone else from the Macon area. I found out from his aide where the meeting would take place. I drove to Macon separately from Robert and decided to pop in and meet with Alonso one more time to plead with him to reconsider telling about Jesse's letter. But he wouldn't. He seemed agitated. I guess he was pissed that I kept hounding him and he was pressed for time. He kept looking at his watch and told me he was meeting with someone else before going on to Savannah. But he never said who with, and they didn't show up while I was there. Maybe that's the person you should be looking for."

Claude, Juan and Rod exchanged glances. "We're comfortable sticking with you for the moment," Claude said. "Tell us about Brad."

"I told you that before. Brad called me that Sunday evening and asked me to meet him at his cabin in Unicoi. He said it was important."

"What about?" Claude asked.

"He didn't say. I assumed it was about Jesse's letter. Although he had assured me he was going to tell Robert, I was hoping maybe he had reconsidered."

"If that was the case, couldn't he have told you that over the phone?" Rod asked. "Or waited until he saw you the following Monday?"

"Ordinarily, I guess. But he told me he had to leave town on urgent business and would probably be gone a few days. He was driving back into Atlanta and taking an early morning flight."

"Did he say where he was going?" Claude asked.

"No. He said it was important I meet him that evening."

"What time did Brad call you, and what time did you get to the cabin?"

"He definitely called me at six-thirty in the evening. I know because I checked the time on my Caller ID. I can't be so sure about the time I arrived because I wasn't looking at my watch. It was maybe around nine or nine-thirty."

"And what happened when you arrived at the cabin?"

"I didn't see a car, but there was a light on inside. I knocked on the door several times, but he never answered. I waited a while to see if he would show. But he didn't. I used my cell phone to call him. All I got was his voice mail. I felt like he was jerking me around, so I left and stopped for some gas on my way back home."

"Marcus, your explanation has done nothing more than strengthen your motive for killing those men," Rod said. "They threatened to expose you. You feared losing your job as a result of it. Open and shut."

"Oh yeah. Like I would have confessed to this if I had something to hide. If I were guilty, do you believe I would give you a motive by admitting to you that those men remained adamant about telling Robert?"

"Sure you would," Rod said. "Because you think we're stupid."

"This is getting us nowhere. No matter what I say, Rod, you're determined not to believe me. You've always had it in for me."

"I wonder why?"

"Should I give you a list?"

"I already have my own."

"Now tell us why were your fingerprints all over one of the bottles containing the GHB?" Claude said.

"What?"

"Yes, the bottle was analyzed for prints. Yours were found all over it. I must say it was slick thinking to stash it in a cologne bottle. Our guys almost missed it."

"A cologne bottle?"

"Yes a cologne bottle."

Marcus rubbed his hand across his head and thought for a moment. "Was it a kind of unique, fancy ornate black bottle that didn't have a name on it?"

"Yes. You described it well for a person who swears he's never seen it," Juan said.

"That's because I have seen it. But not like you think. The bottle you're talking about was given to me by Brad's aide, Lena."

"Here we go," Rod said.

"You may not want to believe me, Rod, but it's true. I received an anonymous note attached to a copy of the letter Jesse sent to the three legislators. I couldn't figure out who sent it. It was somebody trying to mess with my head. I met Lena outside the Speaker's office one Friday. It was . . . the Friday before last. She told me she knew who sent it, but she wouldn't tell me unless she could come over to my loft. She wouldn't give me a time but said she would come over the following Sunday and to wait for her call."

"Did you wait for her call?" Claude asked.

"I waited at home all day," Marcus said. "She called at eight and got to my place about nine. The first thing she did when she came in was hand me the bottle of what I thought was my favorite cologne, Mystique. She said it was a peace offering to make up for being so late and an early Valentine's Day gift. I remember remarking that it wasn't in a Mystique bottle. And she said that was part of the present. She said she got it at a boutique that copies major brands for a fraction of the price."

"What boutique? Did she give you a name and location?" Juan asked.

"Where did she say that place was located . . . ? Oh, now I remember, it's a place in Greenbriar Mall called Perfect Scents. I remember the bottle because she said the keepsake cologne bottles were a popular attraction. She also told me that it was Renae who sent me the note and copy of Jesse's letter. She said that Renae had gotten the original off the secretary's desk and made copies. But I've found out since then that Brad's secretary never opened his mail – either he or Lena did. So it could have been her who sent me the note."

"Our guys found the copy of the letter and note in your desk drawer in the loft." Claude said.

"So you're saying that it was Lena who gave you the GHB, but your prints were the only ones found on it," Rod said.

"Yes. She gave me that bottle with a liquid in it that I thought was cologne. I don't know why her prints weren't on it. All I can say is she was wearing driving gloves when she handed it to me."

"You didn't smell it, or try some on?" Rod said. "You said it was your favorite. Since she had, as you say, gotten it from a knock-off cologne merchant, you didn't try it to see if it was in fact identical to your cologne?"

"No, I didn't. I had just bought a brand new bottle and although I thought Lena was doing something thoughtful at the time, I didn't want to accept a gift from her and had no intention of ever using it. So I put it in the back of the cabinet."

"I go to Greenbriar all the time, and unless it opened last night, I can assure you there is no cologne store in that mall called Perfect Scents. You're lying," Rod said.

"No, I'm not. I'm only telling you what she told me."

Rod shook his head. "You know, Marcus, the sad thing about being a pathological liar is that nobody ever believes you – even on the few occasions when you *might* be telling the truth."

"I *am* telling the truth. I know how important this is. I know you're going to check it out. I'd be a fool to lie about something like that. Lena did give me that bottle, and while she was in my loft, she also went to the bathroom. Who knows what else she could have left in my place!"

"Did she also go in your kitchen?" Juan asked.

"No."

"So how do you explain the GHB found there?"

"I . . . I can't."

"But regardless, according to you, it's all Lena's fault," Juan said.

"She's the one who gave me the GHB. Why don't you ask her why she did it? Why don't you ask her where she got it from? Lena is the person you should be questioning, not me."

"So you're innocent?" Claude said.

"Yes. That's what I've been telling you. I didn't do anything."

"Then if you didn't do it, that means someone is trying to frame you," Juan said.

"Yes. It could be Lena, Renae or both of them. Renae is the one with narcolepsy. Lena told me that Renae thought she was the last person to see Killian alive. Why aren't you investigating her? She's the one who probably planted the GHB in my place. God knows Lena and Renae both have

reasons to hate me. Lena is mad at me for dumping her. And as for Renae
. . . well you already know that story."

"Yes, we know it too well," Rod said. He stood up and walked aggressively
in the direction of where Marcus was seated. "You know, I've always known
you were selfish and arrogant, but you've got a lot of gall. I remember ten
years ago, how you swore up and down you had nothing to do with what
happened to Henry. All the time you knew that you had framed him. Now ten
years later, you're at it again, this time trying to blame his granddaughter, your
half sister, for something you did. You're a vicious, backstabbing liar who
will never change. You killed those three legislators as sure as I'm standing
in front of you, as sure as you're the cause of Henry being dead. Your own
grandfather, and you might as well have killed him with your bare hands.
You're going to get what you deserve, and I'm glad I'm here to see it."

Marcus was not the man to pass up a direct challenge or let an insult slide.
"You self-serving, incompetent punk!" You're so blinded by your personal
dislike for me you don't want to see or hear the truth." Marcus stood up and
was now standing face to face with Rod.

"That's the problem. I want to know the truth, but you're incapable of
telling it. You're a career liar who wouldn't know the truth if it slapped you
down."

"If you call me a liar one more time—"

"You'll do what? What will you do? I wish you would try something. I
wish you would try."

Marcus and Rod were about to come to blows when Claude stepped in
between them. "All right fellas, let's cool down. Step back and take some
deep breaths. Arguing with each other is getting us nowhere."

"Sorry, Claude," Rod said as he stepped back still glaring at Marcus. "I
apologize. That was unprofessional and uncalled for. But this thing between
Marcus and me goes back a lot of years."

"Everything is okay, just cool down," Claude said to Rod and then turned
to Marcus. "I'm going to ask that you accompany me to headquarters for
further questioning."

"Am I being arrested?" Marcus asked, struggling to calm his temper.

"Not at this point, but this would be a good time to reconsider your initial
decision and call a lawyer. If what you say is true, we can get it all sorted out
before it gets to an arrest." Claude clicked off his tape recorder and placed it
in his pocket. "Let's go, Marcus."

Marcus' head was spinning. He knew that going to GBI Headquarters for questioning would be the first step toward his arrest and incarceration. Why else would Claude suggest – not once, but twice – he get his attorney involved? Marcus knew they didn't believe him, especially Rod, who hated his guts. There would be no convincing them of his innocence unless he could prove it. And it would be impossible for him to prove anything from behind bars. He had to get away from them. But how? He knew that Rod wouldn't hesitate to shoot him if he had half the chance.

"Can I have a moment to stop by my office to call my attorney and get my coat and briefcase?" Marcus asked, stalling for time.

"Yes, I'll accompany you," Claude said. "But I don't think you'll need your briefcase."

As they took the elevator up to the second floor, Marcus observed the three men. Claude – the calm, level-headed one, Juan – the edgy, sarcastic one, and Rod – the vicious attack dog. He had to shake these three off his tail and get away so he could think. He would have to make his break before he went into his office. He had never been happier that his office was located close to the MLK Drive exit door and that his parking space was just outside by the sidewalk. Marcus' only chance would come if two of them were distracted. He could take one of them, but not all three.

They exited the elevator on the main floor. It was packed with people. It was Poor Peoples Day, and they had come in droves to let the powers that be know exactly what they thought of punitive welfare reform. Their presence, combined with the crush of school students and other groups, threatened to fill the building to capacity. The many different voices blending together in their own separate conversations produced a roar throughout the building. Marcus caught a fleeting glimpse of Lessye as she led a tour group into the rotunda and wondered how she would react to what he was about to do.

Halfway from the elevator, a security officer stopped Rod; he needed his urgent assistance with a news conference in the south wing that was getting out of hand. As Rod excused himself and hurried off in the opposite direction, Marcus said to himself, one down. A couple of seconds later Juan's cell phone rang, and he was distracted by the call. They were approaching the door to Marcus' office. Marcus took one more glance at Claude. He looked relaxed. Juan was still distracted by his cell phone conversation. Marcus took a deep breath. It was now or never. Suddenly, Marcus bolted for the side door. His sudden move surprised Claude and Juan, and it took them a moment to realize what was happening, recover their composure and start after him. A moment of surprise was all Marcus needed to make his escape. He sprinted through the MLK door, down the steps and jumped into his car. As he screeched away from the curb, the sound of their voices yelling behind him faded into the other desperate sounds of the city.

CHAPTER 50

*I*t didn't take long for Sean to realize Karin had hit pay dirt this time. The information she sold him was worth every penny he gave her. There was no doubt that Marcus was the number-one suspect in the GHB Connection. He would print Jesse's letter in its entirety and also mention the fact that during a GBI search, GHB was found in Marcus' loft. He had called Marcus for a statement, but his secretary said he could not be reached. The Governor was unavailable and his press secretary had no information and no comment. No matter. Sean's news train was pulling out of the station with or without a comment from the bronze prince, the Emperor, or his press aide. The GBI had motive, opportunity and means . . . Soon they would have Marcus. Sean prepared his newsletter for print.

———————————

"They should have found the GHB in his loft this morning," Karin said to Lena as the two had lunch at Mick's in Peachtree Center.

"I'm sure they did," Lena said. "I called Marcus' office to speak with him before coming to meet you. His secretary said he was in a meeting in the conference room on the first floor, so I went down there on my way out. I got there in time to see Claude , Rod and Juan going in to meet with him. It was good thinking to plant some in the kitchen in case the cops overlooked the bottle I gave him."

Karin nodded as she ate chicken penne pasta.

"Did you have any trouble getting into his office to plant those other items we discussed?" Lena asked.

"Not a bit. The guy who cleans that suite of offices listens to gangsta rap through earphones. I could have dropped a drum kit and he wouldn't have heard me. He's also careless. He never locks doors behind him. I planted them in Marcus' desk drawers. The GBI shouldn't have to look too hard to find them."

"My guess, then, would be that it's all over for Marcus," Lena said.

"Oh, I have something to give you." Karin took a key from her purse. "It's the key you gave me to Marcus' loft. I won't need it anymore."

Lena dropped the key in the bottom of her own purse.

"How about that issue with the pharmaceutical company?" Lena asked.

"It pays to have friends in high places who are good at making things disappear and then reappear as needed."

"Karin, I had no idea when we first met as volunteers on the Governors' campaign that we would work together so well."

"One only needs the right incentive."

Lena removed a small manilla envelope stuffed with cash from her purse and slipped it under the table to Karin. "This should add to your nest egg. Courtesy of that stupid racist, Randy Joe. He made my skin crawl but he served a purpose."

"Thank you, Lena. Are you sure you can handle everything else on your own now?"

"I'll manage. Oh, and if I were you, I might think about taking a trip abroad for awhile. Relax on a nice beach somewhere far away, see the sights."

"You must be reading my mind. I've already made arrangements. Say goodbye to Renae for me. I can't say I'm going to miss our telephone chats. She could sure stand to be less anxious."

"I'll be sure to give her your regards."

═══════════════════════════

Marcus had a lot to do and a short time to get it done. He figured it would not be long before every police officer in the city was looking for him. He had to plan. There was no way he could go back to his loft. He couldn't go to Lessye's house or to anyone else he knew. Besides, Lessye was his only friend and the only person who would care enough to help him. And he had to ditch that shiny red Lexus. He was thankful he decided to leave that bag of clothes in his trunk because they would certainly come in handy now, as would the cash in his wallet.

He turned on the radio to a local rock station. Bruce Springsteen & The E Street Band were belting out the strains of "Born to Run."

Marcus knew that chances would be better for his car if he ditched it in an area where cars were always parked. He had an idea where he could leave the car and then blend in with the crowd. He was able to make it to Greenbriar Mall without being pulled over by the police. He parked his car close to Circuit City, got the duffel bag and his leather jacket out of his trunk and went inside the mall. He ducked into the public restroom, changed from his business suit into jeans and a tee shirt, and put on one of his Atlanta ball caps. He then went to the food court and settled at a table to have a hearty meal. He used about three hundred dollars to buy some other items he needed: several more changes of underwear, tee shirts, jeans, sweat shirts, toiletries, and some snacks. He wanted to use his cell phone to call Lessye, but decided against it. She might not be at the desk when he called, and the GBI would surely put a tap on her line because of her association with him.

He asked each of the sales people who waited on him about a cologne shop called Perfect Scents. Each of them confirmed his fear and Rod's assertion that there was no shop of that kind located anywhere in the mall – one more lie Lena told that Marcus could not prove.

Marcus left Greenbriar Mall headed for the 66 Lynhurst-Greenbriar bus that would take him to the Hightower MARTA Station. The early morning rain had subsided, but the icy February wind was blowing colder, and he had to have a place to go into out of the frosty night air. Marcus needed to go somewhere the police would never find him. The last place on earth they would think to look . . .

Capitol Hill employees were buzzing about the new co-stars of the GHB Connection: Randy Joe and Tyrell. All the metro area stations had somehow gotten hold of the videotape, and there was no longer anyone on the Hill who hadn't seen it, heard about it, or formed an opinion. Everyone was truly sad that Randy Joe lost his son in that awful fire. But with this videotape issue, they didn't feel as sorry for him as they probably should have.

After Marcus' escape, Claude got tough. He immediately informed Director Shaw of the latest developments in the case, and they decided that if Marcus did not turn himself in to authorities by 5 p.m. Wednesday, they would immediately swear out a warrant for his arrest. Robert, who reluctantly agreed with them, still believed in Marcus' innocence and knew in his heart there was a reasonable explanation why he ran. He just couldn't think of one at the moment. Marcus was officially placed on indefinite suspension without pay until the matter was resolved, and the senior deputy chief of staff was taking over his duties.

Working swiftly, Claude got a wiretap order for the office and home telephones of Lessye, who was known as a friend of Marcus', as well as Lena and Renae, in case he tried to contact them. Agent Jason Grogan, who had been assigned to tail Renae, now had a new assignment: to shadow Lessye. If she and Marcus even tried to contact one another, they would have him. Claude called in several other agents who conducted a search of Marcus' office to find any clues as to where he might have run to. They failed to find any clues to his whereabouts, but what they did find was an envelope containing a door key. It didn't take them long to find out that particular key fit the front door of the apartment rented by Renae.

CHAPTER 51

After a brief meeting in the Governor's office, Juan returned to wrap up some work at the State Patrol, while Claude returned to his office to get some paper work done. He prepared the evidence concerning the Buford-Reynolds case that he would turn over to the state Attorney General the following Tuesday and checked in with the agents he sent to Peach County to tail Randy Joe. Out of respect for his loss, Claude would give Randy Joe a few days to mourn his son. But come Monday, he would have to be back in Atlanta to answer serious questions.

Claude thought about the accusations Tyrell made against Randy Joe and Nathaniel. Randy Joe clearly had the opportunity to kill the legislators, and the videotape showed he was in possession of GHB at some point. But the motive was weak. Every elected official had political enemies. Would that be a strong enough motive to kill? Also, could Randy Joe have been behind the fire that killed those children? That was too horrible for Claude to imagine, but in his line of work he had seen much worse. The initial investigation of the fire scene turned up nothing suspicious. Just an unfortunate case of candles being placed too close to highly flammable curtains. The two victims, probably asleep at the time, were killed by smoke inhalation before the fire ever touched them. There hadn't been much left to identify. As far as local investigators were concerned, the case was closed. But why would Tyrell make up a lie like that?

Then there was Marcus, who had been adamant that he didn't know anything about the GHB. But yet he ran. Innocent people don't run: They prove their innocence. Marcus said that he got it from Lena, a woman who, coincidentally, was connected with practically everyone involved in this case. And who was the person who called with the anonymous tip about the GHB? The raspy voice could have belonged to a woman. Renae made no secret of how much she hated Marcus, yet it was *her* door key that was found in *his* office. Rod was sure that Marcus was guilty, and with all the evidence against him, that was the most reasonable assumption. But there was also a lot of bad blood between Marcus and Rod, which, no matter how objective Rod tried to be, couldn't help but get in the way. Marcus had framed Henry and, according to Rod, now it was time for Marcus to get his. But the most important question that was still nagging and wouldn't let go was why Brad called Marcus to meet him at his cabin the night he died. Marcus mentioned it to Claude during their first interview. Brad couldn't have wanted to talk about Jesse's letter because that ground had already been covered. Marcus himself said that Brad told him he was going to the Governor. So why did he have a reason for Marcus to drive up to his cabin? And why would Marcus have admitted to Claude and the others that Brad was going to tell Robert his secret if he was guilty? As Marcus said, that would have been giving them motive.

Claude checked Marcus' telephone records that corroborated his story of the time Brad called. He ran checks on Brad's credit cards and found that he had indeed booked two flights, the first leaving Atlanta at 6 a.m. Monday, January 24th to Boston. From there he would fly to New York. What was the purpose of a trip that neither his secretary or his aide knew anything about?

One piece of vital information was missing in this puzzle, and Claude knew that when he found it, he would have his murderer.

———————————

"Lessye, this is serious," Rod said. "Marcus is wanted in connection with three murders. A warrant has been issued for his arrest and as of five o'clock today, he became a fugitive on the run. If you know where he is, you've got to tell me – now."

Lessye and Rod were having a quiet conversation at the tour booth. It was almost six o'clock, and her staff had long gone home for the evening. Lessye was waiting for Aunt Rose who was still on duty in the House gallery. She was desperately worried about Marcus and hoped that while she was waiting, she could find out any information about his whereabouts. Lessye prayed he would give himself up and come in safely. Now Rod was practically accusing her of knowing where he was, and his badgering was only aggravating her more.

"I don't know where Marcus is. The last time I saw him was during my lunch hour. I went to his office to find out about his talk with the Governor. He told the Governor everything. Marcus is telling the truth. He's trying to come clean."

"Then where is he?" Before she could answer he said, "Don't be fooled by his innocent victim routine. He's playing you. Like he did ten years ago when he lied about Henry. Did he tell the Governor that he had GHB in his loft? Or did he tell you for that matter, since he's so big on true confessions these days?"

"If GHB was in his loft, it was planted. Those drugs don't belong to Marcus."

"Then where did they come from?"

"I don't know. You're the police chief. It's your job to find out."

"I already know. The drugs are his, whether you choose to believe me or not. We've known each other a long time, and I would never lie to you — unlike your boyfriend."

"I don't think you would intentionally. But I also think you're letting your hatred for Marcus cloud your reasoning—"

"Like you're letting your feelings for him cloud yours. The bottle of GHB has Marcus' fingerprints on it. He wants us to believe that Lena gave him the GHB in a cologne bottle. Some smaller bottles were also found. His excuse is that Renae must have planted them."

"Then why aren't you investigating that theory? Lena is sneaky and Renae has been acting stranger than usual lately."

"Come on. No one is more sneaky than Marcus. He's still lying and scapegoating. He's guilty – as guilty as he was when he framed Henry. If he could do something like that to his own grandfather, he's capable of anything. I'm not talking to you as a police officer. I'm pleading with you as a friend. I don't enjoy saying things that hurt you, and I don't want you to get hurt trying to protect Marcus. Open your eyes. Don't allow this man to drag you down in the mud with him. Because if you help him in any way and the GBI finds out, my hands are going to be tied. I won't be able to help you. You could lose your job and face criminal charges and do some serious time."

Although Rod's verbal assault was slamming against her nerves, she couldn't help but appreciate his concern. Rod was a dear friend, but Marcus was the man she loved, and she was going to defend him.

"We don't see Marcus the same way," Lessye said. "I don't think we ever will. I told Marcus that although you might not like him, you would always be fair. I believed that then, and I believe it now. You're a good police chief, one of the best. But for once, please look at Marcus as objectively as you would look at anyone else. Forget about the baggage between you and look at the facts of *this* case. I believe someone *is* trying to frame Marcus. I don't know who. But I'll tell you right now, and you can run and tell anybody you want to: If I can help Marcus find out who is doing this to him, I will. You know yourself that both Lena and especially Renae have a reason to dislike him. And if there is any chance that they could be trying to frame him, it's your duty as a law enforcement officer to find out. You can't let your hatred cause an innocent man to lose his freedom. I'm sure if you ask your granddad, he'd tell you the same thing. You owe it to his legacy and your badge. But most importantly you owe it to yourself, because deep down you know what's right and what's wrong. That's one of the reasons I love you so much."

"You know I love you, too. And I understand your points. But I'm also pleading with you to think hard about what I said." With that, Rod walked away.

A few minutes later Lessye's cell phone rang. She answered in hopes that it would be Marcus, or some news about him.

"Hello."

It was Tanya. "Hey. Where are you?"

"I'm still at the tour booth waiting for Aunt Rose and hoping to hear from Marcus."

"Can you drop by here before you leave? My car is in the shop and Kevin is tied up in a meeting. I might need to bum a ride home with you and Aunt Rose."

"Why can't you meet us over here?"

"Cause I don't want to run into any of my representatives, and I have something to show you."

"Okay. I'm on my way," Lessye said, hoping that Marcus would call her on her cell or at home later that evening. Lessye grabbed her belongings and headed in the direction of the Mitchell Street exit door. Agent Grogan kept a respectable distance behind her while talking quietly into a radio transmitter.

"It's all right," he said as he watched her approach the front door of the LOB, "she's only going in the Legislative Office Building."

———————

The suite was deserted except for Tanya, who was changing out of her walking shoes when Lessye walked through the door. All of her representatives were either still at the Capitol or gone for the day, and Amber left during their daily walk around the Capitol building complaining of a headache and slight fever.

"Are you ready? The House was adjourning as I was on my way over, and I don't want Aunt Rose to have to wait long. What do you have to show me?"

"I didn't call you because I needed a ride," Tanya whispered as she got up and locked the front door of the suite behind Lessye. "I called you because I have some information. Come with me."

Lessye dropped her purse and jacket on a chair and followed Tanya down the hall of the suite to Brad's old office, the one Tanya and Amber were now using as their private lounge. "What's up?" Lessye asked.

"You'll see." Tanya turned the key in the lock and opened the door. There, seated on the couch with a jacket and duffel bag beside him, was Marcus.

CHAPTER 52

$\mathcal{C}$ laude went to the Capitol early Thursday morning and the first thing on his agenda was a meeting with Lena in the Speaker's conference room where they could talk privately.

"Lena, during an interview with Marcus yesterday, he told me that you visited him on Sunday, February 6 at approximately nine in the evening. He said that at that time, you gave him a bottle of cologne that you told him was Mystique. Is that true?"

"It is true that I gave him a bottle of Mystique cologne, but I didn't go to see him on Sunday the sixth. I went to Macon to visit with my aunt on the sixth of February."

"Did you talk with Marcus anytime that day?"

"Yes. I called him around eight that evening to let him know I was still with my aunt in Macon and couldn't come over that night like he wanted me to. He had been pressing me to find out who gave him a copy of a letter from someone named Jesse Higgins. I couldn't help him because I didn't know."

"He says you told him Renae sent it."

She shook her head. "That's not true. I would never have told him that. Renae is a good friend."

"The same good friend who despises Marcus."

"From what I understand, she has good reason to dislike him. But she would have had to have access to that letter to send it to Marcus, and I certainly didn't give her a copy. Neither would Brad. We were the only ones who opened his mail."

Claude regarded her carefully. "When did you give Marcus the cologne?"

"I gave it to him at his office. It was about a week before Valentine's Day. It was an early present. I picked up the cologne for him at the Lenox Macy's and had them tie a red bow around it in gift wrap. I think I kept the sales receipt, if you want to see it."

"That won't be necessary, but let me get this straight. Marcus told me that the bottle of cologne you gave him came from a shop called . . ." Claude referred to his notes, "The shop is called Perfect Scents in Greenbriar Mall. They duplicate colognes. He said it came in a special black unlabeled keepsake bottle."

"I don't have a clue what he's talking about. I didn't even know there was a shop called Perfect Scents in Greenbriar Mall. Mystique comes in a royal blue bottle with the name engraved in gold lettering. That's what I gave Marcus."

Claude scribbled into his note pad. "Now you're sure you did not visit Marcus on the sixth of February and the bottle of cologne you gave him was royal blue, not black?"

"Yes. I swear it. Do you have any more questions for me, because I need to get to work."

"No. That's all for now. Thank you for your time."

As Lena got up to return to the reception area of the Speaker's office, Claude made a note to himself to call the nursing home in Macon. He would double check if this place called Perfect Scents existed. Rod had been sure it didn't. Marcus swore that was the line Lena gave him. Claude was duty bound to check it out for himself. One of them, Marcus or Lena, is lying, Claude thought to himself, as he closed his pad. The obvious choice would be Marcus. But Claude had not come this far going with obvious choices.

Before leaving the Capitol, he stopped by Marcus' office to give it another look through. It didn't take him long to find a royal blue bottle of Mystique cologne neatly tied with a bright red ribbon in the bottom drawer of Marcus' desk. He sat down at Marcus' desk, took out his pad and dialed the number of the nursing home in Macon, again speaking with the administrator who transferred him to the head nurse on duty the day in question. After checking her files she found that Lena had signed in to see her aunt at three o'clock on Sunday the sixth and didn't sign out until nine-thirty that evening. According to the nurse, several people including the nurse saw her sitting with the old lady. So she could not have been in two places at one time.

Claude called information to find a number for Perfect Scents. There was no phone number listed for a shop in Greenbriar or anywhere in metro Atlanta. He also contacted the manager of the mall who assured him he could recite by heart every vendor that ever rented a space in the mall and confirmed that Perfect Scents had never been one of them.

Claude went to the Lenox Macy's and dropped by the men's cologne counter. The neatly dressed young man at the counter had no trouble remembering Lena from the description Claude gave.

"Sure I remember her. The finest chick to come in here for awhile. Long brown hair, tight figure, beautiful eyes. Said she was buying a present for a special friend and asked me about gift wrap. All I could do was wish I was him. What a lucky guy."

"Yeah, lucky guy," Claude had said.

So It looked like Lena *had* been the one telling the truth.

But one question nagged on: Why would a man as smart as Marcus make up a lie that could be so easily disproved?

On his way to Rod's office, Claude stopped by the Capitol snack bar and ran into Gus, who was buying a bottle of orange juice. Claude had heard the legend of Gus through the years, and figured that a person as seasoned as Gus could have some good tidbits of information he could use in his investigation. After all, Gus gave Rod the original tip about the GHB, and Rod had introduced Claude to Gus on one of his previous visits to the Capitol. Gus was an old timer on the Hill who knew practically everything that was going on. Maybe Claude could glean some objective information from him about Marcus. Old Gus seemed like a good-natured guy who couldn't hold a grudge if he wanted to.

As was Gus' fashion, it was he who first approached Claude to say hello and ask him about the case.

"Any word on Marcus?"

"Unfortunately, nothing yet," Claude said.

"I heard on the news this morning that an APB was out on him. And that's not the half of it; have you seen the *Capitol Reporter*?"

"No. Why?"

"I have a copy here in my pocket." Gus took the newsletter from his inside pocket, unfolded it and handed it to Claude. The whole newsletter was dedicated to the GHB Connection, and on the front page was a copy of Jesse's letter in its entirety. There was also mention of the fact that investigators found substantial amounts of GHB in Marcus' loft.

"Where did he get all this information?" Claude said. He scanned the newsletter and handed it back to Gus. Since he got rid of Karin, he was almost sure there were no more leaks in the department. But Sean was still getting inside information.

"Sean gets more news than I can, and that's saying something," Gus said as he folded the newsletter, put it back in his pocket, then opened his bottle of juice and swigged it down.

"It's not good for the investigation for all this evidence to get leaked to the media," Claude said. "All it can do is cause confusion and hurt the case."

"I agree. Sometimes it's best to keep some things to yourself. I think that's a lesson Sean has never learned. Everyone on the Hill is talking about this newsletter and Marcus, that is when they're not talking about Randy Joe and Tyrell. It's a wonder any work is getting done around here. Everyone seems to have formed their own opinion."

"Which is?"

"The general consensus is, Marcus should go down whether he's guilty or not. A lot of people are still around who remember that incident with Henry. And although some can't visualize him killing the legislators, they still want him to pay for Henry, big time."

"Gus, you've been around the Capitol a long time. You've got a lot of wisdom and insight about people. In your opinion, what do you think about this mess?"

"I'm willing to bet my paycheck that Randy Joe and Tyrell are guilty. I've known those boys for years, and believe me when I tell you they're capable of anything. I overheard an odd conversation between them."

"Oh?" Claude asked. Rod had briefly filled him in by phone, but didn't go into much detail. There was nothing like getting it first-hand. "What were they talking about?"

"Now, I'm not trying to start anything or spread any rumors, but it's only my duty to pull your coat tail," Gus said. "Randy Joe was talking about putting an end to a relationship his son was in. It was last Thursday right before the Natural Resources and Environment Committee meeting. He was referring to something that was supposed to be done this week. He said Nathaniel was handling the details. Randy Joe's exact words were, 'I don't care who her daddy is. If that tramp thinks she's going to derail my boy's future, she's got another thought coming.' They didn't mention the girl's name. And it wasn't until later that I found out that Ronnie Reynolds was in a relationship with Barry Layton's daughter, Tamika. I believe Randy Joe arranged to set that fire that killed his son and Tamika in Fort Valley. I don't have any real proof other than what I overheard, but I know what Randy Joe is capable of. He's rotten to the core."

Claude's mind flashed back to his conversation with Rod about the fire and what Tyrell revealed during the interrogation. Maybe this theory could stand some checking into. He would assign some agents to check it out.

"What do you think about Marcus?"

"I think he's ambitious. He can also be ruthless when it comes to politics. But I don't believe he's a murderer. My personal opinion is that Marcus is too smart to ever do anything that would make him wind up in prison. He wouldn't survive in prison one week without his fancy designer suits and Italian shoes. Can you see him scraping around the lock up in that ragged orange jumpsuit and prison-issue flip flops? He'd have a nervous breakdown," Gus said and chuckled.

"It is a funny thought," Claude said and smiled. "Have you had much contact with him over the years?"

"Only on a professional level. Somehow I've managed to stay off his hit list. He never seemed to have a problem with me. I guess because I'm an old man, he would let me get away with more than he would most people. He never saw me as a threat. I know how to keep my nose clean."

"I'm sure you do." Claude couldn't help but smile.

"Whenever I've needed Robert's ear through the years, Marcus has made it happen. I remember when Marcus first came to the Capitol; he was always smart and sure of himself. Sometimes when you're overly aggressive, you make a lot of enemies just because. But Marcus didn't care as long as he got what he wanted. I always thought there was something fishy about the Perkins incident, because I knew Henry. He was a good man. Everything they say he stole or tampered with was found in his desk drawer. I don't know of many thieves who would take money and not spend a dime of it. There was no proof Marcus rigged a setup until now. But it's still hard to believe he would frame his own grandfather." Gus sighed.

"What do you know about Marcus and Lena?"

"That attractive aide who used to work for Brad? The one who's in the Speaker's office now?"

"Yes. That's the one."

"I know she had a thing for him. She used to stay in and out of his office so much, it needed a revolving door. Then suddenly that was over. I hear he's seeing that pretty girl at the tour booth, Lessye. She's a sweet thing. She'll be good for Marcus, smooth the rough edge off him. That is, if you ever find him. Although Rod wouldn't agree with me on that. He and Marcus don't get along."

"I've already found that out. How about Lena? Did you think she was good for him?"

Gus chuckled. "Let's put it this way. That's the kind of woman that every boy's mother warns him to not just walk, but run away from. Lena is fast business and an opportunist to boot. Give her the opportunity, and she'll sleep with anybody. Did you know she had a thing going with Randy Joe?"

"I've heard the rumors."

"Those aren't rumors. I've seen them together. Thank goodness, she had the good sense not to let him talk her into going to his hotel suite, because if she had, she would probably be among those other unfortunate girls spread eagle on that videotape."

"So she dropped Marcus for Randy Joe?"

"She didn't drop Marcus. It was the other way around. Marcus – as the young people say these days – kicked her to the curb."

"Say what?"

"Hey, there's no law against an old geezer keeping up with the times is it?"

"Not at all," Claude said and laughed.

"Now, getting back to Marcus and Lena. If you had seen how she was pushing him to let her come over to his place about a couple of weeks back, you'd know what I mean."

"When was this?"

Gus got the serious expression on his face that always settled there when he was deep in thought processing information.

"Now I remember. It will be two weeks ago tomorrow. They were standing in front of the Speaker's office. He was trying to get her to tell him something about a note he was sent. But she told him she wouldn't unless she could come to his place. I heard Marcus mention Jesse Higgins' name."

"Do you remember what day she wanted to meet him?"

"Yes. She told him she would come to his place on the following Sunday. She wouldn't even give him the time. Told him to be available all day. She would call him one time at home and if he wasn't there he could forget it. He was upset with her because I don't think he wanted her in his place. But he agreed. I could tell she was getting on his nerves, especially when she pulled out that mirror and started checking her makeup and dropped a key on the floor. She waited for him to bend down and pick it up. I thought that was a hoot. Chivalry ain't dead and buried yet."

"How do you know it was a key she dropped?" Claude asked.

"Because Marcus told her something smart like if she kept her keys on a keyring like other people, she could keep up with them better. She said something back smart to him and told him to drop it in her hand bag.

"You're sure it was a key?"

"I'm positive. It fell out of her bag when she pulled out a tissue to dab at her face."

"And you didn't see her touch this key?"

"No. She opened her purse and told him to drop it in."

"Thank you, Gus. You've been helpful."

"Anytime."

Claude left Gus and went directly to Rod's office. "Hey, Rod. You got a minute?"

"Sure, Claude. What's up? Any word on Marcus?"

"Not yet. He's still on the run, but we'll track him down. Every law enforcement agency in the area is on alert. Marcus won't get far," Claude said, with the confidence of a seasoned lawman as he walked in and took a seat across from Rod.

"I had a conversation with your friend, Gus, in the snack bar," Claude said. "We talked about his theory that Randy Joe arranged the fire that killed his son and Tamika in Fort Valley."

"I spoke with the arson investigator in Peach County," Rod said. "He told me as far as he could determine, there was no sign of foul play, so they're closing the case."

"They may not have found any evidence of foul play, but Gus is positive about his theory. And in light of the other information we now know on Randy Joe, anything could be possible. During my interrogation of Tyrell, he told me that Randy Joe conspired with Nathaniel, who was the one who handled it. I think it deserves further checking into. I'm going to ask a couple of our arson specialists to closely examine that apartment scene and question some of the neighbors. Maybe they'll find something the local boys missed."

"That's a good idea."

"I met with Lena this morning, and she refuted Marcus' story. She said she went to Macon to visit her aunt the Sunday in question. Lena said she gave him a royal blue bottle of Mystique with a red bow tied around it, at the office, not a black one, at his loft. She said she's never heard of a shop call Perfect Scents and nobody else has either. I went to Marcus' office after I met with her and sure enough I found the bottle of cologne she said she gave to him. I confirmed she bought it from Macy's at Lenox. I called the nursing home in Macon. Lena's story checks out. According to the head nurse, she was there from three until nine-thirty."

"What a shock," Rod said. "I knew he was lying. That man is incapable of telling the truth."

"I'm not so sure."

"You're not so sure . . . You just told me that Lena's story checked out."

"I know. But what's bothering me is Marcus had to know we would talk with Lena. He had to know we would check out that bogus cologne shop. He's no idiot. Marcus is a smart guy. He wouldn't have been stupid enough to make up a lie that could be that readily disproved."

"Take it from one who knows. Marcus is arrogant and pathological. Lies come as easy to him as that fake name he's using now. Marcus is our murderer . . . and the sooner we find him, the better. Personally, I can't wait to slap some cuffs on him."

"I know you can't. I admit it looks bad for Marcus. I was almost ready to believe the Lena version of the story until I talked with Gus who told me that he overheard a conversation between Marcus and Lena outside the Speaker's office the Friday before the sixth. He said Marcus was trying to get some information from her about a note he received. Marcus mentioned Jesse's name. She said she would only tell him if he let her come over the following Sunday. Gus said she refused to give Marcus a time. So he had no choice but to wait for her. Lena told me it was Marcus who asked her to come to his loft, but Gus overheard her pressing Marcus to let her come to his place."

Rod pushed back from his desk, folded his arms across his chest and thought for a moment. "I've never known Gus to get his facts wrong. I have to admit that does sound consistent with what Marcus told us–"

"And that's not all Gus said. He told me that during the conversation, Lena dropped a key. She waited for Marcus to pick it up. And get this, she didn't take it with her fingers. She told him to drop in her purse."

"Is Gus sure it was a key?"

"He's positive."

"Are you thinking the same thing I am?"

"Yes. There might be something to Marcus' theory about being framed after all. Marcus told us he received Jesse's letter anonymously. I received an anonymous copy also. Marcus said Lena told him that Renae sent him the copy that she got off the desk of Brad's secretary. But the secretary did not open his mail. If what he says is true, then Lena lied to Marcus about that letter. Now she told me that there was no way Renae had access to that letter, but I think that Lena has not been as truthful as she would like me to believe. I believe that the key that Lena dropped that Friday while talking to Marcus was a key she wanted his fingerprints on – Renae's key. Also that anonymous tip about the GHB in Marcus' loft is suspicious. Marcus' fingerprints were all over the cologne bottle, but none were found on the box containing the smaller bottles or any of the individual bottles. There was not one piece of physical evidence at any of those crash scenes linking Marcus to the crimes."

"But Lena still couldn't be in two places at one time," Rod said. "If she was in Macon with her aunt until nine-thirty, how could she be walking in Marcus' front door a half hour earlier?"

"She could if she had help. Somebody could have posed as Lena at that nursing home. I don't doubt that Lena was there to sign in, but somebody else could have signed her out. Someone she sneaked into the home and left there sitting with the aunt while she kept her date with Marcus in Atlanta." Claude thought for a moment. "Let me run this by you. What's the single most damaging piece of evidence against Marcus in connection with the murders?"

"Besides the GHB?"

"Including the GHB."

"That would have to be Jesse's letter."

"Exactly. That letter gives Marcus a motive stronger than any other suspect in this case. Somebody who had it in for Marcus, who knew his history could have easily set him up. In each of those accidents, an empty fifth bottle of bourbon was found, almost re-creating Henry's death. Marcus had a strong connection to all three of those dead legislators. They were holding this Henry issue over his head."

"That's a good theory. But it still doesn't explain why Marcus ran. If he is innocent, which I still find it difficult to believe, he should have stayed here to clear himself."

"With all the evidence against him, would you believe him no matter what he said?"

Rod shrugged his shoulders but didn't answer.

"I didn't think so. You know, I can't stop wondering why Brad wanted Marcus to come to his cabin the Sunday he died. I truly believe that if and when we find out what was so urgent that Brad wanted to tell him, we will have our murderer."

CHAPTER 53

*T*anya was busy at work when Lessye arrived in her suite Thursday morning. Amber had called in sick with the flu and would be out until next week. Tanya was sorry Amber was ill, but it couldn't have been better timing. With Amber out, Tanya didn't have to worry about her assistant being involved in this situation, which, before it was over, would probably land her and Lessye in the slammer.

The legislature had not yet adjourned for lunch and the suite was quiet and deserted. Tanya was so thankful they had not told Clarice or Renae about their secret lounge. She gave Lessye the key to open the door, while she remained at her desk.

When Lessye went in to see Marcus, he was reclining on the couch. He got up the moment she came in and locked the door behind her. Lessye had not stayed long enough to do much talking with Marcus the previous evening because Aunt Rose was waiting, and it might look suspicious if she stayed in the LOB too long that late in the evening. Seeing Marcus and knowing he was safe had been enough for her. They had agreed that they would not try to reach each other by phone and before leaving, Tanya placed a sign on the door instructing the cleaning crew that the office was vacant, and they should not clean it. Lessye knew that Tanya maintained an excellent rapport with the LOB housekeeping staff and although they did an exemplary job, she also knew they certainly didn't mind having a lighter load.

"Are you all right?" Lessye asked, dropping her purse and tote bag on the couch. She hugged him tightly and kissed him on the lips.

"I am now," he said. "This is what I needed, you in my arms."

"Are you hungry? I brought you some food from home."

"Oh Baby, that sounds good. But I'm still stuffed from this morning. Tanya went upstairs and got me a big breakfast. I'm good to go right now. I'm going to save this feast for dinner. All I want right now is you," he said, holding on to her like he would never let her go.

They sat down together as close as they could and spoke quietly. "How did you get in here without being seen? Everyone is looking for you."

"I know. I heard they issued a warrant yesterday, but I was already in this building by then – hiding in the maintenance closet. When I first left, I drove out to Greenbriar and ditched my car in the parking lot. I caught the bus to the Hightower MARTA Station and took the train to the Georgia State Station."

"How did you get in the LOB without being seen by the guards or the cameras?"

"A lot of luck and good timing, especially with all the heightened security. I sneaked in the back way through the courtyard while the guard was distracted by a delivery driver. Somebody's always going in and out of the key card access doors closest to the snack bar. I had on my baseball cap and kept my head down so no one would recognize me and took the steps up. When I got to the fifth floor card key access door, I managed to duck in behind a couple of legislative aides. The next hurdle was making sure everyone on this end of the hall, especially Renae, was gone before I came to Tanya's suite."

"Back on the Hill *is* probably the last place they would expect you to come."

"That's what I was thinking. I asked Tanya to help me get a message to you. She had come back in from walking. I think she felt sorry for me. I know I had to be looking desperate and crazy. She practically slung me back here in this office and then called you. She hasn't turned me in yet, so I guess she's one other person who believes in my innocence . . . that is if you still do."

"I know you're innocent," Lessye said.

"I know by now you've heard that they found GHB in my loft."

"Yes. It was on the front page of the latest *Capitol Reporter* – right beside the infamous Jesse Higgins letter." Lessye took a copy of the newsletter from her purse and showed it to Marcus, who stared at the photo of himself looking up from the page before scanning the article.

"Well it's not a secret anymore, is it? All my dirty deeds have come back to slap me in the face. Now I know how Henry must have felt when I framed him. Now I know how it feels to be wrongly accused. Those drugs in my loft were the nails in the coffin. I've resigned myself to the fact that I'm going down for this. But Lessye, whatever happens to me, I want you to know that those drugs are not mine. Please believe me."

Lessye took both of his hands tightly in hers. "I believe you. I told you before, I know you're innocent. And don't be discouraged, we're going to prove it. But first, you've got to turn yourself in. The longer you hide, the more everyone else is going to believe you're guilty."

"Like your friend, Rod. He's probably already chosen my prison EF number and personally sewn it on my cell block uniform. No, baby, I can't turn myself in until I have some evidence that can prove my innocence, especially since nobody but you and maybe Tanya are going to take my word for it."

"Regardless of what Rod believes, he doesn't have the last word."

"But he's got a lot of influence on those who do. Has he been sweating you about me?"

"He thinks I know where you are."

"You've got to be careful. Don't come over here anymore. If Rod, Claude or any law enforcement officer finds out you know where I'm hiding, you're going to be in a lot of trouble. I shouldn't have put you and Tanya in this position, but I needed to see you so bad. I'm going to be out of here tonight."

"No! Where will you go? And who's going to help you prove your innocence? You can't make any calls or do the leg work without getting caught. Right now, this is the safest place for you. Think about it, you're not running at all. You were back in this state office building by the time they swore out that warrant for your arrest. So technically you have turned yourself back in to the state. And we agree this is the last place that anyone would think to look for you. We can use this room to make our plans and see where we go from here. Promise me you won't leave. Promise me when you leave here, it will only be if you are exonerated or turning yourself in. Promise me."

"I love the way your mind works. Okay. I promise you. Thank goodness there are no cameras on the halls and in the suites, so getting to the bathroom won't be a problem in the early mornings and evenings as long as I avoid the security guards on their rounds. And Tanya told me that if I need to use the restroom during the day, I could slip out through the end office next door to this one. The representative who uses that office rarely comes over to the LOB. It leads to a conference room and an old empty copy room that opens onto the hallway. I better make sure I don't bump into Renae or anyone else who knows me."

"What about your car? Give me your keys and I'll get it from Greenbriar and take it home and put it in my garage."

"No. It's much too dangerous. The cops are looking for my car. If you have it, they can make a case that I've contacted you and you know where I am. I'm not worried about the car. It'll be okay. But if anything bad happened to you, I couldn't take it."

As they gazed at one another, talked and kissed tenderly, the time slid by.

"Can I get you anything before I leave?" Lessye asked, rising to go.

"I only want to feel you close to me one more time." Marcus took Lessye in his arms once again and held and kissed her gently. "You're everything to me, Lessye, everything."

━━━━━━━━━━━━━━━

Rod stopped by the tour booth a couple of times looking for Lessye. He intended to try again to convince her to turn Marcus in if she knew where he was. And Rod was almost positive she did.

On his third approach, he asked the part-time guide where she was.

"She took an early lunch. Left at eleven-thirty. I think she went to the LOB. She should be back by one-thirty," Jon said.

"A two-hour lunch during the session?"

"Another perk of being the boss."

"Thanks, Jon. Tell her I stopped by. I'll drop by again later." On the way back to his office Rod walked over to the Mitchell Street exit where he ran into Agent Grogan, who had been assigned to shadow Lessye to see if she would lead them to Marcus. As a long-time friend of Lessye's, Rod was uncomfortable with sneaking behind her back and invading her privacy with tails and phone taps. But as police chief, he knew it was the best, if not only, way of finding Marcus. Unfortunately, sometimes in his line of work, duty came before friendship.

"What's happening, Jason? You keeping an eye on Lessye?"

"Yes. But to tell the truth your girl is not too much more exciting than Renae so far. She's over at the LOB. She sure had a pep in her step getting over there this morning."

"Her best friend works over there. Maybe they had some current gossip. Check you later."

As Rod took the steps down to the first floor, he thought to himself that as long as he could remember, Lessye had taken her lunch break at exactly twelve noon – unless there was an emergency. Sometimes she might be a few minutes late, but never had she taken a two-hour lunch during the legislative session.

CHAPTER 54

*O*n Friday, Lessye again spent a two-hour lunch sitting and talking with Marcus, and along with Tanya, brainstorming a plan to clear him. Between provisions supplied by Lessye and Tanya, Marcus had more than enough food for the weekend. Lessye desperately wanted to visit him on Saturday and Sunday, but both Tanya and Marcus warned her against it, stressing the importance of her not doing anything out of the ordinary to raise suspicions.

Marcus told them about the GBI finding GHB in the cologne bottle Lena gave to him, and the lie she told him about it being his favorite cologne and where she purchased it. He also shared what Lena told him about Renae and Jesse's letter and his suspicions about Renae working with Lena to frame him by planting more GHB in his loft.

Lessye planned to spend the weekend coming up with ideas to help Marcus clear his name and decided the first step would be talking to Lena and Renae to see if she could convince them to tell the truth about what they knew. Tanya volunteered to research GHB and if any pharmaceutical companies in the Atlanta area had conducted GHB drug studies within the past year, and if they had, whether Renae was a participant in any of them. Tanya told them that Renae had a weak stomach and remembered Renae saying that she hoped she didn't get real sick and have to take any drugs because every drug she had ever taken, with the exception of aspirin, had made her so sick she had to stop. They concluded that if Renae had ever been prescribed GHB she probably still had a considerable amount of it because she never used it.

When Tanya left them to get back to work, Lessye and Marcus shared their last few minutes together locked in each other's arms.

When Lessye left Tanya's suite after lunch, she ran into Renae, who was on her way back from the break room.

"Hey, Lessye. Why don't you and Tanya go to the break room anymore? You stay closed up in Tanya's suite by yourselves."

Lessye's antenna went up. Renae was fishing for something. She had to be on her guard not to let anything slip about Marcus. "I've been going through some personal issues lately, and Tanya's been encouraging me with her good pep talks."

"I guess you're worried about your friend, Marcus. I know you're dating. Has he tried to contact you?"

"Marcus hasn't called me," Lessye said, stretching the truth. "What would make you think a thing like that?"

"You two seem close, that's all. He's going to be caught, you know. And when he is, he's going to prison for murder."

"Not if he's innocent. And he is innocent."

"Marcus is anything but innocent. He made his career off the back and blood of my granddaddy. Thanks to Sean, everyone knows what a dog he is. Take some advice from me, you're too good for him, and you're only going to get your heart broken if you don't cut Marcus loose. There is one consolation. When he goes to prison, you won't have any choice but to cut him loose."

Lessye didn't miss the smug look on her face and determination in her voice. "You sound happy about the possibility of Marcus going to prison . . . and sure of it. You seem to know more than the agent investigating the case. How can you be so sure Marcus is guilty?"

"Because of what he did to my granddaddy! Low down people always get what they deserve."

"Don't you mean *our* granddaddy, as in yours and Marcus'? Marcus is your half brother. Your blood."

"That's a lie! You believe that stupid Jesse Higgins theory?"

"What I believe has nothing to do with Jesse Higgins. Marcus told me everything."

"I don't care what he told you! It's another one of his lies! If it was true, my grandparents would have told me. My mother only had one child, me!"

"Renae, please calm down. I didn't mean to upset you."

"You didn't, and I'm sorry I yelled at you. I have to get back to my suite," Renae said quickly, and she was gone before Lessye could say another word.

As Lessye looked behind her, she realized that Renae was in some heavy denial, and she also knew more about this mess than she was telling. Lessye would go to Renae's apartment this weekend. But first she would have to think about how she would approach Renae. Lessye knew she had to handle her carefully, and she couldn't afford to blow it because Renae was probably the one person who hated Marcus most and the one person who held the key to his innocence.

CHAPTER 55

*R*andy Joe was in the middle of a nightmare. But the only difference between this and most nightmares was that he was not going to wake up. Early Wednesday morning, he received the call from home that Ronnie had been killed in a fire – a fire that he was responsible for. He had warned Nathaniel to make sure his son was nowhere around when they torched that place. But when the deal went down, his son had been there, and now he was gone. All Randy Joe's hopes and dreams for his precious boy had been ravaged by that vicious fire.

When he arrived home, the scene had been heartbreaking. The only time his other two children, Kelley and Tim, weren't crying hysterically was when they were tossing and turning in a fitful sleep. And Miss Pearl was in such a terrible state of shock, Randy Joe feared she might never fully recover. She managed to utter that the last she heard from Ronnie was when he came home Tuesday night and yelled that a package had been delivered for her. She was on the phone discussing plans for an upcoming bridge club meeting. By the time she hung up, Ronnie was gone again and several hours later, she received the news about the fire.

Randy Joe immediately guessed that the package must have been that cursed videotape. Randy Joe searched for it but didn't find it. Had Ronnie taken it with him when he left? Randy Joe prayed that the sordid videotape was not the last image of him his son took to his grave.

The infamous videotape had slithered its way to televisions in his district. Randy Joe could tell by the knowing stares that even pity at the loss of Ronnie could not conceal. But no one in this gentile community, adhering to carefully written rules of etiquette and civility, would dare utter an unkind word about it at a time like this – not before he said goodbye to his son. And surely not in front of Miss Pearl – no matter how many unimaginable cruelties they whispered behind their backs.

Miss Pearl was so caught up in her grief, she had not yet seen it. How could he ever explain this mess? How could he explain the GBI agents in the unmarked Crown Victoria who had shadowed him and his house since Wednesday?

Expressions of sympathy poured in from throughout the state, and the kitchen was flooded with food and beverages brought by family and friends. The largest floral arrangements had been from Nathaniel and the CNAA, none of whom dared show their faces at the memorial service – Nathaniel out of fear, and the CNAA out of the need to distance themselves from an embarrassing former member. And of course, Tyrell was nowhere to be found. He was probably somewhere spilling his guts to reduce his potential prison time. Some friend that sour drunk turned out to be, Randy Joe thought bitterly.

The grave side memorial service for his son on Friday had been agonizing, not only because his son was gone, but because his mother-in-law, the stately society doyenne, Margaret Blair Richmond, would not stop glaring at him. Ever since she and her son, Kell, arrived, her razor sharp eyes had drilled accusatory holes into him. It was obvious she blamed him for what happened to Ronnie, and she didn't take long to let him know it.

Late that night after all their neighbors were gone and what was left of his family had been poured into bed, Randy Joe went downstairs to his den to make a stiff drink and do some thinking. His mother-in-law was waiting for him.

"I knew I could depend on you to stumble in here sooner or later to get plastered," Margaret said. She had already finished her first drink and was working on her second. But that glass of liquor in no way impaired her senses or her tongue.

Ignoring his mother-in-law, Randy Joe strode over to the bar, poured himself a glass full of straight bourbon and plopped down in his favorite reclining chair. This den was his domain, his throne room, his refuge. He would not allow anyone, even his tough old bird of a mother-in-law, to ruin it for him.

"Randy, I've never been one to bite my tongue. I speak my mind."

Randy Joe remained quiet, sipping his drink and staring into space.

"You know I've never liked you. I knew the first time that Kell brought you through our front door that you would one day be the downfall of my family. I detested your dreadful notions about people who were not exactly like you. When you married my daughter against my wishes, I gave you the benefit of the doubt. I knew you were all wrong for my girl. I knew she could do much better. But she loved you, and you were Kell's friend. So to keep peace in the family, I tolerated you. But I always knew that you were a terrible accident waiting to happen. And now to my horror, it has."

Randy Joe rolled his glassy green eyes in her direction. "Why don't you hurry up and get to the point and leave me alone." He was sick and tired of hearing her voice scratching against his eardrums like fingernails on a chalk board. He wanted so badly to bust her in the mouth with his fist, but he was already in enough trouble. Besides, knowing his mother-in-law, she might even get the jump on him and beat his brains out.

"Randy, I've seen news reports about the videotape." Margaret was the only person who refused to call him Randy Joe, referring to him by the first of his mismatched names.

"What are you babbling about, old woman? Why don't you finish your drink upstairs?" Randy Joe said, hoping to intimidate her.

Margaret got up from the sofa and advanced in his direction with a force and speed that startled Randy Joe. Her eyes impaled him, and she looked like she was ready to snatch his throat out with her bare hands.

"Randy, you must have forgotten who you're talking to. You might have your sniveling cronies scared to breathe hard in your direction, but I guarantee you it doesn't work with me. I'm talking about the videotape that shows you and Tyrell forcing yourselves on girls young enough to be your children after drugging them. You are nasty and despicable. I'm going to make sure that Pearl leaves this sorry excuse of a marriage for good. If it takes my last breath." She paced back and forth with her hands on her narrow hips. "Randy Reynolds the wealthy peach planter and businessman, the prominent state legislator, the pillar of the community, the church-going man who never misses a Sunday. What a farce."

"You're the most insensitive person I've ever known. I've lost my son, and you can't wait to break up the rest of my family. You can't wait to pounce on me with your venom. Don't you have any compassion?"

"Save the drama. You're no victim. I have compassion for those who deserve it. And you're not one of them. I also have discernment. I watched you at that memorial service. You didn't look sad, you looked guilty and scared. Ronnie was dating a black girl, I understand. I know that didn't sit well with you because you're one of the most hateful people I've ever met. I don't think you would have any compunction about killing someone's child if it was in your best interest and you figured you wouldn't get caught. That so-called *accidental* fire at her apartment seems strange."

"What are you saying!?"

Her piercing blue eyes met his glassy green stare without flinching. "I know exactly what you're capable of. You've done some evil things through the years. But if I find out that you had anything remotely to do with the death of my grandson and his girlfriend, I will do all I can to help her people get the information they need to bring you to trial and get you convicted. But don't you worry about spending one day in prison. I will find a way to kill you myself long before that happens. This is one old lady who won't mind spending the rest of her life behind bars as long as you're swallowing dirt."

The color sliding from his face, Randy Joe knew that Margaret meant every single word she said.

CHAPTER 56

$\mathcal{L}$essye was emotionally drained, and by Saturday morning, the weariness she felt was beginning to show. She resolved to remain strong to help Marcus prove his innocence. Before going home Friday, she made several unsuccessful attempts to catch up with Lena. Afterwards, she darted over to Tanya's to see Marcus one last time before the weekend. She picked up copies of the research material on GHB Tanya downloaded from the Internet. Before leaving, she hugged Marcus so tightly, she thought he might break and again pleaded with him to stay put unless he decided to turn himself in.

She would spend most of Saturday poring through the Internet research and deciding on her plan for getting Renae to talk. Lessye hoped she would have more luck contacting Renae than she did Lena. After several calls to Lena's home and cell phones, she had only connected with her voice mail.

Lessye had the strong urge to talk with her parents and her brother, Brian. When she was sure they were up for the morning, she would call them and ease their minds about Marcus. She was almost sure Aunt Rose had told them about his troubles. Her family had not yet met Marcus, and she had to make them understand that he was innocent.

Aunt Rose questioned her suspiciously as they rode home together on Friday evening. Lessye hated lying to her aunt, but she could not tell anyone of Marcus' whereabouts.

As Lessye lay snuggled under the warm quilts covering her bed thinking about their conversation, she was almost positive her aunt knew she had had contact with Marcus but didn't press the issue.

When the telephone rang, her heart skipped a beat as she answered, praying that it wasn't bad news about Marcus and hoping that Lena had decided to return her calls. She felt a mixture of relief and disappointment when she heard Tanya's familiar voice.

"Hey, girl. You up yet?"

"Just laying here thinking about Marcus. What's up?"

"I'm calling to check on you. You sound like you were expecting someone else."

"I was hoping that Lena would return my calls so I could arrange a time to see her about Marcus."

"I don't want to discourage you. But I wouldn't hold out much hope of hearing from Lena. She's never cared for us, and I don't see her warming up now, especially since you beat her out for Marcus. I would focus on Renae. Although she hates him, she's always liked you. Her nervousness could work in your favor. And you don't have the she-stole-my-man baggage to deal with."

"Maybe you're right."

"As usual. Kevin and his jazz band are playing at the C-Spot tonight. He has a saxophone solo. We want you to come with us – our treat."

"Thanks for the invitation. But can I have a rain check? I'm so tired, and I have a lot to do today."

"If I come over and help, will you change your mind? Come on, Lessye, please say yes. This is Kevin's first big gig with the group and the guys are so excited. They need a strong cheering section of their fans, which at this point are slim to none."

"But I'd only be a third wheel."

"That's nonsense. Besides Kevin is going to be with the band. I'm going to need someone to talk about it with while it's happening. Telling you about it after the fact won't be the same because I might forget something. I called Amber last night. She's still sick. Her doctor has given her five days on bed rest. If you ask me, I think it's all a ruse to keep that cute Kwame hovering at her bedside. I'm going over to visit her this morning to get the four-one-one. You've got to come tonight."

"Okay, okay I'll come, but I've got a lot of work to do first. What time can you get here?"

"I'll be there by one."

"See you then."

Saturday was always a good time for Rod to do his thinking. This would also be a good time to clean out the cluttered storage room in his comfortable restored Victorian-style home located in Atlanta's West End area.

Rod was the product of a nurturing, middle-class, inner-city family whose roots in Atlanta spread back several generations. In 1948, his grandfather, Roger Jennings, had become one of the first black police officers in Atlanta history. In the early sixties, he worked on his first homicide case, a case that wasn't solved until twenty-five years later. Rod's "pop-pop" had been the catalyst in solving one of the most sensational and bizarre crimes in the state's history.

For as long as he could remember, Rod dreamed of following in his pop-pop's footsteps and being a police officer. After graduating from Tillmore College with a B.A. in criminal justice, he enrolled in the Georgia Police Academy. Upon graduation, he joined the Georgia Department of Public Safety as a police officer and swiftly moved up in the ranks to chief of State Capitol Police.

Rod considered himself a fair chief. But wondered whether he was being fair in Marcus' situation. For as long as they had known each other, Rod had disliked Marcus and the feeling was mutual. Rod was put off by his arrogance, the chilly aloofness, and an obvious distrust and disdain for people. Marcus was the exact opposite of Rod, who craved warmth, loved people, harbored no secret agendas and detested power trips.

Rod's dislike for Marcus grew more acute after the incident with Henry. Rod liked Henry. He was a good man. Rod believed that Marcus engineered his firing but never could prove it. The last straw in their already contentious relationship was the firing of one of his favorite employees.

About a week after Governor Baker's inauguration, his wife and some friends attempted to enter the Capitol and the security guard, not recognizing Mrs. Baker, asked her to sign in and produce identification. Mrs. Baker was irritated and related the incident to Marcus. Instead of coming to Rod so he could resolve the issue, Marcus went over his head to the commissioner of the Department of Public Safety, making the case that any police or security officer who was not diligent enough to recognize the Governor's wife, children and prominent state officials should be relieved of their duty. Marcus played it as a critical safety issue. Rod knew it was typical Marcus, being vindictive and slinging around his power. Before Rod could intervene, the employee was dismissed. That was the day Rod's dislike for Marcus turned into hatred. He began counting the days until Marcus got exactly what he deserved, and now, that day had come.

But Rod had to wonder as he thought about his conversation with Lessye. Was he letting his hatred for Marcus blind him to the fact that Marcus could be innocent? Was he so desperate to see Marcus get what he deserved that he would intentionally close his eyes to evidence that could exonerate him? And if he did, then what kind of police chief would he be? Certainly, not the kind that Pop-Pop would be proud of. Lessye was one of his best friends, and she was right. If he kept his eyes closed and refused to help look for the truth, it would tarnish his badge and he would not deserve to wear it. If only his pop-pop wasn't out of the country traveling. He needed a strong dose of his wisdom and common sense. Rod missed his long talks and fishing trips with his granddad who still sometimes called him by his childhood nickname, Roddie.

Rod knew that Claude was beginning to have serious doubts about Marcus' guilt. And after they shared the most recent developments with Juan, he was also swaying in that direction. It would be difficult, but Rod would have to find a way to look at this case through objective and professional eyes. He would have to remove the element of his dislike for Marcus from the equation and consider the facts. Yes, Marcus was a liar, but something in his gut told him that this was one time that Marcus wasn't lying. He had to force himself to stop listening to his heart and start listening to his gut instincts, those pure instincts that had never failed him.

Lessye and Tanya spent a considerable part of the day going over all the research Tanya collected from the Internet concerning GHB and the local pharmaceutical companies that sponsored GHB drug studies during the past year.

Gamma hydroxybutyric acid was classified as a sedative and popularly known as a date rape drug, with most of its victims being drugged when their drinks were spiked. It depressed all brain functions and was usually used to intoxicate, produce euphoria or for growth hormone releasing effects. The short-term effects included drowsiness, nausea, impaired memory and seizures – while the long-term effects produced memory impairment, coma and damage to the heart and lungs. Symptoms of overdose included headache, impaired breathing, loss of reflexes, loss of consciousness. GHB could cause death through the suppression of the respiratory system and the induction of cardiac arrest.

Although it was praised by many victims of narcolepsy for helping them to overcome most of the more severe symptoms of the disease and hailed as the closest thing to a cure, when GHB was misused, it was a deadly drug.

As it related to the fewer than 120,000 victims of narcolepsy, one article read that even the top GHB researchers projected that the final FDA-approved medicinal product was several years from development. And a lot of research was still needed to understand why some people died from the drug while others could overdose as many as fifty times with no serious long-term effects.

One in 200,000 people suffered with narcolepsy and could legally obtain GHB only as a result of being in a study backed by a pharmaceutical company that planned to market it for prescription use only.

Out of five pharmaceutical companies in Georgia that conducted GHB studies in the past year, three were located in the metro Atlanta area. Tanya promised that Monday morning she would contact each of the companies to find out if Renae's name had been on any of the participant lists.

CHAPTER 57

*M*arcus was becoming accustomed to the small office that had now become his refuge. He had better get used to tight small places because the way things were going, he would probably spend the rest of his life in prison, or worse. So much had changed in a few days. It was only Monday when he and Lessye celebrated Valentine's Day. He had looked forward to having her on his arm at the Governor's dinner on Thursday evening. Instead, he was in hiding eluding the police.

By the weekend, he had relaxed to the point he didn't flinch each time the door opened or the telephone rang. His only anxious times were coming now whenever he left the safety of his hiding place to venture into the hall to the bathroom. He had to be extra careful, especially during the weekend. All he needed was to run into a security guard on rounds, and it was all over. Before leaving Friday, Tanya gave him a spare door key, easing his fear of being locked out by a patrolling security guard while on a bathroom run.

He soon became bored with watching television, and he was sick of all the news reports about the case and law enforcement officers proclaiming how close they were to finding him. Poor Robert was catching it from all sides. In a news conference from their home, the Austin men assured reporters that they would not rest until Brad's murderer was brought to justice. Although careful not to make any outright accusations, they questioned why Marcus was allowed to remain the Governor's liaison in the murder investigation when almost from the beginning, he was among the suspects. They made a strong appeal for people to call the police if they saw Marcus or had any knowledge of his whereabouts. They were prepared to offer a $50,000 reward to anyone with information that led to his capture.

Prominent members of the civil rights community, joined by the Black Caucus, had assembled at the Capitol in front of the portrait of Dr. Martin Luther King, Jr. to demand an end to the media leaks and pray that Marcus would give himself up. While they desperately wanted Alonso's murderer brought to justice, they also expressed their hope that the first African-American chief of staff was not being made a scapegoat and being unfairly persecuted by the media and racist political enemies.

The only thing besides Lessye's love that he found comfort in was the home-cooked food she and Tanya prepared for him.

While in hiding, Marcus had plenty of time to be still and ponder what brought him to this crucial juncture. His arrogance and reckless disregard for other's feelings had caught up with him. Now he knew how it felt to be accused of a crime he didn't commit. He knew how it felt for people to accuse him of lying. He knew how it felt for someone's hatred of him to blind them to the truth. Now, he understood how his thoughtless, malicious actions drove a good man to his death. Why hadn't he told Henry who he was? Why hadn't he asked Henry the reason he gave him up to live with his father's family? Why had he been so vicious, stupid and selfish? Now, he could never bring Henry and Martha back. He could never tell them how sorry he was. He could never tell them that when he was seven years old, he loved them so much that it broke his heart to leave them. He could never make it right.

Maybe what was happening to him now was justice. Maybe the moral arch of the universe was calling him to answer for all the cruel and vicious things he had done in his life. Maybe he should turn himself in and accept his punishment without a whimper.

Marcus had a half sister who hated him . . . who was probably one of the engineers of his downfall. And how could he blame her after all he had done? She would never feel anything but contempt for him. One more thing he could never make right . . . What a mess he had made of his life, and he had only himself to blame.

Along with thinking, Marcus did a lot of repentant praying. Before that time with Lessye, it had been so long since he had prayed for anything because he also harbored an anger against God. He thought back and vaguely remembered kneeling beside his bed in prayer with his mother before she died. He remembered them going to church with his grandparents every

Sunday. But when she died and he was given away, everything changed. Marcus had thought that God, like his grandparents, had turned away from him and didn't love him. What kind of God would take his young mother and rip a child from a loving home and cast him into despair? Marcus decided that if God did not love him, he would not love God. He turned away from God. As he grew older, Marcus felt deep down that he was not worth loving. But now Marcus knew how wrong he was. He had been wrong about so many things.

Marcus lay back on the couch facing the window. The sun was setting and night was falling over the city. Soon Marcus would be in darkness except for the small stream of light from street lights outside. He didn't dare turn on the light. It would attract attention. Marcus would have to endure the darkness all alone in his cell with nothing for companionship except his thoughts that were threatening to consume him.

CHAPTER 58

*L*essye took Aunt Rose to Sunday worship service and treated her to dinner. After taking her home, she stopped by the drug store to pick up some toiletries for herself, then went home to change clothes and prepare for her visit with Renae. Lessye thought about calling first but remembered all the unreturned calls to Lena and decided against it. At this point, it would be better to show up unexpected. Lessye decided that surprise would be her best strategy. She would be straight-forward and make an honest appeal for her help. Lessye knew how much Renae hated Marcus. She was reacting to a lot of negative experiences that happened in her life for which she blamed him. Renae and Marcus were alike in many ways. Lessye knew that deep down, Renae was a nice person with a good nature. Lessye planned to use her persuasiveness to force her to bring it out. When it came down to it, Lessye did not believe that in the end Renae would let Marcus go to prison for something he did not do.

Lessye pulled her thick curls back into a ponytail and changed into a pair of comfortable, faded denim jeans, a black cashmere sweater and low heel black leather pumps. She put on her thick leather jacket and driving gloves to fend off the fierce wind and drove to Renae's apartment to find the front door ajar. Lessye knocked several times and called out, but there was no answer. She wondered why would Renae leave her door open if she was going out. Lessye pushed the door open enough to peer into the living room. As she got a clear view, her question was answered. Renae was at home after all. She was sprawled out unconscious on the floor of her apartment. She was barely breathing.

Lessye immediately called 9-1-1 and Rod. Rod called Claude and Juan, and they all arrived at the hospital in time to meet Lessye after Renae's ambulance pulled in.

"What happened?" Rod asked as he and the others rushed toward Lessye, who was almost in tears.

"I don't know," she said. "I went over to visit Renae to try and talk her into telling what she knew about this situation with Marcus. I'm sure Marcus is being framed. And I think Renae is involved."

"I've almost come to that same conclusion," Claude said. "What did the EMTs say about Renae's condition?"

"When they checked her out, they said it appeared to be a drug overdose, but they couldn't be sure. I told them about her narcolepsy, but this was different from one of those episodes. There was a glass on the floor close to her hand and liquid spilled around her on the carpet. It looked like she had been drinking something when she collapsed."

"I'm wondering if that may have some connection to her collapse," Claude said. "I'll make arrangements to get a carpet sample to have it checked out at the crime lab."

"Did Renae know you were coming this evening?" Juan asked.

"No. I purposely didn't tell her. I know how she feels about Marcus. And if I had asked her if I could come over, she probably would have said no. We're friendly, but we don't visit each other much socially. She would have figured anything I had to say to her would be about Marcus."

"Do you remember what time you got there?" Rod asked.

"It was a little past four. Aunt Rose and I went to church and then dinner. By the time I took her home, ran an errand and got home and changed, it was almost four. Renae's apartment on Fairburn Road isn't far from me."

Renae had been immediately wheeled into the trauma room, where one of the attending physicians was working on her. Lessye and the others questioned a nurse who did not tell them anything but assured them that a Dr. Gary Stephens would come out and talk with them as soon as possible. Lessye was the first to approach him when he did.

"Dr. Stephens, I'm Lessye McLemore. I came in with Renae Stewart. How is she? What's wrong with her?"

"Hello, Ms. McLemore, I understand you're worried about your friend, but I'm not at liberty to discuss her condition with anyone other than a family member."

"Doctor, Ms. Stewart doesn't have any close family members," Rod said, not going into detail about Marcus.

"Also," Claude said, showing the doctor his identification, "Ms. Stewart is involved in a major GBI investigation. Anything you tell us will not only help Ms. Stewart but shed some light on this investigation."

"Please, Dr. Stephens," Lessye said with tears in her eyes.

"All right," Dr. Stephens said. "She's critical at this point but struggling hard to hold her own. She is suffering from an overdose of GHB. We're working now to flush it out of her system."

"Is she conscious?" Lessye asked.

"No. She still hasn't regained consciousness. She has a loss of reflexes and her breathing is greatly impaired. Her heart rate has been slowed to dangerous levels, and blood pressure has plummeted. To your knowledge, Ms. McLemore, does Ms. Stewart have a drug problem?"

"No. Renae has a weak stomach. A good friend of mine told me that Renae said drugs and medicines didn't agree with her. But she suffers with narcolepsy. That could explain the GHB."

"Then she was probably taking GHB for her condition and mistakenly ingested too much," the doctor said.

"Maybe . . ." Lessye said. "But considering her dislike for medicines, she would be extra careful about the dosage."

"Thanks for the information," said Dr. Stephens. "I'll keep you updated on her condition." He rushed back into the trauma room.

"Renae told me during our interview that she had never been prescribed GHB." Claude said. "And her background check confirmed it. So the question now is, where did she get it?"

"I'm beginning to think Renae knows more about this case than she has revealed," Juan said.

"She's definitely going to have a lot of explaining to do once she wakes up," said Rod.

"I only hope she does wake up," Lessye said.

===============

Two hours passed, and the doctor had not appeared to talk with them again. Lessye called Tanya, and she and Kevin rushed to the hospital to sit with Lessye. Claude had received an urgent call about a possible Marcus sighting at a Buckhead restaurant that he and Juan left to follow up on, but it turned out to be bogus. Rod was still comforting Lessye when Tanya and Kevin arrived.

"Hey, Rod, You know my husband, Kevin," Tanya said as she rushed to Lessye to give her a hug.

"Yeah, sure. Hey man. How's it going?" Rod said rising to greet them.

"Everything is cool," Kevin said. "What's the story on Renae?"

"The doctor said it's a drug overdose. She's pretty bad man."

"That's rough," Kevin said, shaking his head. The guys decided to walk down to the snack bar and get some coffee to give the ladies time to talk.

"Lessye, what happened? And what was Rod saying about drugs?"

"I went over to talk to Renae about Marcus. When I got to her place, I found her passed out on the floor. When we spoke with the doctor earlier he said Renae overdosed on GHB."

"Renae would never take drugs. They make her sick to her stomach."

"That's what I told the doctor."

"Have you had a chance to see her?"

"Not yet."

"Did you call Clarice and Lena?"

"Yes, I tried them both. Clarice went out of town with friends this weekend. They haven't returned. And Lena is nowhere to be found. I've been trying to reach her all weekend."

The guys had returned with coffee when Dr. Stephens gave them an update.

"Ms. Stewart is still in critical condition. The GHB has been flushed out of her system. But we're going to have to wait and see now. The next forty-eight hours are crucial."

"Doctor, may we see her?" Lessye asked.

"She's in intensive care. When I left her, she was still unconscious. She probably won't know you're there."

"Doctor, we want to see her." Lessye glanced at Tanya for support.

"And if she happens to wake up while we're there, it will mean a lot to her to see some familiar faces," Tanya said.

"All right, I'll make arrangements for the two of you to see her, but only for a few minutes."

"Thank you, Doctor."

Lessye and Tanya entered Renae's room. She was a pathetic sight, attached to blood gas and vital signs monitors with IV tubes running in her small arms. Renae was already thin, but in the hospital bed she looked like a tiny girl, frail and vulnerable.

"Renae, can you hear us?" Lessye asked softly. "It's Lessye and Tanya. We're here for you, Renae. Everything's going to be all right. Keep on fighting." Lessye took Renae's hand gently and Renae weakly squeezed her hand. Renae never opened her eyes but she faintly whispered something that sounded like a name.

"What? Renae, did you say something? Come on, keep talking to me," Lessye said.

"Linda . . ." Renae murmured weakly.

Lessye and Tanya could barely hear her. "Lessye, what did she say? It sounds like she's calling for Lena."

"No. It sounded more like she said Linda."

"What is it, Renae?" Tanya asked. "Do you want us to call Lena?"

"Linda," she murmured again, barely above a whisper.

"She said Linda," Lessye told Tanya. "I heard her clearly that time. But who is Linda?"

"I have no idea," Tanya said, then turned back to Renae. "Who is Linda? Renae, who is Linda? Is she one of your nurses?"

Suddenly, the monitors attached to Renae began going crazy. Several nurses and doctors ran into the room. One nurse ushered Lessye and Tanya outside. Renae was in cardiac arrest. Lessye ran to Rod and Tanya to Kevin as they waited in hushed horror as the medical team worked furiously to revive Renae.

CHAPTER 59

$\mathcal{T}$anya had known long evenings but none as long as the night before when they kept vigil at the hospital until early Monday morning. Renae was revived but had slipped into a coma. Tanya had gotten home with just enough time to shower and change and get to work by eight. Amber was still out, so she knew Monday would be an especially hectic day. Surprisingly, she didn't feel any more exhausted than usual, and the extra work with Amber's absence was sure to keep her alert.

When Tanya arrived at her suite a few minutes before eight, she found a manilla envelope waiting for her on the floor inside. There was a note attached from Kaye who had slipped it under the door. She placed it on her desk and before taking off her coat, went back to check on Marcus. Tanya and Lessye agreed that Lessye would tell Marcus about Renae, and she planned to come over as soon as she arrived for work and made sure everything at the tour booth was in order. Marcus looked surprisingly well and hardy for a man in hiding. He was freshly shaved and groomed, and smelled of cologne.

Tanya went back to the front of the suite to hang her coat on the rack and log in on her computer.

She loved this time of morning, her quiet time before her representatives came. The ones who were on the Hill were either attending breakfast functions or had early committee meetings that kept them out of her hair until about nine. The telephones were quiet. After making coffee, taking Marcus a cup and poring herself a steaming cup with artificial creamer and sugar, she sat down at her desk to look at Kaye's note. Kaye had written that she was sorry she missed Tanya but she had to leave for New York earlier than expected and decided to drop off the photo on her way to the airport. *The guard was nice enough to let me in before seven. Thanks for everything,* she had written, before adding a smiling face.

Tanya opened the envelope and took out an eight-by-ten color photograph of three attractive young women in cap and gown. They were smiling radiantly, and from the look of the people in the background, it must have been their graduation day. Tanya recognized the one in the middle as Lena. Another girl in the photo, except for eye color, looked amazingly like Lena. The third young lady was pretty with a golden brown complexion, cinnamon-colored hair and straight, pearly white teeth. The note to Brad from Vivian Staley of Branton University and her business card were also attached. Tanya was about to place the photograph between two pieces of cardboard, slip it in a clean envelope and address it to Lena in the Speaker's office when she decided to turn the photo over and look at the back. On the back was a label with the full names of each of the young women on the photo in the order they were on the picture. Tanya looked at it closely, then flipped it over to again examine the photo. Turning it over one more time, she said to herself, "This can't be right." Lena was standing in the middle, yet on the back of the photo the label identified the middle one as Linda Michelle Loring. "Linda?" Tanya said to herself as she thought back to their visit with Renae. "Renae had said the name Linda. But how can that be? This is Lena."

Lessye breezed through the door carrying a bag of food for Marcus. "Talking to yourself in your old age? I know we had a long evening, but don't lose it on me now. I called the hospital before I came over here. Renae is still in the coma, but the nurse I spoke with said she's holding her own. Her breathing is almost back to normal. Her blood pressure is slowly creeping back to normal range and her heart rate is steady. The nurse was positive. She said that sometimes comas are a way of helping the body heal." Lessye took a breath and noticed the odd expression on Tanya's face.

"What's wrong?"

"You better look at this." Tanya handed Lessye the photo and Lessye, recognizing Lena, remarked about her resemblance to one of the girls beside her and then Tanya said, "Now turn it over. Look at the order in which it's labeled."

"Yeah, I see," Lessye said. "Lena is in the middle, but this has her listed as someone named Linda? Maybe whoever labeled it got them mixed up."

"Maybe . . . But I don't think so. There's something strange about Renae saying the name Linda last night."

Lessye looked at Tanya for a moment as a light of realization gleamed in her eyes.

"Are you thinking what I'm thinking?" Tanya asked.

"Now that you mention it, I'm thinking it's much too much of a coincidence for the name Linda to have come up from nowhere. On this photo, the girl we know as Lena Lawrence is listed as being someone named Linda Loring. Where did you get this photo?"

"Brad's sister, Kaye, dropped it off this morning on her way to the airport. She asked me to pass it on to Lena. Vivian Staley of Branton University sent it to Brad. She met him during a visit to the campus. Kaye told me Brad had planned to frame it for Lena."

"I think we should give Vivian a call."

"So do I. Why don't you go back and see Marcus, and I'll give her a call."

"It's still before nine. Do you think she's in her office this early?"

"Her home and pager numbers are on the card," Tanya said.

Lessye was happy to see Marcus looking so well. She ran into his arms, hugging him like it was their last time, and they kissed passionately before sinking down on the couch to talk. Lessye told him about Renae.

"I don't understand this," Marcus said. "I don't believe Renae would ever have intentionally taken a drug overdose. And even if she thought about it, she sure wouldn't have done it before having the pleasure of getting even with me. Where's Lena? Did you tell her?"

"Honestly, in all the excitement last night I only called her once while I was at the hospital waiting for Tanya and Kevin. There was no answer at her place or on her cell phone. I only got her voice mail. I've been trying to reach her since Friday to see if I could get some information out of her that could help you, but none of my calls were returned. I haven't called today."

"Maybe you should try her now," Marcus said.

"I don't think that will be necessary," Tanya said as she walked through the door and handed Marcus the photo. "I spoke with Vivian, who promised to fax me all the information she has about the other two women on this photo. Lena Arlene Lawrence is a rich white girl with a deep olive complexion, who has beautiful green eyes, and Linda Michelle Loring is a poor, struggling hazel-eyed black beauty, light enough to pass for her twin. According to Vivian there's a black butterfly tattoo on the back of Linda's neck which is missing from the real Lena. Vivian only heard from Lena a few times since they graduated. Linda is supposedly living somewhere in Europe. My friends, I think that the woman we all know as Lena is an impostor."

CHAPTER 60

$\mathcal{I}$ s Lessye on tour?" Rod asked her assistant. He stopped by, hoping that Lessye had an update on Renae's condition.

"No," Tracey said with a smile. "She stepped away from the desk to run over to the LOB. She told me I could reach her in Tanya's suite if we needed her."

"Tanya's suite? This early in the day? I thought she didn't usually get over that way until lunch time?"

"I guess something important came up. No sooner than she got here this morning, she rushed over there. Do you want me to call her?"

"No. That's okay. I'll see her later."

At that moment, Tracey's attention was distracted by a noisy teenage tour group storming the main door.

"Excuse me, Rod, I've got to go and settle them down before they enter the building. Why don't you hang around a few minutes? I'm sure Lessye won't be too long as busy as our schedule is today," she said before moving swiftly in the direction of the main entrance.

Instead of waiting at the tour booth, Rod decided to walk in the direction of the Mitchell Street exit door, wondering if the reason for Lessye's early morning visit to Tanya had anything to do with news about Renae's condition. He ran into Agent Grogan, who was standing at the door speaking quietly into his radio transmitter.

"Hey, Jason, what's going on? What's up with the tail on Lessye?"

"Nothing to write a report about. Your girl had a somewhat quiet weekend. On Friday night, she went to a dance school off Cambellton Road, stayed an hour, and then went home alone. On Saturday, her friend from the LOB, Tanya Ivey, came over for a visit and stayed half the day. Later in the evening, she rode with Tanya and her husband to this new jazz nightclub on Cambellton called the C-Spot. Sunday morning, she picked up her aunt and went to church. Afterwards they had dinner at Sylvia's downtown. Later on around four, she went over to Renae's apartment and you know the rest."

"Anything with the phone taps?"

"Nada. Marcus hasn't even tried to get in touch. There haven't even been any hang-up calls or suspicious wrong numbers. I just made contact with our man over in the LOB. Lessye's over in Tanya's suite now. Shot out of this door like a bullet about fifteen minutes ago."

"Yeah, I know. Tracey, at the tour booth, told me she was gone. I guess I'll catch her when she gets back," Rod said before heading downstairs to his office.

The tragic death and memorial service for his son had only been the beginning of Randy Joe's torment. He felt as if he was being sucked in a pit of quicksand – sinking fast. Randy Joe could not escape the wrath of his mother-in-law as she stabbed him with her accusatory eyes at every turn. Kell and his family returned home early Saturday morning, but the old battle axe remained, dogging his trail like a rabid pit bull. She vowed to stay with her daughter and the kids until this matter was resolved. Translation: She was determined to stay until she found some — any — evidence that would remotely connect him to the agonizing deaths of Ronnie and the Layton girl.

But what hurt the most was that he knew, deep down, Miss Pearl blamed him, too. Unlike his dagger-eyed mother-in-law, it was not the way she looked at him. It was the way she didn't look at him. The way she purposely avoided his eyes. It was the way she refused to be comforted or consoled by him. She had not spoken more than a few words to him, preferring to stay in the company of Kelley, Tim, and her mother. To make matters worse, she saw a news report about the videotape on Saturday evening. Miss Pearl was a smart woman, and it didn't take her long to put it together that a copy of the video was probably in the package that Ronnie found the day he was killed.

Ms. Pearl exploded in anger. She was furious with Randy Joe, more hurt and enraged than she had ever been. The death of his son and, now on its heels, the revelation of his infidelity had ripped their relationship irreparably apart. And it certainly didn't help having his mother-in-law crouching around instigating.

On Sunday morning Randy Joe, determined to keep the family tradition, attended church service with his remaining two children. Miss Pearl couldn't face being seen with him in public. The thought of sitting in a church beside a man who had made a mockery of all the moral and spiritual laws in which she so strongly believed made her sick. She had no intention of taking any further part in Randy Joe's hypocrisy. As Randy Joe, Kelley and Tim sat solemnly on their special family pew, there was the sad realization that one of the members would never be there again. And another one was so filled with grief and pain that she probably never would either.

The final straw came Sunday night. Miss Pearl lashed out, screaming and cursing at him. There was a deadness in her eyes when she told him she wished that he had died in that fire instead of her son. At that moment, Randy Joe knew that he had lost Miss Pearl and his family for good. The words spoken in anger between them could never be taken back.

On the ride to Atlanta Monday morning, Randy Joe was nothing more than a hollow shell. He thought of the look of betrayal, embarrassment and disgrace behind the sadness in his children's eyes. He thought of the icy coldness of his once warm and loving wife. He thought of the venomous hatred of his mother-in-law. He was now a man ridiculed by his family, deserted by his friends, hated by his political enemies, sought by the GBI, and most of all, devastated and guilty over the death of his own son. He and he alone had killed his precious boy. His blind hatred had ripped from him one of the only people in his life who had ever mattered. Why hadn't he left it alone? How many teenage romances lasted for a long period of time? If he had stayed out of it, the relationship probably would have fizzled out in a couple of months and his boy, Ronnie, would still be alive.

He looked in his rear view mirror. The GBI agents were still earning their pay checks. The same two guys in the unmarked Crown Victoria had been shadowing him almost from the moment he arrived home Wednesday morning. They were parked in front of his house at the end of his long winding driveway. They kept a respectful distance from their family and friends at the memorial service for Ronnie. Now they were keeping an aggressive distance behind him as he made his solitary sojourn back into Atlanta where he would probably be arrested on rape and drug charges the minute he set foot in Fulton County. Tyrell had probably sung enough for the both of them. That sniveling wimp probably told everything he knew and when that spigot of knowledge was exhausted, made up the rest. But he couldn't worry about that now.

Randy Joe exited I-75/85 north on Capitol Avenue and drove the few blocks to his assigned parking space on the upper-level of the number one lot. He would stop by his office and take care of some business. There was one last thing he had to do before he was taken into custody.

As Claude suspected, the dried liquid in Renae's carpet contained trace amounts of the drug GHB. But where did Renae get the GHB? That question, rattling around in Claude's head, would not be answered until she regained consciousness – if she ever did. He checked with the hospital that morning and while she was still in a coma, he was told that Renae was holding on. Her vital signs were slowly returning to normal.

He looked at his watch. The agents assigned to Randy Joe had informed Claude that he was en route to Atlanta with an estimated time of arrival at 9 a.m. Claude had a lot on his plate, and he was anxious to turn the GHB-rape case against Randy Joe and Tyrell over to the Attorney General. Then he could concentrate all his efforts on solving the murder case.

Claude had pretty much ruled out Randy Joe and Tyrell as suspects in the murders of the legislators, as well as Marcus for that matter. Claude was becoming more and more certain that Marcus was being framed. He could not argue that there was compelling evidence against Marcus. But the evidence implicating him was too neat. Why would he have agreed to a search if he knew he had a stash of GHB in his loft where it could easily be found? And why would he make up a lie about Lena coming over to his place and giving him the bottle of what he thought was cologne – a lie that could be so easily disproved? And there was also another issue that would not leave his gut: Why did Brad so urgently want to see Marcus the night he died?

As he sat at the laptop in his office, Claude made a list of everything that he had learned as a result of the investigation. One column was labeled "hard evidence," one was labeled "possible suspects" and the other was labeled "unanswered questions."

For a moment, he thought of his grandmother who always used to say, "Sometimes you find what you're looking for in the least obvious places. So it's best to turn over every rock, no matter how smooth."

Claude thought about Marcus. He was a good looking guy who loved the ladies. It was probably only a woman who could have gotten close enough to frame him. In fact, who else could have gotten close enough to those legislators to spike their drinks with GHB? Who had a motive, the opportunity and the means? Claude feared that the woman with his answer was fighting for her life at Grady Memorial Hospital.

═══════════════

Lessye rushed back to the tour booth in time to take three tours back to back, which combined with the nervous activity in the Capitol building, partially distracted her mind from the revelation about Lena.

Lessye desperately wanted to tell Rod what they found out, but they agreed to wait until after Tanya got the information from the pharmaceutical companies concerning the GHB drug studies. She prayed it would be by eleven when she planned to go over for a long lunch.

═══════════════

Tanya e-mailed all the House secretaries about Renae and they decided that they would take a short break and all say a silent prayer on Renae's behalf.

Tanya divided her time between typing letters and covering the phones for her suite and Clarice's when she had to step out. Both Tanya and Clarice were short-handed so they helped each other the best they could.

Tanya hit a stone wall with the pharmaceutical companies who gave her the same terse answer: Yes, they had conducted GHB drug studies in the past year, but no they were not at liberty to release the names of any of the participants, not even to the secretary of a state representative.

While she sat dreading telling Marcus and Lessye she had come to a dead end, she was startled by the deafening sound of an explosion overhead. Her first impulse was to think that some government-hating, malcontent made good on their threat to blow up the building. But as she listened, it sounded more contained. Then came sounds of stomping and running all in the same direction over her head.

Clarice came rushing over. "Tanya, did you hear that? What's going on upstairs?"

"I have no idea, but I'm going to find out," she said, picking up the telephone to dial security.

━━━━━━━━━━━━━━━━

Being a state representative had its privileges, and one of the best things about being a legislator was being able to bypass many of the rules of security. Legislators with badges did not have to run their briefcases through the Xray machines or even so much as walk through the metal detectors. So it would never be detected if one was to bring a weapon into the building. It was this selective security policy that Randy Joe depended on his last day on the Hill.

He entered his suite as usual, spoke to his secretary, then locked himself in his office. Calmly, he sat down at his desk, put down his briefcase, opened the top drawer of his desk and took out a legal pad and a pen. On the pad he wrote two letters. One was to Claude about his crimes and the death of his son. The other was to his family about his thoughts, his sorrow and his regrets. He said goodbye to his family and asked them to forgive him. He had put them through enough anguish and would not have them dragged through the humiliation of a nasty sex trial. After finishing the two letters he tore them off the pad and placed one in an envelope addressed to Claude. The other was addressed to his wife. He placed the pad and pen neatly inside his top, center desk drawer with both letters on top of it, and then he closed the drawer tightly. His secretary buzzed him. The agents from the GBI were there to take him away.

"Just a moment," he said. "Tell them to have a seat, I'll be with them shortly."

Quietly, he opened his briefcase and took out the gun. He stared at it for a moment with its ominous magnum barrel and deadly hollow-point bullets. Randy Joe had come to the end of his road. He had turned the final corner and faced himself and could not live with what he saw. It was his final curve. There was a tap on his locked door. A man's voice said sternly, "Representative Reynolds, it's time to go."

Randy Joe did not respond but thought to himself, Yes, indeed it is time to go.

Silently, he placed the barrel in his mouth, and as hot tears burned a hopeless trail down his cheeks, he pulled the trigger.

CHAPTER 61

*C*laude jumped in his car and sped to the Capitol as soon as he heard the news. Randy Joe had eaten his gun. This case, with all its strange peripheral events, was turning out to be one of the most difficult in his career. He had not been a Randy Joe fan and was probably going to be instrumental in putting him away on rape and drug charges. But he didn't wish that kind of tragic ending on anyone.

When he arrived in Randy Joe's office suite, Sean was already there dragging his laptop, camera flash blazing and tape recorder humming, arguing with one of the GBI agents who was holding his ground and not letting Sean anywhere near Randy Joe's office.

"Have you guys ever heard of something called freedom of the press?" Sean asked as Claude pushed his way through the crowd of other media and nosy onlookers gathered around the main door of the suite.

"Have you ever heard of something called interfering with a police investigation?" Claude said, then turned to one of the agents. "He gets nowhere near this office until we have concluded this investigation – even if you have to cuff him and take him in, and that goes for the rest of the media," Claude said, glancing in their direction. He didn't hang around long enough to hear anymore of Sean's irritating remarks or see the exasperated look on his face. Instead, he marched straight into the office of the late Randy Joe. When he entered, he found Rod waiting for him amid the gruesome splatter of bright red blood and brains that now stuck to the walls and blinds. The body, limply slumped over the desk, had not yet been moved. The forensic pathologist arrived on the scene, pulled on his rubber gloves, and told them

291

what they already knew, Randy Joe was a victim of a single self-inflicted gunshot wound through the mouth. However, the corpse would still undergo an autopsy to ascertain whether drugs or alcohol played any role in the death.

His distraught secretary had been questioned and then sent home on two-day stress leave, and the Speaker, after hearing the news, spoke with the Lieutenant Governor and both Houses voted to pass a resolution to recess until the following Wednesday morning. The other suite mates who felt uneasy about returning to the office went straight to their hotels or home.

"Hey, Claude. Looks like we've got ourselves a real mess in here," Rod said.

"I guess he *really* didn't want to talk to me," Claude said, then regretted it a moment later. A man had been so distraught that he had taken his own life. The least he could do was be more thoughtful about his off-color remarks.

After the body was bagged and taken to the morgue, Claude and Rod began a search around the office, looking for a possible note or any concrete insight into why he had done what he did. They soon found what they were looking for in the center drawer of his desk.

Claude took both envelopes, placing the one to the Reynolds family in his coat pocket and opening the one with his name scrawled across the front. In the one-page letter that he showed to Rod, Randy Joe confessed to his crimes of rape and drug use and wrote that he obtained the drug from one of the women he was seeing, Lena. The most compelling part, however, was the part dealing with the death of his son. He admitted that the fire in the Fort Valley apartment building was no accident. It was arranged by Nathaniel who was working with two brothers, local thugs that Randy Joe had found out about later — Sonny and Ike Cole. He had asked Nathaniel to get rid of Ronnie's girlfriend, Tamika, but by mistake Ronnie was also in the apartment at the time.

"So Gus' theory was right on the money," Rod said, shaking his head with a mixture of sadness and disgust. "It's true, Randy Joe inadvertently killed his own son."

"Yeah, and so was Tyrell. It's a shame about Tyrell. All that singing for nothing. Randy Joe is dead, and he has nothing left to bargain with. He doesn't know it yet, but that boy is looking at some hard time."

Claude immediately got on the phone and arranged to send a team of investigators to Fort Valley. He notified the Peach County sheriff's office and the Fort Valley City Police to detain Sonny and Ike Cole. He also put out a statewide all points bulletin for them in case they were no longer in the Peach County area. After hanging up, he ordered the agents who had been tailing Randy Joe to arrest and detain Nathaniel until he could be turned over to Peach County authorities for questioning.

Claude then turned to Rod, "I'm going to personally deliver this letter to the Reynolds family. With Sean snooping around, I'm not letting it out of my hands. I also need to check with the local authorities on this fire matter. I'm leaving now, and it will take me a few hours to get there and back. Would you do me a favor?"

"Sure, name it."

"Find Lena, and don't let her out of your sight until I return."

———

Rod went directly to the Speaker's office only to be told that Lena had not reported for work that morning or called to say why she hadn't. She had last been seen on Friday afternoon before leaving early to run some personal errands. He got her phone numbers from the Speaker's secretary, and the home address she had listed on file. He called her several times. There was no answer. He drove to her midtown apartment. She did not answer the door. The mini blinds that provided her privacy from the bustling street outside were drawn tightly shut, and Rod could detect no movement inside.

Upon returning to the Capitol, he went directly to the tour booth to see Lessye. Maybe she knew where Lena was. Surely she had spoken to her since Renae's overdose.

"Sorry, Rod, you just missed her," Jon said. "She's already gone to the LOB for lunch."

Rod glanced at his watch. "Eleven o'clock again?"

"Being boss tour lady has its privileges. Is it true about Representative Reynolds killing himself?"

"I'm afraid it is."

"Man, that's too bad."

"You can say that again. Look, Jon, I've got to run. When Lessye comes back, tell her I need to see her, ASAP."

"Sure thing."

Rod almost went to his office to wait for Lessye, when he decided on a hunch to go over to the LOB. Maybe she and Tanya together could shed some light on this Lena mystery.

He greeted Jason and other members of security in the lobby of the LOB. Jason had been back and forth from the Capitol since Randy Joe's suicide. As Rod approached he said, "She's upstairs, man."

When Rod got to Tanya's suite, he found the main door locked, and she was not out front at her desk. There was no sign of Lessye. He walked into Clarice's suite almost directly across the hall. "Hey, Clarice. Are Lessye and Tanya down in the break room?"

"Hey, Rod. No they're not in the break room. I rarely ever see them in there anymore. They always eat over in Tanya's suite now."

"Well, I don't see them out front, and the door is locked."

"I'm covering Tanya's phone lines, and I saw Lessye go in a few minutes ago. Maybe they snuck away to one of the representatives offices. My door key fits Tanya's. I'll let you in." Clarice darted out and unlocked the door then returned to her desk.

Rod entered the suite quietly and heard nothing. He walked down one end and then down the other. As he approached Brad's former office, he stopped short at the sound of muffled voices in low but excited conversation. One of them belonged to a man. It was the voice of a man who was familiar. Rod opened his blazer and quietly unfastened the holster that held his service revolver and braced himself as he heard movement coming toward the door. He heard Tanya say, "I'm going to give you guys some time alone. Besides, I better keep a look out up front in case anyone is trying to get in the suite."

But it was already too late for that, Rod thought as he waited for her to open the door. When she did, she gasped in surprise as he pushed passed her and entered.

"Well, well, well," Rod said to everyone's surprise. "If it isn't our long lost fugitive."

A couple of secretaries went to the hospital on their lunch hour to sit with Renae and pray. Since the excitement with Randy Joe and the House went into recess, almost all the representatives had vacated the LOB sixth floor, and their secretarial supervisor gave them permission to go as long as they didn't have any pressing duties and their phones were covered.

When the girls arrived they found Lessye's Aunt Rose and Neveleen already there.

"How is she?" one of the girls asked, as they joined Rose and Neveleen. "There's no change, she's still in the coma," Rose said. "We've been sitting here talking to her, singing and praying. Please join us."

They made a semi circled around Renae as best they could without disturbing the machines that were monitoring the fragile state of her life. They all took turns praying for her recovery, calling her by name, beseeching the Lord for a miracle. After they prayed, they began to sing one of Rose's favorite hymns, "Great is Thy Faithfulness."

As they came to the end of the third and last verse, another faint voice joined them. Renae was singing along. The Lord had answered their prayers.

CHAPTER 62

*G*ive me one good reason why I shouldn't clamp all of you in handcuffs and arrest you now?" Rod said, looking like any further provocation would compel him to commence pistol whipping the three of them simultaneously.

"Maybe because you only have one set of cuffs?" Tanya said, trying but failing to ease the tension.

"Keep it up, Tanya, and Kevin will be coming to pick you up tonight from the city jail. Do you ladies have any idea how much trouble you'll be in when I tell Claude you've been hiding a fugitive for almost six days? Law enforcement officers all over the state are looking for this guy. That's money plus manpower wasted." Marcus started to speak, but Rod silenced him with a menacing glare. "I'll get to you later." He turned back to Lessye and Tanya. "And Lessye, I'm especially disappointed in you. I practically begged you to tell me where Marcus was hiding, and you looked me right in my face and said you didn't know where he was. I didn't want to believe you would blatantly lie to me, but something in my gut told me you would where Marcus was concerned."

"I swear I didn't know when you asked me. I didn't find out until after our talk."

"And it never occurred to you to tell me as soon as you found out. And if you had known when I talked with you would you have told me?"

Lessye did not answer, maintaining a guilty silence.

"That's what I thought. You never intended to tell me."

"It's not Lessye's fault. It's mine," Tanya said. "I'm the one who told Marcus he could hide in here. So if you're going to yell at anyone, it should be me."

"As far as I'm concerned, you're both equally at fault, and right now, the GBI would have good charges of obstruction and harboring a fugitive against both of you."

"Rod, we can explain—"

"And it better be good."

"No. Let me explain," Marcus said, refusing to sit quietly and leave Lessye and Tanya holding the bag no matter how harshly Rod scowled in his direction. "Don't blame them. I'm the one who put them in this position by coming here. Lessye and Tanya felt sorry for me because they believe in my innocense. I know you don't believe anything I say, but I am telling the truth. I did not drug and kill those legislators. I know my running looks bad. But after that GHB was found in my place and our confrontation in the conference room and Claude was getting ready to take me in, I panicked. I couldn't give myself up until I had concrete evidence to prove I was being framed."

"And now we can prove it," Lessye said. They showed Rod the photograph that had been delivered by Kaye and told him about the call to Vivian confirming that the woman they all knew as Lena was Linda Loring.

"Vivian promised to fax me some information about the two women," Tanya said.

Rod took a moment to let what they were telling him settle in his mind. "This all makes sense now. I've been trying to track down Lena. Randy Joe wrote a letter to Claude telling him that it was Lena who supplied the GHB that he and Tyrell used. She told him she got it from a friend at the Capitol but didn't give a name. If Brad saw that photo and figured out that Lena wasn't who she claimed to be, that's probably the reason he was in a sweat to see you the night he died, Marcus."

Tanya thought of something else. "Brad took Amber, Lena and me to dinner the week before session. It was a welcome-back dinner for Amber – Brad's treat. We were talking about universities and his trip to Branton. He joked about putting Lena's photo on the Internet under dead-beat alumni. At the time I thought she was irritated, but she was afraid of being exposed. If she thought that Brad already knew her secret . . ."

"She killed him to keep him from talking," Lessye said.

"But what about the other two legislators? What would she gain by killing them?" Rod asked.

"They were close to Brad and joined him on the visit to Branton University," Tanya said. "She didn't know what Brad or Vivian might have told them. Being close to Renae, Lena probably found out about the Henry Perkins history, so she made it look like Marcus committed the murders to keep them quiet about what he had done."

"Lena knew my feelings about Lessye," Marcus said, "She wanted me all to herself. But I wasn't having it. So she solved all her problems at the same time. She got rid of Brad before he could expose her and used all three murders to frame me."

"But Lena couldn't have pulled this off by herself," Rod said.

"We believe she had help from Renae," Lessye said. "Renae knew the whole story. Renae, because of her illness, was the one who could score the GHB. And in the event that Marcus slipped free of the frame-up, Lena could always fall back on Renae as a prime suspect in the framing of Marcus and the murders of the legislators."

"I'm going to call Claude about getting a warrant to search Lena's apartment," Rod said. "But meanwhile, Marcus, I'm going to have to take you in."

"Come on, Rod, not now," Lessye said. "We're so close to clearing Marcus' name. When Renae wakes up, I'm sure she'll put all the missing pieces together."

"I've been here all this time," Marcus said. "I'm not going anywhere now. Please give me a chance to get this sorted out."

"Technically, Marcus is not a fugitive," Lessye said. "He's been right here on state property since before five o'clock on Wednesday when Claude issued the APB. So he had already turned himself in to the state. You just didn't know it."

"Are you moonlighting as an attorney now?" Rod slightly smiled. "Okay, okay. Against my better judgement, I'm going to wait before taking him in. But I want you all to know this, my job is on the line, so no funny business. As for you, Marcus, I'm doing this for Lessye. Because if it were only up to me, I'd take you in now."

"Because you still believe I'm guilty," Marcus said.

"No. Honestly, I had stopped believing in your guilt several days ago. So many things didn't add up. I'd take you in because as a sworn officer of the law, it's my duty. But now I know it's also my duty to find the truth; a good friend reminded me of that." He looked at Lessye, and they smiled at one another.

Tanya told them about her calls to the drug companies and how she hit a dead end.

"I don't think you're going to accomplish much by getting those lists anyway," Rod said. "We did a thorough background check on Renae which included cross checking her name with participants of pharmaceutical drug studies. Nothing came up on her."

"But that GHB had to come from somewhere," Lessye said. "Are you sure there couldn't be some mistake?"

"Anything is possible. We've been wrong before," Rod conceded, not wanting to crush the hope glistening in Lessye's eyes. "I guess it couldn't hurt to try again."

"Will you make the calls and use your authority as police chief?" Tanya asked.

"I'll do better than that. I'm going to the one man with real juice in the pharmaceutical industry, my good friend and their lobbyist, Gus."

━━━━━━━━━━━━━━

It didn't take long for Rod to track down Gus. After Rod told him what he needed, Gus immediately went with him to Tanya's suite and made a telephone call. As their number-one lobbyist, Gus had special clout in the pharmaceutical industry. There was nothing he asked for that he didn't get.

"I requested a compilation master list of all participants in GHB drug studies in the past two years at pharmaceutical companies in the state. As soon as the computer prints it out, my contact will fax it here," Gus said. "It shouldn't be long."

Tanya poured Gus a cup of coffee, and he sat down in a chair sipping it slowly. In less than fifteen minutes, the fax machine started ringing and the nineteen-page list began sliding through.

Rod took the pages from the machine, scanning them for Renae's name. As he suspected, it was nowhere to be found.

Lessye couldn't hide her disappointment. "Looks like you were right, Rod."

Tanya rifled through the list. "Rod, when the GBI ran the check on Renae through the pharmaceutical companies, did you see the list or just cross check her name?"

"We just ran a check on her name – Renae Dolores Stewart."

"But what if she used another name?" Tanya asked.

"It's possible," Rod said. "But I'm sure they would have checked her ID to make sure she was who she said she was."

They divided up the list to look for any variation of Renae's name or any name that could be connected to her.

It was Gus who said, "Does the name Martha Dale Perkins ring a bell?"

CHAPTER 63

Claude made it to Fort Valley in little time. His first stop was a heartbreaking visit to the home of Randy Joe.

His next stop was at the Peach County Sheriff's Department, where the sheriff and the Fort Valley city chief of police were waiting for him. Before leaving Atlanta, he faxed them a copy of Randy Joe's confession. They immediately upgraded the status of the fire-related deaths of Tamika and Ronnie from accidental death to arson-murder.

"Your agents have detained Nathaniel Tucker, and they're on their way here now. We've also got deputies looking for the Cole brothers. Those boys won't get far," the sheriff, a big burly man, assured Claude.

"Our fire investigator and your guys from the state crime lab are going over that apartment as we speak. We'll get to the bottom of this," the city police chief added.

"I'm confident that you will," Claude said, standing to shake both their hands. As he was about to leave, a call came over the sheriff's radio. Sonny and Ike Cole had been apprehended trying to board a private, twin-engine plane at Fulton County's Charlie Brown Airport in Atlanta.

CHAPTER 64

*I*mmediately after the two-day recess was called, the Black Caucus convened a special meeting to discuss the final status of the anti-affirmative action legislation.

"I met with the Judiciary chairman and the Speaker shortly after we heard the news about Randy Joe," said Della. "They agreed that this was a hot-button issue that neither of them was anxious to tackle during an election year, especially in the wake of a scandal. And with the main sponsor in the House now deceased and the primary sponsor in the Senate facing criminal charges, they saw no reason to even call it up for a vote. The chairman is going to bury it in committee until it disappears."

"So this means our battle is officially over," said Charles.

"For now," said Della.

Charles still could not believe the sudden turn of events. "It's as if someone planned it. Who would have thought that two legislators would get caught so cleverly with their pants down?"

"Yes, who would have thought?" echoed Bernard with a slow smile spreading across his face.

CHAPTER 65

*R*od called Claude on his cell phone and told him everything they had found out, with the exception of the whereabouts of Marcus, which he thought better explained to Claude in person. Rod, however, did tell Juan, who joined them in Tanya's suite. Juan agreed there would be time enough to tell Claude about Marcus when he returned to the city. None of her legislators returned after the recess, so Rod and Juan, along with Gus and Lessye, turned the suite into their command center. They cautioned Marcus to continue to remain out of sight until Claude returned and he was officially cleared of suspicion.

Lessye went back to the tour booth after her lunch hour to briefly check on everything, and after assigning the rest of the tours for the afternoon, returned to Tanya's suite.

Clarice came over a couple of times with a quizzical expression on her face.

"What's going on over here?" she asked.

"You know the guys have been in the building all morning because of the Randy Joe incident," Tanya said. "They stopped in to have some coffee and chat."

"Okay. Call if you need me." And she was gone back across the hall.

Another fax transmittal began to come in. This one was from Vivian. As promised, she dug up all the information she could find on Lena and Linda, including the phone numbers and home addresses listed on their school records.

Lena Arlene Lawrence was reared by her favorite aunt, Charlotte Lawrence Spencer, after the death of her parents when she was young. She grew up in the exclusive Boston Beacon Hill section and attended elite boarding schools before enrolling at Branton University. She had a high academic average and although her beauty could have propelled her into one of the most popular girls on campus, she was shy, a loner. Her only extracurricular activities included participating in a few academic-related clubs and the newspaper staff. She first met Linda Loring during their freshman year, and they became good friends. She was impressed by how much they looked alike and how much they had in common, although Lena was an introvert and Linda was a gregarious party girl. Linda was outgoing and popular on campus. She showed Lena a world of excitement and fun she had been missing. They started referring to themselves as sisters.

Sophomore year, Lena and Linda became roommates, sharing a suite in one of the campus' nicest dorms. Linda came from meager beginnings. So it was Lena who graciously helped her out with spending money and defrayed the expenses of their dorm room. Lena grew up a lonely child, starved for friendship. She found it with Linda and Vivian, who was her only other friend.

According to Vivian, she and Linda were frequently invited to spend long weekends at Lena's aunt's estate and Linda often traveled with them abroad. Lena's aunt was a widow who inherited the bulk of her husband's vast estate.

Vivian heard that Lena's aunt suffered a debilitating stroke some years earlier. Vivian wrote several letters which were never answered and tried to call, only to find that the number was disconnected. Soon, Vivian discovered that the family home on Beacon Hill was closed and that Lena and her Aunt Charlotte had moved away to an unknown location. The next pages to come through the fax were dedicated to Linda.

Linda was as sure she had gotten away with murder as she was what her new name would be. She had already acquired the proper documentation to facilitate her transition to a new woman — birth certificate, social security number, driver's license, credit cards, passport and letters of reference. All the professional, untraceable phony ID that good money could buy. Karin had come across a lot of valuable information during her time with the GBI, and several of her contacts came in handy. Linda had hidden Lena's fortune so cleverly, even she had trouble keeping up with it, and she traveled with a ready case of fashionable new wigs and contact lenses that would change her look at a moment's notice.

Linda purchased a used car with cash and drove down highway 16 toward Savannah, what she considered the most beautiful city in Georgia. She would spend some time in Savannah and on Tybee, Island before deciding on her final destination. Linda loved the beach. To her, it was the most relaxing place on earth, and although a chilly sting hung in the winter air, she could still put on a heavy sweater and kick up some sand as the waves crashed against the shore.

Linda thought back about her life. She never knew who her real parents were — only that neither of them wanted her.

All her life she had only wanted one thing: to be truly loved by the people she wanted to be loved by. But things never worked out. Something or someone would always get in her way no matter how perfect she imagined it could be. What she wanted was always so elusive to her. Maybe the fact that her own blood mother didn't want her and put her up for adoption had marked her for failure in relationships. Because when you get right down to it, if your real mother does not love you enough to keep you, who on earth will?

She was adopted and raised by a nice family in Columbus, Ohio, who tried to give her the best that they could, which wasn't much. She made good grades and in high school was one of the few students selected to participate in an exchange program in an elite prep school. A new world opened to Linda, a rich, pampered world that, until then, she had only imagined. She had gotten a taste of the good life and hungered for more. A life of luxury was no less than she deserved. Through contacts she made at the prep school, she received a full-tuition scholarship to Branton, where she met the girl who would eventually make her dream come true.

Linda would have preferred not to kill, but sometimes she had to. Killing came as a natural response to dealing with her problems. It was as natural as breathing. If people refused to do things her way and threatened her freedom or had something she wanted and wouldn't give it to her, it was their fault, not hers. In her mind, they were asking for it. And she wasn't one to lose a moment's sleep over it because deep down she didn't feel she had ever done anything wrong. *She had to protect herself, didn't she?*

It was during a trip to Italy, that the thought first occurred to get rid of Lena and assume her identity. Lena had received the emergency call that her aunt had taken ill with a stroke and went home. Linda remained at the Spencer family villa in the picturesque town of Sorrento.

Everything fell into place. Lena's aunt was pretty much a loner. Their few family friends were dissuaded from coming to the house because Lena knew her aunt wouldn't want anyone to see her that way. What little family they had were in two categories: greedy poor and stingy rich. The latter were spread out across the globe, mostly nesting in Europe. They were of the ilk who kept their distance and rarely visited. They didn't want to risk stumbling across any unfortunate kin who wanted to hit them up for a buck or a favor. Lena often mentioned a favorite cousin named Larry, who lived somewhere down South, whom Linda never met. Lena said that they had been close as children, but as he grew older for some reason, the family had come to the general consensus that it was better he take his trust fund and find his own way. So Lena had no compelling reason to inform any of them of her aunt's illness.

While in Italy, Linda sent a long letter breaking all ties with her adoptive family.

She also sent a postcard to her old friend, Vivian, explaining that she had taken a trip to Italy and planned to stay.

One day Linda received a call from Lena, who told her that all the legal issues, monetary transfers, trust fund and power of attorney, were settled. She had signed the final papers the day before.

Linda encouraged Lena to hire a temporary nurse for her aunt and come back to Sorrento for a few days to relax and soak up some sun. Lena hesitated, but Linda convinced her that she owed it to herself to get away and get some rest. As usual, Linda's persuasive arguments prevailed and a couple of days later, Lena was on a plane back to Italy.

They spent a beautiful week in virtual isolation, relaxing in the sun, sailing on the Gulf, and shopping in some of the nearby towns of Salerno, Amalfi, and Ravello. Then, it was time to leave. For the last sail of the vacation, Linda suggested they go out at sunset. She wanted to remember the setting sun from the water of the Gulf of Salerno. Lena was enthusiastic to join her friend on the sail, never suspecting that this would be her last one.

Lena hadn't felt a thing, which was the way Linda wanted it. She laced her champagne with enough barbiturates to kill her before she ever hit the water. In Linda's eyes, she did her friend a favor. At least now she wouldn't have to be around to watch the aunt she so dearly loved deteriorate into a vegetable.

Linda encountered no real problems in her transition into Lena's life. They were the same height and size. Linda styled her long brown hair the same way. She knew Lena's mannerisms and perfected her signature and vocal quality. The aunt was almost a zombie, and if she noticed the difference, she never gave the slightest inclination. Linda dismissed the temporary nurse hired by Lena and contracted another one through an agency. As in Sorrento, there was no full-time household staff, and the contracted cleaners never looked up long enough to notice anything but their paychecks. The attorney had finished his business so there was no need for him to hang around. And any paperwork she needed was all neatly filed in Lena's desk.

The only nagging problem was Vivian, who would not stop writing. In her last letter, she intimated that she might pop in for a visit the next time she was in Boston. Linda couldn't risk that. Vivian of all people would know who she was. She would wonder why Lena had gone off and left her with a sick aunt. She would have questions and wouldn't stop until she saw Lena, and that would not be good. Out of necessity, Linda ended the life of one person who was dear to her. She didn't want it to happen a second time but would kill Vivian, without compunction, if the need arose. So she decided to pack up Charlotte and move her to a small Southern city where Vivian would never think of looking – Macon, Georgia. She settled Charlotte in an expensive nursing home and checked on her often.

The new "Lena" arrived in Macon as Robert was gearing up his campaign for Governor. After laying eyes on his chief aide, Marcus, she immediately volunteered for the campaign. She worked hard and did anything to gain Marcus' attention. While working on the campaign, she met Brad, who offered her a full-time position as his legislative aide in Atlanta. Her love for politics influenced her to accept the offer, and she took a posh apartment in midtown.

She had gotten Marcus' attention, if only for a short time, and she also set her sights on Brad. Everything was going fine. But then Brad, Killian and Alonso ran into Vivian during a visit to Branton. Vivian said enough to make Killian suspicious about her true identity. Then Brad joked about placing her photo on the Internet as a delinquent alumna. He thought it was so funny. And Killian blackmailed her into sleeping with him. She could only guess what Alonso might know. He had talked with Vivian, too, and Killian and Brad were his friends. They were all toying with her.

At Marcus' instructions, she became friends with Renae. She was in the suite alone with Renae when she had a narcoleptic episode at work. She gained Renae's confidence and found out the whole story about Renae's grandparents and Marcus. Linda was especially interested in the previous association of Killian, Alonso, and Brad in the Perkins matter. After reading Jesse's letter and seeing the photo in Renae's apartment, Linda realized that Marcus and Renae shared the same mother, but never told this to Renae, who obviously didn't know. She got an idea how she could take care of Killian, Alonso, and Brad and shift the blame on Renae by re-creating Henry's accident.

Renae told her about participating in a GHB drug study and that she had a good deal of it in her apartment in the cabinet under her bathroom sink. Linda lifted and copied Renae's door key to have ready access to the GHB as needed. With her cunning it was easy getting close enough to the men to slip them a lethal dose of GHB and plant the empty bottles of bourbon. And by drugging Renae with a small amount, she was able to take her anywhere she wanted. Renae was weak minded and easily manipulated into believing she committed the murders.

When Marcus began turning his attentions to Lessye, Linda became furious and her plans changed. She would make Marcus pay for dumping her. She would frame him instead and use Renae to help her do it. Jesse's letter gave her the perfect ammunition to put the fix on Marcus or Renae, whoever was most expedient. And now Marcus had moved to number one on her hit list.

With the assistance of Karin and Renae, she began her campaign to frame Marcus. But, before leaving for good, Linda had been forced to tie up one of her only other loose ends – Renae.

Renae was too nervous to leave around. Especially after Linda realized Renae knew her real name. Her plan was foolproof. If Marcus ever wriggled free from suspicion, Renae would be the next likely suspect. She hated Marcus enough to frame him. The GHB was hers. She had been at or close to the scene of each of the crimes, and she lied to Claude about why she was in Macon. But Renae was unpredictable. What if she started talking about a frame up and someone believed her? What if she told someone about what she thought had been only a dream? What if Renae realized she overheard the last conversation between Linda and Brad?   Renae would have to go. Now, it would look like she took an overdose of GHB out of guilt over what she had done. Linda smiled to herself.

She went to see Renae on Sunday afternoon. They talked and Renae poured them sodas. When Renae went back to the kitchen at her request for some snacks, Linda spiked her soda with enough GHB to overdose Renae.

As she drove to her new destination and yet a new identity, Linda glanced at her beautiful face in the rear view mirror. Not bad for an amateur, she thought.

CHAPTER 66

*C*laude arrived at the LOB to find Marcus surrounded by a supportive group of believers and converts, including Rod and Juan. After hearing the new evidence, combined with what he already knew and compounded by the fact that the woman they all knew as Lena was an imposter and had seemingly disappeared, Claude immediately called off the search for Marcus, called the Governor and Director Shaw to alert them of the new developments in the case and began making arrangements for a news conference. He would schedule it for Tuesday afternoon. That morning, he would meet with the Attorney General to turn over the last bit of evidence he had collected in conjunction with the GHB Connection. At the news conference, he would announce that due to new information, the focus of the investigation was shifting. Marcus was given permission to return to his loft with a stern warning from Claude: "Don't leave town until this mess is sorted out."

"Don't worry," Marcus said as he held on tightly to Lessye's hand.

"I'll call and give the okay for the release of your vehicle from impound. It was found a couple of days ago at Greenbriar Mall and pulled in. You can pick it up in Decatur."

"As for you two," Claude said, looking at Lessye and Tanya. "Do you ladies have any idea how much money and manpower has been spent looking all over Georgia for someone who you have been hiding on state property all the while?"

"No sir," they said simultaneously in small unsure voices before apologizing.

"You better be thankful for a friend like Rod. And count your blessings that I'm a man with a forgiving heart and a good sense of humor."

While he was in Tanya's suite, the call came from Aunt Rose that Renae was out of the coma. She had regained consciousness and was now resting comfortably.

═══════════════════════════

The Tuesday afternoon news conference broke attendance records in the Capitol north wing. Courtesy of Sean's newsletter and the evening news broadcasts, everyone was following the events of the case like a steamy soap opera and were not about to miss a chance to eyeball its major players.

The solemn bust of James Edward Oglethorpe stared stoically from its perch on the landing over them as Claude announced that due to new evidence, the search for Marcus was called off after he voluntarily turned himself in to Capitol Police Chief Rod Jennings. He had officially been cleared as a suspect in all three murders. Former Brad Austin aide, Lena Lawrence also known as Linda Loring, was currently being sought for questioning as a person of interest.

Marcus, who read a carefully prepared written statement, thanked everyone for coming, especially Lessye, Tanya and Robert who had never given up faith in him. He thanked Gus for his assistance, and Claude and his task force for keeping an open mind and endeavoring to seek the truth in the case as opposed to an expedient resolution. Marcus officially announced that during a meeting with the Governor, he expressed his intentions to tender his resignation as chief of staff.

"I am innocent of these murders, but I do have to answer for what I did to Henry Perkins ten years ago. I feel that giving up my job is a small price to pay for all the harm I inflicted on my family," he said.

Lessye smiled. This was the first time Marcus had publicly admitted his relationship to Henry. She knew that his thoughts were now also with Renae.

"Let me make it clear that Governor Baker did not fire me or ask for my resignation. This is something that I want to do. It's something that I have to do. I had a long meeting with the Governor this morning. He is graciously supporting me in this decision," Marcus said.

Next came the Governor, who commended Claude, Rod and Juan for their perseverance in the case. He thanked Marcus for his service to the state of Georgia and his administration and wished him well in his future endeavors. Director Shaw added his share of praise for Claude and the others who were working around the clock to bring the true perpetrator to justice.

There were questions from the media. Sean's efforts to bait Claude into releasing classified information about the investigation failed.

=====

After the news conference, Claude contacted the hospital and spoke with Renae's doctor, who informed him that if her condition improved, she would be moved from intensive care on Wednesday. He did stress, however, that he didn't feel she would be strong enough to undergo intense questioning until early the following week.

Claude was anxious to talk with Renae about Linda and her overdose of GHB. Lessye and Tanya told him that Renae said the name Linda before she lapsed into the coma. He knew that his interview with Renae would complete this complex puzzle.

There was still no news on Linda, and Claude knew it would be difficult to track her down. Aides were not required to have state-issued photo ID — only name badges. All he had so far for identification was a driver's license photo and the graduation photo Vivian sent to Brad. She promised to pull together as many yearbook and other photos of Linda as she could. There was not a full set of fingerprints on file for Linda anywhere. The sole print on her license would only be useful if she had a legitimate license made in another state requiring one. A few, smudged to the point of uselessness, had been lifted from her apartment, which the building manager confirmed was furnished when she moved in. It was stripped bare of all personal items. All the waste baskets and garbage cans had been emptied and cleaned. The refrigerator, cabinets and closets were cleared, scrubbed clean and immaculate. There was not the slightest clue as to where she might have gone. Her car, also clean of prints, was still parked in her assigned space on the ground level of her apartment building.

Claude did a skip trace on both Linda and Lena, gleaning no more information than they already knew. Linda definitely was not using the same social security numbers. There was no bank account under either name anywhere in the U. S. or abroad. Whatever Linda had done with Lena's money, Claude couldn't find it. She had done a masterful job in hiding Lena's millions and covering her tracks. The last account he found with Lena's name on it was in a small local bank where Linda cashed and deposited her state pay checks under that name. It had been closed and the money withdrawn in cash. It was as if Linda had dropped off the earth.

Claude contacted the Macon nursing home administrator who informed him that the woman she knew as Lena had last been there late Sunday evening. At the time, she told the head nurse that she was beginning a new job and was leaving the state, but failed to give an exact location. The administrator told him that Charlotte Spencer's trust was structured in a way that her bills and expenses would be taken care of, whether her niece ever returned or not. Good news for Aunt Charlotte, bad news for their investigation. He knew that Linda was never planning to come back this way again.

Contact with her family in Ohio also drew a blank. The last they heard from her was by way of a letter they received from Italy several years earlier. They had no recent photos, and her old bedroom had been remodeled into a den. FBI investigators in the Boston area joined city police officers in combing the Beacon Hill neighborhood, questioning residents about Lena and her friend Linda. None of them had any information helpful in tracing Linda. Claude planned to visit Vivian. She could help put him in touch with some other friends who might know of her whereabouts.

Marcus cleaned out his office at the Capitol and said his goodbyes to the staff. Leaving a position of power he had dreamed of all his life, in the end, hadn't hit him as hard as he thought it would. It was a nice feeling not to have any pressure on him. He had never felt this free. All his life he had been trying to escape something, achieve something, get revenge for something, hide something or justify something. The job pressure was lifted and his conscience was clear. There were no more dark clouds of secrecy hanging over his head. In Lessye, Tanya and Kevin, he had found the first real friends of his life.

He concentrated on spending as much time as possible with Lessye, resting, thinking and bolting into a long, hot shower any time he thought of his days cooped up in that office building, having to sneak to the bathroom. He was beginning to wash away the ache and humiliation of the last ten years.

Marcus loved Lessye, and he had a sincere desire to make some radical changes in his life. He had done a lot of soul searching during the time he was in hiding from the police. For the first time, he truthfully faced himself and understood the hurt and pain his actions had caused. He had turned the final corner and faced a person he could no longer live with. But he resolved to make a lot of changes — even if it meant seeking therapy to help deal with the past and put his life in order. He was so blessed to have a lady like Lessye. She promised to stick by him and had already put her job and her freedom on the line to prove her loyalty.

Marcus had saved wisely and invested well, so he was good to go for at least the next three years. By then, he would surely have another position. Maybe he would try his hand at being a pollster or maybe he would launch his own political consulting firm. With his knowledge and experience, there were tremendous possibilities. Whatever he decided, as long as he had Lessye by his side, it would be all good.

Marcus thought about Renae often. He didn't visit her in the hospital because he was sure the sight of him would only worsen her condition. He also thought about the woman he had known as Lena. Who was she? Someone named Linda who had taken another woman's identity and been calculating enough to frame him for murders she probably committed to keep her secret. If it hadn't been for Brad's sister finding that photo, she might have gotten away with it. He, too, wondered what had become of the real Lena.

═══════════════

Lessye, Tanya and Clarice visited Renae that evening after work. She seemed to be getting stronger, and she even talked to them. As they were leaving her room, they greeted Neveleen, who volunteered to sit with her through the night, and Lessye recognized someone else lurking around waiting for a chance to see Renae. She immediately called Rod who contacted Claude.

Claude arrived at the hospital and went straight to Renae's room, only to find Sean skulking around her door.

"Sean, it goes without saying that you are trying my patience." Claude said, startling him.

"Then why are you saying it?"

"What are you doing here?"

"What do you think?"

"I think I have a nice set of handcuffs about your size. So move away from that door. I need to talk to you. Now!"

Sean reluctantly followed Claude to the waiting room at the end of the hall.

"You have no business here, Sean. You're not a friend of Renae's, so I assume you're not hanging around to pray for her speedy recovery."

"I'm working on a story and wanted to ask her some questions since you refused to answer them during the news conference."

"So that gives you license to harass a young woman who is fighting for her life?"

"I don't call a few questions harassment. Besides, I didn't get anywhere near her for the parade of doctors and nurses going in and out and that old cleaning lady guarding her bed."

"Well, you better be glad you didn't. Because if I had caught you in her room, I'd haul you in right now."

"You law enforcement types can't give a hard-working brother a break."

"Save it. For once, I'm sure the Governor would be relieved to get some information in this case before reading it in your newsletter."

"Thanks for the compliment."

Claude shook his head and threw up his hands in disgust. "Get lost."

"This is a public hospital, and I have a right to get answers to my questions–"

"Like you had a right to acquire leaked information about an ongoing investigation?" Claude said. "I haven't forgotten that scheme you pulled with Karin. And I'm warning you, stay away from Renae. If I so much as hear that you have belched in the direction of her room again, I'm hauling you in for interfering with a criminal investigation, and you can print that in your newsletter from the lockup. Do I make myself clear?"

"You're interfering with my constitutional rights. There is freedom of the press and I—"

Claude silenced him with a stern look, as Agent Grogan exited the elevator and walked briskly in their direction. "Remember what I said, Sean. And to keep you from forgetting, Agent Grogan here is going to be on post outside Renae's room." Claude turned to Jason. "If he even walks in the direction of her room, arrest him."

"Sure thing, Claude," Jason said, eyeing Sean as if he were ready to clamp the cuffs on that minute.

"When this is over, Special Agent Henderson, you're going to have to answer some serious questions about the way you handled – or should I say mishandled this investigation. And I'm going to make sure of it."

"Promises, promises," Claude said over his shoulder as he started toward the elevator.

CHAPTER 67

*I*t was late Tuesday evening before they arrived at their destination. Excited, yet apprehensive about the reception they would receive, they looked at each other and sucked in deep breaths before walking slowly toward the front door. Tentatively, they rang the doorbell. It was several moments before someone answered. When the door opened, there was first a stunned silence. Then they were almost swept away on a hysterical wave of raw emotion — disbelief, shock and loud hoops of jubilation and fervent prayers of thanksgiving. To Tamika, who had expected being scolded and lectured for ditching a week of school to run off with Ronnie, her family's reaction was a pleasant, yet, perplexing surprise. But Tamika had a surprise of her own. Just wait until she told them that while they were away, she and Ronnie were married.

CHAPTER 68

*B*y Friday, the Cole brothers and Nathaniel still hadn't cracked. To the surprise of Peach County Sheriff Hugh Bonner, they were sticking to their stories like cheap peanut butter on a slice of thin white bread.

Courtesy of Nathaniel, he and the Cole brothers had acquired Dylan Brantley, one of the best criminal trial lawyers money could buy, who had cautioned them to keep quiet under all circumstances. Nathaniel would have much preferred having separate representation from the Cole Brothers. But he needed to keep an eye on them. Having the same attorney would give the Coles less opportunity or inclination to roll over on him.

"Bonner and the GBI have no evidence linking you to this crime. And they won't as long as you don't give them any," Dylan said. "They are going to try to question you separately. Answer no questions without me. I'll do all your talking. They are going to use all their underhanded interrogation tactics to make you two roll on one another and take Nathaniel with you. Don't fall for it. Let me reiterate: There are no eye witnesses who can place any of you at the scene. And there is no physical evidence at the scene that in any way ties you to that fire. The only evidence they have is a questionable letter from a suicidal, drug-using, admitted sex offender grieving over the loss of his son and looking for someone to blame. His credibility is shot. Boys, when I get through tearing that so-called evidence to shreds, the jury will believe that Randy Joe, himself, set that fire. And that's only if the judge allows the letter to be presented as evidence because Randy Joe is no longer around to undergo cross examination. I hear Tyrell has had a lot to say, but anything he says would be considered hearsay. And right now, he's in a world of trouble of his own in Atlanta. So much for his credibility."

But they all underestimated Hugh's cunning. He had built a career on making suspects talk and getting them sentenced to hard time. This was the biggest case to come his way in years, and he wasn't about to let these guys skate by. But as fate would have it, this time Hugh wouldn't have to break a sweat turning these bums. There had been witnesses after all. Two unimpeachable witnesses who placed all three of them at the scene of the crime.

Against the vehement protests and objections of their attorney, Nathaniel and the Cole brothers were refused bail due to the gravity of the charges and because of the potential flight risk. They were brought from their cells for questioning by the sheriff early Friday morning.

"My clients have said all they're going to, Sheriff," Dylan said. "This is a sham of an investigation. You know as well as I do that you have no physical evidence or any witnesses who can place my clients at the scene of this tragic *accidental* fire."

Hugh waited for him to finish. "That's where you're wrong counselor," he said to the attorney then focused on Nathaniel and the Coles. "I have to admit, the *candles too close to the curtains* routine was good, considering that improperly burning candles are one of the leading causes of fire in college dwellings. But you career firebugs should have quit while you were ahead. You should have sense enough to stay away from the petroleum-based fluids — the ones derived from a natural, yellow-to-black, thick, flammable liquid hydrocarbon mixture found primarily beneath the earth's surface. That's how the dictionary describes them. Well anyway, these and similar fluids don't completely burn and leave residue, which the last time I heard is called arson evidence. Also, it came to our attention yesterday that we do have two credible witnesses who put all three of you at the scene of the fire, that by the way was no accident."

The Cole brothers looked at one another and then Nathaniel who was staring deadpan. They sat quietly as their mouthpiece earned his fat paycheck.

"Where is the official report of this so-called arson evidence or evidence that either of my clients were in possession of any petroleum-based fluids?"

"It's coming," Hugh said.

"And who are these so-called witnesses? We have a right to know."

"I couldn't agree with you more. A young couple recently wed. The witnesses are Ronnie and Tamika Layton Reynolds."

"What?!!" This is absurd," Dylan said, then burst into laughter.

The Coles, as well as Nathaniel, seemed to get a big kick out of this one. Nathaniel's deadpan expression was replaced by a broad smile.

Hugh regarded them like Sunday dinner chickens he was ready to pluck. "Now I know what you boys are thinking. I can almost hear the wheels turning in your idiot brains. You're thinking: He must be out of his mind. No way are Ronnie and Tamika still alive. And this foolishness about them being married is even more ludicrous."

Dylan recovered his serious composure. "So you're a mind reader now? And I don't appreciate you insulting my clients. I knew you could stoop low. But this is pathetic. Those poor children are dead, and you're sitting in here making cruel jokes."

Hugh sucked his teeth out of habit. "This is no joke. And your clients have a lot more to worry about than insults. Didn't I tell you? The teenagers you killed in that fire were Veda Jacobs and Tommy Ramos, not Ronnie and Tamika. Veda was a student at Fort Valley State, a good friend of Tamika's. The Ramos kid, a friend of Ronnie's, was her boyfriend.

"My witnesses left town the night of the fire, but before they left, guess who they saw. You three lurking around the apartment building. They gave an excellent description of what you were wearing. Those items were found during a search of your apartment. Your red and black jacket, Sonny, and your baseball cap, Ike. Ronnie recognized you, Nathaniel, and assumed that his father sent you to find him and bring him home. So he and Tamika slipped out without you seeing them. They borrowed the Ramos kid's Camaro so nobody could trace them. They've been out of the state and got married while they were away. They got back on Tuesday," Hugh said, punctuating this revelation with another suck of his teeth.

For once, the dazzling Dylan was speechless. Hugh watched as the color drained from all their faces. This was the part that Hugh enjoyed the most: the realization in their eyes that they were on a rocky road that led to serving hard time. Almost simultaneously, three mouths started flapping, and the finger pointing began.

CHAPTER 69

$\mathcal{S}$ t. Simons Island, Georgia, could easily be described as heaven on earth – the serene, easy beaches; the luxurious houses and condominiums lining Ocean Boulevard; the scenic tourist attractions; and delectable seafood cuisine. It was a wonderful place for Linda to lay low and get her head together.

Her getaway trip to Savannah and Tybee Island changed her plans drastically. While leisurely shopping in a River Street boutique she met her dream man, a handsome south Georgia real estate investor named Hammond Carson. With his main offices located on St. Simons, he owned or had interests in much of the prime beach-front property on St. Simons, Jekyll and Tybee Islands.

Dressed in her most attractive and professional royal blue pant suit, she walked briskly up Ocean Boulevard. It was a beautiful day. The gleaming sun bathed her tanned mocha skin, and she wanted her hazel eyes to match the color of the cloudless sky. Her hair, now cut to her shoulders had thickened and whipped in the damp, gusting ocean wind. She was en route to the home office of Hammond Carson, a man, who based on the reputation that preceded him, was most intriguing. He was thirtyish, single and wealthy. She had recently taken a job as his special assistant. Not nearly the excitement of working in politics, but it was clearly time for a change in an inconspicuous location. Besides, Claude had probably given her name and description to every State Capitol and government office building in the nation. She couldn't have some over zealous lawman seeing her tattoo and getting ideas. Linda laughed at her cunning. Who would ever think of looking for her in their backyard, so to speak? And the experience that came with a change of occupation would be beneficial. Maybe through Hammond, she could finally unload that villa in Sorrento. She hoped like everything that this time, things would go her way. But if they didn't, she shrugged, she wouldn't lose much sleep over it. After all — accidents will happen and she always carried insurance in case of an emergency.

CHAPTER 70

*O*n Monday, Renae felt much stronger and was sitting up and eating on her own. She was anxious to be released in a couple of days and was ready for questioning.

Claude, Rod and Juan arrived at her room early Monday evening and found Lessye and Tanya visiting with her. Clarice and Amber, now fully recovered from her bout with the flu, had already come and gone earlier.

Claude greeted the ladies and asked Renae, "How are you feeling? Are you up to answering a few questions?"

"Yes, and I feel much better. Thank you for asking."

Claude nodded and looked at the ladies as if to signal for them to leave.

"Is it all right if they stay?" Renae asked. "I would feel much better with them here."

"Well, it's unorthodox, but nothing about this investigation has been routine. Your friends are welcome to stay. Besides, they have a lot invested in this case, too," he said.

Lessye and Tanya were sitting in two of the three available chairs. Claude pulled the other one close to Renae's bed and sat down, while Rod and Juan stood facing her.

Claude took out his note pad, a pen and a small tape recorder. "May I tape our conversation, Renae?"

"Yes. It's all right."

Claude clicked on the recorder. "There are some important questions that we need to ask you. Would you like to have an attorney present during questioning?"

"I don't need an attorney. I'll answer your questions truthfully."

"First of all, we know that you were in possession of the drug GHB. We found out that you participated in a pharmaceutical drug study last March under your grandmother's name, Martha Dale Perkins. You were given a significant amount of the drug as a result of the study. Yet, during our first interview you told me that you had never been in possession of GHB."

Renae remained silent.

Claude and the others realized that Renae did not yet know that the woman she knew as Lena was named Linda. So for now, they would refer to her as Lena.

"Renae, we know that you and Lena were involved in a scheme to frame Marcus for the murder of the three legislators. What do you know about these murders?"

Renae sucked in a deep breath and told them.

═══════════════════

Coming home had been bittersweet for Ronnie. There was an abundance of hugs and kisses, and immeasurable surprise and joy that he was alive after all. But there was also the profound sadness that his beloved daddy was gone. Ronnie knew that his father had done a lot of things wrong, but he still couldn't bring himself to hate the man who, in spite of all his faults, he had loved for so many years. Ronnie would have to come to grips with the fact that his father had conspired to kill the woman he loved but instead killed two innocent people whose only crime was wanting a nice quiet place to be alone. He would have to adjust to the fact that his father thought he was dead, contributing to his decision to commit suicide. Nathaniel, and Sonny and Ike Cole killed his friends, and he would make sure they paid for their crimes.

Ronnie hated the fact that the last image he had of his father was the sordid image captured on the videotape. He destroyed that horrible tape to make sure his mother never saw it. And although he knew that she found out about it, she never asked him if it was the tape that had been delivered to her the night he left, and he never told her.

Ronnie introduced his family to his new bride, and like Tamika's family, they were so happy he was alive, they were ready to accept anything. Ronnie was now the head of his family. His mother and younger siblings would look to him for strength. They would look to him to take the reigns of the family peach empire and lead them into a new era.

He was also a married man who loved his wife with every inch of his soul. In one short week, he had fully transformed from a boy into a man with great responsibility. He prayed he would be up to the task.

———

Barry could not stop thanking God for answering his prayers — for giving his precious baby back to him. He thought about how ironic it was that tragedies put everything in perspective. Two weeks ago, his greatest fear had been Tamika and Ronnie running off to get married. And then he thought that his baby was dead. Now that she was back, eloping turned into the best thing she'd ever done. In fact, he had been so happy to see them that he kissed his new son-in-law. Maybe God was telling him something.

As elated as he was that Tamika and Ronnie were alive, their family also had a deep sadness over the loss of Tamika's friends, Veda and Tommy. Those children lost their lives for nothing. Veda had come to his home many times. It had been hard talking with her family to express their condolences. They would all miss her.

CHAPTER 71

"Why did you use your grandmother's name when you participated in the GHB study?" Claude asked as he made several notes in his pad.

Renae looked perplexed. "I used my real name. I don't know how it got changed . . . unless . . .?"

"Unless what?"

"Well, Lena mentioned that if the police did a check on my name, it wouldn't be good if they found out I participated in a study. But that was all she said."

"I'm thinking maybe she somehow arranged to do the switch," Rod said.

"When I spoke with you before, you told me you were an only child. You said your mother only had one child," Claude said.

"That's true."

"We did an extensive background check on Marcus," Juan said. "He was born DeMarco Norris. It has been confirmed that you two had the same mother. Henry and Martha Perkins were his grandparents, too."

"No! That can't be true. If it was true, then why didn't my grandparents ever tell me about him?"

"I can't answer why your grandparents never told you. I can only assure you that the records we have are not wrong," Claude said.

Renae turned away from them as tears ran down her face. The man she hated all these years shared her blood. Her beloved mother had borne him, too. It was almost too much to take.

"Do you need some time before we go on? You can have all the time you need."

"I'm all right," Renae said, wiping her eyes with a tissue Lessye gave her. "I'm thirsty. Tanya, would you pour me a glass of water, please?" There was a pitcher of water and a plastic cup on the table beside Renae's bed. Tanya immediately poured her a cup, and Renae took several long sips. "Thank you. I'm ready to go on," she said after placing the empty cup on the table.

"Lena talked you into framing your own half brother for crimes he did not commit?" Claude asked.

"At the time we both thought he deserved it. He was responsible for what happened to my grandparents, and he had dumped Lena for you, Lessye. I guess we both had reasons to want to get even with him."

"And now?" Claude asked.

"And now, I want to get everything out in the open once and for all. I'm tired of the lies. Having a near-death experience has made me see everything differently. I have to accept responsibility for the things I've done. The first step is telling you the truth. I'm sorry I didn't do it sooner."

"Maybe you better tell us everything in your own words," Claude said. "From the beginning. From the time you first met Lena to now."

"I first met Lena in the summer when I began working for the House. The session was out, and she only came in maybe twice a week during that time to pick up Brad's mail and handle his special projects. She was nice to me and would come over to the suite and talk with Clarice and me.

"The week before the session, Lena and I were alone in the suite when I had a narcoleptic episode. Clarice had the afternoon off and Lena stayed with me. When I regained consciousness, Lena asked me what was wrong. But I wasn't sure I should trust her. I was hesitant to tell at first, but she had always been so nice, and I knew I had to confide in somebody in case it happened again. So I told her the whole story including my participation in the GHB drug study. She promised she wouldn't tell anyone and told me it would be best if I kept the secret from everyone else.

"During the Wild Hog Dinner, I started feeling bad and wanted to leave early. I told Lena, but she said she couldn't leave because Brad needed her to go to the office on an errand. She went to the bar to get me another ginger ale to settle my stomach, but it didn't. So I went outside to find a cab. That's when I ran into Killian, who was also leaving. He offered me a ride home. I didn't want to accept it because I didn't like him. He was one of the people responsible for firing my granddaddy. But he insisted, and I felt so sick. Getting into his car was the last thing I remember. I woke up at home hours later. The next day, I found out that Killian had been killed that same night in a car accident. A week later, the same thing happened to Alonso. That was the Sunday I wound up in Macon and had to call Clarice, and she and Lessye picked me up. I don't remember how I got there. I had seen Lena earlier that day. That's why I said I had ridden with her to Macon. The next week after Brad was killed and I woke up in that hotel in Helen, Georgia, I got scared. It wasn't until I read in the *Capitol Reporter* that all three deaths were GHB-related and I knew I had some GHB that I realized something was wrong. I had to confide in someone, and Lena had been a friend before."

Claude interrupted, "What was the name of the hotel where you woke up in Helen?"

Renae searched her memory, "I'm sorry, I can't remember. I know it was close to the highway, and it was one of those places that you walk into the rooms from the outside. More like a motel."

Claude jotted some notes in his pad. "Let me get something straight. Now you said at the Wild Hog Dinner, Lena gave you a ginger ale to settle your stomach."

"That's right. Each time I needed something to drink, she volunteered to go to the bar."

"What happened when you saw her the Sunday that Alonso died?"

"We went to church then picked up some dinner in the West End."

"And the Sunday that you wound up in the hotel in Helen . . . had you seen Lena that day?"

"Yes, she had come by after church that Sunday, and brought us some salads for dinner. Why?"

"Why don't you finish your story first."

"All right. When I told Lena what I suspected, she said that if we didn't do something fast, the police would think I did it . . . those three murders. I was already beginning to believe I did do it, and I was scared because Lena said that was the only explanation for why I wound up in Macon and Helen, Georgia. She told me that my problems would be over if we could make everyone believe it was Marcus who killed them. She showed me a copy of the letter that had been sent to Brad by Jesse Higgins. She also told me that she would take care of the planning; she said she had a friend who could help. All I had to do was keep quiet and follow the plan."

"That didn't sound strange to you – that someone you had only known a short time would volunteer to help you avoid a murder rap?"

"No. I guess I hated Marcus so much, I was willing to jump on any excuse to bring him down. Besides, she was mad with him, too, for dropping her for Lessye."

"Who was this friend she mentioned? Did you know who it was?"

"No, I never knew her name. I only spoke with her on the telephone and never from my desk. I had a number to reach her. I would call from the telephone booth on the first floor of my building."

"Do you still have the number?"

"No. It was on a slip of paper in my phone book, but I must have misplaced it."

"Or Lena took it," Rod said. "Like she got your door key."

"What?"

"Did your plan include giving her a copy of your apartment door key?" Claude asked.

"No."

"Well, she had one that she planted in Marcus' office. It had his fingerprint on it."

"That wasn't part of the plan. We were only going to send the letter and a note to Marcus and one to you and call Sean. We were going to plant GHB in his place. Lena said nothing about my key. She knew I hated him. I would never want him to have my door key."

"It seems that there were a lot of things that Lena didn't tell you. For instance, did she mention that her real name was Linda Loring?"

Renae shook her head. "She never told me that. Are you sure?"

"Yes, I'm sure. How much do you know about this woman you called your friend?"

"I know she worked on the Governor's election campaign. That's how she met Marcus and Brad and became his legislative aide. She went to school up North, Branton University. She also had a nice apartment in midtown."

"Did she tell you anything about her family? Where she originally came from? Anything else about her personal life?"

"She mentioned that she had an Aunt Charlotte in Macon, but I never met her. She never talked about her parents. She said they died when she was young. She told me she grew up in Boston. That's all I know. When we were together, she always encouraged me to do most of the talking. I guess I don't know as much about her as I thought I did."

"To your knowledge, was she taking any kind of medication?"

"No, I never saw her with any pills, except aspirin, and that was rare."

"The day of your overdose, can you tell us what happened?"

"I went to church Sunday morning and picked up something to eat on the way home. She came over later. We had some sodas, and she asked for some snacks. When I came back with some chips, I drank my soda. That's the last thing I remember."

"Did you ingest the GHB on your own?"

"No. I would never take GHB again. I tried to continue after that drug study, but it upset my stomach. So I stopped using it and stored it under my bathroom sink. That's where it stayed until she came up with the idea that we could use it to frame Marcus."

"Not all of it. I think she had been into your stash before," Claude said, glancing at the others. "You were drugged by Linda. We believe she not only drugged you with the GHB, but she also drugged you on the Sundays when the legislators were killed. I think she did it to confuse you and make you believe you committed the crimes."

"But that still doesn't explain how I got to Macon and to Helen, Georgia."

"I think it does," Claude said. "If she drugged you with a mild sedative or a small amount of GHB, she would have been able to get you into her car and take you anywhere she wanted you to go.

"We now believe Linda was the one who killed the legislators to conceal her true identity," Claude said. "And the only reason I can figure that would make her desperate enough to kill is to keep it secret that she had already gotten rid of the real Lena. Brad and the others came close to discovering her true identity, and she wanted to get rid of them before they could figure it out. After she read Jesse's letter, she had the perfect scenario for either Marcus or you. Marcus' motive would be to keep them quiet about framing Henry, yours would be one of revenge for your grandfather's death. It has also come to our attention that she was the source of the GHB used by Randy Joe and Tyrell. Randy Joe wrote it all down in a letter before he killed himself. That played into her plan, as well. If Randy Joe and Tyrell were in possession of GHB, that would also make them good suspects in the murders. Linda was sleeping with Randy Joe. She knew he and Alonso didn't get along. She probably also knew about the meeting that Randy Joe had with Alonso in Macon the day he died. And if all else failed, she could leave you holding the bag because the GHB she used was yours. She used you, Renae.

"As for why she spiked your soda, maybe she thought that you would eventually realize she was guilty and talk to the police or say enough that would start us wondering about her. She wanted to keep that from happening, and she would have succeeded if Lessye hadn't taken the chance and come by your apartment when she did."

"Thank you, Lessye, for everything."

"You're very welcome." Lessye said.

Renae cleared her throat and looked at Claude. "Are you going to press charges against me? Am I going to jail?"

"Don't worry. You've been through enough," Claude said. "You were just as much a victim of Linda's as the others. You had no idea who she really was or what she was up to so you're not an accessory. The only thing you're guilty of is your part in framing Marcus and lying to me. I'm not holding that against you. And I'm willing to bet Marcus is not going to take action against you."

"I know he's not," Lessye said, squeezing Renae's hand. Lessye turned to Claude. "Since I am partly responsible for Renae being here, may I ask something concerning Linda?"

"Go ahead," Claude said.

Lessye thanked him with her eyes. "Renae, you said earlier that Lena never mentioned to you that her real name was Linda. Are you sure she never said that name to you?"

Renae looked puzzled. "No, she didn't."

"But, the night of your overdose, you said the name Linda a couple of times. Why?"

"I don't know."

"That name had to have come from somewhere," Lessye said. "Are you sure Lena never mentioned the name Linda to you, ever?"

"No . . . But . . . I think . . . I dreamed about it one night."

"What?"

"Yes. I think it was the night that Brad died. I had this weird dream that was so real. I was in a cabin in the woods. Lena was there. Brad was yelling at her, and she was begging him for another chance. The strange part was he didn't call her Lena. He kept calling her Linda over and over again."

CHAPTER 72

*L*essye used all her powers of persuasion to talk Renae into seeing Marcus, and out of gratitude to Lessye, Renae agreed. "Okay, when I get out of the hospital." Renae may have said it reluctantly, but it was definitely a start.

On Wednesday as Lessye stood at the tour booth between tours, Rod stopped by to inform her that Claude was going to New York to meet with Vivian and would probably be there a couple of days. He also informed her that Claude arranged surveillance for Renae.

"Claude isn't sure what Linda might try and doesn't intend to take any chances."

"That should make Renae rest easier. Did you guys have any luck finding the number Renae used to contact Linda's accomplice?"

"Renae was able to remember the area code and first three digits which narrowed the search. All the numbers are accounted for except an untraceable cell phone number. We'll probably never find out who was helping Linda."

"That's too bad. How's the Governor getting along without Marcus?"

"He's surviving. I hear his new chief of staff is growing into the position nicely. She's ripped a wad of chapters out of Marcus' ball busting book of management." Rod smiled. "By the way, while we're on the subject of your boyfriend, how is he?"

"He's fine, adjusting slowly but surely. He's kicking back, enjoying the rest."

"From what? Backstabbing?"

"Here we go again."

"Let's face it. I don't like Marcus any more than I ever did. And I probably never will. But I'm confident he's innocent of murder, and I'm glad everything turned out the way it did. I still think you could do much better. But since you love him, and he loves you, I wish you both the best."

Lessye raised an inquisitive eyebrow. "So you no longer think he's using me?"

"I can say a lot of things about Marcus. But now the most important one is he is definitely in love with you."

"Thank you, Rod. That means a lot."

Before leaving for New York Wednesday evening, Claude had meetings with Director Shaw, as well as the Governor and his new chief of staff, whom Claude found to be an extremely sharp woman who would be a new and powerful force to reckon with on the Hill. He also received a call from the Fulton County DA, who had been asked by the state Attorney General to handle the Buford case personally. Tyrell had been forced to resign his Senate seat. With nothing left with which to bargain and an overwhelming mountain of evidence against him, it was widely speculated that he would enter a plea of guilty to all charges and spare his family and former Senate district the further embarrassment of a long trial. Claude predicted that after it was all over, it would be a long time before Tyrell was back on the street again.

After poring over the case files, and studying Renae's interview, he checked with all the hotels close to the interstate in the Helen, Georgia area. No one remembered seeing or registering either Renae or Linda. He guessed the room where Linda dumped Renae had probably been arranged by the silent and still unknown partner.

Claude did his best to piece together all the information he had thus far on Linda in order to try and figure out her next move. He was convinced that Linda was a cold-hearted killer whose victims were usually people whose confidence she gained. In his opinion, this type of person harbored the worse kind of evil.

CHAPTER 73

*C*laude met with Vivian on Thursday morning in her office at Branton University, on a small, lush campus with beautiful brick Tudor-style buildings covered by a bed of snaking ivy. Her office on the second floor of the building, referred to as Alumni House, included expensive-looking antique walnut furnishings and African art objects creatively scattered on the ample window sills. Vivian a personable, attractive and professionally dressed young woman, greeted him warmly.

Vivian gave him a list she prepared, including the names, last known addresses and phone numbers of classmates Linda might contact. She also gave him all the photos she collected. Although she hadn't heard from Lena or Linda for some time, she candidly told him everything she remembered about them and gave him a good insight into Linda's personality.

"Linda was smart, outgoing, methodical – almost a perfectionist. She usually got everything she wanted. She didn't like to take no for an answer. She would use her charm to wear a person down to her point of view whether it was the instructors or her peers. Linda hated making mistakes of any kind. Looking back on it, she always took it harder than the average person. Lena's Aunt Charlotte adored Linda. She always seemed to say the right thing in a sincere way, never phony. But at the same time, she was also somewhat of an enigma. Nobody was ever allowed to get too close. She was the best friend in the world when you needed a shoulder to cry on or someone to confide in. She was the type of person who encouraged you to talk about your past, your feelings, your pain. But she never let anyone inside her world the same way. She was always careful not to let her guard down."

335

"Didn't you think anything was strange about that?" Claude asked.

"Not really. She was adopted, and I figured she was sensitive about it and generally afraid to trust anyone too much. Not knowing who your real parents were and why they gave you up can mess with a person mentally."

"I guess you're right."

"Do you believe that Linda is capable of murder? Do you think she killed Lena? She truly loved Lena like a sister."

"Yes, I do. I believe she killed Lena for the most basic of all reasons: her money. She killed the legislators to keep from being found out. You're one of the only people who knew both women well enough to pose a threat to her."

Vivian shuddered. "That's a scary thought," she said, regaining her composure. "You think she might try to kill me?"

"I don't want to frighten you, but anything is possible, especially if she feels you're enough of a threat and she can get to you and get away without being caught. You need to be careful and observant of your surroundings. If you hear anything from Linda or even imagine you've seen her, call the police immediately." Claude handed her his business card. "You can always reach me at one of these numbers. Under no circumstances do you meet with her alone."

He scanned the list she had given him. "Did Linda have any interest in or use drugs to your knowledge?"

"No. She never used recreational or illegal drugs. She started having trouble sleeping during our senior year, so she used a prescribed sleeping aid. I believe it was Nembutal capsules."

"Did she tell you this?"

"Not before I found them by accident. One day I was visiting with her and Lena in their room and her purse spilled over. The bottle of pills fell out and I picked it up. That's when she told me. It was an awkward moment. I could sense that was something she didn't particularly want me to know, but it would have been strange if she hadn't said anything."

"Do you know why she was having trouble sleeping?"

"Linda only had one real boyfriend during the whole time we were in school and that was during senior year. His name was Tony Gerardo. He was a real good looking Italian and a popular frat boy. He was the one who talked her into getting the tattoo. She seemed to care about him, but I never thought he shared her affections. They went together for only a few months, and it ended badly one night after she attended one of his frat house parties. There were some real ugly rumors that something bad went down during that party and Tony and Linda were involved. Some people were whispering that it had something to do with a bet, but no one who was there would admit anything. It was like some kind of code of silence. I guess the frat was afraid of getting thrown off campus if it got out, or maybe even worse. Linda never talked about it. But she and Tony were definitely through after that. That's when she started using the sleeping pills."

"Where is this Tony Gerardo now? I don't see his name on the list."

Vivian hesitated for a moment. "Tony is dead," she said slowly. "He was killed in a tragic car accident about a week before graduation. The police said he had been using drugs . . . You know, now that I think about it, Linda was so cunning and methodical that if she did kill Lena to steal her identity, poor Lena will probably never be found."

Claude spent the next couple of days in New York contacting people on Vivian's list who were still in the area. Many of them resided in Hartsdale, Larchmont, and White Plains. A few had addresses on Long Island and Manhattan. The night before, the Westchester County area had been covered with a fresh blanket of snow that glittered like diamond-flecked satin in the sunlight. He took the train down to Manhattan to interview alumni currently working and residing in the trendy Tribeca section. He drew a blank on Long Island.

Claude obtained a copy of the Westchester County medical examiner's report that confirmed Vivian's account of how Tony Gerardo met his fate. Gerardo had been under the influence of alcohol and barbiturates when his car careened off the road into a deadly ravine. He had probably been Linda's first victim.

CHAPTER 74

*T*he following Monday, Renae returned to work. It was the first full week of March, and the cool, breezy weather was a welcome introduction to the warmth of spring. A lot happened during the two weeks she was out, and she was happy to be alive and able to come back. The girls surprised her with a cake and made a colorful banner across the front door of her suite that greeted her.

The legislature was in recess on Monday and Tuesday, a usual occurrence during the last few weeks of the session. So they were able to throw Renae a welcome-back party later that morning in one of the conference rooms. It was attended by most of the secretaries in the LOB and a few of Renae's friends from the Capitol, including Lessye, Neveleen, and Aunt Rose.

After the party, Neveleen stayed around to chat with Renae.

"You gave us all a real big scare, baby. I'm so glad you're all right."

"Thank you, Miss Neveleen. I'm glad to be back. There was a time I thought I wasn't going to make it. But I did, thanks to all your prayers and thoughtful care. I appreciate you staying nights with me when I was in the hospital."

"It was my pleasure, baby. Now we've got to work on fattening you up," Neveleen said, giving her a motherly hug. Renae, who was already rail thin, had lost even more weight during her illness.

"My stomach was upset for a while probably from all the hospital medications. But my appetite is coming back. And I'm eating a lot of starches and drinking some protein shakes. I should be back to normal pretty soon."

Neveleen regarded her seriously for a moment and then said, "You know honey, I'm one of the few people still around here who not only remembers your grandparents but was close to them. When you were a baby, Henry and I talked about you a lot, especially after your mother died. He was always saying that he hoped he would live to see you get grown, and his prayers were answered."

"Yes, barely."

"I'm not trying to get in your business, but have you talked to Marcus since you got out of the hospital?"

"No, not yet. Lessye talked me into agreeing to meet with him. I said yes only because she saved my life. But otherwise, I wouldn't. I have no reason to talk to Marcus. We don't run in the same circles and never will," she said bitterly.

"You may not like him, but he's all the blood family you've got. You can't deny that he's your brother. He was your mother's baby, too. And I'm sure she loved him as much as she loved you. But she died early. She couldn't help it. It was one of those sad things that happen and only God knows why."

"What are you trying to say?"

"I'm saying that your granddaddy loved his grandson, too. He hated the fact that he gave that boy up. He never forgave himself when his father's people cut off all contact with your family. Marcus probably had a hard life—"

"So I should forgive him and forget everything he put my family through because he had a hard life? Who hasn't had a hard life? We all have. But we didn't make the decision to kill an old man because of it."

"Marcus didn't kill Henry. He made the choice to get drunk and then get behind the wheel of his car. When Henry was fired, I tried to tell him it wasn't the end of the world, that the truth would come out one day. He still had his family, and he had some skills. He could find other work. I told him he had to stay strong for you and Martha. But he didn't listen. He only seemed to find comfort in the bottle. Yes, Marcus was wrong for what he did. He should not have lied on Henry and set him up. He was cruel and malicious, but Henry made some mistakes, too. He should have made more of an effort to keep in contact with his grandson."

Renae couldn't believe what she was hearing. "Are you blaming my granddaddy!"

"No, baby, I'm not blaming anyone," Neveleen said in the voice of a soothing grandmother, patting her arm gently. "I'm only saying that all people make mistakes. They're not reserved for some people like Marcus. You knew your granddaddy. Tell me something honestly – knowing the kind of man he was, do you think he would still be holding a grudge against Marcus for what he did, or do you think he would have forgiven him?"

Renae was thoughtful for a moment. "I know he would have forgiven him."

"Well if your granddaddy could forgive him, how can you do any less? Honey, you're only hurting yourself with this attitude of yours. Don't you think it's way past time you tried to put all this hatred and bitterness behind you? Don't you know it takes much less energy to love?"

Renae couldn't answer. Neveleen hugged Renae tightly as she fought to choke back tears. She knew Neveleen was right. It was time she rid herself of the bitterness that had been eating away at her insides for ten years. She had no idea where she would go from here with Marcus. She had no idea how she would begin the steps needed to forgive him. But she did know two things. God worked a miracle and spared her life for a reason, and she was tired of hating and hurting.

CHAPTER 75

*T*he following Sunday, as Marcus arrived for dinner at Lessye's, he was nervous. Renae was coming, and this would be the day of their first meeting. He had faced-down and intimidated some of the most powerful officials in government with ease. But when it came to meeting with his own sister, his stomach felt like it was twisted in knots.

After dinner, Lessye would leave them alone so they could talk privately. For the first time in his life, he would have a conversation with the woman who was his half sister; the woman who shared his blood; the woman for whom he had harbored a mixture of hatred and jealousy all his life; the woman who hated him enough to help frame him for murder. It was now time for them to make peace. He felt as if he and his half sister were two major powers struggling against each other, having been on the verge of war for many years.

Renae arrived about fifteen minutes after Marcus. It took her a little time to get up the nerve to go in. They greeted each other stiffly but cordially. Somehow between the meal and Lessye's determined efforts to keep pleasant conversation going, they managed to get through dinner without incident. Then the dessert was served and afterwards Lessye went upstairs and left them alone to talk.

For the longest time, they sat and stared at one another, neither of them wanting to be the first to bend or break. Renae had harbored her animosity for ten years, and Marcus, for almost a lifetime. The wall was not about to crumble in a day.

For the first time, Renae could see the striking physical resemblance between her and Marcus and wondered why she never saw it before. They both inherited the mysterious light brown eyes, high cheek bones, dark wavy hair and smooth bronze complexions from their mother. Marcus possessed a seriously strong jaw and powerful physique that probably came from his father. Renae, the reedy thinness and keen nose evident in photographs of her father. They were both tall like their mother had been, Renae standing only a few inches shorter than her half brother.

It was Renae, who after her talk with Neveleen, called Lessye to ask her if she would arrange the meeting with Marcus at her home. Lessye invited her to Sunday dinner before she could change her mind. Now, as she sat almost tongue-tied, not knowing what to say or how to start, all she could think of was keeping her cool, not having a screaming fit, and above all else staying conscious.

"Thank you for coming," Marcus said, breaking the heavy silence. When Lessye told me you called her, I was surprised. It had to have taken a lot for you to do that. And I want you to know that we both appreciate it."

"You didn't have to come either," she said. "I'm glad that you did."

"How are you feeling . . . I mean . . . I didn't come to see you in the hospital because I figured . . . I mean I didn't want to upset you. I was pulling for you to get better."

"Lessye told me why you didn't come, and at the time, it was the right decision. I wasn't ready. I'm feeling much better. Thanks for asking. Have you made any plans since resigning from the Governor's office?"

"Not yet. I'm taking it easy for a while . . . thanking God that I'm free of pressure and suspicion. The last few weeks have been a real roller coaster. I'm still adjusting to the fact that it's finally over."

"Well . . . in spite of everything . . . I hope it works out for you."

"Thank you."

"And thank you for talking to Claude and the DA in my behalf."

"It was the least I could do. Claude's a good man and the DA was looking for big fish. You never had to be afraid of going to jail."

There were only so many pleasantries they could exchange. Now that her illness and his job situation were out of the way, all that was left for them to talk about was the weather, unless they got down to the root of the matter.

"Lessye is so nice, and she means well. But I don't know what she was hoping to achieve in getting us together. We both have a lot of negative baggage between us, and one dinner and a few kind words are not going to solve our problems."

"You're right. But maybe Lessye just wanted us to get together and talk – like we're doing right now. We've never, ever had a conversation before about anything."

"Did you agree to this to make points with her? Do you think by hanging around her that some of her kindness will rub off on you, or are you using her, too?"

Marcus grimaced. It was obvious that her words stung him.

"I'm sorry," she said. "I didn't come here to insult you."

"It's okay. You're being honest, and it's important that we're honest with each other. No. I'm not using Lessye. I care for her deeply. And, yes, I do pray that someday her sweetness will spill over on me. Meeting with you is something that I wanted to do. It's time we talked. What made you decide to meet me?"

"At first, it was only because Lessye asked me to. But then I thought about the fact that I came close to dying a couple of weeks ago. Being that close to death gave me a new perspective on a lot of things. There's a strange peace that comes over you. When you come that close to dying, you don't think so much about life or where you've been.

"I had a talk with a good friend of my granddaddy. She made me face something I had refused to think of before. She made me face the fact that whatever you did to my granddaddy, he would have forgiven you. He was a good, kind man who could never hold a grudge against anyone. I'm tired of the bitterness. And if talking to you can help it go away, then that's why I'm here. Why are you here?"

"I'll never have a chance to apologize to Henry for what I did to him. I want you to know how sorry I am for what I did. I am sorry for all the lies and hurt and pain I have caused you. I was hoping that someday I would be able to make it right with you."

"Make it right? Exactly how can you make it right? My grandparents are both dead. They died way before their time because of you. And you sit here . . . you can't even refer to him as your granddaddy. You still call him Henry, like he was some guy you knew, some guy you did wrong. There are some things that can't be made right by just saying I'm sorry."

"Don't you think I know that? I'm carrying a guilt in me that will never go away. That's the worst punishment I could ever have – never to be able to close my eyes without remembering. I never meant for it to end up this way. If I could change it, I would. But I can't, and you can't. The best we can do is salvage the pieces we have left and try to go on from here. And if I'm wrong for not referring to him as grandfather, you are equally as wrong for refusing to accept the fact that he belonged to both of us. Not once have you referred to Henry as *our* granddaddy. He's always *your* granddaddy, like you have special dibbs on him. I know he was my grandfather, too. He was also the man who threw me away when I was seven years old. He kept you, the precious baby girl. But he gave me up to suffer hell. So excuse me if I can't see him as the great man you think he was."

"You're wrong! Granddaddy never threw anyone away! I can't believe he would have done that. It had to have been your father's family who came and took you away."

"You must be kidding. Those people were poison. They never wanted a child for anything but slave labor. And you were only a baby when all of this happened. You couldn't know what went on, but I remember everything. You didn't even know you had a half brother. If Henry and Martha were good people, why didn't they ever tell you about me? Why didn't they even *try* to keep in touch with me?"

"I don't know the answer. Maybe we will never know. But why didn't you take the time to ask him while he was alive? Why didn't you tell him who you were? Why did you keep it all in and sneak behind his back?"

"Because I was sick of being hurt! All my life had been nothing but rejection. I couldn't take any more. If I had told Henry and he still rejected me . . . it would have destroyed me–"

"So you decided to destroy him first?"

"Yes. I did. I wanted to take his job and maybe see him spend a few years in prison. But I never, ever wanted him to die. The hatred that I had built up against Henry, Martha and you had been growing inside me a long time. It consumed me. It got out of control, and I have suffered the consequences for it in a big way."

"Lena . . . I mean Linda told me you had her spying on me. What were you planning to do, set me up to be fired, too?"

"At first, I thought about it. But then, I settled for having the upper hand of knowing who you were, while you were in the dark about me. I'm sure you were eager to help when she decided to frame me."

"I wouldn't exactly put it that way."

"How would you put it?"

"She convinced me that if we didn't do something, I would probably be accused of the murders. She came up with the idea of framing you. I hated you. So it didn't take much persuading for me to agree."

"How do you feel about it now?"

"I know it was wrong, just as wrong as what you did to granddaddy. And I know I should be sorry, but . . ."

"You think it's what I deserved after what I did to Hen . . . our grandfather," Marcus said.

"Yes. I have to be honest. I think it's what you deserved. After all, you're still alive. Everyone knows you're innocent, and you get to go on with your life. Our grandparents were not that fortunate."

"Can you ever forgive me for what I did, and where do you see us going from here? Do you think we could ever have any kind of relationship?"

"I don't know. I wish I could say yes. But I don't know. I want to believe you've changed. But I don't know if I can ever trust you."

"I feel the same way. But I want to . . . I need to try. Can we take that first small step?"

"We already have."

CHAPTER 76

The first three weeks of March rolled around quickly. The previously hectic reception schedule of February now slacked up to a manageable crawl with the Jefferson-Jackson Dinner – a huge annual Democratic fund raising affair – being one of the last big events of the legislative season. Finally, the day that Tanya and the other legislative secretaries dreamed of since the first day of the session arrived – the fortieth day of the session, sine die. Sessions were always hard on everyone, and there was a general mood for enjoyment.

The Black Caucus, among others, planned a huge sine die bash at a downtown hotel. Tanya and Kevin, Amber and Kwame, and Clarice and a new boyfriend she was dying for everyone to meet, along with Rod and his date, attended. Lessye talked Marcus into going, but Renae declined the invitation to join them. Since their first conversation at Lessye's, Marcus and his half sister had spoken a couple of times. They accepted the fact that there was still a long road ahead before either of them could look optimistically at forging a true familial relationship, but they were not giving up.

Gus promised to bring his five oldest great grandchildren to witness the ending of the session from the floor of the House, a Stanton family tradition since his own children were small.

Sean had gotten his chance to talk to Renae after she left the hospital, and his series on the Capitol murders was almost complete, with the exception of the final chapter, the arrest and prosecution of Linda. That morning, he received an overseas telephone call from his old friend, Karin, who promised to give him an exclusive on her role in framing Marcus only in the event Linda was caught and only if he promised never to reveal her whereabouts to the authorities. Also, in the tradition of the opportunistic Karin, there would be a hefty fee involved.

For now, however, Sean would have to console himself by digging up dirt during numerous sine die parties.

━━━━━━━━━━

Claude, who had returned from New York with no further leads on Linda, spent the last day of the session cleaning out his temporary office at GBI headquarters. What he had left to do on the case could be handled as well from his home office in Americus. He was also tired of being away from his family and longed to go home to his wife and his own bed each evening instead of in some cramped up hotel room. His relocation in no way diluted his intensity in solving this case. Claude never had an unsolved case, and he wasn't about to let Linda outsmart him. He was confident he would catch her. It was only a matter of time before she slipped up and did something stupid. A flamboyant girl like Linda couldn't hibernate for long. It wasn't in her nature.

━━━━━━━━━━

At exactly twelve midnight on the fortieth day of the session, Lessye, Tanya, Amber, Clarice, Rod, Kwame, Gus and his great grands (who had all taken naps early in the evening in return for getting to stay up that late), gathered in the main aisle of the House Chamber, courtesy of Della, to witness the sine die. Lessye had been there for ten years but always felt the excitement of looking from the House across the balcony of the rotunda to the Senate as the Speaker and Lieutenant Governor banged their gavels simultaneously ending the session. The Speaker would come down from his podium, bow to both sides, then sprint out the side anteroom door closest to his office as the members of the House threw up the confetti.

During the after-party, Marcus and Lessye held each other close and danced away the early morning hours. As they danced and kissed in rhythm with a Marvin Gaye favorite, "Let's Get it On," Lessye whispered to Marcus. "You still haven't answered my question."

"And what question is that?"

"How are we going to celebrate sine die?"

"I thought that's what we were doing."

"Okay. Be smart and miss out."

"I was only teasing. I have a wonderful idea how we can celebrate sine die. In fact, if you agree with this idea, we'll possibly have the greatest post sine die celebration ever."

———

The wedding of Marcus and Lessye was every bit of the great celebration Marcus promised Lessye.

It was a welcomed bright spot in the midst of the depressing darkness that had held them hostage since the beginning of the legislative year. Hundreds of their family, friends and coworkers were on hand to witness their exchange of vows in Lessye's church on a sunny Saturday in early June. Standing with Lessye were Tanya, her matron of honor and Renae, who agreed to be a bridesmaid. Kevin and Lessye's brother, Brian, stood with Marcus. Along with seeing her nephews and her parents who flew in from Philadelphia for the occasion, what made Lessye especially happy was that Renae agreed to be in her wedding. She knew it took a lot for Renae, who was still struggling with her relationship with Marcus, to share their special day. Renae and Marcus agreed to seek professional counseling to help heal their many emotional wounds.

Their exquisitely catered champagne reception, fittingly held in the rotunda of the State Capitol, was a wedding gift from the Governor and included a five-tier pineapple-flavored wedding cake with delectable cream cheese icing.

———

Honeymooning in the Grand Caymans, when Marcus gently lifted Lessye in his arms, all the emotions he was feeling, had felt and knew were to come welled up in tears in his eyes, as he whispered, "Lessye, I love you."

Marcus knew that in Lessye he had found an enduring love that would never hurt, reject or betray him. He had found a love that would nurture him and inspire him to be the man he should be. He had found another human being with whom he could freely share all of himself and was no longer afraid to be vulnerable. He had found his soul mate. As the twinkle of early light peered through the curtains in their room, he knew that like the coming of the pristine day, his beautiful new life had begun.

CHAPTER 77

O ver a year had passed since the murders. Another legislative session had come and gone. The legislators, who had won the special elections to complete the terms of Killian, Alonso, and Brad were handily re-elected the following November, and although they could never replace their predecessors, they were quickly carving positive names for themselves in and out of the General Assembly.

Marcus, still nestled in the bosom of marital bliss, enlisted the assistance of Della and with the support of the Governor and Secretary of State, Henry Perkins' name was officially cleared. His pension was finally granted and awarded in a lump sum to Renae.

There was still no sign of Linda and to Claude's surprise, she made no attempts to contact Vivian or finish the job she started on Renae. This lack of action on Linda's part confirmed Claude's fear that she had become so hidden and entrenched in a new life with a brand new identity, that she was not going to risk doing anything stupid that might get her caught. And if she didn't do anything stupid, they probably would never find her. Claude took it especially hard because not only was a callous, methodical killer still on the loose, he had failed to accomplish his objective.

To make matters worse, Robert had taken a real beating over the past year. Amid media allegations of power grabbing, he had gone and done what to some had been unforgivable — backed the Black Caucus in their efforts to change the Georgia State Flag. They had successfully removed an offensive symbol which kept the state sinking in the hate-filled quicksand of the past and replaced it with a hopeful beacon of a promising future of tolerance and inclusion. As the new banner whipped in the wind in the shadow of the sparkling gold dome, hoards of irate "flaggies" were following the Governor around the state denouncing his actions and warning him he would feel their wrath come next election.

Although Senator Windsor "Sammy" Nokes had linked arms with Robert in front of the television cameras in his home district and proclaimed his loyalty and support long enough to secure funding for his tri-county library and medical center, he had seized the opportunity amid the flag flap to break ranks with the Democrats and joined the Republican Party. It was speculated that he would oppose Robert for the office of Governor the following year.

Without Marcus around to threaten enemies, call in favors from friends, and trouble shoot, Robert's boat was sinking fast. In spite of it all, he was a man of true courage and he needed some good news for a change.

═══════════════

"Claude, you've got to stop sulking over that case," his wife Carmen said. "You'll find that woman eventually. She can't hide forever. Pretty soon I'm sure she'll do something to give herself away. She'll probably turn up in a place you least expect. But until that time comes, we're way past due for that vacation you promised me. My brother needs an answer about the trip. I want to go. The boys have gone back to school, and you don't have any major cases at the moment. We haven't had a real vacation in over a year and we'll only be gone for two weeks. Come on, Claude, don't let me down."

The sweltering, hazy days of late August were the last gasp of summer, and the heat was making Claude restless. After about a week of cajoling by his wife, his depression over the unsolved case, and a need he didn't know he had to get away from it all, he broke down and agreed to the trip.

"Okay, baby, let's do it. What's the plan?"

His wife detailed the plan for a wonderful two-week vacation in Hawaii. "Sherman and Martia have a friend who has extended an invitation for all of us to spend some time at one of his homes in Maui. We're also going to spend several days on what is described as 'Hawaii's most exclusive island,' Lanai. Sherman says he's wealthy. He's footing the bill for the whole vacation, including transportation on his private jet."

"Sounds almost too good to be true," Claude said. "Why is he being so generous where we're concerned? He doesn't even know us."

"According to Sherman, he invited another couple who had to cancel at the last minute. He asked Sherman if he knew anyone who might want to go in their place and he suggested us."

"That was thoughtful. Who is this guy who's being so generous?"

"Hammond Carson, a south Georgia real estate investor. He sold them their condo on St. Simons way below market value. Almost gave it away. Sherman told me he comes from old money up North, and he just got engaged. According to my brother, he's anxious to meet us."

"I know that Sherman has told him all about his baby sister," Claude said and smiled playfully. "When do we leave?"

"I thought we would drive to the coast on Friday and spend the weekend at Sherman's. We leave for Hawaii Monday morning."

Their conversation was interrupted by the ringing of Claude's cell phono. He gave his wife a quick peck on the lips before answering. It was his office patching through a call from the Jekyll Island police.

After doing most of the listening, Claude said, "Thank you for calling, I'll arrange to come down as soon as possible. Goodbye."

"What's going on?" Carmen asked as soon as he ended the call.

"That was the Jekyll Island police. Baby, our plans are going to have to change."

"Please don't tell me we're going to have to cancel our trip."

"No. But we're going to have to leave tonight for the coast."

"Why, what's wrong?"

"The body of a young woman washed up on the beach on Jekyll Island last night. It appears to be a suicide. She has a black butterfly tattoo on the back of her neck. They think it may be Linda Loring."

CHAPTER 78

$\mathcal{L}$inda was tired of laying low. And now it was time to get rid of Hammond. She would get even with him for breaking her heart. Why couldn't he love her like she wanted him to? She gave him her charms for months, only for him to dump her for another woman. She would get rid of Hammond the same way she did the others. Why couldn't the men in her life ever just love her? Tony Gerardo had been the first. Now Hammond's time had come.

Everything was going so well. Linda had gotten the job as Hammond's special assistant under the name of Lisa Lanier, like the Georgia lake she often enjoyed. She endeared herself to him and his small staff and started an intense, yet, secret relationship with the wealthy real estate magnate. She thought that Hammond was the one, with his rippling physique, curly dark hair, mysteriously deep brown eyes, and rich olive complexion. But it all started to unravel when his former girlfriend showed up. She had left town to travel and play rich girl, now she was bored and wanted to return to Hammond. So Linda had to go. Linda was crushed to find out Hammond had been seeing that woman romantically. They were in love. Now they were engaged. They were on their way to Hawaii to celebrate. He had invited friends to join them. Hammond was looking so forward to his vacation. That was one vacation he would not live to enjoy.

Linda had made preparations to cover her tracks and leave town right after getting rid of Hammond. She had made a big deal of resigning her position two weeks earlier and told Hammond's staff she had found a new position in New York which required her to leave immediately. If the staff was questioned after Hammond's unfortunate tragedy, they could tearfully tell police that the woman they knew as Lisa had resigned and left town two weeks earlier.

It wasn't all a lie. She did plan to go to New York, but not for a new job. She would pay a surprise visit to her old friend, Vivian. It was time Vivian had her long-awaited reunion with the real Lena, and Linda would be too happy to make it possible.

Linda arranged to meet Hammond on his luxurious 120-foot motor yacht, *Victory*, in the Jekyll Island marina. It had been the scene of many of their secret romantic trysts. Tonight it would take him to his watery grave. Darkness was settling in, and the dock was deserted. There was only a faint light visible from Hammond's yacht. He was waiting for her when she arrived. The six-man crew, always conveniently missing during Linda's visits, was once again in absentia.

Linda admired the interior colors of *Victory*, dominated by beige and gold with teak-brown woodwork and trim. It included a spacious master stateroom and three smaller cabins, a large saloon and dining room, a smaller more intimate saloon, a game room, two fully equipped galleys, and a hot tub on the top deck. His "toy" was a floating mini-mansion, worth more than four million, but according to Hammond was worth every cent. He went to the bar and poured them drinks as she settled back on the overstuffed sofa in the expensively appointed smaller saloon.

He returned with the drinks, and she took a short sip. "Thank you, Hammond," she said. "Would you happen to have some chips or something? I'm a little munchy."

"Sure." He placed his drink on the coffee table in front of her and went to the adjoining galley to get some pretzels.

While he was gone, she took a small bottle of GHB from her purse and emptied the contents in his glass.

He returned with the pretzels and sat them on the coffee table and she ate a handful.

"I know my engagement has come as a shock to you," he said. "But you must know that I've known Deanna for a long time. Our relationship started about five years ago. She left town partly because of my failure to commit to her."

"But all of a sudden, you can commit to her now, although we were in a relationship," she said, and sipped her drink.

"I should have told you in the beginning that there was someone else. I regret that I didn't. You're right, I did end our affair abruptly, and I'm so sorry if I hurt you. Can I offer you a peace offering, a sort of parting gift?"

"Yes, as a matter of fact. I would love it if we could sail together one last time."

"Now? Tonight?"

"Sure. We're already on this fabulous boat. It's a beautiful, clear evening, and I don't want to remember my last night on *Victory* standing at attention. Pleasssse."

"All right. You've talked me into it. Let's do it," Hammond said.

Linda joined Hammond in the pilot house, and he took the helm. They cruised slowly out of the marina into the St. Andrew Sound and slightly northeast into the Atlantic Ocean.

A few miles out, Hammond stopped the vessel, and they drifted for awhile. They took their drinks to the upper deck to enjoy the soft breeze and the silvery glow of moonlight.

"I have something else for you," Hammond said, with a sparkle in his eyes.

"What?" She could barely contain her excitement. If there was anything she loved more than her reflection and money, it was the promise of a gift.

"Not so fast. It's a surprise." He handed her a black, silk blindfold. "First put this on, and then I'll give you your present."

Linda squealed with delight as she covered her eyes, the anticipation of the gift momentarily taking her mind off the deed she would later perform. "You are a naughty boy. But I love it."

Hammond smiled. "You're a beautiful woman, especially tonight, even though you're not wearing any makeup. You're dazzling without it."

"I know."

He went down to his stateroom and, moments later, returned and placed a long velvet jewelry box in her right hand.

"Okay, take off the blindfold." She did and immediately opened the box containing a beautiful antique gold bracelet engraved with the initials *LL*.

Linda gasped. "It's beautiful," she beamed, putting it on her wrist. "I'll treasure it forever."

Hammond took a long sip of his drink. "It's the least I could do. That bracelet has been in my family for many years. I thought it only fitting that you should have it tonight. It originally belonged to my mother's brother who gave it to his wife on their fifth wedding anniversary. They died when I was a child. It would have gone to their only daughter, but she's also deceased. It's one of the most expensive and precious pieces that I own."

"Thank you. But why would you give something so expensive and sentimental to me?"

"There is no price I can put on your broken heart."

"That is so sweet and how coincidental. Your aunt had my same initials. What did they stand for?"

He pulled her close and brushed his lips against hers, then looked into her eyes. "The only thing important is what they stand for now . . . Lisa Lanier."

She giggled at his thoughtfulness. "Have I told you what a wonderful man you are?"

"Yes." Hammond said and glanced at his watch.

"I know you have to go," she said.

"Yes, but we have time to finish our drinks." As they finished their drinks, he talked about how excited he was about his upcoming trip.

Linda watched him intently. In spite of everything, he had been so sweet to her, and he was so happy. It was a pity she still had to kill him. So sad that the new life he looked forward to with that witch, Deanna, would only be a dream he would never realize.

He was still talking about his trip when, suddenly, he grabbed his stomach and doubled over in pain.

"Hammond . . . Honey are you sick? Do you want me to take the boat back in? You know I can."

He groaned. "No, it's just a wave of nausea."

"You look drowsy, too." Just like the others, she thought.

"No. I'll be all right. I feel a little funny. I'm sure it will pass."

Just like a man. Never admit when something is physically wrong.

"Let me rest here for a moment. And then we'll leave."

Hammond was leaning against the starboard railing. This was the time to do it. She wouldn't be as kind to him as she had been to the real Lena. She wanted Hammond to know every second of what was happening to him.

Hammond was sagging now. He could barely keep his balance as she moved toward him with a vicious look in her eyes.

"Wha . . . What are you doing?" Confusion registered on his face.

"You're getting ready to take a nice, long swi . . ." Before she could finish her sentence, she lurched forward in pain and stopped abruptly.

"Wha . . . What's wrong?" Hammond asked weakly.

She clutched her stomach and leaned over the railing and vomited into the water. "I . . . I don't know. All of a sudden I got real nauseous. My stomach is cramping and my head is pounding . . . I . . . I— "

"W . . . well," he began stammering, and then finished in a strong, icy voice. "Could it be, Linda, that you have been drugged?"

"Wha . . . What did you call me?"

He laughed a loud, nasty, hollow laugh. "Linda Loring, of course. You *are* the one who killed your best friend, Lena, stole her identity, along with her money and who's now being hunted by the GBI for killing three Georgia legislators. I know you've done much more, but I fear you're not going to last long enough for me to recount all of your crimes."

Her voice trembled with growing terror. "What have . . . you done to me?" She looked deep in his eyes, and for the first time, she saw it – the look she had seen in the reflection of her own eyes so many times before, the look of satisfaction that accompanied coming in for the kill. Hammond was like her, he was her, and he was killing her. For an instant, several faces flashed through her mind: Tony, Lena, Killian, Alonso and Brad, Marcus and Renae — all the people she had killed and done wrong.

"Let's say I've given you a strong dose of your own medicine. Don't you think I know why you wanted me to bring you out on my boat, so you could drug me and kill me like you did Lena in Sorrento?"

"What . . . How do you . . .?" She slumped to the floor of the deck.

"Yes, I know all about it. And to think all I had to do was bribe you with a gift to get a blindfold on you long enough to switch drinks with you. The look on your face when you thought I was about to pass out was priceless," he said, reaching down, grabbing her wrist and unhooking the bracelet. "I'll take this back now, if you don't mind."

"How did you? How did you?" she slurred, the drowsiness was kicking in and her vision was beginning to blur.

"Speak up. I can barely hear you. Are you asking me how I found out about you? Oh, that was easy because I'm not a fool. I knew who you were the moment I saw you. You look so much like Lena. Except for that cheap butterfly tattoo and eye color, you could have almost been twins. Lena talked about you often. She loved you like a sister, and you repaid her by killing her.

There's a picture of you on the GBI most wanted list. I toyed with the idea of turning you in, but you know how I like games. You were so anxious to be with me. I wanted to see how far you would go. I wondered what it would take to trigger you to want to kill me. So I gave you a push. And sure enough, you didn't disappoint. You made your move. I knew you would because I know you. I know your type. That's another thing we both have in common. We always get exactly what we want. Isn't that right?" He looked at her eyes that were now closed. "Well, maybe not always. Are you still with me?" he asked, shaking her.

Linda had slipped into unconsciousness and was unresponsive.

"Oh well," he said, looking at her limp body sprawled on the deck. "I guess now it's time to say goodbye." He started the boat and traveled out about fifty miles. He then cut the motor, picked up Linda's lifeless body and tossed her overboard. He watched as she hit the water with a violent splash and disappeared into the dark silence below. The glass, laced with GHB, went in behind her.

"So long, Linda, Lisa and whoever else you were," he said.

As he started the return trip to the dock, his thoughts again turned to his trip to Hawaii. Sherman Baptiste, his wife, Martia, and Sherman's sister, Carmen, and her husband, Claude, were also coming. Claude was the GBI agent who was chasing Linda. Should he tell him where she was now? Nah, smart man that he was, he would figure it out soon enough.

Hammond Lawrence "Larry" Carson couldn't help laugh to himself about what a silly girl Linda was. Did she honestly think that he would let her get away with killing his cousin? That simple woman didn't realize that there was room for only one psycho on St. Simons Island, and he wasn't about to relinquish that title. Now . . . on to Hawaii and his new life with Deanna . . . well . . . for as long as that lasted.

AUTHOR'S NOTE

The Final Curve is a work of fiction which combines my love for mystery and suspense with a keen interest in Georgia history and government. It embodies a mixture of suspense, enlightenment, and entertainment. All characters are fictional and are the products of my imagination. Any resemblance to any actual persons, living or dead, is entirely coincidental. Fictional circumstances were created by my imagination to make the story interesting, keep it moving and fuel the suspense and intrigue. The glimpse into Georgia history and government, as well as any references to real events, businesses, organizations, locales and contemporary or historical public figures are used fictitiously and intended only to give the fiction a sense of authenticity and reality.

I hope you enjoyed this book as much as I enjoyed writing it and accept it in the spirit of what it is – a piece of fun and interesting fiction.

ABOUT THE AUTHOR

*M*adge D. Owens is a native Atlantan and graduate of Clark College (now Clark Atlanta University). A professional business and creative writer, and public speaker, she is the author of two novels: *To Silence Her Memory* and *The Final Curve*. She is also the author of numerous unpublished short stories, as well as a collection of poetry. Madge weaves intricate tales of mystery and suspense, and seeks to use her writing as a vehicle to entertain, educate, and celebrate the positive aspects of inner-city life.

To Contact Author:

Post Office Box 38288
Atlanta, Georgia   30334
(404) 280-5029
writepagemo@yahoo.com

Printed in the United States
46603LVS00004B/121

9 781420 892154